He Who Holds My Soul

THE FIRE AND SILENCE SERIES

BOOK ONE

SHANNON V. VELZEN

Cover Design: @Liverosess (Instagram)

Internal Artwork: Shannon V. Velzen

Editor: @ebbandflowediting (Instagram)

Formatted with Vellum

For the morally grey.
The emotionally unhinged.
For the girls who prefer to worship the devil.

Welcome home.
Korithax will see you now.

P.S, He's seven feet tall.
Of course it's big.

Her grief will drown the stars.

— Velentha

TRIGGER WARNINGS

He Who Holds My Soul is a dark romantasy that delves into intense emotional, psychological, and supernatural themes. While this book centres love, vengeance, and personal reclamation, it also explores trauma, grief, and the consequences of power.

Please proceed with caution if any of the following may be distressing:

- Parental abuse and betrayal
- Gaslighting and manipulation
- Emotional trauma and breakdown
- Suicidal ideation and suicide attempt
- Identity loss and dissociation
- Physical assault
- Blood rituals and self-inflicted harm
- Murder and vengeance killings
- Sexual assault threat/attempt
- Childhood neglect
- Power imbalances and coercion

- Explicit sexual scenes - (consensual, intense, primal/blood elements)
- Power-exchange dynamics (D/s undertones)
- Obsession as a romantic motif
- Grief and loss

This book is not intended for readers under 18.
Please take care of yourself, and skip any scenes you need to.
Your well-being comes first. Always. 🖤

PROLOGUE

She dreams of ash.

It curls in the air like falling snow, silent and slow, blanketing the shattered world in soot and distant memories. The ground beneath her is cracked and scorched, glowing faintly with dying embers that pulse like a fading heartbeat. It hums beneath her, ancient and angry.

Screams sound in the distance—or maybe they're echoes of screams long since silenced. Here, sound doesn't die. Here, everything remembers.

Something that once resembled a crown lies discarded at the base of a blackened throne. Half-melted. Twisted. Warped by fire or fury—it's impossible to say.

Who did it belong to?

She reaches out with trembling hands that are blistered. Smoke unfurls from her skin like she's burning from the inside out. But she doesn't feel pain, not here, not in these dreams. Only the weight. Gods, the weight. It's the type that suffocates, like the silence before a guttural scream that could crack the sky itself.

She tries to turn, to move, to run. But she can't. Something holds her still, like fate itself is holding her completely frozen, pressing down on her shoulders.

"You were warned."

The voice is everywhere and nowhere. Male and female. Divine and monstrous.

The ash begins to swirl faster now, like a storm, a reckoning. It stings her eyes, her throat, filling her mouth with a taste of dust and betrayal.

A shadow rises in the distance. It has no face; it never does. Just a silhouette of absence, a walking void.

"She will return."

She wakes with a gasp, sweat-slicked and shaking. Her hands tremble as she touches her chest.

She can still taste the ash on her tongue.

CHAPTER 1
DAISY

There's something about the sound of sneakers squeaking against a gym floor that feels like home.

The echoing slap of soles, the rhythmic bounce of the music, the swell of laughter. God, I love it. The whole gym smells like floor polish and faint sweat, and somehow, it's comforting and familiar. Like everything's in its right place.

"You ready, Sandoval?" Ezra calls out, grinning from where he's practicing his tumbling on the far end of the court.

His bright ginger curls are tied up in a bun; his face already glistening with effort. He sticks the landing of his back handspring and throws his arms up like he's won gold at the Olympics.

I throw him a dazzling smile and give him a thumbs-up. "Always!"

"Ugh, how are you this perky after such a long day?" Talia groans from the stands where she's tying her laces. "What kind of unholy pact did you make to be this alive without caffeine?"

"Easy," I chirp. "My soul is powered by glitter, chaos, and the unshakable belief that today is going to be a good day."

She snorts, and Ezra whoops. "That's our Daisy!"

I twirl once on the spot, my golden ponytail bouncing as I do, arms outstretched in cheerleader glory. The gym lights catch the shimmer of my uniform—the deep navy and silver of our college colours—as I flash the kind of smile that could blind someone if they weren't careful. Because this moment? This is mine. People always underestimate cheerleaders, like we're just glorified pom-pom holders. But they don't see the bruises, the torn ligaments, the late practices. They don't see the tumbling drills, the lifts that demand complete trust in your team not to let you crash to the ground. We fight gravity every damn day. And I made sure I made it look as easy as freaking possible.

I grab my water bottle and jog over to the mat where Ezra's now stretching with dramatic flair, legs out, arms above his head like a ballerina.

"I'm feeling good today," I say, bouncing on the balls of my feet. "What's our lineup?"

"Full stunt routine," he says. "Coach wants to nail it before the game next week. You're flying."

"Perfect," I beam.

Flying is my favourite. There's nothing like the moment your feet leave the ground and the world disappears for a breath of air. That second where gravity forgets you exist, and you're just free... untouchable. Like maybe all the pain and bills and grief down below can't reach you up there.

As the team begins assembling, Coach blows her whistle and shouts for us to circle up. I stand shoulder to shoulder with my squad, clapping my hands, radiating sunshine. Because that's who I am.

Daisy Sandoval: Psychology major. Cheerleader. Optimist. Chronic overachiever. The girl who always has snacks in her bag, a first-aid kit on hand, and a smile for everyone. The girl who can hold her world together with sheer force of will. Who can pay rent, take extra shifts, and still hit every mark on the routine like it's nothing. No one sees the cracks. Not Ezra, not Talia, not my professors. And especially not my drunk of a father who hasn't been sober a day since my mom died. And that's exactly how I like it. I'm not broken. I'm bright. I'm the sun. And I don't burn out.

"Focus up, sunshine," Ezra sing-songs from behind me. "You're two seconds behind, and it's throwing off my entire centre of gravity."

I spin on my heel with a grin. "Maybe if you didn't do that dramatic shampoo commercial hair toss every time we hit a pyramid, we'd all be better off."

Ezra gasps, full drama, one hand clutching his chest. "You love my hair toss. It's iconic. It's theatrical. It's—"

"—Distracting," Talia yells from across the gym with her hands on her hips. "Reset! From the top!"

Ezra winks at me, his green eyes glinting with mischief, and mouths, *"She's scary,"* before spinning into position beside me. I bite back a laugh and pop back into formation. We run the same routine again. Step, kick, twist, catch. The routine blurs into sweat and rhythm, our bodies moving as one. My thighs burn, my lungs ache, and my face hurts from smiling too hard through it all, but it's the kind of ache that feels good. Here, in this sweaty gym with blaring pop music and scuffed floor lines, I feel untouchable.

When we finish, the whole squad collapses to the floor in dramatic groans and gasps. Sweat drips down the back of my neck as I lie back on the mat and close my eyes.

Ezra flops down beside me like a dying Victorian heroine. "Tell my story," he wheezes.

"You flipped once."

"And what a flip it was," he croons. "May I rest in glittery peace."

I giggle, unable to help it. "You're so dramatic."

He smirks. "You love it."

"Unfortunately."

Talia walks over, her high chestnut brown ponytail swinging with her steps. "You two done playing dead?"

Ezra points at her without lifting his head. "I'm not playing dead, I am dead, and I'm going to haunt your stanky-ass locker."

"Rude. Mine smells like peaches." She huffs.

"Then I'll make it smell like the despair I'm currently feeling with this damn routine you're killing us with."

"Mmhm." She smiles. "I earned this cheer captain title, and I don't plan on being an easy captain because my two best friends are whiny bitches." She laughs and tosses a water bottle at him, misses, and then hands one to me with a little squeeze to my shoulder. "You good, Daze?"

"Perfect." I beam, throwing in a thumbs up for extra sparkle.

She narrows her eyes at me. "Liar."

"Sunshine never lies."

"Sunshine lies so much," Ezra mumbles into the mat.

We all burst into laughter, half brought on from the sheer exhaustion of yet another brutal practice with Talia directing us like an army instead of a squad.

By the time we shower and change, the sky outside the gym is fading into cotton-candy hues. Talia insists on a 'post-practice snack run,' so we end up crammed into a booth at our favourite diner, sticky menus open and laughter echoing. Ezra orders three milkshakes—one vanilla, one strawberry, and one 'mystery flavour.' Talia keeps stealing my fries, so I retaliate by sticking a ketchup packet to her elbow. Moments like this make me forget everything else.

"Okay," Ezra says between mouthfuls of whipped cream. "If you were a flavour of milkshake, what would you be?"

"Vanilla bean," Talia answers confidently.

"Boring," he scoffs.

"Uh, no, it's classic." She retorts.

Ezra turns to me. "And you?"

"Sunshine swirl," I reply immediately.

They both snort, Talia shaking her head at me before stealing another fry. "Is that a real thing?" She asks.

"No. But it should be." I respond, shrugging my shoulders.

"You'd be like... lemon and hope," Ezra muses.

"Exactly."

THE SUN'S dipped below the horizon by the time I walk home. I don't drive, but it's fine because the three blocks from campus to my apartment aren't too bad to walk. Just dim... and a little eerie. The kind of walk that makes you clutch your phone a little tighter and makes you keep your keys between your fingers. Just in case. But it's not too bad.

By the time I climb my stairs to my apartment, my whole body's humming. Not from fear, but from fatigue. My building smells like burnt toast with a lovely undertone of regret. The carpets are always a little damp, and it's a place where no one smiles in the hallway, but someone is definitely always watching from their little peephole.

I lock the door behind me and let out a breath. Home. If you can call it that. Mails piled on the counter, mostly for 'Jim Sandoval.' Bright red FINAL NOTICE stamps scream at me from every envelope, but I don't throw them away. I don't know why... Maybe some part of me still hopes he'll come back. But I won't admit that out loud.

I toss my bag on the couch and head for the bathroom, tugging my shirt over my head on the way. I pause in the mirror, glancing at my weird little birthmark. A faint swirl of lines sits just below my shoulder, like a curling flame. It's almost invisible, but it's never gone away. My fingers brush at it out of habit. It means nothing; it's just skin. Just me. My mom used to say I looked like a bottle of sunlight—freckles, blonde waves, that kind of skin that never truly tans in the summer but has a nice glow to it anyway. Sometimes I see her in my own reflection: the curve of my nose, the way my smile tugs crooked when I'm nervous. But my eyes—those are all my dad. Ocean blue, a little too honest and a little too tired.

I drop my hand, strip the rest of the way, and step into the shower. The water is slow to heat, but I stand under it anyway, letting the chill wash away the sticky scent of sweat from practice, running my hands through my tangles in my hair. Gods, I ache everywhere. By the time I shut the shower off, the water's back to being barely warm. I wrap myself in a towel and wipe the steam from the mirror with my hand so I can see better. My reflection's a little clearer now, but the circles under my eyes look darker in this light. I press my palm flat against the glass, then pull away, leaving a foggy print behind. The bathroom light flickers once, making me grit my teeth as I stare at it. *Not now. Please. Not now.*

I DON'T BOTHER with a real dinner, just spoon straight from a tub of mint choc chip ice cream while scrolling through my phone. My hair's still damp when I flip onto the sofa in leggings and my favourite oversized tee—an ancient cheer shirt that has more than a few little holes that smells like lavender detergent. My phone buzzes, a text popping up on the screen.

Dad

Hey sweetheart, can you send me $100? I wouldn't ask if I wasn't desperate. Just until Friday. Promise.

The air leaves my lungs on an exasperated sigh. I stare at the message, my heart sinking into a familiar cold place. I check my bank app: Fifty-two dollars and eighty cents. Not enough for him, gods, it's barely enough for me. I type back out a reply, chewing on my lower lip:

I can't right now, Dad. I have to pay the electricity bill and buy food.

The typing bubbles appear, disappear, reappear. Then nothing, just utter silence. Every month without fail, there's a new crisis with my dad. Rent he can't pay, a bill that's overdue, money he swears he'll get back to me. It's always my problem, even though he doesn't live here anymore, and hasn't for a while. But his mess still lives in my mailbox, my texts, my voicemails, and deep inside my chest.

I lay back on the couch and toss the phone on the sofa, pressing the heels of my hands into my eyes until stars burst behind them. For over half of my life, I have been the responsible one, the one who finds money, or makes money. The one who handles bills, debts, food, life, whilst he spent those thirteen years with his head buried in the sand, piled high in debt, with a drinking problem and a gambling addiction. We both lost the sun in our lives, but where losing the sun turned me into a stronger version of myself, it turned him into a mess.

People say I'm resilient, bright, that I make things look so easy. Good. Let them say that, let them believe it. Because someone has to be the sun. And if not me—who?

CHAPTER 2
DAISY

I loved Tuesdays.

Maybe it's the promise of the weekend looming closer, or the fact that I managed to get through Monday with nothing more than a smile and a pep in my step. But even with four hours of sleep and a coffee cup that should've been retired yesterday, I am unstoppable.

My alarm blared at six thirty a.m., and I rolled out of bed with all the grace of a newborn deer. My hair looked like a crime scene, and my favourite hoodie had migrated somewhere under the bed (RIP). But still—up I got, because sunshine doesn't sleep in.

Now, standing outside of campus with the cold morning air kissing my cheeks, I balance my thermal filled with cheap store-bought coffee in one hand, and my psych notes in the other. I am a vision. Sort of.

"Daisy Sandoval, is that you radiating divine energy this early in the morning?" A voice calls from behind me.

I don't even have to turn around to know who it is. "Only if divine energy comes with chronic exhaustion and a side of coffee."

Ezra sidles up beside me, fully decked in glitter eyeshadow and a scarf that was so thick it could double as a freaking quilt. "You say exhaustion, I say edgy glow."

We walk onto campus together as Ezra scrolls through TikTok whilst I read a paragraph on my phone on Freud for the third time. I still can't decide if he was a genius, or really just needed therapy and a good sandwich. The entire campus is buzzing with energy as students crowd the quad, expensive cups of coffee in hand, looking far too alive for people running on deadline panic and vending machine diets.

I wave at a few familiar faces, most waving back, some even smiling at me first. That's the thing about being the 'sun', people tend to just like me. Professors remember my name, strangers hold open the door, and I get invited to almost everything, even when I rarely go. I guess people assume sunshine equals stability. They don't see that I haven't bought groceries in four days despite having next to no food, or that I've had the same voicemail from my dad sitting unopened in my inbox because I'm too tired to listen to whatever mess he's in now. No one sees that, and I make damn sure of it, too.

I BREEZE through my first two lectures, taking colour-coded notes, nodding thoughtfully, even asking a question that makes my ethics professor raise her eyebrows like she's both impressed and terrified of how seriously I take everything—because being a failure is not an option. By the time classes end, I've taken four pages of notes, answered two questions aloud, and handed out three pens to strangers who forgot theirs, of course, not getting them back. Thankfully, I have a lifetime supply of gel pens at home. I'm not sure when I started collecting them, but now I have at least three drawers full of them in a range of colours. Some sparkly, some neon, and some that write in a funky bubble writing.

After class, I meet up with Talia at the student union for our usual Tuesday smoothie ritual that I absolutely cannot afford to obtain. She's already waiting at our table, tapping away on her laptop, with her hair twisted into a sleek bun and her eyeliner sharp enough to cut anybody who pisses her off. And that happens to be a lot of people.

"I got you mango-pineapple," she says, handing me the straw with one hand and still typing with the other. *Psycho*.

"You're a goddess among mortals," I say, sinking into the chair and taking a long freezing sip.

"And you're late," she mutters.

"I was having a full-blown existential crisis in the library bathroom about deadlines. You know... Tuesday things."

She finally looks up, snorts, and flips her screen toward me. "Wanna read the paragraph I wrote about maternal bonding and identity projection through the mythic archetypes?"

"Only if I can cry about how I still haven't finished mine."

Ezra appears with a beaming grin, plopping into the seat beside me. "Good news! I convinced the theatre department to lend us fog machines for the next cheer showcase. Bad news... they said if we break them, we owe a grand each."

I blink in utter confusion. "... Ezra. Sweetheart. Why do we need fog machines?"

He sips his iced mocha, letting out a dramatic *ahhhh* of satisfaction. "Because the spirit of cheer demands it."

We burst into laughter loudly, earning a few glances from annoyed students. But I don't care. This right here is my favourite part of college. Not the grades, not the accolades. But this—laughing until your ribs hurt with the people who make your world glow, who keep you sane. The ones who let you continue to be the sunshine, even when you're running on fumes. Ezra had been my best friend since high school, and every year I've watched him turn more sparkle-obsessed than the last.

His bright, long, softly curled ginger hair and his freckle-splattered face match his fiery personality. If I were the sun, he was the sunset. Beautiful, breathtaking, and demanding of attention. His green eyes were a match for emeralds, like little sparkling gems that were always so full of life. He was the breath of fresh air in my life, my anchor, my platonic soul mate. We even made a pact that if we both weren't married by the time we were forty, we would just marry each other, despite the fact that he most definitely was not into girls.

He tried to convince himself he was straight in the final year of high school, and even dated a girl for a while. Of course, it didn't last, and he ended up sleeping with her brother instead. He low-key deserved the slap she gave him.

If Ezra and I were the bright sunshine and sunset, Talia was the night. Sexy, seductive, and everything I wished I was. She oozed confidence, her chestnut brown hair never out of place, her honey brown eyes always lined with an eyeliner wing I could only dream of achieving. She was utterly beautiful, and she knew it. She refused to settle down, despite Bradley Everington trying for the best part of a year to get her to. In her words, "I am way too young and sexy to be anchored down to just one man." I admired that about her, being a 'free spirit', as she liked to call herself.

I've been with Ethan for six months now, and I truly think I'm in love with him, even if neither of us has said it yet. Where Talia enjoys having casual sex, I'm the polar opposite. At twenty, I'm still a virgin. I don't know why. I guess I've just had so many other things going on in my life that I've just kept putting it off, despite Ethan's eagerness to go further. I've done other stuff, like giving him head, but he refused to return the favour and go down on me.

Apparently, that was 'gross,' and he didn't do that because only girls were supposed to go down on guys. Talia said he's a 'fucking loser', and only 'little bitches' don't go down on their girlfriends, but I don't mind; it's not like I know what I'm missing out on.

After smoothies, I head to work at the campus cafe, and like always, the shift is busy. Students and faculty swarm in like caffeine-starved locusts. I wear my apron and my customer service voice like armour and keep the smiles coming until my cheeks ache. I recommend a cinnamon chai to a girl who looks like she's seconds from tears, and she lights up like I gave her a free puppy.

Sometimes, that's all it takes—a little light in someone else's day to make everything better. Even if mine is stitched together with cheap coffee and poor coping mechanisms. On the plus side, work means I get the good coffee for a change, not the cheap crap that sits in my cupboard at home.

By the time my shift ends, I'm sticky with syrup and feel like I've been steaming milk for a decade. Not to mention the unbearable amount of Taylor Swift that has blasted over the radio for hours. I step outside into the fresh air, cheeks flushed, and take in a deep breath. It's a good day. I mean, sure—I've got two essays due, a stack of laundry taller than my fridge, and a voicemail I'm still ignoring. But the sun's out despite it being freezing, my friends are weird and wonderful, and I'm still standing. So, that has to count for something. But despite my utter exhaustion from work, I still had one more thing to do: cheer.

~

The football game runs late, again. The sky's gone from golden hour to dusky pink, and sweat sticks to me as I re-lace my shoes. My legs feel like jelly, and I can already tell I'm going to regret those final stunts in the morning.

"Nice work today," Coach yells as the squad starts packing up. "You're clean on timing. Keep it tight!"

We all groan in half-unison, some collapsing dramatically onto the turf. I grab my water bottle and take a long sip before standing and stretching myself out.

My eyes scan the field, spotting him almost instantly. Tall, dark brown eyes and messy brown hair. Ethan stands by the bleachers, helmet tucked under one arm, sweat-soaked jersey clinging to his broad chest. He's already grinning when our eyes meet, and it takes all of two seconds before he's jogging toward me, his brown hair sticking to his forehead.

"Hey, baby," he says, pressing a quick kiss to the side of my head. His hand settles low on my waist, then lower, fingers curling possessively around my hip. "You looked hot out there."

I smile, but it's strained as I focus on his hands lowering down my body. "Thanks. You guys looked good, too. Congrats on the win!"

He shrugs off the compliment, then slips his hand from my waist to my lower back, pulling me into his side. "You wanna come hang for a bit? Some of the guys are heading out for drinks."

"I can't," I say, not quite apologetic. "I have a paper due Monday, and I'm tired from work."

Ethan's jaw tightens for a fraction of a second, his usual calm exterior slipping. "Always so tired from working," he mutters, like it's a flaw.

The problem with Ethan was that he came from money; he didn't have to get a job. He had a full-paid scholarship thanks to being the football captain, and his parents were literal millionaires. He didn't understand that not everyone had their parents' money to live on; he definitely wouldn't understand that my dad basically lived off my money.

"I like having electricity and food," I say sweetly, stepping back just enough to breathe.

He laughs, but there's no warmth in it. "Maybe it wouldn't hurt to miss a meal or two, you're not starving babe," he says, poking at my belly.

I take a sharp inhale, his comment stopping me in my tracks. I wasn't thin, I knew that, but I wasn't overweight either. I was curvy, with naturally larger hips, thighs, and bum. I weighed around 185 pounds, which I knew was more than the rest of my squad, but I was still healthy. He'd never mentioned my weight being an issue before.

He smiled, "I'm kidding, Daze; no need to get your panties in a twist." He pulls me close, his hand brushing my ass as he leans in again, his mouth close to my ear. "You sure I can't convince you to blow off doing your paper? I've been thinking about you all day."

I stiffen in his touch, preparing myself for more of his pushing about having sex with him, despite me constantly telling him how I wanted to wait a little longer. I don't actually know what I'm waiting for, or why I'm waiting. But I know for certain, I'm not ready yet. Ezra appears out of nowhere, throwing an arm around my shoulders like he's rescuing me from a predator.

"Hey, lover boy. She's got a paper to write. Chill."

Ethan's smile drops, just for a second. "What does this have to do with you, sparkles?"

"Just looking out for my girl," Ezra says brightly, but with a bite to his tone. "Someone has to."

Talia's beside us now, too, arms crossed with one of her eyebrows arched in disapproval. "You know, Ethan, I've met actual dogs with better manners."

He chuckles, but there's tension in his posture now. "Relax. We're just talking."

"No," Talia snaps. "You're pawing."

I step between them before it turns into something worse. My friends are extremely protective, and they're especially protective when it comes to Ethan.

"Guys, it's fine." I smile brightly.

"It's not," Ezra murmurs, but he lets it go.

Ethan leans in one more time, lips brushing my cheek. "I'll text you later."

I nod, but I already know I'll pretend to be asleep when he does, so I can avoid his need for constant sexting and nudes. It's like the guy's brain is hardwired to one topic only after nine p.m., and it really wasn't something I was in the mood for today. Or any other day, for that matter.

"So," Talia says, chewing the cookie she pulled out of her bag, "what the hell's up with your boyfriend grabbing onto you like he's trying to stuff you into his gym bag so he can take you home and use you as a sex doll?"

I blink. "Wow, what a subtle way to approach that conversation."

"You know what isn't subtle?" Ezra says, his voice low. "The way he touches you. Like you're a prize he won at a rigged carnival game."

"He's just... affectionate," I smile.

"No, babe. I'm affectionate,' Ezra says. "Ethan's a hungry narcissist with boundary issues and the emotional depth of a doorstop."

Talia nods, forcing back her snort and high-fiving Ezra for his doorstop comment. "He treats you like you're supposed to be grateful he shows up. Like he's doing you a favour by dating you."

"He's not that bad," I say automatically. Then I pause.

Is he that bad? He wasn't always like this. When we first met, he was sweet. Charming even. Funny in a slightly try-hard kind of way. He used to walk me to class, send me dumb videos, and bring me chocolate after late-night shifts. But lately... It's all felt heavier. Like every conversation is a negotiation. Like I owe him something just for being my boyfriend.

"You don't have to defend him just because you've already invested time," Talia says, softer now. "Time doesn't make it love, Daze."

I roll my eyes, "I know."

And I do know. Somewhere deep down, I know Ethan is a storm coming, not the shelter. But it's easier not to look up when the sky starts to darken. Besides, he hasn't given me an actual reason to have to break up with him, and I'm pretty sure you need one of those to end a relationship, right? I internally groan. I know absolutely nothing about relationships. That's probably why I stay with Ethan.

I pull my jacket on, my shoulders aching, and wave goodbye to Talia and Ezra as I head away from the campus gates to walk home. It's late, and the streets are emptier now without the bustling students. The stars are out, but dim, the kind of night that feels too quiet to be real. It's peaceful in comparison to my daily life, filled with rushing, working, studying, and practicing. I pull my phone from my pocket, noticing there's not a single new message. Not from Ethan, not from my dad, absolutely nothing, and it just adds to the peace. I walk the familiar path back to my apartment, one foot in front of the other. Tired and hungry, a bite of Talia's cookie doing nothing to fill the pit in my stomach. My bones ache from a long day of using and abusing my body. I hum a little under my breath to fill the silence, a melody I don't ever remember learning but one that comes back to me constantly. When I reach my building door, I glance back, and the atmosphere feels slightly heavier than it did moments ago. I scan my surroundings, just in case, but there's nothing there. Just me. Just home.

CHAPTER 3
KORITHAX

The mortal realm is so loud and cluttered.

Ceiling fans click like broken bones, and pipes groan in protest. Half the lights flickered as if debating whether to keep existing. And yet somehow, it's the glitter-covered calendar on the fridge that offends me most. Bright pink lettering with the words "Smoothie date <3" and "Exam prep!" scrawled across it like the ramblings of a preppy cultist. Gods, I hate it here.

I pace Daisy Sandoval's tiny apartment with the coiled irritation of someone who's not only been summoned against his will, but summoned to this chaos. Mismatched mugs, a laundry pile the size of a corpse, books stacked in unnatural places. There's a system here, but it's pure fucking madness. The couch sags like it's been through a war, and there's glitter everywhere.

"I should've killed him where he stood," I mutter to myself, brushing a stray hair tie off the counter onto the floor.

A mug near the sink reads Good Vibes Only, and I resist every urge in me to break it. Instead, I sit on the edge of the couch, wings folded tight against my back, my shadow leaking across the floor like spilled ink. The summon still tingles through my body, the magic of the deal sealed, buzzing in my palm. A deal with a drunk. My jaw ticks at the memory of the event:

He stumbled into my circle like a man already half dead. Whiskey on his breath, tremor in his fingers. His soul tasted like rot and regret—just the kind of man who sought out demons when life had stopped giving him answers. Jim Sandoval. Mortal. Pathetic. Reeking of desperation.

"I need money," he slurred, eyes too bloodshot to hold mine for more than a second. "Enough to fix everything. Get out of debt. Give her a life I never could."

At the time, I assumed he meant his wife or a trashy side-piece. Most men did.

"How noble," I replied, my voice dry. "And what will you offer me in return?"

He hesitated. Then pulled out a photograph—creased, worn. A little blonde girl, beaming through a missing tooth.

"My daughter," he said. "She's bright. Pretty. People like her. She... she could be something, y'know?"

I didn't blink, just glared at him.

"You're offering me your child's soul?"

He didn't flinch at my tone, just nodded.

"She'll survive. She's strong. Stronger than me. She'll find a way out."

It wasn't the worst offer I'd ever been made, but it was among the more pathetic. I took the deal. Not because I needed the soul. But because something about it itched behind my ribs, the kind of itch that I was desperate to scratch. I marked the contract in flame, and he signed it in blood that he was too drunk to realise he'd spilled.

And here I am—sitting in his daughter's home—among the glitter pens and gaudy mugs. I lean back, wings draping across the couch. Her scent's everywhere, it's sickeningly sweet with a hint of lavender. But underneath it, I can sense the grief and fatigue that lace the aura of her home. It's a kind of sadness that doesn't shout to be heard; it just lingers in the air like smoke. It annoys me. She annoys me, and I haven't even met her yet.

I KICK my boots up on the coffee table and scowl at a photo frame. She was with two other mortals—one with ridiculous eyeshadow and bright ginger hair, the other a dark-haired girl with a face that says *I think I'm a goddess*. They stand on a beach, arms slung around each other, smiling like they don't have a fucking thing to worry about. Well, that was quickly going to change for the little sunshine.

I sense Daisy's energy the moment she reaches the front door. Her light aura brushes against me like a dandelion against stone, soft and pure. I don't bother moving. I want to let her see me instantly. Let her understand exactly what her father's desperation has bought her.

The key turns in the lock, and she steps inside without a care in the world. That is, until she sees me.

She freezes, and we stare at each other across the room. There I am, lounging like a serpent on her couch, and she stands clutching a tote bag, blinking in disbelief, her mouth slightly parted.

"You're early," I say blandly. "I was enjoying the thrilling tension between the lights and your unpaid electricity bill."

She drops her bag. "Who the hell are you?"

"Rude." I stand slowly, wings spreading just enough to shadow the room. "I'm the one who's been waiting to collect on a very, very stupid deal."

CHAPTER 4
DAISY

I don't scream.

Which, in hindsight, is either incredibly brave or incredibly stupid. Because standing in front of me is a literal demon.

Tall, so tall his head nearly brushes the ceiling, and what the... horns... those are horns. Curled from his skull, looking like polished obsidian in the dim light. And behind him, drape large, black, leathery wings. His eyes are midnight black. Not brown, not dark. Hauntingly black.

But it's his face that unsettles me the most. He's beautiful, in a way that's completely inhuman. Sharp cheekbones, full lips, a jaw carved like he was born from storm and stone. He has pointed ears that poke out of his long black hair, which sits at shoulder length. Power radiates off of him, humming like a wire stretched too tight, ready to snap.

He's wearing a tight black shirt, which is rolled up to his elbows, revealing his muscled forearms that are intricately tattooed in swirls and patterns. His hands are huge, veins protruding from them, showing the strength behind what I imagine is a lethal grip. His black pants hug his legs in a way that makes them look like solid stone, ending tucked into black combat boots. Good god, he's death incarnate.

"I'm sorry," I say slowly, still frozen by the door. "But did you just say you've come to collect from a deal?"

The man—creature—whatever he is, lifts one eyebrow, like I'd just asked if the sky was blue.

"Yes, from your dad. Keep up." He gestures vaguely toward the kitchen. "I'd say offer me a drink, but your fridge is a shrine to sadness and expired dairy."

"My dad wouldn't," I say, my voice barely a whisper.

"He would. He did. And frankly, you should be flattered. He could've offered up his rotten soul, but no, he went with you, his 'precious girl.'" He sneers the words with a mocking undertone.

My legs remember how to move, barely, and I stumble toward the kitchen counter, gripping onto it for some sense of stability.

"This is some kind of joke."

"If only." The demon sits back down, leaning back against the couch, his wings shifting with a leathery rustle. "Do I look like I do jokes?"

He has a point. He looks like he does wars, or plagues, or poetry slams where the poems are just death threats.

"This is a dream," I whisper. "A very weird, stress-induced, demon-laced dream, brought on by too much caffeine and too little sleep."

He rolls his eyes. "Yes, because your subconscious definitely knows how to sculpt such perfection. Sit down, Daisy."

I don't sit, instead opting to pace. Although there isn't much room to pace in here, it's more like taking two steps forward, turning on the spot, then repeating the process the other way.

"How do you know my name?" I ask.

"Your father gave it to me." His tone changes, just a fraction. "Along with your soul."

And just like that, my body feels like ice. I know my dad's bad with money. I know about the gambling, the drinking, the times rent wasn't paid. I'd scraped coins from couch cushions just to keep food in my belly. But this? This was worse than anything I'd imagined.

"You're lying."

"I'm not," he says. "And I'm bored now. So, unless you'd like me to start packing your things for the trip to Hell, I suggest you get a grip." He stands, crossing his arms across his broad chest.

"Trip to Hell?" I repeat, voice rising with panic.

"Figuratively speaking. For now." He smiles like he's enjoying watching me short-circuit. "You've been claimed, sweetheart. That means a few things, one of which involves me keeping close until I'm ready to collect."

I blink. "So... what? You're like, haunting me now?"

"No. More like, babysitting what's mine."

The rage hits before the fear, and I slam my hands on the counter before marching toward him and jabbing a finger at his chest. Well... his torso, because this man is a damn skyscraper.

"I don't care who or what you are," I snap. "You don't get to waltz in here, insult my fridge, and act like I'm some kind of possession."

He looks down at my finger, then back at me with an arched brow. "You touch me again, sunshine, and I'm turning your bathroom into a portal that leads to a screaming abyss, and I'm fucking pushing you through it."

I drop my hand, but refuse to back down.

He sighs like I'm giving him a migraine. "You're really going to make this difficult, aren't you?"

"Absolutely."

He grumbles something under his breath that I'm pretty sure was a curse word, and sits back down with the wariness of a demon realising he's been assigned to the worst possible human going.

"Of course, I had to agree to take the soul of a cheerleader. With the glitter and the unbearable sunshine aura."

"Excuse me for not decorating in death and brimstone."

He raises both of his eyebrows at me this time, and I just glare at him with as much hatred as my face can muster.

"I didn't come to collect," he says, after a moment. "Not yet. Just figured I'd meet the girl who was worth more than her father's soul."

"And?" I ask.

"And I'm disappointed." His smirk sharpens. "You don't look like much."

The words hit me, but they don't hurt like he probably intended. I cross my arms over my chest, chin lifted despite the tremble in my knees.

"Well, you're not exactly the Prince Charming I imagined either," I mutter. "Too many horns. And you tracked smoke onto my rug."

Something flickers across his face, a noise threatening to leave his throat. A laugh, almost. But it's gone as quickly as it came. He stands and takes a step toward me, making me push myself as far as I can against the door to recoil away from him. The closer he gets, the more heat I can feel radiating from his sun-kissed skin. He lifts my chin with a long finger, making my eyes meet his dark gaze. He grins, a smile worthy of dreams and nightmares.

He tilts his head again at me, "I'll be seeing you, Daisy."

And just like that—he's gone. No flash. No sound. Just a ripple in the air where he stood, and the lingering scent of fire and musk. Even the smoke from my rug has vanished. How considerate of him.

I slide down the door until I'm sitting on the floor, knees pulled to my chest. I don't scream, I don't cry. I just sit there, staring at the empty space where he was. And I wonder how many more things in my life are going to be taken from me before anyone ever thinks to ask me what I'm willing to give.

~

THE ROOM IS deathly quiet after he's gone, like the walls are holding their breath. I sit there on the floor for what feels like hours, the imprint of his presence still pressed into the air around me, the feel of his finger on the underside of my chin still burning. I stare at the floor where my bag fell, its contents spilled all across the floor.

That didn't happen. It couldn't have happened. Demons aren't real. Fathers don't sell their daughters' souls. Except... mine might have.

I press my hands to my head, slowly dragging them down my face. They're shaking, my breath stuttering in and out like my lungs have forgotten how to work.

"It wasn't real," I whisper. "It was just stress. You're tired. You haven't slept. You hallucinated. People under stress hallucinate all the time."

Oh great, now I'm talking to myself too. This is normal. Everything's absolutely fine.

I peel myself off the floor and move toward the kitchen on autopilot, stepping over the contents of my bag without bothering to clear it up. My throat feels tight, my head buzzing. My body is moving, but my mind is pacing in circles and screaming.

Denial:

It was a dream. A waking dream. You've been working too much. Not eating enough. You just imagined it; people imagine things. It happens.

Anger:

But why him? Why a demon? Why not a faceless shadow or a monster under the bed? Why a voice like thunder wrapped in silk? Why a man who looked like sin carved into something holy? And why did it feel so freaking real?

Bargaining:

Maybe you're crazy. That's better, right? That's fixable. You can take meds, go to therapy. Maybe you've snapped, and you don't know it yet. Maybe this is what losing your mind feels like.

I start moving through the kitchen to look for something to comfort me. I open the fridge and stare blankly inside. There's nothing there. Nothing but a small piece of cardstock placed carefully on the middle shelf.

I freeze.

No. No, no, no.

I reach for it with trembling fingers, my breath catching in my throat. It's smooth, black, and the edges are gilded in gold, catching the fridge light.

There's only one line printed in silver ink:

Your soul now belongs to me.

- Korithax

My knees almost give out. I grip the counter, the card clutched in my fist, heart pounding so hard I think I might be having a heart attack.

He was real.

He was real.

CHAPTER 5
DAISY

I didn't sleep.

Not because I was scared. Okay, maybe a little scared. But mostly because I was absolutely, completely, cosmically baffled. I mean, there was a demon in my living room last night. A demon. Horns, wings, and a voice like molten sin. That's not normal. That's not how my Tuesdays go.

Now the card sits on my nightstand, silent and smug and all too mocking for my liking. Matte black with golden edges and silver foil lettering, like it's some VIP invite to Hell's Met Gala.

Your soul now belongs to me.

- Korithax

The writing looks too elegant for the threat it carries. Like something written on wedding invitations. Except this one's promising eternal damnation instead of cake and bad dancing. How rude. I keep hearing his voice. That dark, silky tone that held such power behind it that my skin instantly broke out in goosebumps when it caressed my ears. The way his shadow filled my apartment, and how the air itself shifted around him, as if the laws of physics personally stepped aside to make room. And every time I blink, I see him standing there. Boots planted, arms folded, not a care in the freaking world. Honestly? Kind of iconic... if you forget the part where he owns my soul.

I TRY to go about my morning like I haven't just been told I'm literally soul-deep in demonic debt. Because really, what could I do? Make a complaint to demonic customer services? I brush my teeth and change into leggings and a bright yellow hoodie, the weather turning a little too cold for my usual bright and floral summer dresses, and twist my hair into a messy bun. Padding bare foot across my cramped little flat, the cold floor cold against my toes, I make a smoothie with the last little bit of milk in my fridge and the banana that could've been thrown out a few days ago, as well as some frozen berries.

My place is tiny. Like, cupboard-under-the-stairs-but-with-bills tiny. But I love it. Fairy lights drape over my little bookshelf, which is jammed with every fantasy paperback I could afford second-hand. My bed is a nest of mismatched pillows and blankets, the walls are plastered in sticky notes, and I have precisely one working lamp.

Even though I know I need to nourish my body, I throw the smoothie away after just one sip. Everything tastes wrong now, with my stomach constantly churning like a never-ending storm. I can physically feel the anxiety and dread eating away at me; it feels like my body is in fight or flight. Except, there is no flight. And I highly doubt I could fight against a demon and win. So what? Instead of fight or flight, it's... bow down and surrender? Yikes.

Still, despite everything, I go to campus anyway because after a morning of staring at my web browser, I had run out of things to Google. Not like I really knew what to look for in the first place. 'How to reverse a soul bargain made by your alcoholic father with an ancient demon?' Safe to say, there wasn't a Reddit thread for that, no matter how hard I tried to will one into existence.

By the time I get there, I've convinced myself this is fine. Totally fine. Everything is sooooo fine. Except it's not. Because apparently, demons are real. Demons. I've read almost every fantasy series I could get my hands on, and not once did I ever expect to be starring in one. Where's my sword? Where's my prophecy? Why is my magical inheritance an ancient blood pact forged by a drunk dad with a devil man who looks like a cursed Calvin Klein model?

I flop onto a bench near the arts building and try to study—which is going really well if the goal is to draw increasingly chaotic doodles of little flame emojis around the word HELP.

"You look like you wrestled a demon in your sleep and lost," Ezra says, flopping down beside me.

I almost laugh, a choking sound leaving me instead. The irony of his words wasn't lost on me.

"Do you mind? Some of us are busy suffering in silence."

He sits swinging his legs off the side of the bench, his purple eyeshadow extra glittery today. "Hmm. Suffering loudly is much more therapeutic. Trust me."

"You would say that. You're literally the loudest person I know." I scoff.

"And you love me for it." He beams.

"Undeniably." I smile. Because it's impossible not to when Ezra's around. He smells like sweet marshmallows and has a constant chaotic aura surrounding him.

"You okay, Daze?" He adds, softer now.

"Fine," I chirp. "Just discovering that Hell is real and I have a personal demon. You?"

Ezra blinks. "Is this one of your books that you're reading or...?"

I wave it off. "It's fine. I'm fine. Everything is fine." My voice cracks on the last word, and I fake a cough to cover it.

He stares at me, any hint of amusement gone from his face. "Daisy..."

"Seriously. Let's talk about you! Did you finally steal that glitter gel pen from Talia?"

Ezra gasps dramatically. "That freaking pen was mine first! She borrowed it two years ago, and I've been manifesting its return ever since."

A snort escapes me. He was just as manic about his gel pens as I was. He links his arm through mine and rests his head on my shoulder. My giant human-weighted blanket.

~

Psychology 210 is brutal. It's not the material—it's me. Professor Doyle is lecturing us about trauma responses. Fight, flight, freeze. The human brain under duress. Maybe we should add a new one: 'freak the hell out but pretend you're fine and spiral internally.' My pen is in my hand, but for once, I'm not scribbling down every word with intensity. He says something about dissociation, and my stomach twists. When the mind can't handle what's happening to the body. It splits. Creates distance.

Dissociation. Yep. That's what I'm feeling right now. Like I'm floating six inches outside of myself, watching from behind glass that I can't seem to break through. I don't realise I'm digging my nails into my thigh until I feel the sting of skin breaking. Someone behind me laughs, the sound sharp and jarring. I flinch, my breath coming in too fast, as I try to calm myself down. You're safe, Daze. It's okay.

The girl next to me leans over, whispering, "Hey, you okay?"

I nod, offering her a warm smile, despite the fact I feel like I'm dying inside.

After class, I aimlessly walk. Past the library, past the quad, and through one of the little gardens some of the students had planted a few years back. I keep walking until the noise in my head gets quieter, and I end up under my favourite tree. It's half-dead and split from a storm three years ago, but it keeps growing anyway. I like that about it, that despite the odds stacked against it, it continued to grow and flourish. My kind of girl. Maybe I could do that, maybe I could still have a long, happy life, and ignore the impending doom that's awaiting me on the other side.

I press my back against the bark, the sharp wood digging into my flesh as I pull my knees to my chest. I reach into my bag and pull out the card again, idly flipping it between my fingers. *Your soul now belongs to me.* I could burn it. Tear it. Deny it. Instead, I opt for texting Talia.

Me: If I die, delete my browser history.

Talia: Oh, gods, what did you Google?

Me: "What to do when a demon claims your soul."

Talia: ... so no coffee today?

I snort. She knows me too well. I look back at my phone and stare at the contact I need to speak to next. Dad. My finger hovers over it for a second too long, then I tap call. It rings. Once. Twice. Four times. Then his voice picks up.

"I had a visitor last night," I say. "Tall. Horns. Looked like he models for Hell's annual calendar." Silence. "Do you know anything about that?" More silence. "Dad?"

"Shit," he mutters.

"That's your response?! You sell my soul, and all you can say is shit?"

He tries to explain, but I hang up before he can finish. Because I'm not interested in whatever excuses he's got. I'm interested in surviving this, and doing it in the most aggressively cheery way possible.

I close my eyes, resting my head against the tree, letting the wind brush against my face. My dad had been a perpetual ass since my mom had died when I was seven. Breast cancer, the kind that moves fast. The kind that steals everything before you even understand what's happening. They said breast cancer was one of the better cancers to get, that it was the most easily manageable. But they were wrong, because it had spread long before they found it. She was bright and kind, she smelled like vanilla and flowers, wore sunflower earrings, and used to sing off-key in the car like she didn't give a damn who was listening. Mom told me I could survive anything, and that I was the sun. But then she was gone, and I soon learned that, in fact, she was the sun. Because the world became so much duller without her shining in it. But for her, I tried so very hard to be the sun, and would continue to do so, no matter what. My dad started drinking not long after she died, and I learned what it meant to become strong just to keep someone else from falling apart. But no matter how strong I was for both of us, he still crumbled away, into a shell I no longer recognised as the loving, doting father he once was.

I wipe my eyes with the back of my hand to clear the tears and sit up straight. I am so angry. Angry at my dad, angry at this demon who walked into my life like I'm just another line in some infernal ledger. But I'm also scared. So, so scared. Still, I won't break. I'll hold my head high and continue to be the sun in everybody else's lives. I will continue to sing in the shower, offer my help to strangers, and brighten up everybody else, whilst ignoring the fact that life has thrown another curveball at me.

"Be the sun," I whisper, taking a long, deep breath.

CHAPTER 6
KORITHAX

Hell doesn't burn. Not in the way mortals expect.

It isn't just a landscape of fire pits and shrieking souls. That's Gehenna, a southern wasteland full of lava rivers, boiling stone, and damned screams. But Hell itself? It's a continent fractured by purpose—each with its own horrors, laws, and rulers. A monarchy of monsters held together by threats and blood oaths. And I sit at the centre of it, awaiting to wear a crown I never even wanted.

I sit alone, lounging on the obsidian throne of Zeriavoss, the northern capital. My leg hangs over one carved armrest, and I'm nursing a headache that refuses to die. The throne is too tall, too obnoxious. My castle sits beneath a never-ending sky, with winged sentries on constant guard. Below, it's ringed by molten rivers on its outer edges, daring trespassers to try to enter my kingdom. Gothic spires cast long shadows through the stained-glass windows, and still, somehow, it bores me to tears.

The distant glow of Gehenna's smoke stains the horizon. That's where the newest batch of sinners are likely already burning—priests, liars, and a child-killer. I used to attend every judgement at the Welcome Circle, where the soulstone cliffs whisper the truth of every mortal to enter our realm. Now, I leave that to the lesser demons because the screams and excuses are always the fucking same.

Nobody ever believes they'll end up here, facing the wrath of their wrongdoings. But it's always the same beg for mercy, the same desperate, pathetic pleas. They're escorted in, placed on the podium, and the circle of judges, normally six of us, sit around them and listen to their sins. They have a chance to explain themselves, often coming up with bullshit excuses as to why they behaved the way they did, and then their judgement is made. Some only have to reside in Hell for a period of time, for petty sins that don't require a lifetime of suffering.

However, some are children, their tortured souls sent to us to help them heal before they are moved on to their final resting places. They go to the realm of children. A softer western dominion, ruled by Vailith, the Goddess of Mercy. Children's souls go there, those broken far too young. They tend to gardens that have soft winds, where glowing spirit willows dance between the plants and trees. They're given power, a choice. Forgive, or punish those who wronged them. Neither choice is wrong; neither choice makes a difference in their stay here. And sometimes, the children even choose to stay instead of moving on. Not out of fear, but because love has anchored them to her little sanctuary. The only corner of Hell where pure laughter is continuous, and not full of pure madness.

I SHIFT on the throne again, glaring at the carved edges as if I can will them with my mind to be less uncomfortable. This throne used to belong to my father, Korran. The High King of Hell and former manipulator. A man carved from pride and deception, who wielded control with a smile as sharp as his blade. He handed me this throne not out of trust, but strategy. A transition masked as inheritance, but built on secrets and blood deals. Conveniently, his whore of a second wife disappeared after he handed away his throne. Not a shocker that's for sure.

He still lurks, of course. Creeping around the halls of Hell when he has the energy, advising where he isn't welcome, whispering to the few allies who still call him king. He wants me to rule the way he did—with cruelty mistaken for order. He sees my defiance as weakness, my restraint as failure. But I am not him, and I never will be. Despite the fact that it was long before my existence, the constant whispers all tell the same story of the betrayal, the lies, the deceit. And one day, when the right moment comes, I will burn the last remnants of his reign from these walls.

We don't even speak, not really. I spare him a hello every now and then, but other than that, he may as well be a stranger who lurks the halls with a lopsided crown upon his aging skull.

He may technically still be king, but as far as I'm concerned, he is nothing more than a thief of oxygen whose time is running out. Removing him from the throne permanently is the only thing that makes me want to take a bride. But even so, I cannot. Not yet. I have too many things to focus on before shackling a woman to a lifetime beside me. I have no interest in love or women, other than using their bodies for a quick fuck to release tension.

I lean my head back and let out a slow breath. I've got no interest in any politics today. No patience for court games or fake smiles. My thoughts continue to drift back to the girl in the cluttered apartment. Daisy. Stupid name. Stupid sunshine attitude. But damn if she didn't stare at me like I wasn't the worst thing to ever walk through her door. The way she didn't scream makes my skin itch in the most irritating way. In fact, she was sarcastic as fuck and acted like I was just an annoying inconvenience in her little pathetic life. Mortals are supposed to crumble when they meet their end.

I'd checked her file. Dead mother. Gambling, drunk of a father. A girl caught between trying to survive and pretending she's not breaking from grief. Death was such a big deal to mortals, something

I didn't understand. Maybe it was because their lives were so short in comparison to us immortals. Gone in the blink of an eye. My mother had also died, but I did not mourn or grieve. Death was a part of the process, even as an immortal. Or maybe I just didn't have enough time with her to be able to grieve her. I barely remember her, only her lavender eyes that sometimes appear in my dreams, like even in death she's checking on her only child.

MID THOUGHT, the summons arrives on parchment that smells like self-righteousness and stardust. The seal is golden—pressed with their wretched emblem: six interlocked rings. Six beings who believe their authority is divinely ordained just because they sit higher in the sky than the rest of us. The Divine Six. The Uppers. The creators and rulers of everything that is and ever was. They want a word. Of course they do. I let the scroll burn to ash in my hand before stepping through the portal I summoned with a flick of my hand.

The chamber of the Divine Six is made of pure light. Not the warm kind, but the blinding, blistering, and suffocating kind that scrapes at your skin like it's judging you the second you walk in. And gods, does this place give me the feeling it's disappointed in me. It shouldn't hold form the way it does. Pillars stretch impossibly high. The air here tastes like purity laced with lies. I absolutely hate it here, and now my headache is so much worse.

They're already seated, a perfect crescent of celestial arrogance. Three women and three men, each one glowing in a way that would make you believe they've never known shame. Spoiler: they have. They're not smiling, they never do. Miserable bastards. They're like judges in a cosmic court, yet you can guarantee to never expect fairness when it comes to them.

They say nothing at first; they never speak until they want to. It's all power games and arrogance; the delay meant to come across as dominance, but it just comes off as insufferable bullshit. A whole performance meant to remind me I'm the one they can summon whenever they please, and that they hold my strings like just another one of their puppets in their fucking games. I don't offer them the respect they so desperately crave. I don't bow, don't blink in awe like they expect. Because I don't give a shit about a single one of them.

Finally, Seraphiel rises like the leader she wishes she were. The Voice of Judgement. Drenched in silver and polished chrome, a helmet hiding what little humanity she might've had. Her wings stretch behind her, crystal clear, flawless, and as cold as her dead heart.

"You were summoned. You are late."

I sigh, already bored to near tears. "I'm here, am I not?" I lift a hand with dramatic flair. "Try not to faint."

There's a musical laugh, soft, sweet, and fake as hell. Amarithe. The Manipulator of Light and Reality. She glows like a sunrise made of gold and honey, but underneath the warmth is the chill of illusion. She could stab you with a smile and convince you to thank her for it.

"Still alone, I see," she purrs. "No partner. No... anchor."

She doesn't say bride, none of them do. But it's what they mean. Because without a queen, I'm just a boy playing king in their eyes. They believe that I am not fit to rule without a queen.

Velentha speaks next—though it's not speech so much as weeping. Because, unfortunately, everything with her is melodrama and mystery. Tears of pure white light train endlessly from beneath her hood, vanishing into the marble beneath her feet. Time runes twist across her arms in constant motion, shifting futures looping like ribbons around her. She doesn't look at me. She doesn't need to, because she sees all. Every possible future and outcome, she knows it. Of course, fate changes every second, so she sees many possibilities.

"The threads tangle," she murmurs, voice distant. "Too many paths... too many endings. You tempt the storm, Child of Ruin."

I bristle at the name, but I say nothing. I impatiently await the next one to speak because it's always the same. They speak their riddles, their warnings, each thinking their voice should shatter the sky. All it actually does is raise my bastard blood pressure.

Calrix leans forward—because of course the militant asshole wants in. The Spear of Order. Divine Warfare's golden boy, who claims to be the protector of the realms. He's flame wrapped in armour, his wings ablaze, and his eyes burn with the fury of a sun held back by chainmail.

"You should not be here," he growls. "You stain the light."

I snort. "First of all, I was invited. Secondly, if I'd known I was walking into a celestial poetry slam, I would've brought wine."

Calrix's sword ignites in his grip, the fury in his eyes sparking even brighter as he stares me down. I swear, he lives for the drama. Seraphiel lifts a hand, and he instantly lowers the weapon like the obedient bitch he is. Across the crescent, Elaron smiles. His voice, when he speaks, is so gentle it almost slides past you unnoticed. Despite his soft voice, he is just another manipulator, his abilities allowing him to mess with your thoughts, memories, and dreams.

"The realm quivers. Strange dreams ripple through the mortal veil. Something stirs."

His hair is starlight, and his eyes are gentle, yet unblinking. He smiles like a friend, but the whispers within the realm are that he was the one who erased the old queen's soul. Honestly, it wouldn't surprise me.

"Do you feel it, Korithax?" He asks me. "The little sparks waking in the dark?"

I stare back at him, my expression deadpan, and say nothing. I won't give them the satisfaction of asking them what the fuck they're talking about. My eyes track over to Mal'Thariel. He doesn't speak, never does. His body is a monolith of marble and glass, ancient beyond comprehension. The original creator of everything. And he just... watches. Like a god who sees every flaw in your soul and decides you're boring anyway. The laws of the universe get quiet around him.

I roll my eyes. "Gods, don't all speak at once for a change, will you?"

"You mock us," Seraphiel says, her voice cutting through the atmosphere like a blade. "You forget who we are."

"No," I mutter, straightening. "I remember exactly who you are."

Show time. I raise a finger to point, a cocky grin plastered on my face. "One: Judgement in the form of a silver bitch." Seraphiel glares.

"Two: Manipulator of perception." Amarithe's eyes narrow in amusement. "Three: A weeping time witch." Velentha doesn't react. She never does. "Four: A flame with a stick up his ass." Calrix flares hotter. "Five: A walking celestial gaslighter." Elaron smiles wider. "And six," I say, landing on Mal'Thariel, "a mute slab of cosmic furniture."

Amarithe hums a low, silken sound. "Your arrogance continues to amuse."

"And your obsession with control continues to bore me."

"You speak as if you matter," Calrix growls as his wings flare wide, flame licking the edge of his shoulders. "You're nothing but an heir still unproven. Without a throne. Without a queen."

There it is, the blade they always swing. And it lands. Not deep, but enough to care. I keep my expression flat, not deigning to give these assholes the reaction they so desperately crave.

Velentha's runes flicker. "Time bleeds faster than you realise. The cycle closes."

Elaron leans forward, "Tick, tick, Child of Ruin. The crown slips from fingers too long unclaimed."

"You all love your riddles, don't you?" I say, smiling without warmth. "Just say it. Just say I need a bride. Say I'm running out of time. Say you're all terrified of what happens if I ascend the throne without one."

"You will not ascend," Seraphiel says, final and smug. "Not without balance. That is the law."

"Your law," I growl.

"The only law that matters." She counters.

Amarithe tilts her head, lashes fluttering. "Unless... you've found someone?"

Every eye turns to me. Six points of celestial pressure, suffocating and bright. I lift my chin. "You'd be the first to know if I had."

Velentha tilts her head, ever so slightly. "Would we?"

That's an insane question from the bitch who sees literally fucking everything. But I've had enough, so I let smoke begin to coil around my shoulders in warning. "We're done here."

"You leave," Seraphiel says, "with no answers to our questions."

"I never get any in return," I shoot back with a smirk. "Seems fair."

The portal hums open behind me; this bullshit realm rarely lets me just teleport in and out. It's like a power play from them—or fear. Making sure I'm a little weaker magic-wise because portals require more power than teleportation. I turn to the portal to my world. But before I step through, I glance back once.

"When I do choose," I say, voice low, "You'll feel it. Or your little all-seeing eye over there will tell you."

And then I'm gone.

CHAPTER 7
DAISY

The hunger didn't come in waves anymore.

It just hums. A constant, gnawing ache in my stomach, I've learnt to ignore. I pour black coffee into a chipped thermos, hoping the bitterness will fuel me enough to get me through the day. It won't, but I like to pretend it does. Just like how I pretend I'm not tired, or worried, or fraying at the edges. Because pretending has become somewhat of an art to me.

My apartment smells faintly of toast, burnt as always. I shove my textbooks and work apron into my battered tote bag, checking the fridge one last time to see if it's still tragically empty. It is. Half a stick of butter, one egg, and a bottle of off-brand ketchup glare back at me.

My walk to campus is soggy in the bitter fall weather, but it's peaceful. The cracked pavement glistens with rain, and leaves cling to my boots, my college looming ahead like a tired giant made of grey brick clad in ivy. The surrounding buildings are a mix of hopeful modern renovations and a weary old library that smells like dusty books. My favourite smell alongside coffee.

Rent was due next week, and my last paycheque from the coffee shop barely covered the electricity bill. I'd already sold my mom's old earrings, and yesterday morning, I finally gave up her necklace—the delicate gold one with a tiny engraved heart. I pawned it without looking the guy behind the counter in the eye.

"I just need enough to float me until next payday." I'd said.

He didn't ask questions, just handed me sixty bucks and a receipt I wouldn't use. I knew damn well the necklace was worth more than that, especially sentimentally. But sentiment didn't pay the bills.

By the time I reach the coffee shop where I work part-time, my socks are wet, my hair is a mess, and I'm ten minutes early because I couldn't stand being alone in my apartment any longer.

"Morning, daydream," my manager calls as I clock in.

I flash him my brightest smile as I pull on my apron. Work is its usual blur of overly complicated orders and cracked hands from over-washing. I joke with the regulars, write silly doodles on the to-go cups in my assortment of glittery gel pens I keep in my apron pocket, and silently mourn the smell of pastries I can't afford. I sneak a broken cookie from the tray when no one's looking. Sweet, sugary salvation.

It's just past noon when my saving graces arrive.

"You look like sunshine got punched in the face," Talia says, dropping onto a stool.

"And still glowing, thank you," I say, wiping my hands on my apron.

Ezra slides a paper bag across the counter like he's sliding me drugs. "A flaky croissant for our flaky ray of light."

"Poetic," I say, tearing into it like a gremlin. "And you guys are the best. Did I mention I love you? Because I really love you."

Ezra leans over the counter despite my never-ending warnings about him doing that. "You're not eating enough again, are you?"

"Ez," I mumble around a mouthful of heaven. "Let me have my carbs in peace."

. . .

THEY STAY FOR A WHILE, chatting about their latest drama. A group project disaster for Ezra, who absolutely despises having to work alongside people that aren't Talia and me. Talia's drama was yet another problem with yet another Tinder date. Apparently, this one was 'overenthusiastic', whatever the hell that meant.

Ezra slaps his hand on the counter. "We need a night out. I'm thinking: neon lights, terrible music, and maybe a bouncer named Blade."

"I have class tomorrow, and uh... we aren't old enough," I remind him.

He rolls his eyes like he completely forgot we were still under the legal drinking age and flops back on his stool like I'd just broken his heart.

~

ETHAN SHOWS up at my apartment like a rom-com boyfriend knockoff, holding a greasy pizza box, his too-perfect smile shining.

"Figured you hadn't eaten," he says, stepping inside without waiting. "You get snappy when you're starving."

He doesn't say hello or ask how I am. He just sets the pizza on my coffee table and settles on the couch like he owns the place.

"Thanks," I say, dropping onto the couch. "How... generous."

"Generous is my middle name," he jokes, kicking off his ridiculously priced designer trainers.

He smells faintly of cologne and gym sweat. And the already tiny apartment shrinks a little with him in it, though I can't explain why. I eat in silence as he talks about himself, then his coach, his gym progress, and finally, his ex, who 'totally wants him back.' I nod when appropriate and smile when expected. I slowly eat the pizza, despite wanting to inhale the entire thing. I don't want another comment on my body from him, even though he's the one who brought the damn thing over here.

His hand lands on my thigh halfway through some action movie

I didn't ask to watch. I watch as he rubs slow circles above my knee, making my body freeze.

"Ethan," I say softly but firmly.

"What?" He grins. "You're tense, so I'm helping."

I shift my knee away from his touch. "Don't. Not tonight."

He leans closer, lips brushing my neck. "Come on, babe. Don't be like that."

I turn my head to him with a soft smile as my heart pounds. "Ethan, I said no."

He pulls back, rolling his eyes. "Jesus, okay. Chill."

I curl into the couch, arms crossed across my chest. "I'm just... tired."

He exhales sharply. "Right. Tired. Always fucking tired."

He suddenly stands, grabbing his keys from the table and slipping his shoes back on.

"Are you mad?" I ask, even though I already know the answer.

He just shrugs. "Guess I'll book a reservation next time I want to touch my own girlfriend."

He storms out the door, slamming it behind him, causing me to flinch, and leaving me alone in the quiet. I sit staring at the now-closed door, the half-eaten pizza still sitting on the table, as something hollow presses against my ribs. I didn't do anything wrong, but I still feel like I did. That familiar guilt creeps in like fog. I switch the TV off and curl my knees to my chest, staring at my reflection in the dark TV screen. I look so tired, so not me.

Maybe this is me now. Because it's not just Ethan, it's everything. The bills piling up, the empty fridge, the way I flinch every damn time my phone rings, in case it's my dad calling to ask for money he knows I don't have. And as well as all that... the deal. The one I never made, but somehow got thrown into anyway.

I keep pretending it's not real, that it's a hallucination, and that I'm just severely mentally ill. I laugh softly. I must be going utterly insane.

"If anyone out there's listening," I whisper up to the ceiling, "maybe throw me a goddamn bone?"

Nothing answers, of course. Just the drip of the kitchen tap and the gentle creak of the floorboards above. I think about my mom. What would she say if she saw me like this—tired, scared, nearly starving, and desperate? Would she be disappointed in me? Or would she hold me and tell me I'm stronger than I think I am? My throat tightens. I miss her. I miss her so, so much.

I let the silence settle, heavy on my chest. And still, somehow... I smile. Because tomorrow, the sun rises again. And so do I.

CHAPTER 8

She dreams of ash.

It drifts like snow through a dead sky, weightless but heavy, covering everything in silence. The stone beneath her bare feet is cracked, pulsing faintly with a dull, embered glow—like a heartbeat buried too deep to rise.

There's screaming in the distance. Or maybe they're memories. Or maybe they're her own screams, tearing from her throat until it's raw.

Something sharp glints near the foot of a blackened throne—half-melted, twisted into something that once meant power and now only whispers ruin.

A crown. Or what's left of one. She reaches for it—her fingers blistered and trembling, skin blooming with smoke. There is no pain, there never is. Just the unbearable weight in her chest, pressing down like grief carved into stone.

She cannot move.

She cannot run.

The air thickens.

"You were warned."

The voice comes from everywhere and nowhere. It's not cruel, but it carries no mercy either.

The ash begins to swirl faster, like it's being pulled by something unseen—spiralling in on her, around her, into her.

She opens her mouth to speak, but her tongue is thick with soot and flame. She tastes betrayal.

A figure rises from the smoke. No face. No name. Just shadow.

"She will return."

Her knees buckle. The throne burns brighter behind her. The stone at her feet cracks wider, light pushing up from below—hellfire or memory, or something worse.

She falls—

CHAPTER 9
DAISY

Two weeks.

That's how long it's been since Ethan stormed out, since I pawned the necklace, since my last semi-decent night of sleep, too.

Work's been steady, college has been overwhelming, and the rent is still unpaid. And Korithax? Yeah, he's been as absent as my dad—hauntingly present in my thoughts, yet never actually there. I keep expecting to see him in mirrors, or lurking on street corners, or lounging in my damn closet like some cryptid with wings. But no, not even a flicker of his smoke. Just silence, and recurring nightmares. They're the same ones I've had since I was a kid. Always dark, always having me waking up, clawing at my sheets like they've tried to swallow me whole.

I visited my mom's grave last weekend. I try and do it at least once a month, to go by and visit her. This time, I ended up staying so much longer than usual. I didn't say much, because what could I say? "Hi, Mom, I miss you. Also, turns out demons are real, and one of them may or may not technically own me now. Hope you're proud." Instead, I brought along some daisies which are her favourite. I know, how ironic. And sat cross-legged on the grass whilst I tried not to cry. I succeeded, instead opting to watch the clouds and telling her about everything that I could say. That I was tired, but I was trying so very hard to always be the sun.

My dad hasn't called since the last conversation. No surprise there, though, since I'm used to it now.

When I reach campus, it's buzzing. Noisy in the way only October on a college campus can be. Everyone's excited, high on the scent of fall and pumpkin-spiced caffeine. And there are bright flyers taped to every lamp post, tree, and available flat surface. Neon orange and dripping in glitter:

"THE UNHOLY MASQUERADE"

Costume Party — Saturday Night. Bring your alter ego. Make sure it's sexy.

Talia finds me outside the cafeteria, practically vibrating with excitement. She's flapping one of the flyers at me like she's won a golden ticket.

"You're going!" She declares. No questions, just demands.

I blink at her. "Good morning to you, too."

She loops her arm through mine. "No distractions, no excuses. Costumes, mystery, potential makeouts. Maybe even blood sacrifices, who knows? It's college." She shrugs, grinning from ear to ear.

"I don't think blood sacrifices are actually legal," I mutter, tugging my hoodie sleeves over my hands to hide them from the cold.

Ezra appears beside us like a conjured spell a moment later, iced coffee in hand, dripping with rhinestones and oozing chaos as usual.

"I already have my outfit picked out," he announces, swirling the straw. "It's glam. It's dramatic. It may involve body glitter. Ugh, you'll love it!"

"Of course it does," I say, cracking a smile.

"You need this," Talia says, tugging me closer with a look that says no arguments. "Just one night. One party. No Ethan, no stress. Just music, glitter, and pretending we're not all having existential dread over deadlines. Come as something dangerous for once."

I laugh, but hesitate.

"She's tempted," Ezra singsongs. "I can see it in her sad little orphan eyes."

I shove him playfully. "Fine, I'll go. But I am not wearing anything ridiculous!" I say in a stern tone, specifically to Ezra.

Talia and Ezra exchange a look that's nothing short of villainous. Gods above and below, what the Hell have I gotten myself into?

~

FRIDAY COMES FAST, too fast.

Somehow, time manages to crawl and spring at the same damn time. I'm broke, I'm tired, and I've skipped three proper meals this week, unless you count espresso shots and breath mints. But for once, I'm kind of... excited? Not in a scream-it-from-the-rooftops kinda way. More like a quiet little flutter in my chest that doesn't feel like dread kind of way. Ethan has a game the night of the party, some inter-college thing with a team whose mascot looks like a depressed walrus. So he'll be occupied, which means I'm officially free to enjoy myself without side-eyes, passive-aggressive comments, or that weird habit he has of checking my phone screen when he thinks I'm not looking.

I'm curled up on my couch in my favourite oversized jumper, dog-earing pages in a fantasy novel I've read three times before. Something about cursed lovers, enchanted knives, and a heroine with absolutely unhinged energy. It's my comfort read, and I even put a sparkly gel pen bubble around my favourite quote: "Remember that even the sunshine can be deadly." I smile at that one every time.

My tiny apartment smells like vanilla wax melts and cheap perfume, which honestly feels like an absolute win compared to last week's burnt toast and sadness combo. I've even lit a birthday cake scented candle to elevate my mood.

There's a knock at my door, one so rhythmic and dramatic I just know it's Ezra.

"Your saviours have arrived!" He declares the moment I open the door.

Talia sweeps in behind him like a woman on a mission, marching straight into my bedroom and tossing a garment bag onto my bed with a devilish grin.

"Costume delivery. No refunds, no take-backs, and absolutely no refusals."

I follow her through the bedroom, glancing down at the mystery bag. "I didn't order anything."

"We know," Ezra says from the kitchen.

I can hear him opening the fridge and cringe, knowing it's utterly freaking bare.

"Still empty." He mutters. Ass.

I pad over to the bed and unzip the bag, already bracing myself for disaster. And—oh no. Oh no no no. It's red, skimpy, and sinfully short. Oh gods, there are horns... and a freaking tail.

"You got me a devil costume?"

"A sexy devil costume," Ezra corrects, leaning over me to pluck the tail from the bag. "With glitter. You're welcome."

Talia flops onto the bed, positioning herself against my pillows. "We figured you'd hesitate or wear something boring. So, we took creative liberty."

I pull out the headband, the horns sparkling like pointy disco balls. They're most definitely not to scale if my memory serves me right. I stare at them, then at the costume before tracking my eyes to my best friends who are lying together, practically vibrating with anticipation.

"You're wearing it!" Ezra says with an exaggerated finger wag. "And you're coming over to my house to pre-game. Your shift is covered."

"You what?" I ask, plopping the outfit back into its bag.

"The manager owed me a favour," Talia says sweetly, kicking her shoes off so she can get comfortable. "I cashed it in. You're off the hook, sunshine."

I open my mouth to protest, but—ugh. They're right. I haven't had fun in forever, and the idea of dressing up, dancing, and not having to go to work on a Saturday? It sounds magical. I sigh, but I can't contain the smile that lights up across my face.

"Fine. I'll wear the stupid costume."

Ezra claps dramatically, springing to his feet so he can jump up and down on my bed. "The sun becomes a slutty devil. I love it!"

"I'm not wearing the freaking tail," I cut in, narrowing my eyes.

"You say that now," he grins, flopping back down on the bed, panting for air. He reaches for his tote and pulls out a bunch of eyeshadow pallets, spreading them out across the bed. "Just wait until you see what I have planned for you."

He beckons me over, and I giggle as I plant myself on the bed by him whilst he opens each palette one by one, pointing at different shades of reds and pinks. I love listening to Ezra talk about makeup; his entire face just lights up whenever it's the topic of conversation. He settles on a deep red and a sparkly black colour, claiming they'll make my 'ocean blue's pop'. Whatever the hell that means. I look at my two incredible best friends and smile, thinking about the party. Gods help me, I think I'm actually excited.

EZRA'S BATHROOM becomes my transformation chamber.

I stare at myself in the mirror. Red corset. Fishnets. Horns tilted slightly. The tail dangles mockingly from the counter, because absolutely not. I look insane, in the best kind of way, but still insane. Like I fell out of a "Devils Who Slay" Pinterest board and landed straight in Hot Topic's clearance aisle. And for some reason, that makes me laugh. Not a cute, ladylike laugh either. A full-bodied, wheezing, ugly-cry giggle that has my eyes watering and my stomach cramping. Just a few weeks ago, my soul was sold to a demon with a lethal face card. And now here I am, dressed up as a dollar-store version of a dominatrix from hell with dark red eyeshadow, lipstick to match, and winged eyeliner, ready for a frat party. It's not funny... but it also kind of is. Because if I don't laugh, I might cry, and I refuse to cry tonight. Because tonight, I'm going to have fun, I'm going to drink, and I'm going to dance until my thighs hurt.

When I finally calm down and step out of the bathroom, Ezra's apartment is vibrating. Bass-heavy pop thunders through the speakers, the scent of setting spray, cheap vodka, and overly sweet perfume clings to the air. Talia's lounging across the arm of the couch in a black leather catsuit so tight I'm pretty sure it'll have to be surgically removed. Her chestnut-brown hair's slicked back into a high ponytail, her cheekbones contoured so sharply she's bordering on looking like Maleficent. She's sipping pink tequila from a mason jar and scrolling through her texts, probably seeing who she's going to hook up with tonight.

Ezra's in a full vampire costume, with drag queen glam. We're talking floor-length black velvet cape, red glitter eyeshadow, highlighter blindingly bright, and sharp little fangs that make his smile look even more adorable. His ginger curls are swept up into a half-up bun, with sparkling glitter dusted throughout. His boots are heeled, and his nails are a sparkly black. He looks like a freaking vision.

"There she is!" He yells when he sees me. "Miss Sin and Suffering herself."

Talia lets out a wolf whistle. "Look at our little devil. Who knew damnation came with a pair of banging tits?"

I bark out a laugh and flop onto the couch beside her, adjusting the corset for the hundredth time. "I feel ridiculous."

"You look hot," Talia replies, bumping her shoulder into mine. "Like the kind of girl who could ruin a man's life with just a wink."

"Honestly?" Ezra says, handing me a solo cup filled with pink liquid. "If I were into boobs, I'd be worshipping yours right now."

I giggle, shaking them at him for effect before sipping the drink. It tastes like melted candy with a strong after-burn. Perfect. We keep drinking, and Talia puts on Doja Cat, making us scream the lyrics into hairbrushes as we dance around the room. Ezra spins, his cape billowing around him as he lip syncs for his life, whilst I do my very best not to trip over in my heels. It's nothing short of chaotic, and I've never felt so alive.

Talia swipes up Ezra's phone, scrolling through his playlist with a smirk before putting on a track she knows is going to break us all. Sleep Token - Take Me Back to Eden. The room stills for a breath, then the first haunting notes slide through the air. We don't speak, we freaking belt. Every single lyric and crescendo. Talia clutches at her chest dramatically, and Ezra throws his head back, howling the bridge like it's being torn from his soul. When it ends, we stand there panting from our efforts, and Ezra throws a handful of glitter into the air like confetti and yells, "TO THE FRAT!"

THE LAMBDA HOUSE looks like it's been doused in the stuff that oozes from glowsticks, wrapped in fake cobwebs. Pumpkins line the stairs up to the door, fog machines pump out thick mist, and lights pulse red, purple, and eerie green through the windows.

Ezra spins as he steps into the foyer, his cape flapping around him. The party is buzzing. Bodies are everywhere—angels with glitter halos, cowboys in crop tops, there's even a guy in a banana suit doing the worm. The music thumps through the walls, and I swipe a drink off a tray, downing it in one gulp alongside Talia and Ezra. We move straight to the middle of the main room, Ezra grinding on me like a horny teenager, and neither of us gives a damn. Talia's surrounded by a flock of frat boys, every single one of them dressed as something shirtless. Ezra barks at them. Literally barks, to make them go away. One of the guys stumbles back, eyes wide. "Jesus!"

"I bite!" Ezra says as he barks again, and I burst into a fit of laughter.

Talia kisses his cheek as a thanks, then begins to vanish into the crowd with someone way too old to be in a college house. "Back later!" She calls with a wink.

Ezra turns to me, glancing over my shoulder with a sparkle in his eye. "Don't let the frat goblins steal you. I'm off to seduce Batman."

I turn to look over my shoulder and spot him across the room. Tall, blonde, definitely Ezra's type. He's wearing black eyeliner and cat ears.

"Go get him," I say, shoving him forward. "Flash him your fangs, maybe he'll let you bite him."

He winks and struts off, hips swaying as his cape trails behind him. Menace.

I SPOT him before he sees me. Ethan, standing in the doorway, flanked by three of his teammates and riding the high of an obvious victory from the game he just crushed. His letterman jacket hangs open, red solo cup in one hand, half his shirt untucked. He's grinning like the party was thrown just for him.

He wasn't supposed to be here. He said that he would be too tired after the game, that he would need to rest. But here he is, loud, drunk, scanning the crowd. I don't know why, but some small part of me prays he doesn't see me. But of course, his eyes land on mine.

"Daisy!" He shouts over the music, grinning from ear to ear as he walks over.

I force a smile as he pulls me into a one-armed hug. "You won?"

"Crushed 'em, babe. You look—" his gaze sweeps over me hungrily, lingering just a little too long. "Jesus, you look hot."

I step out of his arm, pushing a strand of hair behind my ear. "Thanks."

"Here," he says, thrusting a drink into my hand. "Catch up."

"I'm good, really—"

"Come on, it's a party. Don't be a bore." He demands, cutting me off.

He stares down at me until I take a sip, pushing the cup back to my lips when I go to pull it away. He holds it there until I finish it, and he smirks before handing me another.

He pulls my back to his chest, gripping my hips as he grinds himself against me to the music. His friends all surround us, cheering and laughing, and I just let myself fall into it, trying to enjoy the party. When the second song finishes, it feels as though the room is spinning. My legs feel unsteady, and my thoughts feel like they're sticking to the sides of my brain like honey. Everything's loud, then quiet, then loud again. The colours blur, and voices seem to distort around me. But Ethan stays close, his arm wrapped tightly around me. I feel him lowering his fingers, and I try to brush them off, but I feel horrific.

"I don't feel good," I manage to slur out.

I didn't drink that much, did I? Not enough to feel this drunk. Gods, I feel wasted, and not in a nice way.

Ethan leans close, his breath hot at my ear. "Let me take care of you, baby."

He pulls me towards the stairs, keeping a tight grip on me as I stumble forward. I slowly blink as the bass fades, and he opens a door and pulls me into a darkened, quiet room. I don't recall even climbing the stairs, yet somehow, now I'm up them and entering a bedroom. I'm so tired. I just want to lie down. Just for a second.

The bed dips under my weight, the cold sheets welcoming against my too-warm skin. My body feels heavy, wrong, like it doesn't belong to me anymore. My eyes fall on Ethan, and I see him pull a condom from his jeans, ripping the wrapper open with his teeth.

"Ethan," I whisper. "Wait..."

But he doesn't. My thoughts fragment, and I try to move, to sit up. But I can't. My body is not cooperating with me at all.

"Just relax, you'll like it." He whispers as his blurred form slips off his jacket.

His hands are on my thighs, pushing the skirt of my costume up as I try to protest. He's not listening to me. His weight pins me to the mattress. I try to push him back, but my arms feel full of cement.

"Stop," I murmur. "Please stop—"

His mouth crashes into mine. He tastes like vodka and sweat and cigarette smoke. I turn my head to evade the kiss, but he grabs my face in his hands to turn me back to him.

"I promise, it'll be fun," he mumbles between sloppy kisses that I try to avoid.

I try to push away again, but he doesn't notice, or he just doesn't care. My eyes sting as tears begin to fill them. Everything feels too loud and too far away all at once. This isn't happening. It can't be happening.

I hear his belt buckle clatter as he forces my thighs apart, and I give one last attempt at stopping him from doing this to me.

"Please, Ethan," I slur, begging him to stop what he's doing.

He forces himself inside of me, my body so unprepared I hiss in pain at the brutal contact.

"See, doesn't that feel good?" He grunts as he buries his face in my neck.

I go still. Not because I give up, but because it feels like the only way to survive. My body is too heavy to obey me anyway. I stare at the ceiling through bleary eyes at the blinking red light of some forgotten smoke detector. I count each blurry blink, trying to pretend I'm somewhere else. I feel the sting between my thighs as Ethan mumbles my name against my neck and I grip at the sheets for some form of control, some form of safety. My body feels limp, almost lifeless, as he uses me for his own pleasure. My mind floats away, trying to focus on anything other than what's currently happening to me. I lie entirely still until Ethan climbs off me.

"Now you have no more reason to say no to me. It's done, nothing to be scared of anymore, baby." He says before placing one last wet kiss on my mouth. He gets up, buckles his belt back up, and leaves the room without looking back. He doesn't even bother to fully close the door, leaving me to lie there, vulnerable and used. I still don't move. I just stare at the ceiling, hot, wet tears tracking down my temples into my hairline as I try to come to terms with what just happened. And even though my mouth is full of cotton, even though my body betrays my need for flight, frozen like I'm still strapped beneath his weight—a single name slips out of me, soft and broken.

"Korithax."

Then everything goes black.

CHAPTER 10

KORITHAX

I'm halfway through my second glass of whiskey—top shelf, smuggled from the mortal realm by one of our more sticky-handed lower demons— and it's the closest thing I've had to peace in weeks.

Mortals are shit at most things; they're weak, loud, and impressively stupid, but fuck, they make good liquor. But, of course, the peace never lasts in this place. Not when you're surrounded by idiots who think 'summon the demon prince' is a fun Tuesday activity.

A familiar tug pulls at the base of my spine. That irritating little spark that comes whenever some desperate soul decides to invoke my name with candles, blood, or a butchered Latin chant they found on some dark web thread.

I groan, dragging a hand down my face. "Again? Are you all fucking bored up there or what?"

It used to happen maybe once a week, if that. Some back-alley ritual. A wannabe warlock. An idiot selling their soul for a bigger dick. But lately? It's been constant. My name is continuously tossed around carelessly by mortals with no idea what they're actually calling for.

I know exactly who to blame: Lucifer—Satan. He thought it was hilarious—telling mortals, with that smirking, too-white grin of his, "Oh, if you want real power, try summoning the Prince of Hell. He still takes deals." Fucking bastard. He knew damn well that until I ascend fully with a crown and queen, I was still bound to the old laws of infernal commerce. Which meant I had to answer summons. Not all of them, mind you, but the ones that slip through the cracks... yeah. The ones spoken in just the right tone of desperation or fate? They crawl under your skin like a tick and fester until you show up.

And Satan? He laughs. Of course, he laughs. Because every time some mortal gets me instead of him, he adds another tally to his imaginary scoreboard titled "Annoy the Hell out of Korithax."

I enjoyed competition, especially when it put me at the top. But not for summoning. I could happily leave that winning title to Satan any day. Summoning bored me to death, same shit, different day. But clearly, his competition was with himself, and how much he could make me suffer. Asshole.

I swirl the whiskey in my glass, contemplating whether it would be considered a war crime if I just started ignoring these calls outright. I crack my neck, about to choose ignorance, when a knock sounds.

"What?" I growl.

Aran steps into the room, all composed elegance and deadpan disappointment. "Before you ignore that summons," he says mildly, "I'd think again."

I squint at him. "How the fuck do you do that?"

"Do what?" He responds.

"Know shit."

He shrugs, perfectly casual. "I just do. It's part of my charm."

I narrow my eyes at him. "It's unnerving. Stop it."

"Can't. Anyway... this summons is from Daisy Sandoval, sire."

Ah. That name. That irritatingly bright, stubborn little sunspot in human form. My brows lift in interest, and a grin unfurls across my mouth before I can stop it.

"So..." I say, rising slowly from my chair, "the sunshine has finally come to beg. My favourite part."

THE STENCH of humanity hits me first—cheap beer, sweat, and whatever godawful cologne they pretend smells like masculinity. There's a pulsing bass that drills straight into my skull, and laughter rising like bile through the floorboards. I appear in what can only be described as the most offensively beige bedroom I've ever seen. The door is cracked open, letting a strip of hallway light slice across the bed. I smell her before I see her—tequila and lavender and something sharp that makes my jaw clench. She's there, unconscious and so very small. Her limbs are slack and twisted, skirt hiked high, her underwear halfway down her thighs. I don't move for a long moment. I stare and catalogue my surroundings. Red solo cups litter the floor, and there's one beside her on the bed, sticky and still half-full. Glitter clings to her skin, and mascara has carved black rivers down her temples and cheeks. She's silent, limp, and exposed. An offering left out for the vultures.

My nostrils flare. Not from pity, I don't do pity. I do wrath. And this? This is a soul-rot level of fuckery that deserves the worst wrath can offer. I drag a hand down my face, inhaling once, slow and shallow. My eyes track the little outfit she has on. She came dressed like me. Well... a horny mortal's version of me. Horns, glitter, and blood-red fabric that's hugging her curves like she was made to wear sin itself. And someone looked at her and thought, 'Yes, that's mine and I'm taking it.' Without permission, thinking there would be no consequences.

I step forward, my boots crushing something underfoot. Plastic, probably. Doesn't matter, nothing in this house matters other than this room and the scene in front of me. I kneel by the bed, my movements almost mechanical as I tug her skirt back down. I'm not gentle or affectionate, but I am precise. Because even desecrated altars deserve to be covered.

"You called for me," I murmur, my voice low. "But why now, sunshine?"

I don't expect an answer from her; she's too far under. Her skin is fever-warm, her lips parted on a soft sigh. There's a little smear of blood along her inner thigh. My fists clench so hard at the sight that my knuckles pop. Rape is one of the few mortal sins that guarantees rot. A slow, eternal kind. It's an unforgivable offence. I don't give a single shit about most things—but this? This infuriates me.

I gather her into my arms, her head falling against my chest. She's soft, way too soft. Fragile in a way I hate, because fragility invites monsters. And the monsters came. I glance down, and her ridiculous glittery horns are still perched crookedly on her head. One side of her lipstick is smeared, her hair tangled like a fallen angel who crash-landed straight into the worst corner of the world.

"She's mocking me," I mutter, lips twitching into something that isn't quite a smile. "Even now."

I turn toward the dark slit in the wall, the tear in the veils I opened to return home. Without another word, I carry her through it. Hell may not be gentle, but it is mine. And unlike this place, it knows what to do with broken things.

WE RETURN TO ZERIAVOSS.

The instant my boots strike obsidian, the fortress responds, flames flickering higher in the sconces. This is my realm, carved from shadow, sins, and soulfire, and every inch of this palace knows my presence. I take her to one of the lesser guest chambers. It's still grand by mortal standards, but modest by mine. The walls are a smooth blackstone veined with molten soulthread that pulses gently like a heartbeat. The bed is wide, framed in polished darkwood, layered in deep crimson and onyx silks. A single fire crackles in the hearth. The air smells faintly of smoked cedar and ashberries. It's silent here, peaceful. Deceptively so.

I place her on the bed gently, because her body still trembles with the aftershocks of being desecrated in a realm that never deserved her.

"Bring a cleansing tonic," I bark to the nearest attendant. One of the servants bolts instantly, robes fluttering behind him. "HURRY."

They return quickly, elixir in hand. I prop her up just enough, sliding the vial past her parted lips. She swallows on instinct, the warmth of the brew chasing away the poison left in her blood stream. That's a good girl.

I pull up a chair and sit, waiting for the elixir to do its work. She stirs minutes later, her eyes fluttering open, ocean blue and swimming in confusion. Fear hits a moment later, her gaze flicking to mine as she jolts, clutching the blanket to her chest like it'll protect her from me. I raise a brow at her in confusion.

"You summoned me," I mutter, my tone sharp. "Now you act afraid?"

She blinks, the world clearly still tilting under her. Her gaze drops, catching sight of her torn stockings that are poking out from beneath the bedding. Her eyes fill, a tear slipping down her cheek as she curls further into herself, her small body shaking. I exhale through my nose, irritation simmering through me. I'm not irritated at her, not entirely. I just hate this shit. The vulnerability, the mess, the weight of human fragility pressing in on my realm.

"What happened, Daisy?" I ask, a little softer, so I can get answers.

"It doesn't matter," she whispers. "Thank you for helping me."

She looks around, brows knitting together. "Where am I?"

"Zeriavoss." Her blink is slow, like I'd just spoken fucking Latin. "Don't make me ask again."

She shakes her head, pressing her face into her knees, burying herself in silence. I clench my jaw, count to five, then let it all go in a single snarl.

"Daisy. Who fucking hurt you?"

She flinches at the sudden tone change. Then she finally breaks.

"My boyfriend," she chokes. "He... He..."

I take a slow inhale, my hands gripping the arms of the chair hard enough to make the wood groan. The fire behind me flares higher in response to my rising anger, a single spark leaping into the air.

"Did he rape you?" I ask, my voice demanding, ensuring there's no room for lies.

She pauses for what feels like a century, then raises her head to look at me. Her eyes—fuck, her eyes—are drowning. Glassy and raw, shining with something worse than sorrow. I tilt my head, studying her. So innocent, so fucking breakable. And yet fate keeps throwing her to the wolves. She nods once.

I rise. "I'll be back shortly."

"Where are you going?" She sniffles.

I glance back, my voice ice cold. "To see if your boyfriend can take advantage of an actual Devil."

THE PARTY IS STILL GOING. I disguise myself in mortal form using a glamour potion created by one of the mages in the palace. Tall, clean-cut, and entirely forgettable. I glance back at the bed where she was lying. There's blood on the sheets. Her blood. The rage nearly blinds me. I don't remember the walk downstairs, just the absolute fury racing through my being. I feel the way it floods in my chest, slow at first, like lava crawling beneath my ribs. No one here knows what he did, no one here heard her call for help. They laughed, danced, and drank, all while she lay upstairs and bled.

I walk over to a girl in bunny ears and an outfit that leaves very little to the imagination, asking her where Ethan is. I know his name, what he looks like, everything about him. That's the thing about being the Prince of Hell; I know fucking everything about everybody. She points her finger at him, and I follow. He stands with a red cup in his hand, his shirt unbuttoned, revealing a mediocre body at best, fucking laughing with his friends. I take him in, looking him up and down as I approach. He was her first. He took it from her while she couldn't fight back. My fingers twitch, and I don't disguise the fury on my face as I walk toward him.

"Ethan," I mutter.

He turns, a half-drunk smirk on his face. "Yeah?"

I grab him by the throat before he can speak again, his cup hitting the floor, causing people to scatter. His friends shout—but I don't focus on them. I drag him back up the stairs, past gawking eyes, into the room. The room where the sheets are still stained, the air still sour. I slam him against the wall so hard the drywall cracks.

He coughs, wheezing. "Who the fuck—who are you?"

I smile, "Korithax, motherfucker."

"What do you want? I haven't done anything wrong." He shouts, trying to push me back.

His attempts are futile; his strength is basically a soft breeze compared to mine.

"You raped her," I snarl.

His face twists, realisation taking over his smug fucking face. He knows that I know exactly what he did.

"No—I didn't. She's my girlfriend. She wanted it!"

I punch him once. Then again, and again, until his lip splits and blood splatters across the carpet. Thankfully, my mortal form also weakens my strength; otherwise, he'd already be dead.

"She said no," I growl, grabbing him by the jaw and forcing him to look at the blood on the bed. "Do you see it? Do you fucking see what you did?"

He tries to speak, but I don't let him. I let a little of my immortal form bleed through before I throw him across the room, his body crashing into the desk. His shoulder dislocates with a sickening snap, and he screams. Good.

I walk over, stepping on his chest to pin him as he writhes. "You hurt something that belongs to me, Ethan," I whisper. "And in Hell, there are rules even devils do not break."

I kneel beside him, watching the confusion etch across his face. I pull a knife from my pocket, dragging it down the centre of his chest lightly, not enough to pierce. Yet.

"Rape," I say, "is one of them."

I grab his arm and break his wrist with a flick of my hand. He screams again, louder.

He begins begging, pleading, "I didn't know—please—I didn't mean to—"

"Shut up," I hiss.

I grab his leg and twist until I hear the bone crack, then do the exact same to the other. He vomits all over himself whilst I stand, looking down at him as he sobs. Pathetic fucking excuse of flesh. I truly do despise the mortal species.

I drag him by the shirt, leaving a trail of blood, and throw him onto the bed. "Look at it," I growl, shoving his face into the sheets. "Look at what you did!"

"Please—I'm sorry."

I scoff. Sorry, fucking sorry. Like that fixes anything that he did to her. She's the fucking sun, yet when she awoke, she looked like a long-dead star—cold and dim—and he did that to her.

"I own her soul," I growl. "You defiled something that belongs to me. Something that is mine."

His sobs turn choked and pathetic. I turn him onto his back so he can see me. He tries to scramble away as I release him, but his mutilated body doesn't get very far. I stand over him, my body shifting—my true form bleeding through the glamour. My wings unfurl, large with whisps of smoke coming from them. My horns appear, curling from my temples, my eyes blacker than the void, gleaming with the promise of death.

He looks up, his eyes going wide. The stench of piss fills the room as he starts hyperventilating.

"Say her name," I demand.

He stutters. "D-Daisy—"

I smile slowly, not an ounce of warmth behind it. "Good boy."

I grab his throat, bringing us eye to eye. "I'm going to fucking kill you. And when you get to Gehenna, Ethan. I'll be waiting."

He tries to beg for his life, but it's too late. I crush his larynx with one hand, watching as he gurgles and splutters, choking on his own blood. He twitches as I hold onto him, his blood pouring over my hands until he stops moving altogether. His soul tries to flee, but I catch it mid-flight. It screams in my palm as I open the gate directly to Gehenna. Gehenna holds the pit where the worst of the worst rot forever in agony. I shove his soul through without an ounce of hesitation. I'm going to ensure he suffers forever, with no chance of judgment.

Silence settles in the room, and I glance one more time at the blood-stained bed, no longer knowing what's Ethan's and what's Daisy's. Then I turn and walk away.

~

I RETURN to Zeriavoss with blood on my hands and the memory of his screams still echoing through my skull. I expect to feel better, but I don't. It should've satisfied me, yet it didn't.

I stride through the obsidian halls without pausing, gore still slicking my hands, my face locked into a scowl so deep the lesser demons scramble to get out of my way without even needing to be told.

She's awake when I reach the guest wing; the wards I had placed earlier prevented me from teleporting or opening a portal anywhere near here. I can feel her presence, soft, uncertain, but conscious. Her presence presses against the walls of my palace, impossible to ignore. I don't knock when I arrive. I push the door open and step into the room, still drenched in Ethan's blood. I make no effort to hide it, she should know exactly what summoning me costs.

The room is warm and low-lit, the velvet drapes muffling the wind outside. She's sitting up in bed, still in that glittering devil costume. The horns have been discarded, but the mascara streaks still sit beneath her wide, wary eyes. Her gaze catches on me, and she freezes entirely, her breathing hiccupping. I don't bother speaking; instead, I just cross the room and drop into a chair by the fireplace, blood crusting against my forearms, spattered across the torn collar of my shirt.

She opens her mouth, closes it, then tries again.

"You came to the party..."

"You summoned me," I say flatly.

She looks down, fingers knotting into the blanket. "I remember everything."

I lean back, crossing my arms. The chair creaks beneath me as I make myself comfortable. The scent of blood is strong in the air, clinging to me like a second skin.

She swallows, her delicate throat bobbing. "What... what did you do to him?"

I tip my head, my voice dropping into a growl. "Whose blood do you think this is?"

She flinches.

"Ethan, wasn't it?" I continue, casually examining a bit of dried gore beneath my nail. "I didn't bother asking, I know everything. Comes with the nature of my job. But I'll admit, watching him scream my name was fucking satisfying."

She recoils, horror painting her expression. I let it settle between us, let her stare at me with disgust, let her truly see what she called.

"He's in Gehenna now," I say, voice bored. "Lucifer will keep him company. Probably let him rot in his favourite pit for a few decades before getting creative."

Her lips tremble. "You... killed him?"

"No," I say with a humourless smile. "I ripped his soul from his body, shattered it into pieces, and hand-delivered the pieces to the most sadistic being in the universe. Wait... that was after I finished destroying his mortal body. So technically—yes. I killed him."

Silence falls in the room, and I can hear her heart hammering in her chest, scenting her fear.

A knock splits through it, and I grind my teeth. "What?"

A young servant pushes the door open an inch, face pale, eyes wide. They're barely into adolescence, their tiny horns barely sprouted. It's pathetic that my father lets them be pushed into service this early. Just another cog in his fucked up little machine.

"S-sire," they stammer. "A scroll just arrived. Marked urgent."

"Read it," I snap.

The servant unfurls the parchment with shaking hands.

"Thanks for sending me Ethan Lawson personally. It's not often Your Highness delivers new toys to my gates. I'll have extra fun with this one until you come and explain why he was handed over by the Prince of Hell himself. -Lucifer"

I smile, sharp and joyless. "Fucking fantastic." The servant lingers, unsure if they're dismissed. I roll my eyes, waving a bloodied hand. "Out." The door clicks shut, and I turn my gaze back to the little mortal still shaking in bed.

"You're... the Prince of Hell?"

"Yes," I answer, tone clipped.

She looks like I slapped her. Her fragility truly was starting to grate on me.

"Why didn't you tell me sooner?"

I rise, pacing up and down the dark marbled flooring. I don't look at her. I don't want to look at her. Because when I do, I see it. I see that flickering sun behind the damage, still trying so hard to shine. I fucking hate it. I hate how fragile she is. I hate that she thought he was safe.

"I'm tired," I snap. "Tired of mortals thinking the title means I give a shit about their suffering. Tired of being summoned like some glorified bodyguard."

A beat passes, and I see her expression change.

"I shouldn't have summoned you," she whispers. "I didn't mean to. It just—it came out. I didn't know you'd—"

"Kill your boyfriend?" I finish coldly.

Her lips part, but she doesn't respond. She can't even deny it. She doesn't even correct me when I say the word boyfriend. My vision darkens, and I cross the room before I can even register the movement. She gasps as I slam my hands down on either side of her, pinning her beneath me.

"You're still calling him that," I snarl, "after what he did to you?"

She chokes on a sob. "Please. Get off me."

I don't move. Instead, I inch further into her space.

"He drugged you," I bite out. "Violated you. Left you bleeding in a strange fucking room, the door open for anyone else to come and take what they wanted."

"I know," she cries. "I know—please—"

"And you care that he's dead?" My voice is a low growl. "You still want to believe he loved you? That you mattered to him?"

Her tears fall down her face, her nose turning red, her cheeks splotchy. She's shaking beneath me, like her body is struggling to hold itself together.

"You weren't anything to him but a game, Daisy. A conquest. Something to win."

"Stop," she sobs. "Please!"

"I should've left you there; maybe he would've come back for round two. I should've let your mortal little world swallow you whole, and let him destroy you more than he already has."

Her cry breaks into a scream of grief, her entire body curling inward, like she can hide away from me. I step back, my chest heaving.

What the fuck am I doing? I look down at my arm, her handprint bruised into my skin like a brand. I turn away and face the fire, grinding my jaw.

"I'll have the help bring tonics. One to prevent pregnancy, one to heal. Take them or don't. I don't care." I move to the door, gripping the handle. “When you’re done, you’ll be sent home. Aran will arrange it.” Her silence presses against my spine, and I hate the feeling of it. I glance back, just once. “And don’t summon me again, Daisy. I don’t have time for your mortal bullshit.”

Then I’m gone.

CHAPTER II
DAISY

He's gone.

The door slams shut behind him, making the entire room shudder. My bones do too. For a moment, I just... exist. Still and silent, blanketed in the kind of quiet that weighs heavily. I don't move. I can't move. I'm still half-curled into myself, knuckles white where I'm gripping onto the blanket for a sense of grounding. My body trembles—whether from fear, or rage, or humiliation, or all three in a nauseating cocktail, I honestly couldn't say. The tears keep sliding down my cheeks, soft and endless, soaking the pillow in a realm I was never meant to see.

He yelled at me and pinned me down. And I just let him. I didn't even fight. Just like with Ethan. I thought... gods, I actually thought Korithax might've cared. Even if it was just a little bit, since he came when I called. What kind of idiot sees the Devil himself and thinks, yeah, but maybe he's different?

I sit up slowly, and everything aches. My arms, my legs, my soul. The costume feels like it's made of lead now. Cheap fabric clinging to the bruises I haven't dared to look at. I don't need a mirror to know they're there. I can feel them like they're burned into my skin.

"I'll have the help send you a tonic," he said. "Don't summon me again."

A bitter laugh bubbles in my throat. I didn't mean to summon him in the first place. I didn't do a freaking spell or some ritual. My body shut down, and my first thought was of the seven-foot demon that had infiltrated my life.

The knock at the door is soft, but I don't respond. Eventually, it creaks open, and a servant slips in, their bubblegum pink hair plaited on top of their lowered head, their vibrant orange eyes averted, with arms full of vials. They set two of them down with practiced care, informing me which vial is which, bow once, and leave. I stare at the vials. One vial pulses a bright amber, the other a deep green, swirling with flecks of silver. Like starlight caught in a bottle of swamp water. One to stop a life from starting. One to heal the pieces left behind.

I reach for the first one with trembling fingers, but without a single ounce of hesitation. It burns down my throat as I drink it with one large swallow. It burns like the truth. The truth of what happened to me... what I let happen to me.

The second vial sits in my hand, cool against my palm. My fingers keep tightening around it, but I don't drink it. Some awful, insidious voice whispers that I don't deserve it. That I should feel every ounce of pain still throbbing between my thighs. That healing is for people who fought. Not for people who froze. I sit like that for what feels like hours, the green liquid seeming to glow faintly as the silence fills with my heartbeat. The echo of Korithax's voice, low and angry, still rattles in my head. *Don't summon me again.*

THERE'S ANOTHER KNOCK. This one's soft, almost hesitant.

"Miss Sandoval?" A masculine voice says through the door, sounding almost professional. "I've been sent to return you to the mortal realm."

I close my eyes. My throat is raw, and my head is pounding. I don't answer, I just nod, even though they can't see it. The door opens slowly, and a man steps inside. He's tall with emerald green eyes, dark black hair that's short and a little wavy, and two horns that match the colour of his eyes that slightly curl from his temples. They're not as big as Korithax's, but they're larger than the younger servants I've seen around here. He's neatly dressed in a simple black suit, and a face that is just as pale as mine. He looks like he doesn't know how to smile. Not cruel, not kind. Just... neutral.

"Are you ready?" He asks.

No, not even a little. But when has that ever mattered? I push myself upright and stand on unsteady legs, wincing slightly as I straighten my skirt. My shoes are missing, and the horns are still sitting on the nightstand. Those stupid glittery horns. I give them one last look and then leave them behind, along with the green vial. He raises a hand and conjures a portal that looks like a thin shimmer, kind of like glass warping in the air. I watch with fascination, my eyes not quite believing what they're seeing. Maybe I'm still unconscious at the party, maybe I'm still lying in that bed, Ethan still... still...

I shut the thought down, taking a small inhale whilst looking at my apartment at the other side of the portal. Home is waiting on the other side. My life is awaiting. The world where none of this makes any sense.

"This will be painless," he says. "Step through when you're ready."

I nod, swallow, and step forward. I pause, glancing back at the room. The bed, the blanket, the bottles, one still full. The place where the Prince of Hell himself carried me, covered me, and then shredded me with words sharper than a dagger. Something shifts in my chest. Not grief, not anger... something that feels older than both, something that feels like it's trying to wake up.

I step through the portal, the glass-like hole closing behind me with a soft snap, and I fall to my knees and scream.

. . .

THE QUIET OF the apartment presses in on me, thick and suffocating. I'm both physically and emotionally exhausted. The rawness of what happened lingering in my chest. A dull ache that sits just beneath the surface. I sit there, curled up in the corner of my couch, blankly staring for what feels like hours.

I spot my phone on the kitchen counter, and it buzzes as I look at it. I force myself up to grab it, the screen lighting up with an abundance of notifications.

54 messages.

Ezra: Are you okay???

Talia: WHERE THE FUCK ARE YOU?

Ezra: Daze, please respond.

Talia: I swear to god if Ethan did something, I will bury him alive.

Ezra: Daisy. It's bad. Please call us.

Talia: Ethan's dead. Daisy. His bones. His fucking bones.

Before I can even begin to process that last message, a loud bang sounds at the door. Panic floods through me, my pulse quickening to an alarming rate as I freeze. Ezra's voice breaks through the silence, and I exhale sharply, the panic leaving my body as quickly as it came.

"Daisy?! Open the door. Please!"

I stumble across the room and pull it open. They're both standing there, Ezra's eyes wide and Talia's face is streaked with mascara, her body trembling like a live wire ready to snap. Their eyes sweep over me, over the devil costume I still have on, the bruises marring my arms, and my tear-streaked cheeks. There's no need for words, because the silence says it all.

"Daisy?" Ezra says, his voice breaking. "What the fuck happened?"

Talia doesn't wait for an answer. She pushes past me, storming inside. "Did you know about Ethan?"

I don't answer at first, I just close the door behind them, leaning my back on it, slowly sliding down until I'm once again sitting on the floor, hugging my knees. I take a slow, deep breath and start speaking, the floodgates opening. It's a rush of words, broken and jagged, pouring out of me like vomit without a moment to spare for breath. Because if I stop, I don't know if I'll be able to continue.

The bargain. The demon in my apartment. The party. The drinks. The drugged drinks. The bedroom. The plea for help.

Korithax.

I mechanically stand, walking over to my counter to grab the card that the Prince of Hell left me after his first visit, handing it to Ezra. His message seems to taunt me:

Your soul now belongs to me.

They're both silent for a moment too long as I nervously chew my bottom lip, tears brimming in my eyes.

"Holy shit," Ezra breathes, eyes wide.

"I'm gonna kill him again," Talia snaps. "I don't care if he's already dead. I'll go to Hell myself."

I want to laugh, but I can't. The weight in my chest is bearing down too heavily for me to do anything other than breathe, and even that feels like a struggle. We sit on the couch, Ezra turning the card in his hands over and over again, trying to process everything I've just spewed at them. Talia's arms are folded tight across her chest, her thumb in her mouth as she bites at the skin along the side of her nail.

Then, with no warning, a vial appears on the table in front of us. Dark green, swirling with the faint shimmer that I've convinced myself is starlight. A note is tied to the neck in scrawled, angry ink:

Just fucking drink it, Daisy.

Ezra nearly jumps out of his skin. "Okay, what the actual fuck," he gaps, grabbing the vial. "I thought you were bullshitting, but I just watched this appear out of nowhere. What is it?"

He sits, lifting up the bottle and inspecting it, scrunching up his face as he watches the liquid swirl around.

"A healing tonic," I whisper. "He gave me one to... to prevent pregnancy," I sniffle, the tears filling my eyes again. They both go deathly still. "I haven't taken this one," I add.

Talia's eyes blaze. "Why?"

"Because I deserve to suffer," I sob. "I didn't fight. I didn't stop him. I just—I just let him. And now he's dead because of me."

Talia loses it, her voice sharper than I've ever heard it. "No. No, fuck that, Daisy. You don't get to do this to yourself. He raped you. That is NOT your fault. And if anyone says otherwise—hell, I'll summon that bastard demon myself and thank him for what he did to Ethan. Then I'll ask for a knife and do it again."

Ezra is crying quietly beside me, but he doesn't look at me like I'm broken, and I'm truly thankful for that. Talia pulls me into her arms, and I let her, despite the repulsion of feeling someone touch me and my broken, dirty body. I let her hold me, her strength wrapping around me like a shield, and I break all over again.

~

LATER, Talia is the one who makes me drink the tonic. She holds the little bottle up to my lips and doesn't move until I've swallowed every last drop. The warmth spreads inside me, like honey with an airy feeling to it. I don't feel any instant miracle, no golden light shining through my body, or magical transformation. But the sting between my legs begins to dull, and the bruises on my body no longer seem to ache.

"There," Talia whispers, brushing the hair from my face. "One less pain to carry."

Ezra disappears into the kitchen, muttering under his breath as he furiously taps on his phone. He's halfway through ordering three different types of takeout by the time Talia's helping me into the bathroom. She doesn't ask what I want or need; she just runs the water. I don't flinch when she peels the devil costume from my skin with quiet, careful hands. She doesn't ask any more questions, doesn't look at me like I'm disgusting or broken. She just moves around me with a kind of gentleness that you'd reserve for shattered things.

"You're safe," she murmurs, guiding me into the shower. "You're not alone."

The tears come again, but this time, they feel different. They're not just from pain—they're from the weight lifting off me, piece by piece. I let the water pour down, washing away the remnants of what happened. When I step out, Talia's there, a towel in hand, wrapping me up tightly.

Ezra's waiting with clean clothes when I shuffle out—an oversized hoodie, sweatpants, and fluffy socks. He doesn't say anything, just opens his arms and lets me fall into them. I quickly dress, then move to curl up between them on the couch, our food going cold on the coffee table whilst we sit there, lost in our shared quiet. Ezra turns on a dumb reality show we've seen a thousand times; the familiarity of it becomes a comfort, and I can't help but smile faintly at the normality of it all.

"I ordered you groceries," Ezra says quietly. "They'll be here tomorrow. I made sure I picked out all of your favourites."

I smile softly at him, thanking him with a gentle squeeze of his hand.

Later, just before dawn, we head outside. Talia has the devil costume in her hands, and we stand in the alley behind my apartment as she douses it in lighter fluid and tosses a match. It catches immediately, flames curling around the red fabric, slowly burning the cheap material to ash. We stand hand in hand, watching it burn together.

"Fuck him," Talia says simply. "And fuck this costume."

Amen to that.

THEY STAY THE NIGHT, the three of us wrapped on the pullout part of my couch in a nest of pillows and old blankets. When morning comes, they don't want to leave. I can see it in their eyes that they're afraid I'll break the second they go. But I insist.

"You need to go to class," I murmur, my voice rough. "I'll be okay. I just... I need a week to breathe."

Ezra hugs me so tightly it knocks the air from my lungs. "You call us for anything. Groceries, murder, emotional support—anything!"

Talia grabs my face in both hands. "If you need me to come back and read Korithax the riot act, I will. I don't care if he's a demon or the Prince of Hell. I bite." She gnashes her teeth together for added effect before winking at me.

I laugh. It's hoarse and broken, but genuine and real. "I believe you."

They both give me one more hug and then they leave, and I'm all alone again. This time, it doesn't feel so heavy, and the silence doesn't suffocate me. I'm still broken, but with a little part of me put slightly back together again by the two people who mean the most to me in the world.

CHAPTER 12
KORITHAX

She didn't take the fucking tonic.

Of course, she didn't. Why would she do the rational thing when self-punishment is so much more appealing? Mortal logic. It's insufferable. I clench my jaw and teleport to Gehenna before I can throw something through the palace wall.

Gehenna sits at the southernmost point of Hell, and reeks of agony. Not metaphorically—literally. The scent of burning flesh, molten stone, and soul ash clings to the air like rot. The screams are endless, echoing from the pit so deep it may as well kiss the centre of the universe. Even the rocks seem to bleed. Rivers of lava coil like serpents through canyons lined with spikes that are carved from bone. No blue sky. No mercy. Only blood-coloured clouds and red lighting splitting the air without warning. The walls rise in uneven ridges, jagged mountains that have been gnawed raw by time. There's no horizon here—only down. Down into the pits where the most wretched are torn apart, re-stitched, and torn again. Redemption does not exist in Gehenna; this is where the universe forgets you.

I hate it. It's too hot, too loud, too fucking much. I'm glad this part of my realm belongs to someone else. I find said someone else by the obsidian pillars near the deepest gorge.

He's lounging like a man on vacation, wearing a black tailored suit that is utterly pristine, not a wrinkle in sight. He looks like any well-dressed mortal. Handsome and smiling, but it's all a costume. His true form peeks through in subtle wrongness. His eyes, glowing red, molten like the rivers below. Horns, a deep blood red, curling from his temples like a crown of sin. His wings are sharp and the colour of arterial gore, stretching lazily at his back like velvet made from nightmares.

Lucifer.

He's beautiful, I'll give him that. A perfect nightmare crafted from the very core of Hell.

He grins when he sees me. "Ah, Kori, finally. I was starting to think you'd ghosted me."

I ignore the nickname; it's not worth the energy.

Lucifer jerks his chin towards the gorge. "You sent me quite the gift, by the way. That boy's screams? Chef's kiss. Top ten material. Might even bump Sir Thomas the Thief off the list—remember him? Anyway, his legs are fucked for the next century, and we haven't even started act two of torture." He chuckles. It's a dark, velvet sound that slithers under the skin. I say nothing, just stare, tensing my jaw.

He watches me carefully, then cocks a brow. "This one's personal, huh?"

I don't answer; instead, I walk to the edge. The pit yawns below, vast and alive. I find Ethan immediately, well, what's left of him, twisting and screaming. Each breath he takes is met with fire crawling into his lungs. One of the tormentors—a faceless demon with hands of long, brutal talons—drags him across jagged stone, while another pours molten lava into the cracks of his shattered legs. His voice is a threadbare rasp, basically gone. His suffering, however, will never be gone. It will never end. For as long as Hell exists, so will his torment.

Lucifer steps up beside me, tsking. "Still not gonna tell me why you personally delivered prey? That's a new one."

Silence.

He leans in slightly, grinning. "Let me guess. Has something to do with that sweet little blonde bitch he stuck his dick into?"

I don't think before I move. My hand wraps around his throat, and I slam him into the stone wall behind him. The force shatters the rock, cracks splintering through the cliff face. Lucifer's feet leave the ground, dust falling all around us, yet his grin doesn't falter.

"Don't ever call her that again," I snarl, voice low, guttural. "Do you understand me, Lucifer?"

He raises both hands lazily. "Relax, Kori. Touchy subject. Message received. No slander against your golden girl."

I drop him. He lands lightly, brushing imaginary dust from his lapels like I hadn't just tried to snap his neck.

"You know," he muses, "I really should start keeping a tally for how often I do piss you off. What are we at now? Eighty-seven?"

"Ninety-three," I mutter.

He beams. "We've passed ninety already? Gods, time flies when you're being violently throttled."

I narrow my eyes. "How many times have you been summoned lately?"

He lets out a sharp laugh. "Lately? Shit, I've barely had time to shave. The priests are on speed dial."

I scowl. "Did you leak more of my summoning details?"

"I might've let a few scrolls fall into the wrong hands." He shrugs. "They were fun hands." He winks.

"You're a fucking menace."

"And you're a dreamboat when you're furious." He winks. "Honestly, Kori, you should get pissed more often. It really brings out the murder in your eyes." I turn my back on him, already heading for the ridge. "You should visit me more often; you light up the place." He sing-songs.

"I don't care how long you've ruled Gehenna, I am still to be your king. If you ever speak of her like that again, I will throw you into these pits and let the tormentors use your bones as cutlery."

His laughter follows me, and I roll my eyes. I turn to look back over my shoulder before leaving, "Make him suffer more than required."

"Overachieving is kind of my thing," he drawls.

"I mean it. Understood?"

Lucifer gives me a grand, mocking bow. "Understood, Your Highness."

I bare my teeth at the title, but he only smirks and flashes me a wink. The bastard's enjoying himself far too much.

I DON'T TELEPORT OUT, instead choosing to walk.

The winding trail out of Gehenna stretches for miles, carved into the walls of fire and stone. I take each step slowly, letting the heat claw at me, letting the distancing screams settle into my bones. I climb, higher and higher, until the scorched path gives way to the cracked earth that leads back toward Zeriavoss.

Red and black roses bloom across the ashened earth, their petals edged in shadow. I pass through the field, ignoring how they lean toward me like they can smell my blood. The sky above never ceases to amaze me. A brilliant blue—but streaked with bolts of red lightning, constantly alive with tension. Yet it's nothing compared to the storm raging in my mind.

She didn't take the fucking tonic. She said he was her boyfriend. Even after everything.

I rake a hand through my hair and growl, pushing back the strands that have fallen loose from the wrap holding it back from my face.

Why do I care, and why did it make me angry? She's a mortal. Yes, her soul is mine, but that is it, nothing more. I owe her nothing, and she means nothing. So why did it feel like something broke when I saw her curled up in that bed? Why did I want to tear the world in half the moment I realised what he did to her? And why does it feel like my soul is fucking drawn to hers by a tightline?

THE PATH to Zeriavoss winds out of shadow and fire, rising steadily towards the highest parts of my domain. It's not a short walk, but I welcome the time. My boots crunch over obsidian and root, passing under arches carved from blackened bone and crystal that separate my kingdom and its surrounding area from the uncharted areas and Gehenna. The smoke clears, and the valley spreads wide ahead of me, and there it is—Cinderspine.

It lies nestled between the clawed peaks of the Ashen Mountains, where snowcaps kiss the sky year-round, the main village of Hell hums with life, and the air always carries the scent of warm bread and blooming ash-blossoms. This is where the majority of the kingdom works and lives. There are smaller villages throughout the other domains, with outposts in the wastes, communes along the cliffs, but this is the beating heart. The rooftops shimmer with obsidian tiles, curved in elegant sweeps, making the village constantly warm. The homes—crafted from dark stone and wood—are dotted about the land inside the borders, each with their own small gardens with iron fences, blooming a range of flowers and shrubs. Ash-blossom trees sit on the outskirts, their red and white petals drifting lazily in the air like confetti in slow motion. Children's laughter echoes in the distance—gleeful and alive.

Demonspawn. Little ones, chasing each other with ribbons of flames, horns barely budding, some with wings twitching with glee. There's a schoolhouse to the north, ringed with glowing runes and playgrounds made of shimmering crystals and obsidian. Farms stretch towards the cliffs, where massive flamebeasts graze in peace, keeping a watchful eye on the crops grown there, protecting them from thieves and other vile creatures. At the edge of the village, a forge. Its clangs can be heard for miles. It's run by a one-eyed brute named Garan, who once cracked my nose for calling his daughter pretty. She's now one of my lieutenants, one of the most lethal I know. And toward the centre of it all: the bakery. Stone walls, ivy-covered, with a red awning. The scent hits me, and my mouth instantly waters. Pyreloaf, emberfruit jams, and smoke-warmed spice. The castle looms behind it all, perched atop a cliff, its towers scraping the skies. Waterfalls pour from beneath the entrance, crashing down into a crystal-clear river that cuts through the valley. The sound of it is like distant thunder. It's too beautiful for hell, which is exactly why I slowly made it this way, back to something whispers once claimed it was.

Whispers begin as I descend upon the village. Not fearful whispers, not exactly. I'm not known to be half the brute my father is. They bow—quickly, respectfully—but no one lingers, and nobody gets in my way. I've never asked to be loved, though, nor have I made the effort to be loved by my people, only obeyed and respected.

I grunt a greeting to a passing farmer, nod at a trio of guards-in-training, and scowl at a merchant who stares at me for just a little too long. My wings are folded tight to my back, my jaw tense. The weight of Daisy still clings to me, her voice ringing through my head when another pulls me from my thoughts.

"Prince Korithax!"

Ah, only one voice in this entire realm that dares to sound happy when she says my name. Marta, the bakery matron. Ancient and sharp as a knife. She's raised half the village and probably terrorised the other half. I step through the open door to the warm scent of spiced sugar and fireroot honey, the smell instantly making my mouth water. The stone interior glows with enchanted warmth, ivy trailing from the ceiling beams. Fresh loaves cool on wire racks and tarts gleam behind the glass like treasure.

"You're late," she sniffs, not even looking up as she boxes something behind the counter. "I almost gave your tart to one of the coal-runners. Lucky for you, I don't like him much."

"I didn't say I was stopping in," I grunt.

She glances over her spectacles, one brow arched in that way that makes me feel like a scorned child. "You always stop in, boy. Like clockwork. You come stomping through my door, all shadows and brooding and 'woe is my eternal crown', and then you eat sugar and feel better about the world. And don't even try to lie about it."

I try not to smirk, but I fail miserably. "That predicable?"

"Like the sunrise." She slaps the box shut and hands it over. "Your usual. Now take it before I change my mind and give it to the flame beasts."

Inside is a tart—golden in colour, flaked with crystallised sugar, filled with emberfruit so ripe the filling seems to glow faintly. I take a bite before I even turn to leave. The pastry melts, the fruit hits my tongue with that perfect smoky-sweetness, still warm from the oven. For a single second, the taste pushes everything else away. Just for that breath of time, all that exists is this sweet, warm peace.

"You look tired," Marta says behind me, her voice gentle. "Tired and angry. Which means you're either about to kill someone, or you already did."

"Both," I mutter.

She snorts. "Well, at least you're consistent in your ways."

I take another small bite of the pastry, savouring every crumb.

"You want to sit for a minute?" She asks. "I've got fresh hellmead steeping, and a chair that doesn't judge. Or at least, not out loud anyway."

I shake my head. "Not today."

She sighs like a mother, the tone laced with disappointment. "Fine. Go stalk around the village like a cursed storm cloud then. But you come back before week's end, you hear me? If I don't see that smug face in three days, I'm sending Garan to drag your royal arse in here by the horns."

I raise the tart in a salute. "Noted."

"And don't think I won't do it," she calls after me. "I've tanned your hide before!"

"That was a long time ago," I mutter, amused despite myself.

"I still have the paddle," she says sweetly.

I bite back a chuckle as I step into the light again. The village buzzes with life as I dust the crumbs from my fingers. My cloak trails behind me like thunderclouds stitched from shadow, but just for a moment, there's warmth beneath the storm.

~

ARAN IS WAITING in the war room, bent over a map littered with pins —black for guard stations, red for incursions, and a sickly, glowing green for the unnatural.

"The Moirvath are moving again," he says.

Of course they are. The bark-skinned, nymph-like horrors never rest for long. Too many eyes, too many teeth. They cling to the blackened forest at the edge of Hell like rot, slipping from the Whillowing's shadowed roots to raid the bordering farms. They kill for sport, breed like parasites, and feed on anything warm-blooded and smaller than themselves. Flamebeast younglings, ember hounds. Even children, if they can find them. I hate the little bastards. Just when you think you've exterminated them all, another hundred appear, crawling out from the trees.

"Move the eastern guard," I say, stepping closer to the table. "Pull them from the central line and post them at the base of Whillowing. Double the rune traps and notify the flamebeast keepers. It's hatching season, and the younglings will be perfect targets for the Moirvath."

Aran nods, quickly scribbling notes without even asking me to repeat myself. He's loyal as blood, and I trust him more than anyone. He gets the job done, is always by my side, and acts more like a brother than an assistant.

"The northern fields are stable," he adds. "No breaches since the last cull. Cinderspine's been quiet."

"Good." The main village holding. I can breathe easier knowing the forges are running smoothly and the children can laugh in peace.

"We got a whisper from Sovarith this morning," Aran continues. "Another revision from the Codex scribes—something about lineage clauses and succession threads. I told them you'd look it over when the world isn't on fire."

I grunt. "Smart."

He finishes writing, then glances at me from beneath his brow. "Vailith sent a message. She requested your presence in the Realm of Children."

Of course. The quiet guardian of the dead and innocent always has impeccable timing. I sigh, rubbing the bridge of my nose. "One thing after another."

Aran smirks faintly. "Welcome to ruling Hell."

The Realm of Children is always quiet and peaceful. The air is sweeter here, sitting in the western side of Hell, where the skies are softer, and it's away from any of the other threats that lurk in this godforsaken realm. The building is bright white marble, surrounded by glows that emanate from the spirit willows. It's not a place of punishment, but of healing—where the broken souls of children, victims of war and abuse, come to be mended.

Vailith meets me near the healing grove. She stands beneath a flowering tree, its pale flowers glowing faintly in the dusk. Her presence radiates calm and motherly, glowing with a soft soul light. She doesn't walk, she glides. Her robes shimmer with thread woven from memory and peace, white and grey like fog kissed by moonlight. Her long silver-blue hair flows in waves behind her, complementing her gleaming skin and soft, golden eyes.

There are children running through the wildflower beds, their laughter cutting through the quiet like birdsong. Others tend to the vegetation that they help grow for the realm as part of a peace project, helping them learn healing and nurturing. Some of them cower in my presence, one even steps behind one of the teacher's cloaks to hide. I paint on the kindest smile I can manage before turning my attention back to Vailith. They don't need a warlord here;

they need soft, calming beings around them. Something I will never be, but I can pretend for them.

Vailith's arms open, and she pulls me into a soft embrace before holding me at arm's length. She smells like jasmine and old libraries.

"Korithax," she says gently. "It's worse. Too many children come now, and I cannot care for them all. Earth is becoming more corrupt by the day, and these sweet babies continue to suffer."

Her voice trembles, and I see it, the grief buried under layers of calm. She's held too many tiny hands through death. Buried too many souls too young to know what death even meant.

"I'll find someone to help," I promise. "I'll reach out to Solara and Fjellheim Heights. Perhaps we can relocate those ready for warmth and light outside of Hell. Somewhere peaceful, somewhere they can begin again."

Her eyes brim with grateful tears. "Thank you."

"Of course," I step gently out of her reach. I can give my word, my time, my soldiers. Anything except softness. "Is there anything else?"

"I think I need another teacher," she admits, offering a smile that flickers with exhaustion. "They learn well, but as the group grows too large. It's harder to manage. Maybe we can split their lessons and make smaller groups." She smiles softly.

"Consider it done. I'll have Aran vet someone suitable and send them within the week."

Her smile grows. "Your help never goes unnoticed, Korithax. You're a true king. Would you like to stay awhile?"

I shake my head, "I cannot, I still have other matters to tend to."

She nods in understanding. "Safe travels then."

I turn towards the arch that leads back to the teleportation point, pausing just briefly. The children are laughing again, chasing spirit moths that glow pale blue. Vailith hums something low and soothing under her breath, a hymn old and full of memory. I don't belong here. But I'll protect it. I teleport, fading from the peace and into duty once more.

. . .

I LAND at the Welcome Circle. A large amphitheatre carved into the south-eastern soul stone cliffs, where new arrivals are judged.

The head judge bows. "Too many are coming, my prince. We need more judges."

"I know, I'm working on it." I sigh. "But we vet those who want to be a voice of judgement thoroughly for a reason. You remember what it was like before."

He nods grimly. Corrupt judges once ruled the Circle, sentencing the undeserving to Gehenna for their own sick pleasure, or letting souls go for bribes. Souls who only needed growth were sent to suffer for eternity. It took me three hundred years to go through the souls and ensure the ones who didn't deserve to be in the pit were removed and offered magical remedies to help them forget what they had endured.

"We will not repeat history," I tell him. "Even if it means slower judgement in the meantime."

He nods again, thanking me for the work that I'm doing. The truth was, I just came up with the answers; Aran and the small council I let him be in charge of were the ones doing all the hard work. I was the face, but he was truly the brain.

I MAKE my final visit of the day to the training rings. New soldiers spar in sandy arenas lined with roaring flames. One of the newer recruits—a smaller boy with freshly sprouted horns—is being brutalised. Calrix circles him like a predator, the sight reminding me of his brutality throughout my childhood. I step into the ring, placing myself between Calrix and the boy.

"That's enough," I snap. "You will not treat my soldiers the way you treat me as a boy."

Calrix sneers. "Then make them stronger. Look at him, he's pathetic."

I growl, stepping up to him, towering over him by at least six inches.

"I am. By teaching them that cruelty does not equal strength."

He storms off, cursing my name as he goes to find some other poor bastard to bully and intimidate.

I kneel beside the boy. "Your size is not your weakness," I say. "You will grow, but what matters is how you wield your weapon. Do not rely on your height and muscles to get you by. You will die. Be smart, and know how and when to strike."

He nods, barely holding back tears. Unfortunately, until I am officially king, there are some things I cannot change. That includes how young the help and soldiers are. It has been a priority of mine to change the starting age to a minimum of a thousand years old. My father has them starting as young as five hundred, making them just children. It's unacceptable.

By nightfall, I'm back in my chambers alone. My cloak lies discarded over the back of a chair, and my hands are stained with ink and blood from training with my soldiers for a while. Documents have been signed, orders sealed, decisions made that will change things for better or worse.

I didn't visit Nox'thraxis today. I rarely need to. The Shadowfolk don't require my supervision. They whisper beneath twilight skies, threading through their inverted towers in silence. They feed on secrets and regrets like wine, but they are loyal to the crown in their own peculiar, eerie way. House Nytherian rules there—ancient blood, cunning, and cold. If something's wrong in Nox'thraxis, I'll hear it in my nightmares. I also avoided the Shuddering Waste. That place has no ruler, just ghosts and echoes of names long devoured. The wind there howls like something dying, and the sand is made of bone dust and broken identity. The Diminished roam those dunes like wolves without memory, devouring whatever remains behind of themselves and others. I only go there when I absolutely must, when something's gone so wrong that the Waste itself reacts. But not today. Today, other fires needed tending.

• • •

FIFTY THOUSAND YEARS my father has ruled. A tyrant obsessed with control, with punishment, with power. Korran built his throne with betrayal and radicalism and called it a legacy. He never ruled, though; he reigned. He enforced, and he suffocated. And when he finally stepped away from the throne, crippled by age and bitterness, placed on bedrest like some crumbling monument, the weight he left behind nearly crushed me. But I carried it anyway, and still do. And I did more than survive it. I took that weight and moulded it with my bare hands into something better, something worthy. I rebuilt the trade systems, I forged peace with realms my father even refused to name, and I opened our gates again. Cinderspine now flourishes, the school and businesses run without fear, our warriors train with pride rather than terror. Even the ashroses bloom again.

I haven't taken the crown yet, but I already rule like a king. And when the day comes that I finally sit that obsidian throne with a crown upon my head, I will make sure this realm looks less like him and more like the whispers say it did under the rule of the first queen.

CHAPTER 13
DAISY

It doesn't get better.

Everyone says it does. They say that time is a healer, that the days get easier, that if you just keep breathing, eventually the weight will lift and you will one day wake up and feel... human again. Spoiler alert: they lied. Because it's been a week, and my ribs still feel like they're folding in on themselves every time I inhale. Like my own body is trying to smother me.

It's been a week of absolutely nothing. No classes, no work, no cheer. I couldn't even tell you what day it is without checking my phone. Morning bleeds into night, and I spend all of it right here, camped out in the same spot in my bed like a tragic little ghost. The outfit hasn't changed. Hoodie. Sweats. The same ones. The fabric is always damp with either sweat or tears, sometimes both. The last time I saw shampoo was when Talia threw me into the shower, so my hair's a bird's nest I keep scraped into a bun so tight it's practically a facelift.

The groceries Ezra bought are currently starting a silent protest in the fridge. Fuzzy things are growing, and I'm pretty sure the apples are evolving into something entirely new. I can barely manage a bite of toast without feeling nauseous, which is fine because the bread is now hard enough to be considered a weapon. Talia keeps dropping off more food. Fresh, lovingly selected, with little post-it notes that say "Eat something, bitch." With a little pink heart scribbled next to her words. It's sweet, it's guilt-inducing, and it's ineffective.

Ezra texts me memes and sends me voice notes every damn day. Sometimes dramatic reenactments of some crime documentary he's watched; sometimes it's heartfelt reminders that he loves me and he's worried. He even leaves my favourite coffee at the door. He always knocks three times, always waiting, but I don't answer. I just take the stuff from the doorstep when they give up trying to make me open the door. I can't let them in. Because I am not the Daisy they know, the Daisy they love. Not the girls who lit up rooms, who twirled in hallways. I'm not sunshine anymore. I'm static.

I hear the words in my head like a sick joke:

Be the sun. Always the sun.

My mother's voice, so full of warmth, of hope. She believed in light, in strength, in finding beauty in everything, even the worst. I promised her I'd keep shining, keep being the sun. But how do you shine when the light's gone out? How do I be the sun when I don't even feel the smallest bit of warmth? I don't know who I am anymore. But I know I'm not her.

~

I'M LYING IN BED, staring at the same spot on my ceiling that I have been staring at for the past week, when the knock comes. Sharp. Repeated. I stay still, ignoring the knocks just like each one that came before it.

A voice calls out my name, one I don't recognise. "Miss Sandoval? It's the police. We'd like to speak with you."

My heart pounds in my chest like a trapped animal as I slowly rise from my bed. My legs nearly give out, but I manage to make it to my door, opening it with trembling fingers. Two officers stand there, an older man with salt and pepper hair, and a younger woman, bleach-blonde hair styled into a slick-back bun.

"We'd like to ask you a few questions about Ethan Lawson."

They don't say much more, other than telling me to grab my things and that I need to come with them.

The station is cold, but not as cold as their questions. They sit me down in a windowless room with flickering lights, a coffee sat in front of me that I don't touch.

"There were... inconsistencies," the guy, Mark, says, fingers steepled. "Blood on the bed. His, and yours, Miss Sandoval. The scene was brutal."

I stare at the table. Why was I being questioned in a police station when I was the one who was raped? I was the victim, not him. He might be the one who is dead, but I'm the one who has rotted away.

"Miss Sandoval," the young woman says, pulling me from my internal battle. "What happened that night?"

I breathe in slowly, and then I lie. Not because I want to, but because I have to. Besides, how could I tell the truth? "Oh, he raped me, and then a seven-foot demon killed him because he owns my soul?" I'd be institutionalised; they'd never believe me.

"I don't remember much," I whisper. "He gave me a drink, then... I... um."

My voice cracks, and I feel my anger rising inside of me. How can I still not think about it or speak about it without breaking? I'm pathetic.

I clear my throat, still unable to look either of them in the eye. "He raped me," I grit out. "He raped me, and then I passed out."

They don't even flinch at the confession, skimming past it like it's a minor detail just because he's dead.

"Do you know who could've hurt him?"

Yes. "No, I don't."

They ask me the same questions six different ways, trying to catch me in a lie only I know I'm telling. My throat burns from the effort of keeping my voice level. I feel like I'm going to throw up.

After what feels like hours, they finally release me. No charges, not yet, because they don't have enough to hold me. I walk home like a ghost, haunting the streets with my misery.

I CALL my dad that night. I don't know why. Maybe I needed to hear something—anything—remotely comforting. Something fatherly, like he used to be when I was younger. It rings, and rings.

He finally answers. "Hey, sweetheart."

"Hey, Dad, I—"

"You got twenty bucks I could lend?"

I blink. "I—Dad. Something bad happened. I—"

"I just need it to cover this bet. It's important, Daisy. Please."

He doesn't hear the break in my voice, but why would he? I hang up the call, not bothering to try and speak to him further. It was stupid enough of me to even think he'd care, never mind try and convince him to listen to me. He wasn't the father I knew when I was young, just like I wasn't the daughter he knew either, not anymore. I climb back into my bed and train my eyes back onto the same spot on my ceiling as the tears begin to fall again.

BY THE END of the second week, I stopped pretending.

The textbooks gather dust like the forgotten relics of a girl who thought she had a future. My makeup bag stays sealed, and the mirror in the bathroom is covered with a towel. I can't stand to look at her, the girl who let it happen. The girl who was brave enough to face a literal demon, but somehow couldn't stop her boyfriend from raping her. I eat enough not to die; I drink when my lips crack too much to ignore it. But that's it, I'm just doing the minimum of both so I don't rot away. My body feels too heavy and too hollow all at once.

I spend my days in bed, chewing at my lip until it bleeds, whilst I pick at the skin around my fingers mindlessly. I know I can't keep doing this. I can't sit here and sink further and further without an end in sight. But every time I think about moving, about healing, I feel like I'm choking. Hope is something sticky and toxic that I'm not allowed to touch anymore.

Then comes the quiet. It always finds me at night, when the world goes still, and the thoughts are unbearably loud in my head. That's when the weight in my chest crushes down on me. It's suffocating.

"I can't do this anymore." I grit out into the silence.

I throw off my blanket and make my way to the bathroom, my limbs feeling foreign. I rip the towel down from the mirror, and for the first time in weeks, I look at myself, truly look at myself, and despise what I see looking back. It's not me. It's some hollow-eyed ghost of a girl who used to be sunshine and sass. The dark circles under my eyes are dark enough to qualify as bruises, looking like I've been awake for a year straight. My skin's gone grey, my blonde hair, usually so bright and bouncy, hangs like brittle straw. Everything about me is dull, the furthest thing from the sun possible.

"I'm not the sun," I whisper. It becomes a chant, loud and laced with fury and pain. "I'm not the sun. I'm not the sun. I'm not the fucking sun."

I open the cabinet under the sink, staring at the bottles that line the shelves, untouched until now. "I'm weak. I'm weak. I'm weak."

I pull out the bottles of pills and take them into the shower, switching on the water. Not because I plan to wash, but because it's easier to fall apart under noise. I sink to the floor, curling my knees to my chest as the cold tile bites through my skin. A scream rips from me, loud and desperate. I slam the back of my head into the wall repeatedly, like I'm trying to knock the shame out of my skull. With shaking hands, I open up the bottles, and I start swallowing.

One.

Two.

Three.

The pills go down like stones, each one heavier than the last.

"I'm sorry, Mom," I whisper, throat tight. "I really tried. I tried to be the sun. I really did."

CHAPTER 14

KORITHAX

It's been two weeks.

Two fucking weeks of riddles, visions, and celestial parasites breathing down my neck. The Six have made it their personal mission to lecture me like I'm a petulant teenager, and not the demon currently holding this realm together with scorched hands and thinning patience.

Every day it's the same sanctimonious bullshit. Find a bride, restore the balance, do your divine duty. Seraphiel's voice still echoes in my skull like a hammer to glass.

"Without a queen, your claim weakens."

"Your authority fractures."

"Your reign is untenable."

No one ever asks anything. They demand, dressed in prophecy and veiled threats, smiling through teeth sharpened on the bones of royalty. I've heard the whispers of what they did to the first Queen. They tried to erase her. Buried her name, her legacy, her power. But whispers are hard to kill.

I haven't murdered one of them, yet, but by the fifth time

Amarithe alluded to "the ticking clock of succession," I very nearly snapped her neck, just to hear her finally shut the fuck up.

And if the Six weren't enough, I've handled ten new soul bargains landing on my desk this week, all thanks to Lucifer and his delightful little marketing spree. Apparently, the bastard has been leaking the rites at every given opportunity. More mortals than ever are lining up to sell their souls like it's a fucking Black Friday sale. I'm tempted to throw him in his own lava pits and watch him laugh all the way down.

Not one of the bargains has been remotely interesting. It's all the same sob stories, same sins, same desperate attempts to cheat their way out of accountability. I sign them, bind them, and move on.

I've spent more time than usual in the training grounds, just to keep myself from throttling anyone important. I drive my fists into stone columns until either they shatter or my skin splits, my blood spilling across the sandy floor. I keep going until my muscles scream, and the sweat pours down my spine, coating me like a second skin. I've been keeping an eye on the young recruit Calrix was torturing, and it seemed he had taken my words to heart. He was now wielding his weapons so much cleaner, each strike aiming true. I'd gone in the sparring ring with him, and he managed to get a few hits on me, even when I wasn't holding back. I don't give compliments, but the little shit's going to make a fine soldier.

Yet still, none of it helps. Even torturing Ethan. I go to Gehenna daily now, and the demons practically throw a parade when I arrive. They love it because they think it's an honour to have me with them, helping carve apart a man who destroyed something so soft, something so innocent. I've broken every single one of Ethan's bones three times over, poured molten iron into his lungs, and even crushed his fingers one by one. But it still is not enough. It never is. No amount of torture can make up for the pain he inflicted on her. It's not guilt for her, obviously. It's not personal, it's not attachment. It's about the violation, the offence. He defiled a soul I own, one marked by me. That's why I'm furious. That's why her fucking face haunts me every time I close my eyes. Ocean eyes filled with tears, lips trembling, voice cracking. That's why I can't seem to claw her image out of my skull. Not because I care. Gods, no. She's insufferable, loud, mortal. Fragile in the way all humans are—emotional wreckage wrapped in skin and poor decision-making. This isn't about her. It's about what was mine, and what he dared do to it.

~

I STEP INTO MY CHAMBERS, shirtless, sweat still glistening along my chest. My arms are wrapped in torn bandages from sparring with the northern devourers—the feral bastards tasked with guarding the upper edge of Hell, the last border before Zeriavoss. They don't fight clean; they fight to kill. Just how I like it.

Steam curls from beneath the stone door to the shower, hissing like it's eager to peel the blood and sweat from my skin. My knuckles are raw, a feeling I welcome.

She's waiting for me. Naked, sprawled across the silken sheets of my bed like an offering I never asked for, but always take. She's one of the regulars. No name necessary, no conversation. Just teeth and skin and the promise of release.

"You're late," she purrs, eyes alight with hunger.

I say nothing as I cross the room. She knows better than to ask questions. Her hands are on me without saying another word, nails dragging across my skin like she's carving me apart.

"Use the blade," I murmur against her throat.

She doesn't hesitate. The dagger on the nightstand gleams as she picks it up, and when the point kisses my chest, I close my eyes and let it bite. The pain is sharp and immediate. Blood slides over my ribs in slow, lazy rivulets. She moans like it's for her, but this isn't about her. I grab her throat as I push her beneath me, hard enough to bruise. She gasps, but I don't ease up as the bed groans beneath us. The heat of her body blends with the sting of the blade, and just for a moment, I don't think about anything except this.

A knock sounds, sharp and urgent.

"Your Highness?"

I grit my teeth. "Aran," I snap, without looking. "What the fuck have I told you about calling me that?"

His voice cuts through the air from the doorway. "Apologies, sir, but it's urgent."

I sigh, rolling off the woman beneath me without so much as a glance. "You know, I'm starting to think your use of 'urgent' is just an excuse to pester me when I'm busy."

Aran steps in, the door clicking closed behind him. He tries not to look at the woman sprawled on the bed, and tries even harder not to react to the blood still sliding down my chest.

"I know you did not request this of me, but I've been watching Miss Sandoval in the viewing chamber. In my spare time."

My entire body stiffens. The woman in my bed sits up like she might speak. I raise a hand without looking and growl, "Out."

She scrambles without a word. Smart move on her behalf.

I turn back to Aran, jaw tight. "Why?"

He swallows. "I had a feeling that it would be important to do so."

"She is of no concern to you. Or to me," I mutter, heading toward the shower, "Not until her soul is freed from its mortal shell."

I pause, glancing back over my shoulder, "So, what's so gods-damned urgent?"

He shifts, and I see the stiffness in his spine, the hesitation he rarely allows. "She's taken an overdose."

Everything stops. Sound dies, thought dies, and rage is all that's left. It floods my skull in an instant, hot and acidic. My teeth threaten to crack from how hard I grind my jaw.

"When?"

"I don't know exactly. When I checked the scrying mirror, she was unconscious in her shower. Fully clothed, surrounded by pill bottles. I don't know if she's—"

"She's alive," I snarl. "She has to be."

I slam my fist into the obsidian wall hard enough to split the stone. Cracks splinter outward like lightning, a blade clattering from its mouth onto the floor.

"FUCK!" I bellow.

I'm gone before Aran can say another word.

THE APARTMENT IS dark when I arrive. Quiet.

I move through it like a storm toward the bathroom door. I twist the handle, but the door doesn't budge. Of course it's fucking locked. I grit my teeth, anger coursing through my veins. She locked the fucking door to stop anyone from helping her. How poetic. I don't waste time. One brutal kick and the door explodes inwards, splintering into shards.

I stand in the doorway, looking down at her tiny body in a heap on the floor. She's in the corner of the shower, dressed in a hoodie that swallows her small form and pants that are also way too large for her. I approach, the cold water hitting me as I drop to my knees and grab her. Her lips are a pale blue, and her skin is clammy to the touch. I look her over, noticing her chest is barely moving.

"Fuck." I whisper. I shake her gently, but she doesn't stir. "Daisy," I snarl. "What the fuck is wrong with you—"

I shove two fingers down her throat, forcing her to gag. She lurches forward, vomiting violently onto the shower floor. Half-dissolved pills and bile spill out, mixing with the water, swirling down the drain like poison. But she still isn't waking up, and her breathing seems to only be getting worse.

I scoop her into my arms, flicking off the water before pressing her head to my chest to stop it from lolling about.

"You stupid, stubborn, self-destructive girl."

I teleport us back to Zeriavoss, the walls of her old guest room forming around me in a flash. Teleporting is usually rough on mortals, but considering she's basically comatose, it shouldn't make much difference to her. The bed is already made, and I lay her down, brushing back soaked hair from her face.

I step into the hall and roar, "GET ME THE HEALERS. NOW!"

The castle shudders beneath my voice, Aran scrambling to get the healers. I step back into the room and don't move from her side. I sit in a chair by the bed and stare at her almost lifeless body, jittering with restrained violence as I let my heat wash over her to dry out her sodden clothes.

Whilst the healers arrived fast, it wasn't fast enough. Three of them enter in a rush, their hoods drawn, arms filled with salves, vials, and spell books. The oldest begins muttering the diagnostic spell, her fingers twitching above Daisy's forehead whilst one of the books flies open, pages fluttering by in a blur before landing on a page. Another one hovers near her chest, checking her pulse with a trembling hand.

"She's fading," she mutters.

"Her soul is tethering," the oldest whispers. "We can feel it slipping. The overdose reached her bloodstream far too long ago."

She looks me in the eyes, stepping away from Daisy.

"Mortal healing methods take time; we no longer have time—"

"Then make more time," I growl, standing so abruptly the chair flies backwards. The room stills, and the eldest healer lowers her head.

"I'm sorry, Your Highness. We... we do not think there is anything we can do for her."

No. Those words don't belong here. My hand lashes out before I can even register it. The healer gasps as I grab her by the throat, lifting her off the ground with one hand.

"You were not summoned to tell me what you can't do." I snarl.

"P-please—" she chokes, heels scraping against the stone as she dangles, eyes wide with fear.

"You were summoned to fix her."

"Kor," Aran says, his voice now shaking. "Please, she's an elder—"

I twist. There's a sharp crack, and the room goes silent. The healer's body slumps in my grip, and I drop her to the floor like trash.

"Get me someone who can help," I growl, stepping toward the others. "Now."

They don't argue, they just scramble, Aran's eyes wide. He has been my assistant for many years, but not once have I ever killed the help. I can feel my sanity slipping, the darkest parts of me taking over as a vibrating feeling pulls from my core, directly towards the mortal girl half dead on the bed.

I sink onto the edge of the bed, my breathing ragged, my eyes not straying from her face. Daisy's body lies pale and motionless before me, and I can feel it—her soul flickering like a candle in a storm. Each second, it grows dimmer; each second, she slips further from life. I don't know why that idea makes something twist in me. It's not grief or fear. It's something else, something darker.

Her lips part—but no breath follows. Not yet. You do not get to leave like this. I take her hand in mine, and it's ice cold.

"Don't you fucking dare," I whisper. "You hear me, little flower? You don't get to die."

Why? I don't know. I just know that I won't allow it.

"I swear to every god above and below," I breathe, voice low and shaking. "If you leave, I will burn this entire fucking universe to ash."

THE HEALER FINALLY ARRIVES, one even older than the last. She has silver hair, is half blind in one eye, and smells like parchment and old ink. Unlike the others, she doesn't tremble when I meet her eyes.

"You know mortals?" I ask, voice low and ragged from exhaustion.

She nods at me, looking down at Daisy. "Better than most, if not all."

I follow her eyes to Daisy's body, her soul still flickering.

"She's dying," I snap. "You can't let her die."

I can feel my temper rising all over again, the emotions causing me to feel even more drained.

"She won't. But if you want her to live..." she pauses, placing a hand just above Daisy's chest, not quite touching her. "I have to place her in a coma. A deep one. Mortal methods won't work fast enough, and immortal methods will only kill her if not done slowly and carefully. Her soul needs time to root itself again, her body time to purify itself."

A silence stretches. I can feel how tense my jaw is, my wings twitching with each grind of my teeth. I take a slow, deep inhale through my nose. "Do it." I say.

She nods, and I step back to give her room. My pulse hammers through my ears as she starts the spell to place Daisy into a coma, her face seeming to look more relaxed than before. But just as the spell stabilises, the summon hits me, the magic tugging at my spine with enough force to make me flinch. Fucking Hell. Whoever wants me, wants me desperately. They must be using every possible avenue to get me to them. I nearly ignore it. I've ignored worse. But the energy feels familiar. It's an energy I have felt around Daisy before. Fuck.

I RIP THROUGH THE VEIL, materialising into a shitty apartment. I land in the middle of the circle like a storm wrapped in flesh, wings half-unfurled and my eyes burning with pure fury. The two mortals are surrounded by incense, chalk circles, and what looks like a poorly translated print out from a summoning book I had personally banned in three other realms. How the shit did they get their hands on that?

"Lucifer." I mutter to myself. "You have five seconds to explain why the fuck you thought summoning me was a good idea." I growl.

The sparkly one, Ezra, screams like a banshee. "FUCK—"

My head whips towards him, watching as he throws something at me. It splashes across my chest—cold, odd smelling. Did he just throw fucking Holy Water at me? I just stand there, dripping. It steams against my skin but doesn't burn. I stare down at him, a sneer pulling across my mouth.

"I will not snap your neck for that," I say coldly. "Only because she cares about you. However..."

I take a step forward, out of the circle I know damn well they thought would hold me in place, and back Ezra against the wall.

"If you ever try that again, I will peel you open slowly."

"Ezra!" The girl snaps. Talia, I think. She throws herself in between me and the sparkly male, like she could actually stop me from killing him. Bold.

"Where the fuck is she?" She demands.

I roll my eyes. "You summoned me because you thought I took her?" I take a step back so I don't kill them both.

"She told us!" Talia barks. "She told us about you! About the card, about Hell, and Ethan. She told us what you did to him."

"She told you?" I laugh, dry and bitter. "Of course she did."

Ezra swallows hard. "We didn't know what else to do."

"Apparently summoning a fucking demon was your best plan?" I sneer, pacing the edges of the circle. "Well done. You nearly summoned Lucifer with this garbage. That would've gone great for both of you."

I pace the small room, looking back down at the methods to summon me. Smart, I'll give them that. They used nearly all of my calling methods. I quirk my lip up at the corner slightly, noticing that one of them even had the balls to use a little blood.

"So, is she with you?" Ezra asks, voice cracking.

I turn to them, annoyed by the panic, the mortal emotion seeping out of their every word. I forget how fragile they are

"She's in Hell," I say flatly.

They both gasp, and Ezra throws a dramatic hand over his mouth before flopping himself into Talia's arms as she scowls at me.

I roll my eyes, "Not that part of Hell, you morons. She's in Zeri-avoss. Alive, and being taken care of."

They go deathly quiet, Talia going pale despite her tanned skin.

"I found her overdosed in her fucking shower. She nearly died. She's in a coma now, by my order, but she's not out of the woods yet. And I suggest if you truly care for her, you won't summon me again. I won't be as forgiving next time."

They're both crying, but I don't care. They mean nothing to me. The only reason they're still breathing is because of the girl lying in my kingdom, soul tethered by the thinnest thread.

Another summons tingles down my spine, and I resist the urge to groan. This is one I cannot ignore.

I DISAPPEAR through the veil without another word, materialising in front of the most insufferable beings this universe has ever vomited into existence. The Divine Six. Of fucking course. Because apparently my day wasn't going bad enough already.

They're already seated in their favourite little theatrical arrangement on pedestals carved from glowing marble, sitting in the shape of a crescent moon. It's a shrine to their own egos, six thrones of divine arrogance. And true to form, none of them even bothers to greet me. How charming.

"You've brought a mortal into Hell. Again." Seraphiel begins, her voice cutting through the atmosphere.

There she is. Kicking off the sanctimonious parade as per usual.

"She needed help." I bite back, folding my arms.

"You are meddling where you should not." Amarithe adds, her lips pursed into something between a pout and a smirk. Her head tilts just enough to flash the soft gold of her circlet. What useless ornamentation for someone who hasn't lifted a finger in a few thousand years.

Velentha lifts her head, the time runes on her arms glowing faintly, pulsing like veins of prophecy. "You do not own her soul, Korithax."

Of course, they know. You can't do anything around here without her fucking knowing about it.

"I did." I say flatly. "Her father traded it like cheap coin for his own worthless skin."

"And yet, it is not in your possession anymore." Elaron murmurs, tone smooth as glass. "Why?"

There it is. The question I didn't want to answer, not now. Not like this. I'd planned on telling Daisy myself, when she was old, ready to cross over to the other side. I didn't want to discuss it here in this sanctimonious hellhole, in front of six relics trying to play ruler. I hold in my sigh, because I will not give them the satisfaction of seeing me irritated.

"I gave it back."

A pause, the room going deathly silent. Here we go. Velentha tilts her head, her face unreadable beneath her hood.

"That does not answer the question, Child of Ruin."

There it is again. That fucking nickname. I clench my jaw until it clicks. I don't ask why she calls me that. I don't even want to know. Whatever she's seen in some bullshit web of fate she crawled out of is none of my business.

"I owe you no such answers," I say, voice low and laced with venom, "because it does not concern any of you."

A beat passes and I flash them a cold, crooked smile. "Now, if you'll excuse me, I have far more important things to do than sit in a room with pretentious assholes who've forgotten what it means to get their hands dirty."

Calrix's sword flares and Mal'Thariel's eyes flicker with an emotion I don't care to read into. None of them deign to speak further, and none of them stop me as I move to leave, vanishing before they can even blink.

Back in Zeriavoss, I'm pacing.

I don't pace. Ever. Pacing is for anxious mortals and over-caffeinated scribes. But I can't sit still. Daisy's body lies motionless in that godsdamned bed, her chest rising and falling in a slow, artificial rhythm. And that tether—that thing—between us won't shut up. I can feel it tugging. Anchored deep like a hook caught in my soul. Low and quiet, with an almost ancient feel surrounding it. For the life of me, I can't fucking explain it. A mortal shouldn't be able to bond with an immortal one. That's not how it works. It shouldn't be possible, but how this feels, sounds exactly like how people describe soul bonds. And I hate it. Why does it feel like if she doesn't wake up, something in the realm, in me, is going to snap? Maybe this is some residual from the soul bargain that I didn't remove properly. A tether from her end for some strange reason. Yeah, something she did. Definitely not me. Definitely not.

Fuck.

For the rest of the first day, I don't move. I sit beside her, hands braced on her bed as my wings twitch in time with the grinding of my jaw. I keep my head bowed as the healers come in and out, ensuring that she remains in the protective coma. I zone in on the feeling of her soul flickering—barely tethered, barely there—and all I can think to myself is: If she dies, I'll burn every fucking plane of existence until there's nothing left but ash.

The second day, I don't speak to anyone. Not even Aran, who hovers nearby like he wants to say something useful and knows better than to try. The healer brings water to dab her lips, and I glare at her hands the whole time, daring them to shake, daring them to falter. If they so much as tremble, I'll break her fingers one by one.

"She's stable," the healer says.

Stable. Like that's supposed to reassure me. I don't want stable. I want her blazing. Radiating. I want her laughing at something dumb and rolling her ocean eyes like she's too good for the world. Not this—pale and silent and still.

The third day is no different. I move only when absolutely necessary. I ignore food, ignore Aran's updates. I chew on the occasional ashberry when the hunger pangs claw too deep. Hell can run itself for now. Let the councils argue, let Lucifer keep leaking summoning rituals to idiotic morals. Fuck, even the world can burn for all I care.

I reach for the dagger on my belt sometime in the late hours, when the silence starts to stretch too long and too loud. My fingers curl around the hilt, and I draw it across the palm of my hand with clinical precision. Blood wells up instantly, the crimson fluid grounding me. The pain helps. It pulls me slightly away from that damn tether, from whatever the fuck it is. Because it isn't a bond. It isn't real. I'm not attached to her. She's a mortal. A stubborn, emotional, unpredictable mortal, and I've known a thousand like her. But no soul bargain has ever tethered to me like this, and it's utterly fucking infuriating.

I wipe the blood on my thighs and press a thumb into the wound until the sting dulls. She's not special. And yet, I haven't left her side once.

THE FOURTH DAY, the Divine Six summoned me again.

Their realm is so sickeningly bright, it hurts my eyes, my bones, and my blackened soul. I'm getting real fucking tired of their obsession with me.

"We have given you a few days to cool down, Korithax. But we cannot ignore that you have brought a mortal girl into Hell twice." Seraphiel says as I arrive, arms crossed over her silver-plated chest.

"I do what I want," I growl. "And something that's mine needed saving."

My nostrils flare as I meet her gaze. She does not intimidate me. None of them do.

"She is not yours," Amarithe says softly, with that fake sweetness that curdles my blood.

"You do not own her soul," Elaron adds, again.

"I did own it. Her father traded it. It was legally signed and sealed." I am so bored with the same conversation. Why do they care so much about a mortal girl? It's not like she can do them, or anyone in Hell, any harm.

"Yet, her soul is not in your possession now, Korithax." Calrix rumbles, his grip never leaving the hilt of his sword like he's afraid I'll strike him at any moment. Gods, if they carry on questioning me like an insolent child, I just might.

"I told you. I gave it back." I growl, and the silence that follows feels suffocating.

Velentha finally speaks, her voice quiet and distant, her hooded face turned towards me. "You still avoid the true answer to the question, Child of Ruin."

Again, with the Child of Ruin. "What do you know?" I snarl. "Why do you always call me that gods forsaken name?"

She doesn't reply; she only watches me, unmoving. She knows something. She's always known something. But she only reveals what she wants to, even to the other five celestial assholes sitting in front of me.

"This is a dangerous situation, Korithax," Seraphiel says. "You are too close."

"I was close to a mortal soul I used to own. Yes. However, she is nothing now."

"You lie poorly," Amarithe whispers, smirking at me.

I want to rip that smirk straight off her face. Maybe I will. Maybe I will use Calrix's sword to do it.

"You must not bring a mortal to Hell, Korithax. It contaminates the realm. She contaminates the realm." Mal'Thariel spits.

This guy and his obsession with contamination. He acts like everyone is fucking plagued or something. It's the only time the asshole ever deigns to speak. I just flip him off, smirking when he looks shocked at the gesture. I notice Elaron tilting his head at me and I inwardly groan, knowing I'm not going to enjoy whatever this asshole is going to say next.

"Why does your soul flicker when we speak of her, Korithax?"

I clench my fists. "I owe you no answers."

"You brought her to Hell," Seraphiel says, her voice like frost. "You are playing with divine boundaries."

"I have been dancing around your fucking boundaries for centuries. What's one more step?" I ask.

"You forget your place, Child of Ruin." Velentha murmurs.

"And you forget your power." I snarl. "Or rather, lack of it. You sit on thrones and whisper secrets while the rest of us fight to keep the balance. I'll bow to you the day you've bled for something."

I turn to walk away when Calrix's voice rumbles through the air. "Careful," he warns.

"Or what?" I snarl. "You'll swing that sword of yours and cry about 'order'? You think because you erased your queen that you're anything other than cowards?"

I know I'm crossing a dangerous line. Nobody is allowed to speak of the First Queen. Every damn thing about her was erased, down to her sigil, but nothing can be hidden when you're immortal. Those who lived through the queen's reign continue to whisper about her legacy, despite the laws. Despite the lack of respect I have for the Uppers, they do have more power than any leader of any of the realms. The ones I know of, and the ones I do not. They could strip me of my title, they could kill me. But they won't. I am the only one in the line for the throne of Hell, and they know damn well that chaos would reign if they tried to find another.

I watch a flicker of emotion cross all of their faces. A twitch, maybe guilt? Pff, no, never. They say nothing more, and I decide to leave before I let myself burn their perfect little sky realm to ash.

~

By the fifth day, the healer says Daisy's vitals are improving. Who gives a shit? She's still unconscious, still lying there like some pathetic cautionary tale, and I'm still stuck in this fucking room with her like I've been cursed by some divine joke.

I sit by the window, my jaw seeming to never unclench, watching the sparkling river beneath the cliffs of Zeriavoss. Red and white blossoms fall from the trees beyond the glass, so pretty, perfect, and delicate, and I have to resist the urge to tear the curtains closed just to block it all out. The tether between us hums, low and insistent. I hate it. I hate the way it pulls at me, the way it aches in my chest. Why her? I've claimed hundreds of souls, thousands even. Mortals are nothing new. And this one? This broken, messy little sunbeam? She's truly nothing special. She's stubborn, reckless, and so very painfully fragile. She's so loud and dramatic and evidently clingy. She infuriates me so much. And yet, the pull is like nothing I've ever known. It can't be her soul trying to come to its owner, because I no longer own it. I couldn't hold on to it. Not out of mercy—don't mistake the act for sentimentality—but because the entire thing felt wrong, unclean. I didn't want that in my domain. She didn't belong in Hell, not even in punishment. And maybe I didn't tell her because some bitter, unidentifiable part of me wanted to see what she'd do when she thought she was damned. Maybe I liked watching her squirm. Maybe I wanted her tethered to something she couldn't escape.

SIX DAYS.

Six fucking days and she still hasn't moved, and I still haven't slept. I've barely eaten, just consuming a few bites of fruit. I'm starting to see the walls pulse, the stones themselves thrumming with the same frequency I feel inside my ribcage. The healers have stopped trying to talk to me. I stare, breathe, and wait.

At nightfall, the chamber is silent. No aides, no footsteps, just the dying crackle of the fire and the infuriating sound of her weak, steady breathing.

"I don't understand," I mutter to the empty room. "I do not understand what you are doing to me, little flower. But whatever it is, I want it to stop."

I flex my hands before curling them into tight fists. I can't sit here any longer. I need violence, I need pain.

CHAPTER 15
DAISY

I wake to the feeling of my chest inhaling deeply.

Which sounds basic, I know, but trust me—when you've actively tried to stop breathing, waking up mid-breath is... disappointing. It's like someone else had taken over the controls for a while and just handed them back with a cheerful, "Good luck!" My entire body feels like it's been used as a punching bag for the Grim Reaper and then politely returned.

There's a fire crackling, and the silk sheets whisper as I wiggle my toes. There's a warmth surrounding me that absolutely does not belong to my tiny, crappy apartment. Oh no.

My eyes snap open. Dark walls, that faint scent of sulphur with a hint of floral undertones. Zeriavoss. Hell. Again.

I sit up far too quickly and immediately regret it. My vision whites out like I've been flashbanged, stars sparking across my eyes. Gods, everything aches. My muscles feel like they've been filed down with sandpaper. When my vision returns, I glance down, noticing I'm wearing a soft green linen dress, and my hair's braided in one, long simple braid that hangs over my shoulder.

The door slams open, causing my aching body to jolt. Enter: The

Worst Welcome Committee Ever. Korithax steps in, shirtless, towering, blood coating his knuckles. Looking every bit like the villain in a dark fantasy. I flinch on instinct. He doesn't say a word, just glares at me like I've inconvenienced him by surviving.

"Why am I here?" I ask, voice cracked and raw. He doesn't move, nor speak. "I didn't die... did I?"

The disappointment in my tone doesn't go unnoticed by either of us, his nostrils flaring at the question. Still, he says nothing. Just that judging silence that burns its way straight into my soul.

"Did... did you help me again?" I whisper, and honestly, I hate that I sound so small. He turns, stalking back to the door. "Korithax—"

"I do not care for your questions," He snaps, cutting me off. He swings the wooden door open, "Tell the help she's awake."

Then he's gone, the door slamming behind him. Okay then, eff me for asking.

Before I can even process the whiplash of all that, the door creaks open again, this time much more politely. Several figures enter, and to my surprise, none of them look like they're here to disembowel me. One of them is young and quiet; her deep purple eyes glowing beneath her long, thick lashes. She has small horns protruding from her temples, the colour of them matching her eyes. Another one, much older—muttering what I presume is insults under her breath—approaches with a tray of food and several vials that all glow softly. She has a deep skin tone, lined with wrinkles, and deep-set emerald eyes that look friendly, despite the scowl on her face. I offer her a small smile that she does not return.

They help me sit up slowly, adjusting the pillows behind my back like they've done it a thousand times before. The older one puts a warm hand on my shoulder and presses one of the vials into my fingers.

"For strength," she murmurs.

I drink it without question, the citrus flavour burning the back of my throat, causing me to cough. Once they seem satisfied with how I look, they leave, and the room is eerily silent again until the door creaks once more. I hesitantly raise my eyes to the door, expecting to find the demonic prince of angst standing there. Instead, it's the man who escorted me out of Hell last time. He's wearing another tailored suit, with silver buttons that gleam like tiny stars. He has such an unreadable face, it makes an uneasy feeling creep up my spine, despite him being one of the kinder beings I've come across in this place.

"Miss Sandoval," he says, stepping closer. "My name is Aran. I'm Korithax's right-hand demon."

"Right," I clear my burning throat. "The assistant."

"Yes." He stops a few feet away, eyes flickering over my face with a concerned look that makes my throat tighten. Realisation sets in quickly, his expression leading me to a conclusion I'm brave enough to voice aloud.

"You've been keeping an eye on me, haven't you?" I say slowly. "Not Korithax."

He nods. "I saw something... off. So, I watched. When I went to check in the scrying mirror and saw you in that... state. I told him."

I frown, my annoyance getting the better of me. "Why?"

"I couldn't say. Just a feeling, miss." He hesitates. "But, when I told him, I have never seen him react that way. He destroyed a wall, and he nearly killed three people on his way to retrieve you."

I stare, my mind whirring with so many thoughts. I lay my head back on the pillow to look up at the intricate ceiling above me. So many swirls and patterns carved into the stone roof, some looking like the tattoos that cover Korithax's body.

"He came for me?" I barely choke out.

"Without a second of hesitation," Aran says softly, coming to the side of the bed to sit in the chair next to me. "He brought you here. Called the best healers, and stayed by your side every moment, right here in this chair. The only time he left before last night was when he was summoned by the Divine Six or your friends."

I blink, lifting my head off the pillow so fast the stars return in my eyes. "Wait—my friends?" I gasp.

He sighs, rubbing at his temple. "Yes. They summoned him. Desperation, I think. One of them even threw holy water on him."

I choke back a laugh, despite the horror of the situation. "Are they alive?" I ask, my heart stuttering.

"Yes. Though you may wish to tell them to never do that again." He gives a thin smile. "The sparkly one nearly had his neck snapped. But Korithax didn't harm him because you care about them."

That shouldn't make my stomach twist, but it does. He was summoned, doused in holy water, and he didn't kill them? That doesn't sound very demonic of him. I exhale shakily, my fingers fiddling with the sheets.

"And, the Divine Six?" I ask, confusion etched across my face as I nervously chew my lip.

Aran's expression dims. "They're not pleased. A mortal was brought to Hell twice. A soul once claimed, now returned. It unsettles them."

My chest tightens. "Returned? What do you mean, a soul once claimed has now been returned?"

Aran's eyes widen like he just told me something he probably shouldn't have. "Uh... that is not for me to disclose, Miss Sandoval. Please forgive me," he stutters.

I let it drop, despite wanting to know what on earth he was talking about. For some strange reason, I didn't like seeing him so flustered.

"Are these Divine Six powerful?"

"The most powerful." Aran nods. "Seraphiel, Amarithe, Velentha, Calrix, Elaron, and Mal'Thariel. Each one represents a force of the cosmos. Judgement. Light. Time. Order. Dreams. Fate."

My eyes widen. Maybe I'm still dreaming, or maybe I have died, and this is my torture. My head goes fuzzy again from the new information. So there isn't just Hell, and demons, and princes who take soul bargains from idiotic mortals—there's a whole system of divine creatures.

"They summoned him, because of me?"

"Not entirely. They're pressuring him," Aran responds. "He cannot ascend the throne without a bride. Law of balance, as they like to remind him often."

"A bride?" I whisper.

He shrugs lightly. "He needs someone who balances him. Anchors him. They believe love is weakness, yet still demand it as a condition to rule, of stepping up in the line of hierarchy."

My heart skips, not able to stop myself from blurting out my next question, "Does he have someone?"

"No." Aran studies me, a small smile tugging at the corner of his mouth. "But perhaps one day, he will choose someone worthy, made from fire."

The words sink in, spreading through me. Made from fire. What a strange thing to say. Before I can ask more, Aran stands up from the chair, brushing imaginary dust from his suit.

"I shall have more food brought for you soon. You'll need your strength if you are to fully recover. And when you're ready, I would be honoured to show you around. Help you stretch your legs. But first, rest, eat, and heal."

He strides towards the door, but glances back over his shoulder, "He won't say it, but we are both glad you made it, Miss Sandoval."

With that, he leaves, the door clicking softly shut behind him. I lay back against the cool pillow, my head spinning. Hell. The Divine Six. A throne. Korithax.

I don't know what any of this means. Only that I survived, again. Did I want to survive? I most certainly didn't when I took that overdose, but now, I'm not so sure.

THE DAYS in Zeriavoss blur together, but at least my body doesn't feel like it's dying anymore.

The tonics burn less each day, and I can finally sit up without tipping sideways, even managing to keep down an entire slice of something called pyreloaf this morning—blackened crust with ash berries, and some kind of warm fruit preserve that left my lips tingling. I've also stopped flinching every time a demon enters the room. Mostly.

Aran visits often, always knocking softly first, unlike everyone else, who just enters as they please with no warning. His presence is steadying and oddly comforting. Korithax hasn't come back, though. Not even a glimpse of his shadow through the doorway, or anywhere, for that matter. It shouldn't sting... but it does.

By the fourth day of being awake, I'm begging to go home, despite enjoying my time here more than I should. It's strange that despite the trauma, despite everything, there's something about Zeriavoss that calls to me. Maybe it's the sky, so vibrant and always with skittering crimson lightning. Maybe it's the gardens: lush, filled with spiralling obsidian statues, emberfruit trees, and an assortment of flowers that are breathtaking. The trees look like those back home, but are so much more vibrant, growing the most intoxicating fruit I've ever tasted. It's so sweet, with a hint of smokiness that makes me groan every time I bite into it.

Aran must've picked up on my restlessness because he's been taking me around the palace several times a day, even letting me venture into the kingdom gardens to get some air. Today, he's taken me to the outer balcony, high up in the palace. From here, I can see nearly all of Korithax's realm.

"Ready?" Aran says, gesturing for me to join him at the edge of the stone railing.

I nod and step forward, resting my hands on the warm Blackstone ledge. The view almost knocks the breath out of me.

Below, and far beyond the cliffs Zeriavoss sits upon, stretches a world unlike anything Earth could ever hold. To the south, far off in the distance, an ominous red glow pulses like a heartbeat.

"That's Gehenna," Aran says, following my gaze. "Where Lucifer rules. The traditional Hell—lava pits, screams echoing through canyons. Mortals think it's all like that, but as you can see, it's just one region. The place was built for justice, though it's grown twisted over the millennia. Torment isn't chaos there; it's structured. Ritualised."

I shiver. "Sounds... horrifying."

"You'd be correct." He responds.

He shifts, pointing west. "See the white spire glinting near the horizon? That's the Realm of Children. Vailith's territory. It's quiet there. Peaceful."

I blink, looking at him with my mouth popped open. "Children?"

He nods. "Souls who passed young. There are gardens, willow spirits that glow. It's a place of healing. They're cared for until they choose what comes next. Some choose to reincarnate, some ascend. A few stay to help others. Vailith offers them the one thing life didn't."

My chest twists at that. Aran turns slightly, gesturing to a jagged stretch of pale cliffs between the southern and eastern reaches. They shimmer faintly, like lightning frozen in stone.

"That's the Welcome Circle. Where all new souls arrive. The cliffs whisper your name, your sins, your truths. Nothing is hidden here. Lower judges determine where a soul belongs. It isn't a trial, it's more like a sorting. Stripping everything away until what's left is real."

"What about that forest?" I ask, pointing eastward, where a sprawl of gnarled black trees seems to writhe in place.

Aran's expression hardens. "The Whillowing. A forest that eats everything. The Moirvath live there—bark-skinned beings with too many eyes. They don't take kindly to trespassers."

Noted. No forest strolls.

"The black desert just beyond that," he continues, "is The Shuddering Waste. A no-man's-land for broken souls. Sand made of bone dust. Night beasts. The Diminished wander there—souls who've lost everything, even their names."

"Why does it exist?" I ask.

He looks at me. "Because some people don't belong anywhere else."

I shudder again and turn to the southeast, where something dark still looms. A chasm. Inverted towers spiralling downward into the abyss. The sky above twilight, despite it being day.

"Nox'Thraxis," Aran says softly. "The Shadow Realm. Ruled by the House Nytherian. The sun never touches that place. It's cold and silent. The Shadowfolk feed on secrets and regret. They serve as spies and interrogators. But they're not an evil species, just curious."

I don't say anything. There are no words, only awe. Closer to Zeriavoss, I spot something more normal. A village. Smoke from chimneys, the distant sound of laughter.

"That's Cinderspine," Aran explains. "Our civilian hub. Bakers, smiths, merchants, and a school. The forge is down there, powered by soulfire. It's where our Ember-born make enchanted weaponry."

"Wait, there are schools? Bakers?"

Aran smiles. "Hell is more than torment and fire. It's a civilisation, a kingdom. Even those who've sinned still live lives here—some reformed, some rebuilding."

I don't realise I'm smiling until I catch the warmth of it on my lips.

"And that," Aran says, gesturing southwest. "Is Sovarith. The Council Spires. Where bureaucracy lives and dies. Every soul contract, every ancient law—it's all written and archived there. The Obsidian Codes sit in the highest spire. They say it knows the name of every ruler who's ever held Hell's crown..." His eyes meet mine, "And everyone who will."

I take a step back, completely overwhelmed. Everything I thought I knew about Hell has unravelled. This place isn't terrifying;

it's incredible, beautiful, alive. Not like I really believed a place like this existed anyway.

"Well," Aran says gently beside me, "when you're feeling up to it, I'd be honoured to show you around properly. Cinderspine is always lively around dusk. But for now..." he nudges a small cloth-wrapped bundle into my hands, "you do need to eat more."

I unwrap it and bite into a warm coal-coloured cake filled with what Aran says is ashberry jam. Gods, it's divine. As I chew, I stare out across the realm again. Smoke. Flame. Forests. Villages. Secrets. Hell. Somehow, impossibly, it doesn't feel so much like a prison anymore. But it doesn't feel like I belong either, because I'm no resident. I'm a mortal, brought here by a demon who seems to hate me for reasons I can't explain.

By the sixth day of being awake, I've decided that I've had enough. As amazing as this place is, I want out.

"Take me home," I demand, arms crossed, even though I still look like I've gone five rounds with the Reaper.

Aran just gives me this soft, exhausted sigh that says, 'I wish I could.'

"There are... matters to be settled first," he says delicately.

His voice tells me the decision isn't his to make and I decide not to push. Not because I'm feeling cooperative, but because I can't bring myself to be an ass to him.

It's the seventh day when the shift comes. It feels like the magic that constantly surrounds the air changes. It thickens, like walking through syrup made of static and dread. It crawls under my skin, curling around my lungs, and every instinct in me is suddenly screaming to run. The hairs on my arms rise before I hear the knock, like my body knows something bad is coming. Aran enters, wearing a dark robe over his suit, stitched with glowing silver thread. His face is set in a way I've never seen before, somewhere between reluctant and deeply apologetic.

"They wish to speak with you," he says.

My mouth goes dry. "Who?"

His pause is just long enough to twist the knife. "The Divine Six."

I freeze, my breath faltering. "Korithax—"

"Will not be there." He says gently. A little too gently, in a way that has my stomach in knots.

Aran doesn't say anything as he walks me through the winding halls. The castle is truly beautiful, shimmering black obsidian that reflects the light shining in from the floor-to-ceiling windows that line the corridors. There is no beauty in the silence that accompanies us, though. Only dread. Each step echoes too loudly, each corridor feels longer than the last.

Eventually, we stop before a massive door, pulsing with soft golden light. Aran turns to me, placing his hands gently on my shoulders.

"You answer only what you must. Be honest, and do not anger them. You are about to enter their realm, Daisy. I cannot help you, but I will be with you, okay?"

The door opens before I can nod and light floods everything, making my eyes squint as it consumes me. It's pure and sharp in a way that feels wrong. Like the light itself is measuring me and finding me lacking. The chamber feels like it's carved from pure energy, looking like it was shaped in a dreamland. Six thrones arc in a cresent, arranged like a celestial tribunal. And on them sit six beings that don't belong in any reality I know. They're not beautiful, not really. They're unreal. All carved from crystal, flame, shadow, time, light, and god-knows-what-else. And I hate them. I don't know why, I can't explain it. But something deep in my soul hates them with a fire so pure it burns through me, causing my hands to shake.

They don't look at me with welcoming warmth as I walk into the centre of the room with my head held high, despite feeling the smallest I have ever felt. I've memorised Aran's rundown of who's who. Seraphiel, Judgement. Amarithe, Light. Velentha, Time. Calrix, Order. Elaron, Dreams. Mal'Thariel, Fate.

Seraphiel speaks first. Her voice is strong, like a verdict being handed over to me without a conviction. "You should not be here."

I swallow. "I didn't ask to be."

"And yet, you are," Amarithe says, eyes cold despite her golden glow.

"The soul was returned," Seraphiel continues. "You do not belong in Hell."

"Returned?" I repeat, confused. "What do you—"

"Korithax gave it back to you," Elaron says, almost gently, his starlight hair fluttering around his face. "He burned your contract. Your soul is no longer claimed."

My heart thuds, my head spinning at the information so casually given to me, like my entire world has not just been flipped. Again.

"Why would he do that?" I whisper to no one in particular.

"It was his choice," Calrix says, his voice like thunder given form. "But it raises questions. Too many questions."

"You are a contamination." Mal'Thariel grates. His voice is like broken stone grinding against glass. "Your presence distorts the laws of the underrealm."

My fists clench at my sides. The fear that was once rooted in me bubbling into something much hotter.

"I didn't ask for any of this," I snap. "I didn't ask to be sold, I didn't ask to be dragged to Hell. Or to survive when I didn't want to." My voice breaks slightly at the end, much to my horror. But none of them react.

"And yet he did save you," Amarithe murmurs, fingers lacing under her chin. "Curious, isn't it?"

My eyes drift to Velentha, the one who hasn't spoken. The one with glowing runes up her arms and an expression that feels... off. She's staring at me, and her lips part, the whisper too soft to anyone but me. "She remembers the ash, even if she does not know why."

I wouldn't have caught it if I were not watching her. I frown at her, waiting for somebody else to respond to her mumbles. The room goes deathly still, all of them seeming to stiffen at her words.

Seraphiel's head turns slowly towards her. "What did you say?"

"Nothing of importance," Velentha replies smoothly.

But her eyes don't leave mine. The runes crawling down her arms seem to pulse brighter, trembling, as if something inside her is trying to break free.

"You do not belong here, Daisy Sandoval," Seraphiel says again. "When your body heals, you are to return to your realm on Earth and stay there. You are not to cross the veil again."

"For your own safety," Elaron adds.

"And ours." Mal'Thariel growls.

I nod, though my jaw aches from clenching it. My legs tremble, but I refuse to fall under the strain. Aran steps forward from the shadows. "It's time to go." He says gently.

I turn to him, relieved. But before either of us can take a step, the door explodes inward. A shockwave of heat and smoke slams through the chamber, and Korithax storms in like a supernova given form. His eyes are pitch black, wings stretched wide, and his face looks like it has been carved from fury itself.

His gaze locks on me, then shifts to them, filled with nothing short of pure hatred.

"What the fuck do you think you're doing with her?"

CHAPTER 16
KORITHAX

There is no word in any tongue, mortal or immortal, that accurately captures the horror of the Drekkar.

The sky above the Northern Ridge is alive. Blood-red lightning streaks across the expanse, making the sky appear like it's bleeding. Crimson clouds roil over jagged peaks, the ground trembling under the weight of the creature in front of me. The air crackles with dread and terror, the kind that even makes the most sinister of demons pause. Towering over forty feet tall, the Drekkar is a twisted behemoth of scale and shadow. Reptilian in structure, but corrupted far beyond anything that can exist naturally. Its body is armoured in jagged obsidian plating, each scale edged with a venomous green substance that pulses through its veins. Leathery wings sprout from its back like broken cathedral windows, too large for its disgusting body, with membranes black and iridescent, stretched taut over gnarled bone.

Its head is elongated, draconic—but where eyes should be, are hollows of shifting emerald green flame. A maw that splits open wider than physically possible, layered with rows of serrated teeth, roars its deafening sound all around us. It sounds like a thousand dying screams, enough to make me slam my hands over my ears.

I don't take my eyes off its clawed hands, each digit long enough to impale a full-grown man. One successful swipe and I know I'm a goner. Its back has a dozen spiked tendrils—tentacle-like extensions that move with sentience, coiling and uncoiling each time the beast moves. This monster is the reason the north of Hell remains heavily guarded, and the exact reason I'm out here with my strongest soldiers.

This one is massive. Larger than any I've faced before.

"Fall back," I bark to the nearest commander. "Get your men out of the way."

"But sire—"

"NOW," I growl, not giving room for any argument.

The Drekkar lunges before the words are even cold on my tongue. I dodge the first strike, its scorching green flames streaking behind me. It's fast. Too fast. I unfurl my wings, shooting into the sky as it quickly follows, its bone-trembling roar making my ears throb. We clash mid-air, and one of its claws rips through my side, tearing straight through flesh. I hiss through my teeth, hoping that it only managed to slice its way through skin and nothing else. I move fast, countering its strike with a blade of soulfire, the hottest flame in Hell, driving it deep into its neck. It shrieks—a sound that instantly ruptures my eardrums, making the surrounding mountains tremble. I can feel the blood trickling out of my ears as I watch the reptilian bastard fall, its wings slamming into the nearest cliff face. The Drekkar's talons gouge the earth, leaving large gaping grooves across the ground. My blood spills freely from my side, dripping down to join the rivers of molten lava that freely run down the mountainside.

I don't stop, because this is what I was made for. This is why I am to become King of Hell. It takes hours to bring the bastard down, my body aching. I take my final swing, the explosion of power pouring out of me, my hellfire intertwines with the soulfire in my blade, causing the entire realm to tremble. I stand over its corpse, breathing hard, drenched in black blood and my own. Half of my soldiers' cheer, the other half stare at me in awe. But I don't take notice, I just turn and walk away, grateful I've finally had a match to compete with my strength and rage.

I'M HALFWAY to my chambers, too exhausted to try and teleport, when a healer intercepts me.

"Your Highness—" her eyes widen, taking in my appearance.

"What?"

"Miss Sandoval isn't in her chambers for her tonic. She's been summoned by the Divine Six."

I stop dead in my tracks.

"They summoned her?"

"Yes sire. She is still with them now."

Rage floods me, fresh and scalding, consuming me entirely. I summon the little power I've not already burned through and attempt to rip a hole straight into the Divine Six's pretentious sanctum, but it's locked down tight. Those bastards knew I would try and breach it the second they called her. Fine, guess I'll do it the old fashioned way.

I appear in front of the golden threshold of their domain in Zeriavoss instead, smoking peeling off my skin in waves. I'm instantly met with guards trying to intercept me. I snap the first one's neck with barely a flick of my wrist, bone crunching like dried reeds. The second, I grab by the throat and slam into the wall until he stops twitching. I don't break stride. I throw the doors open like a god of war. Smoke trails behind me, my footsteps thundering across the marble. My eyes land on Daisy.

She's stood there in the centre of the Divine Six's chamber. Surrounded. Small. Confused.

"You fucking dare bring her here?" I growl, my voice echoing around the room like a thunderclap.

Seraphiel rises. "You are not permitted—"

"Drop the fucking shield so I can take her back to her chambers. Now!"

"She does not belong in Hell," Seraphiel continues. "Her soul was returned. We do not understand why."

"I SAID—DROP. THE. SHIELD." The words aren't a command, they're a threat laced with promise. I take a step forward, my wings spread wide. My hands curl into fists that glow with dark black fire. They know me, they know exactly what I'll do. I will burn this room, I will tear down every gilded edge, shatter every rune, crack the spines of the immortals until they feel what wrath really is.

The shield drops. I don't wait for permission, I stride straight to her, her eyes wide with fear. She doesn't fight me as I scoop her up into my arms. I can hear her heartbeat thrumming wildly, feel it pattering against my chest. I vanish before they can even breathe another word.

We land back in her room, and I'm shaking. My arms are still around her, my skin slick with blood. Her wide eyes look up at me like I've just walked out of a nightmare.

"Why did you give my soul back? She asks, voice barely above a breath. "Why didn't you tell me?"

I don't answer, instead, I place her down on the bed gently. The second her body is out of my grasp, my anger resurfaces tenfold.

"Why did you go to the Uppers without me?" I snarl.

"I didn't know they—"

"I should break Aran's fucking neck," I interrupt, pacing up and down the room.

"No—don't. He helped me," Daisy stutters, stumbling over her words.

I whirl on her, eyes blazing, but quickly look away before I do something I'll regret. I can't look at her, not like this. They set this up. They planned this. The Drekkar attack wasn't random. No creature that massive, that brutal, just manages to wander that far inside my borders. They sent it. They waited until I was distracted, then grabbed her. My lip curls as a snarl forces its way out of my throat.

She watches me, trembling. "When can I go home?"

My eyes turn to her, my breath catching for half a second. She's splatted in my blood. The sight of her skin streaked in crimson, my crimson, does something ugly to me. I love seeing the women I fucked marked in my blood, but seeing her this way? Fuck.

"Go shower," I snap, "you're covered in my blood." I turn my gaze from her. "The healers will bring the rest of your medicine and I'll have Aran take you home in a few hours."

I exit the room, slamming the door behind me on a growl.

In my chambers, I tear the ruined clothes from my body and storm into the obsidian and marble tiled shower. The water burns as I turn the temperature up to the highest it can possibly go. I plant my palms against the cool stone, letting the heat sting down my back, watching the blood and grime wash away down the drain. I slap my hands against the wall, then pound the sides of my fists against them.

It's not enough. It's never, ever enough. I rear back my arm, driving my fist into the wall once. Then again and again, until my knuckles bleed and my breath comes in broken snarls.

She's leaving. Good. She doesn't belong here, she never did. Not seeing her again will be a good thing. Yet for some inexplicable reason, the thought of never seeing those godsdamn ocean eyes again has my ribs feeling like they're splintering open.

I RETURN HOURS LATER, buzzing with irritation.

"Aran's busy," I mutter as I stride into the guest chamber. "I'm taking you."

She opens her mouth, but I lift her into my arms before she can even form a word and teleport us back to her realm. We land in the middle of Daisy's apartment. It's dim, quiet, smelling faintly of lavender and familiarity. Her medicine lands with a quiet thunk on the table seconds after we arrive.

"You will not see me again, Daisy," I say flatly

She blinks in surprise. "But... what if I want to?"

Her voice is too soft, too raw. It sounds like a plea, like a wish, like she believes there's something in me that makes me worth her time. I force myself to look at her, really look. The way her hair's fallen loose around her face, a piece curling against her cheek. Without thinking, without meaning to, I brush it gently behind her ear. My fingers skim her skin in a moment that's too intimate. I instantly snap the thread, my jaw locking. I step back sharply, arms falling to my sides.

"And why the fuck would you want that, little flower?" I sneer, forcing ice into my voice.

She flushes, embarrassed by her own honesty. "I... I don't know."

The blush rises up her throat, and gods help me, I like it. I take two long strides away, trying to put as much space between us as I can without tearing open the walls.

"You will not see me again," I growl. "Get your fucking self together, and don't try kill yourself again. Just get on with your life, Daisy."

She flinches, tears lining her eyes. "Why are you so hot and cold with me? I don't understand."

I take a slow, deliberate inhale and rake my eyes over her—not with lust, or tenderness, but with forced disdain. "There is nothing to understand," I say, venom lacing every syllable. "You are a pathetic, weak little mortal, who has been nothing but an inconvenience to me since your wretched father sold your soul to me like it was trash. You were so beneath me, I gave it back. I do not want you in my life, my realm, not even in the fucking depths of Hell."

I watch her expression crumble as I tear her down with words I know will scar. Not because they're true, but because if I don't burn the bridge between us, I feel as though I may never stop crossing it. I don't give her another chance to reply as I vanish straight back to my chamber, leaving her behind forever.

I lean against the wall, breathing hard. The taste of my cruelty is bitter in my mouth. Good, I tell myself. But my hands are shaking from an emotion I'm struggling to place. And when I lay down in my large, cold bed, the broken way she looked at me is the only thing I see as I close my eyes. And I fucking hate myself for it.

CHAPTER 17
DAISY

The apartment is too quiet.

He's gone. Just like that. The room still smells faintly of his scent—a smoky and earthy smell with a hint of rich spice. I stay frozen for a minute, leaning against the counter where he set me down like I was weightless. Like I was nothing more than a problem that needed discarding. My heart feels hollow and my limbs ache with a kind of weariness that goes bone-deep. I stare at the spot where he vanished, my thoughts spinning around the way his eyes had changed—just before the cruelty. That fleeting moment where he looked at me like I was something, and then he burned it to the ground. I take a long, deep inhale, my eyes shifting to the coffee table. The medicine, glowing in the tiny little vials sitting there like a slap in the face. A small bit of proof that he cared about my recovery at least, despite his words and actions saying otherwise. Aran had said he was worried about me, but all I saw was a man who couldn't wait to be rid of me.

My eyes lock on my phone laid next to the gleaming bottles, my heart pounding in my ears. I scoop it up, instantly irritated when I realise it's dead. I plug it in with shaky fingers and wait, pacing in a tight circle in the cramped space of my apartment, running one hand through the loose strands in my hair, whilst chewing my thumb on my other hand. As soon as it powers up, the notifications flood in.

42 missed calls. 18 voicemails. 97 unread messages.

Talia. Ezra. My boss. One from Professor Doyle.

Saturday, November 18th. I blink. I've been away from them all for a month. Gods. Two weeks of shutting down. One week in a coma, one week begging to come home. Four weeks of the world moving on without me. My job, my classes, my life.

I blow out a breath, everything slowly overwhelming me. I lean back against the wall, my eyes scanning my empty, quiet apartment. Everything looks so normal, like the last two weeks didn't even happen. My eyes snag on the shattered bathroom door, my heart instantly thundering when I remember what had happened the last time I was in there. I shakily walk into the bathroom, my feet dragging because it's the last place I want to be, but I know I have to go in there and face what happened. The light flickers, casting everything in a pale glow thanks to the lack of windows in the cramped space. And there they are. The bottles. Still scattered around the shower floor, some empty, some not. I walk into the cubicle, my eyes spotting the small dried-up puddle of bile and partially dissolved pills staining the floor next to the plug hole. I lower myself slowly to the ground, curling my fingers around one of the bottles. I hold it to my chest and sob, my head resting back against the cool tiles on the wall. It pours out of me—ugly, loud, and broken. I release every ounce of pain I've been holding on to, my cries turning to screams as I feel my heart shatter all over again. My eyes burn, my throat raw from hysteria. Why did he save me? I had made my choice, and he took that away from me. All for him to then treat me like I was a burden. It wasn't fair, none of this was. I didn't ask for a single thing this fucking life kept throwing at me, yet here I was, constantly broken and bruised.

Eventually, I leave the bathroom, grabbing my phone to text the group chat with shaky fingers.

Me: I'm home. Can you guys come over? Please.

Talia replies instantly: On our way.

They arrive in under ten minutes, Ezra bursting through the door first, flinging himself into my arms. His warm vanilla scent wraps around me, the familiar smell making me feel instantly at ease.

"You dumb bitch, don't you dare scare me like that again," he whispers against my shoulder, squeezing the life out of me.

Talia follows silently, dropping her bag and pulling me into her arms. She doesn't say anything, just holds my face in her hands, pressing her forehead against mine gently as we both softly cry.

We collapse onto the sofa together, our limbs all tangled, our hearts bruised. Talia strokes my hair whilst Ezra sits squeezing my hand tightly like he's afraid I'll vanish.

"I can't believe you summoned him," I whisper.

Ezra raises his brows. "Summoned him? Babe, we demanded him. I think we used every method we could find. Candles, Latin, chalk circles. We were like two witchy gremlins trying to perform an exorcism in reverse." He flaps his hands dramatically like he's reenacting him casting some weird spell. "And holy fuck, Daze, your demon is so hot. Like. Sinfully hot. I kind of want to die just to see him again."

I actually laugh, a sound I never thought I would hear leave my throat again. Then I shake my head. "I'm not bound to him anymore. He gave it back. My soul."

Ezra gasps. "Wait. You're not?"

I shake my head. "Nope," I respond, popping the 'P.'

Both of them freeze, staring at me with open mouths.

Talia's voice is quiet, laced with confusion. "He did?" I don't miss the way her fists curl in her lap.

"Yeah. He told me before he left. Said I was a 'pathetic, weak little mortal.' Then he said he didn't want me in his realm, or his life."

They go silent as I look down, fiddling with my fingers, softly biting my lower lip to stop it from wobbling. I can see Talia scowling out the corner of my eye, but she chooses to stay quiet, which is so entirely unlike her.

"So... takeaway and a sleepover?" I mumble to remove the tension from the atmosphere.

Ezra nods. "Bitch, yes. We are eating, cuddling, and watching chick flicks until your serotonin levels have risen from the grave."

Talia orders the food as Ezra loads up mean girls on the shitty TV I have in my living room. And that night, after the food had been devoured and the second movie we watched ended, we all cram into my bed, a tangled heap of limbs and blankets. They both demanded I lay in the middle, wrapping their arms around me, and for the first time in a long time, I fell asleep without nightmares.

They leave later the next day after ensuring I ate breakfast and got a shower, making me promise that I'll come back to college after the weekend is done. I promise, hooking my pinkies through theirs before they leave. I clean up the apartment, even managing to throw away all the rotting food from my fridge that was left uneaten. It was clear that leaving this life behind wasn't an option for me, because apparently I had a demon that hated me so much he wanted me to continue living for as long as possible, so I could endure more suffering.

~

Monday comes too soon.

I dress slowly in jeans that hang a little too loose, and a sweater that hides my frame. My reflection in the mirror looks like someone I don't know. Pale, tired, but at least my eyes are steady. I pull my hair into a low bun, two blonde strands hanging down either side of my face, and drag myself to campus. My feet are bricks and my stomach sits in a tight knot at the thought of returning to reality. The first thing to tick off my list is my job. Gods, I might not even have one anymore.

I walk into the cafe, scanning for my boss, spotting him behind the counter, tapping on a screen. He looks up and freezes when he sees me.

"Daisy?"

"I'm so sorry," I blurt the apology out before I can even think. "I should have called. I know I messed up. Please don't fire me. I need this job. I'll do extra shifts, I'll clean the staff bathroom for a month, I'll—"

He holds up a hand, cutting me off, his face softening a touch. "Stop, you're not fired."

I stand silently, my eyes wide, trying to catch my breath from the absolute word vomit I'd just spewed at him.

He sighs. "You scared the hell out of me. Just don't disappear on me again, okay?"

I nod, choking back relief. "Okay."

Thank the gods for that. He even explained that he was letting me have my time off as PTO so I would still get some sort of a wage. I swear I nearly knocked him on his ass the way I dived on him to give him a hug.

Talia and Ezra beamed when they saw me, both of them telling me how proud they were of me for returning to college and managing to keep my job. Talia winked at Ezra when I had told them that my boss had let me stay on, and even gave me PTO for some of the time I was away. I'm guessing the two of them hooking up a few times had something to do with it, but I wasn't going to question it when it meant I still had a way to pay my bills.

The rest of the day was uneventful, life seeming to be back to normal despite everything that had happened to me in the month I was gone. I have a butt-load of work to catch up on, and I have to make up one of the assignments I missed. But thankfully it was nothing too overwhelming, and something I should be able to do easily, thanks to all the notes I took before my life went downhill.

At cheer practice, the coach frowns when I show up. "Uniform?"

"Mine's too big," I admit. "I, uh, lost some weight."

She rakes her eyes over me slowly before giving a soft smile, like she can see the reason for my weight loss wasn't purposeful. "We'll find you a spare."

In the locker room, I catch sight of myself in the mirror. My collarbones seem slightly more visible, but thankfully, I don't look all too different—other than my eyes, that seem more shadowed. I smile anyway, bright and sunny, typical Daisy.

"Nothing's changed," I whisper. "Sunshine only."

The routine comes back like muscle memory. I fake energy, falling into the steps and stunts like I'd not missed an entire month, smiling like it doesn't hurt to exist. After, a girl from our squad approaches hesitantly.

"Hey," she says. "I just wanted to say... I'm sorry. About Ethan."

I freeze, my blood turning to ice. She means well, I know she means well. But she doesn't know. She doesn't know that he's dead because of what he did to me. She doesn't know he's dead because someone who owns my freaking soul killed him.

"Thanks," I murmur. "I'm... still processing." I offer her a small smile and vanish before she can say anything else.

LATER THAT DAY, I visit Professor Doyle's office. He's kind, but stern, with salt-and-pepper hair, his reading glasses on a chain around his neck.

"You've missed four weeks, Miss Sandoval," he says, steepling his fingers. "But your early coursework was strong. You'll need to write two makeup essays, and complete the group presentation for Psych 324 with Ms Everson. Your partners have been holding it down for you."

I nod. "Thank you. I'll get it all done."

He studies me carefully. His brown eyes seeing wholly too much of my fractured soul. "Are you all right?"

I smile. Bright. Too bright to be anything other than fake. "Absolutely. Never better."

He catches me up on other parts of the lectures that I've missed, then dismisses me with a 'maybe you should sign up for counselling.' Charming. Clearly the fake smile wasn't convincing him either.

By the time I get home that evening, I've forced myself to believe the lie that I am perfectly alright. That I'm fine. That none of it touched me, and that he doesn't haunt me in every shadow. I sit on the couch, flipping through my notes, acting like I didn't almost die and get dragged to Hell, almost believing a demon prince with eyes like ruin actually cared about me.

"I'm fine," I whisper.

~

It's December.

Christmas is creeping in through the fairy lights strung up in shop windows, through the sound of carols on repeat. On the outside, I do what I always do. I smile. I laugh. I help Ezra and Talia hunt down the perfect presents, pretending it doesn't sting every time I walk past a cute couple sharing hot chocolate, or taking cute Christmas photos. I perfect the role of playing pretend. I make Christmas-themed drinks at the cafe with precision—peppermint mochas, gingerbread lattes, cinnamon-dusted cappuccinos. My fingers seem to constantly smell of vanilla syrup, nutmeg, and burnt espresso. But despite everything, I secretly love it. The songs play on repeat—All I Want For Christmas Is You, Last Christmas, Have Yourself A Merry Little Christmas. They're on a loop at work—and damn them—I hum along constantly, even when they're not playing. Because Christmas is still my favourite time of year, even now, when nothing feels the same. This was supposed to be my first Christmas with a boyfriend. With him. Before it all went sour, before he got too touchy, too demanding, I imagined snow falling outside while we curled up together in my too-small apartment. I imagined his fingers tangling in the lights as we put them up, going on about football and other stupid stuff I didn't care about, and then pretending not to enjoy it when he inevitably got the star perfectly centred on the top of the tree.

And now? Now I drink cheap wine in candy cane pyjamas and sit by myself in the dark, pretending it doesn't hurt that I'm alone. Worse, his parents will be spending Christmas without their son, and that guilt settles into my chest like frost. I know I shouldn't feel responsible, Ethan made his choices. But I do. I feel it like a bruise to the heart every time someone says "Merry Christmas."

The winter ball comes and goes. Ezra begged me to go with them, promising a magical night of fake snow and photos by a glittering tree. I made excuses, making Talia look at me like she didn't believe half of the crap I was saying, but she didn't push. Instead, I worked, volunteering to do the late. I scrubbed countertops and refilled napkin dispensers while the other staff all went home early.

At night, I sit in my dimly lit apartment with the glow of the tree Ezra helped me decorate. It's a chaotic disaster—tacky, bright, but absolutely perfect. Glittery bows, mismatched baubles, multi-coloured lights. There's an ornament that's shaped like a flamingo, a taco, a tiny demon with a Santa hat that Ezra insisted looked like he who holds my soul. There are presents under the tree, wrapped in obnoxiously glittery paper and aggressively large bows. One from Talia, one from Ezra, one from my boss. The kindness of it all makes my heart ache.

CHRISTMAS EVE QUICKLY COMES AROUND, college and work making the festive period fly by in a bright, hazy blur.

I'm curled on my sofa in the same candy-cane pyjamas I've worn all month, blonde hair in two braided pigtails, the lights on the tree blinking quietly in the corner. The bottle is halfway empty, no longer giving me the same buzz it used to when I first started turning to wine to numb the darkness that often creeped into my mind as day turned to dusk. The Christmas movie ends, and I find myself starting to cry. Not loud sobs, just soft tears sliding down my face as I stare at the tree softly glowing in the corner of my tiny apartment. I find myself missing Aran. His soft words and his calm presence. The way he let me be human without pitying me for it. I even miss the halls of Zeriavoss—the stone beneath my feet, the smell of fire and intoxicating fruits. I dream about it constantly, because for some strange reason, I'm homesick for a realm that told me I didn't belong.

And worse—I miss him. Korithax. Even after everything, even after his words broke me open. I wake up some nights after dreams of him, his realm, gripping my shoulder, where the birthmark hums faintly like it's remembering something I've already forgotten.

Ezra had offered for me to go to his family's house for Christmas, telling me about all the wonderful things he and his parents get up to over the festive period. Talia joined in and told me her family's traditions also. I had smiled at them, my heart genuinely warming up knowing my friends had such amazing homes to return to. I declined Ezra's invitation, making a lie that I had agreed to go spend Christmas with my dad. He was suspicious, constantly questioning me on the run-up to his leaving for the festive break. He knows that my relationship with my dad had been strained since my mom died, so he was shocked to hear I'd agreed to go spend my Christmas with him in his home.

Of course, I wasn't actually doing that. Despite Christmas being my favourite time of year, this year, I wasn't feeling very festive at all. Ezra and his parents didn't deserve to have my bad energy bringing down their Christmas spirit. They deserved peace and happiness, not a depressed twenty-year-old ruining their holiday.

I glance at the time on my phone and drag myself up, opting to leave the rest of the bottle on the coffee table. It was time for me to crawl into bed, the thought of tomorrow filling me with dread. Maybe I'll just sleep through it and pretend this year that Christmas doesn't exist.

I push open the door to my bedroom, sleepily rubbing my eyes, when a presence makes me freeze entirely. I don't even have to look up to know who's in my room, but I do anyway.

There he is, sitting on the edge of my bed like he didn't leave me over a month ago, departing with pure hatred pouring from his mouth. He's sitting so nonchalantly like he didn't shatter my entire being after having me put back together by his healers. A small box rests in his hands, wrapped in a deep black paper, tied with a red silk ribbon.

My breath stutters. "Korithax?"

He looks up, lips curling into something too sharp to be called a smile. "Merry Christmas, little flower," he murmurs, lifting the gift with a sadistic look in his eyes.

And my world stops all over again.

CHAPTER 18

KORITHAX

The preparations for my coronation should have consumed my focus.

They didn't. Not when I could still feel the tether between myself and the small mortal girl I'd dumped back on Earth. Aran kept me informed, of course. He always did, despite my protests, despite me telling him that I did not give a shit about her.

Daisy was alive. She went back to her college classes and back to work. She smiled when she needed to, laughing and joking with her friends. But I knew better, because I had seen it myself. In the moments when I would awaken from nightmares plagued with her tear-filled ocean eyes, I would go and allow myself to check the scrying mirror. I would catch glimpses of her life—the wine bottles that consumed her nights, the dark circles she hid under makeup during the day. I would see her mindlessly fiddling with her hands, lost in her thoughts. I hated the way she would force her way into my head like a festering wound. She was, after all, a weak, pathetic mortal. But it would appear I was also weak, because night after night I would find myself sitting for hours, watching her, like a crazed, obsessed stalker.

. . .

ALAS, I had bigger things to deal with. My father, the 'great' former King of Hell, had finally fallen to permanent bed rest, his ancient body giving up under the weight of too many soul bargains, and too many betrayals. Whilst yes, we were classed as immortal, immortality didn't last forever, just a really fucking long time. Soon, Hell would be mine. Officially and wholly mine.

I commanded the war hounds at the northern borders. I redrew alliances between some of the other realms that had grown distant from us under my father's reign. I oversaw the cleansing of the corruption from the Welcome Circle. Some of the judges being a little too happy to send undeserving souls to the pits. I ruled, and I ruled well. A force to be reckoned with, they said. A king who would shake the foundations of the realms themselves, they said.

I was reviewing plans for the coronation when the fucking summons arrived from the Divine Six. Again. Did these assholes not tire of seeing my face, because I sure as shit got tired of seeing theirs. The amount they demanded to see me, you'd think Hell was the only realm they conjured up. Fuck knows how much time they spend sticking their noses in other realms' businesses.

THE CHAMBER of the Six's was as insufferable as ever. Blinding light, cloying sanctimony, and six pairs of eyes that still believed they could command me. It's been a solid fifteen thousand years of them trying—since I was just merely five thousand years old, a small boy —I'll give them respect for their commitment, that's for sure.

"You will not ascend without a bride," Seraphiel declares the second I arrive, her voice slicing through the room, angrier than usual. The others nod, silent but with heavy judgement.

I laughed, loud and bitter. "You keep saying, yet here I am, planning my coronation. It's almost like I do not care about what you have to say." I say, with a shrug.

Amarithe's false smile stretches wide. "Without balance, there is no rule, Korithax. It is law."

Law. Their favourite fucking word. They're acting like they can't change the law, like it's something that is solidified in stone. I know they can change it; I have seen them do it before with Noxthrallia. The realm became so corrupt with dark magic that anything they did just went ignored. So the Divine Six chose to look the other way, because it was too much hassle to do otherwise. But I think Hell would freeze over before they did anything like that for me.

"No bride, no throne, Korithax," Seraphiel continues.

"You may not take us seriously. But if you try to ascend that throne without a bride, your kingdom will be burned to ash," Calrix declares, his flaming sword burning brighter to emphasise his point.

"Is that a threat?" I growl, staring Calrix directly into his glowing, hate-filled eyes.

"It is a promise, Prince of Ruin. I have seen the outcome of you not taking a bride. Time is ticking," Velentha whispers, looking horrified at what she has seen.

I leave without bowing, untamed smoke curling at my heels as I vanish. Burn my fucking kingdom to the ground? Over my dead body.

When I return to Zeriavoss, I find Aran waiting outside my chamber door, arms crossed.

"I heard," he says simply.

"Of course you did." I shove past him, but he follows like the annoying shadow he is.

He hesitates, then, with the fucking gall of someone who had nothing to lose, he mumbles, "You could offer a marriage of convenience."

I stop dead in my tracks, looking at him for any sign of a joke. He just stares back at me with a deadpan expression. I bark a sharp, humourless laugh. "Who the fuck would agree to that? Everybody in this damn kingdom wants that throne. I could not trust anybody with a marriage of fucking convenience, Aran."

He shrugs. "You only need the ceremony to do as the Uppers wish. Then she stays on Earth, and you rule Hell. No mess, and no real connection."

"And who, exactly, would I be proposing this to?" I ask, venom dripping from every single word.

He smiles. "Daisy."

I stand there for a moment, waiting for him to laugh, for him to say he's joking. There was not a single chance this fool was truly suggesting what I thought he was. That I marry a mortal. He's lost his godsdamned mind.

"Even if that was a possibility, she hates me," I mutter.

"She's alive because of you," he counters. "And whether you admit it or not, she's tied to you."

The second he mutters the words, I feel the tether tug. I'm still not entirely sure what the tether is, nor do I know how the hell he knows about it. She is not my soul mate, that's impossible. It's only possible between mortal and mortal, immortal and immortal. Maybe I accidentally did something when I returned her soul, maybe some of it stayed latched onto me somehow. She was clearly dying for someone to fill the void in her life, so maybe her soul was clinging to me out of sheer desperation.

I sneer. "I told her she's pathetic."

Aran winces, whistling low. "Ouch. Okay. Maybe it will be harder than I initially thought to convince her, but—"

I shake my head, fury rolling through me as I cut him off, "She'd say no. I am not wasting my time, Aran, not on her."

"She might say no," he counters. "But what's the alternative? Find a demoness who'll stab you in your sleep? A celestial spy who will sell you out?" He raises an eyebrow at me. "At least with Daisy, you know she's too stubborn to betray you, and too weak to kill you." He shrugs.

I don't answer because I hate that it actually made sense.

"I CANNOT BELIEVE I'm doing this," I grumble, holding the little box in my hand. "You think this will make her say yes?"

Aran nods, chuckling at the box. "If I know Daisy, and I believe I do after our short time together, that will absolutely make her say yes."

I growl, irritated at the fact that I let him actually talk me into this. I have never had to ask for anything in my godsdamnned life. If I wanted it, I took it. Yet I'm about to ask a fucking mortal girl to be my bride, with the added risk of her telling me to go fuck myself. I have never wanted to strangle the Divine Six more than I do right now. Their stupid fucking laws about stupid fucking marriage and their stupid fucking threats. I clench my fists, cracking my neck before slowly exhaling.

"You'd better pray to any God that will deign to listen that she says yes, Aran," I mumble before vanishing out of Zeriavoss.

I APPEAR in her room silently, sitting on the edge of her bed like a shadow among the little twinkling holiday lights that are wrapped around her headboard. I can hear her TV playing in her living room. I shift uncomfortably, impatience getting the better of me. Before I can storm into the living room, I hear her shut off the TV, the silence seeming deafening now. I take a deep breath, preparing myself to be an absolute fool. She enters the room a few minutes later, wearing ridiculous Christmas-themed pyjamas that have little candy canes all over them, rubbing at her eyes as she pushes the door open. She doesn't even look at me before her body registers that I'm here, like she, too, can feel the tug between us. Her eyes snap up to mine, and she freezes.

"Korithax?" She whispers, rubbing her eyes again, then blinking rapidly at me.

"Merry Christmas, little flower," I say, lifting the present slightly, the corner of my mouth twitching up in an attempt to smile.

She stands staring at me like she isn't sure whether or not she's hallucinating. I rise, offering her the small box with another half-smile. Her eyes quickly glance at it, but she doesn't take it.

"Why are you here?" She asks.

Straight to the point. Good. I exhale slowly, "I'm here to propose something." She frowns, not deigning to offer me a response, so I continue, "Marriage. A marriage of convenience."

Silence. Gods, why was my heart hammering in my chest? I fucking hated this. She stares at me for a few more seconds, and then she laughs. A sharp, bitter laugh that feels like a slap across the face.

"You're insane," she says, shaking her head. "You're actually insane if you think I would ever say yes to that."

I grind my teeth. "It benefits us both. I get a queen and shut the Divine Six up, and in return, I will offer you anything that you desire. Wealth, protection, anything."

She folds her arms, chin tilting high in defiance. There she is, the stubborn little sunshine. "The Divine Six literally told me I don't belong in Hell," she snaps.

"Even more reason to marry you." I grin. "It's a way I can piss them off even more than you can imagine."

Her mouth trembles, her eyes sparking with rage as she begins pacing back and forth in front of me. "Leave," she snarls. "You're a fool for ever thinking I would help you. I would rather rot than owe you anything." She stops dead in front of me, poking a finger into my chest, her hand raising over her head just to reach. "A fool!"

I step closer, grabbing hold of her wrist, pulling it away from my chest. "Just remember, Daisy," I say with a low growl. "Not only did I give you your soul back, but I saved your damn life."

She stiffens, looking at my hand wrapped around her small, fragile wrist, then whispers, "And look how that worked out. I'm depressed, I drink myself to sleep every night, and I am more heartbroken each day that passes because I woke up from that day in the shower."

I flinch before I can stop myself, the words hitting me harder than any blade ever has. It's a direct shot straight to my chest, her words landing a hard blow for some strange reason. She still regrets waking up; she still hates the fact that her attempt on her life didn't work. I bare my teeth, the only emotion I'll allow on my face, hiding how her words have affected me.

"Fine," I bite out, forcing her hand away so hard she stumbles a step backwards. "Forget it." I disappear without another word, leaving the gift to sit abandoned on her floor.

"How did it go?" Aran asks as I appear back in my chamber, his presence making me startle.

I turn to him and punch him straight in the face before storming off to the training grounds.

"Not very well then," I hear him mutter on my way out.

CHAPTER 19
DAISY

I don't cry, I refuse to cry.

Tears are what he wants as one kind of proof that he still has power over me. That he can rip the floor out from beneath me, and I'll jump to his commands, like I didn't just spend the last month clawing my way out of the depressive pit he left me in.

Anger surges through me hotter than any sadness ever could. How dare he come here, after a month of absolute silence, after leaving me to drown in my own mess? He just vanished, and then has the absolute audacity to show up on Christmas Eve, carrying a perfectly wrapped present to offer a proposal like he was offering me a glass of mulled wine and not his freaking hand in eternal wedlock.

A marriage of convenience. Like I'm nothing more than a contract he needs signing. Not a woman he abandoned, bruised and broken, who he then spat venomous words at when I was finally strong enough to stand again.

I storm to the trash can in the kitchen and hurl the stupid, perfectly wrapped gift into it without a second glance. It hits the bottom with a satisfying thud, the sound calming some of my unadulterated rage. I hope it breaks. I hope whatever is in that godforsaken box is shattered beyond repair. Just like me.

I march back into my bedroom, yanking off the sheets, so not even where he had the audacity to sit has been defiled by him and his stupid scent. I scream as I throw the balled-up bedding into the laundry hamper.

No contact, no help, nothing from him for over a month. Then boom, "Oh, become my bride." What an absolute maniac. I frantically pace up and down, ranting and muttering to myself like a mad woman. What the FRICK was that? No, "how are you?" No apology, no softness, no affection, and certainly not even a flicker of guilt. Just "marry me."

Like that's a thing normal people do after emotionally eviscerating someone and then vanishing. He acts like I'm something on his to-do list. Acquire her soul, check. Destroy her mental well-being, check. Return her soul, check. Crush her spirit, check. Leave, check. And ooh, one last final thing to do, propose marriage. CHECK. Did he get confused and think this was the Hallmark channel? Is this what we're doing now? Is this my twisted, demon-fuelled Christmas special?

I climb into bed, still vibrating with rage. My jaw aches from how tightly I'm clenching it. I toss and turn, I punch my pillow, I scream into it. But eventually, exhaustion wins, and sleep drags me under. And of course, he's there, in the haze of my dreams, his obsidian eyes following me like shadows made flesh. His voice slithers through my subconscious, repeating over and over:

Merry Christmas, little flower.

THE NEXT DAY, I don't bother pretending to be festive, despite my candy cane pyjamas. I sleep until the afternoon, cocooned in my bed with my phone buzzing endlessly somewhere under the covers. After what feels like the hundredth buzz, I finally drag myself up, finding my phone tucked into the depths of my bed, and lie my back against the pillows to read through it. It's all messages from Talia and Ezra, as expected. I text back a half-hearted 'Merry Christmas' into the group chat, making them instantly flood the chat with emojis, selfies, and stupid jokes. I smile at the screen, happy knowing my friends are having an amazing Christmas, despite the ache in my chest, gnawing away at me. I scroll through social media for a few more hours, the sinking feeling in my chest deepening at each happy Christmas photo I scroll by. Smiling selfies, family photos, present hauls. They all fill my screen, a tear rolling down my cheek despite my best effort to hold myself together.

At around six p.m., I finally forced myself to crawl out of bed and open the gifts my friends and my boss had left for me. Talia had gotten me a pair of fuzzy socks in my favourite colour—yellow—and a little jar filled with handwritten notes, the label on the outside saying 'Reasons We Love You'. Ezra, being Ezra, had gotten me a ridiculous oversized hoodie that said 'Sunshine Incarnate' across the front in glittery gold letters, and a box of my favourite candy. I clutch the little notes in my hands for a long moment, heart throbbing painfully. I open the gift from my boss next, a packet of coffee beans from the cafe that I won't be able to use because I don't own a coffee machine. Well, it's the thought that counts.

I swipe up my phone, deciding to text my dad since it was Christmas after all:

Merry Christmas, Dad.

The little 'read notification pops up, but when a few minutes pass without a response, I just close the thread. I'm not surprised, but it stings all the same.

I sit on the couch in my living room, the twinkle of my tiny Christmas tree throwing soft, colourful shadows across the walls. Everything just feels hollow. And no matter how hard I try not to, my eyes keep dragging back to the trash can. To that stupid present. I clench my jaw. "Don't you dare, Daisy. You're better than this. You don't care about some stupid gift from some stupid demon." I mutter to myself.

Five minutes later, I'm stomping across the room, cursing under my breath. I open the lid to the trash can, staring down at the little box before yanking it out, glaring at it with as much hatred as I can conjure up. I shuffle back to the sofa, tearing away the wrapping paper and throwing it on the floor. Opening the box, I gasp, my eyes widening at the little present. Inside is an orb, small and delicate, and glowing above a stand made of intricate golden branches that curl upward like reaching hands. I pull it out of the box, watching as it levitates above its stand. It freaking levitates, looking almost weightless as it pulses with a warm, gentle light. I stare at it, mesmerised by the magical little globe. I glance back down at the box, a small folded note tucked inside. I hesitate before placing the orb on my coffee table and picking up the note with trembling fingers:

Since you are the sun,

I brought you your very own ray of sunshine. Taken from Solara—the home of light, where Earth's sun comes from. Tap once for midday, tap again for sunset, tap again for sunrise.

- K

Solara, another place I had never heard of. A realm, a whole realm dedicated to sunshine. The light in the orb is soft, yet impossibly bright, like the sun distilled into something I could hold in my hands. I pick it up, tapping it once. The orb shifts instantly, and I watch in awe as the colours melt into the brilliant orange-pinks of a sunset, the kind my mother used to love watching from the back porch. Another tap, and it transforms into the delicate pastel golds and blues of a sunrise, soft and full of sleepy hope of a new day. I sit there, staring, unable to move, unable to think. My chest tightens painfully, my vision blurring. My mother would have loved this.

I pad into my bedroom, setting the orb carefully on my bedside table, watching the colours shifting peacefully. I curl under my blankets, pulling my knees to my chest as I lie on my side, watching the sunset glow of the orb until my eyes grow heavy. For the first time in weeks, I don't cry myself to sleep. Instead, I fall asleep wrapped in the light of Solara. Still furious, still broken, but with a tiny little orb bringing a semblance of peace to my heart.

THE NEXT MORNING, the orb still sits on my nightstand, glowing softly, casting a warm halo across the room. I stare at it for a long time, hating how much it comforts me, hating it even more because it reminded me of a certain seven-foot demon who had flipped my entire world on its head.

I drag myself out of bed, the Christmas wrapping paper still littered across my floor. The presents from Talia and Ezra sitting on my sofa, little pieces of them warming the cold edges of my heart. I wrap myself up in Ezra's ridiculous hoodie, tracing my fingers over the lettering that reads 'Sunshine Incarnate'. Because, honestly, I need the lie today.

~

THE DAYS between Christmas and New Year's blur into one long, sluggish crawl. I go through the motions. Smiling when Talia and Ezra text, frowning when my boss tells me that I have to work the first day back after Christmas break. I even manage grocery shopping, acting like a fully functional human being for the first time in what feels like forever. But inside, I remain stuck, floating somewhere between fury and heartbreak.

New Year's Eve crept in like a ghost. Talia and Ezra begged me to go to a house party with them—offering everything from pizza bribes to promises of no gross frat boys hitting on me—but I declined. I blamed it on still being tired, on needing to rest before I went back to work. The truth was, I wasn't ready to go to another party just yet. Honestly, I didn't know if I would ever be ready again. Images of Ethan flash through my head, making my palms break out in a cold sweat. Nope, I don't think I will ever be ready to go to another party as long as I live.

By eleven thirty p.m., I was sitting on my old sagging sofa, wrapped in the fluffiest blanket I could find, staring out of the window. The streets were alive outside, bursts of laughter filling the air, flashes of cheap fireworks already starting to explode in the distance. I hug my knees to my chest, letting the cool glass of the window chill my face as I lean against it. I'd brought the orb from Solara from my bedside to my coffee table, casting the soft hues of a sunset across the otherwise dark room. I tap it once with my finger, watching it shift to a sleepy sunrise, ready for a new day, a new year.

It was supposed to make me feel hopeful, but I still just feel empty. Like an echo chamber was in my chest, residing where my heart should be. The first fireworks of the new year explode in the sky as the clock turns to midnight, painting brilliant purple and gold against the dark. I press my face harder against the glass, watching the lights scatter across the city as I hold tightly to my empty bottle of wine.

"I wish you had never saved me," I whisper into the empty room. "And I wish you had never left."

I take a glance back at the orb on the table, wondering just how bad a marriage to the Prince of Hell could be.

CHAPTER 20
KORITHAX

The mortal whisky burns like acid as the amber liquid slides down my throat.

Good. Maybe it'll cauterise whatever rot seems to be festering inside of me. I lean back in the worn leather chair of the viewing chamber, the scrying mirror suspended above the blackened stone table like a frozen moon. It hums with magic, flickering with the image I can't stop watching. Her apartment is quiet and dim, messy in the way I've grown to know how she likes her space. And there she is, sitting by the window in that absurdly oversized hoodie. The one with the words Sunshine Incarnate scrawled across the front like some kind of bad joke. The orb sits on her coffee table, casting hues of soft light across the room. The same orb I know she threw in the trash. Yet, there it is, illuminating her space. Her knees are pulled up, an empty wine bottle swinging in her fingers as she stares out at the fireworks illuminating the sky. I swirl the whisky in my glass, letting the silence stretch between us, despite her not knowing I'm there with her.

"If you hate me so much, little flower," I murmur, voice rough from the burning spirit that laces my throat. "Why do you sit with my gift?"

She taps the orb, the colours shifting from sunset to sunrise. Even now, she's always choosing the light. Always pretending her life, her world, isn't made of shadow.

I down the rest of my drink in one go, the glass thunking against the stone with a hollow sound that makes my jaw twitch. It's been well over a month since she left my realm. Well over a month since I told her to get on with her fucking life, since I let the venom spill from my tongue just to stop myself from falling at her feet. And I've watched her every night since. Pathetic.

But I have bigger problems. The Divine Six have made their threat. A noose tightening. A deadline. One more moon cycle to find a bride, or they'll provide one for me. Tick fucking tock. They gave me three options, all of them insufferable, each one worse than the last. Zerithia of the Eastern Flame Tribe that reside in the pits. Strong lineage, a decent warrior, but has tried to assassinate two of her previous fiancés—one of them successfully. It turns out, she also does not want marriage, and is being forced into it by her parents. So if she can't have her own way, she'll just keep trying to kill those who get in her way.

Then there's Iralen of the Wretched Vale, part of a realm Hell cut trade with a long, long time ago. Poison in a gown. She kissed me with daggers behind her back, already asking me what I'd leave her in my will. I'd give her credit for being so upfront if it wasn't for the fact that I knew damn well she wouldn't waste time on stabbing those daggers straight into my jugular the second the ceremony was over. I'm pretty sure she was only putting herself in the running so she had a chance to kill me as revenge for Hell cutting the trade deal. It wasn't even my decision; it was my father's and the Divine Six who decided they weren't worthy. But now all of a sudden, one of theirs was potential bride material. Make it make sense.

And finally, Alorith. Some highborn royal from the Crystalline

Peaks, a realm too far away from here for me to ever even consider visiting. She had come here, though, to make herself a contender. She was absolutely beautiful, well-polished, yet so painfully dull that I'd forgotten her name twice during our meeting. I'm pretty sure I'd fall asleep fucking her, she was that boring.

None of them inspired anything in me apart from dread. But the Six weren't bluffing this time. Something in their voices—especially Seraphiel's—felt different. It felt final. The kind of warning that doesn't repeat itself. This isn't just politics anymore; it's war prevention. Legacy protection. In their eyes, I'm not just a ruler—I'm a loaded gun with no safety, and they want me tied to something. Anything. Something they can predict and control. So naturally, I went to the only person who ever made me feel utterly out of control. And she laughed in my face. And then she screamed. The memory of her fury is still ringing in my ears. The venom in her voice, the way she hurled my gift into the bin like it was nothing more than trash. It should've angered me. Instead, it wrecked me.

I rub at my jaw, staring at her silhouette through the mirror as the fireworks outside her window erupt in colour. She just watches, hollow and still, a wine bottle swinging from her fingertips like a pendulum, counting down the seconds until she finally breaks again. She is so small, so mortal. So utterly fucking mine in a way I can't explain. And yet I sent her away, told her she was nothing.

The irony is, I've never wanted anything the way I want to break her heart and then beg her to let me hold the pieces. But I don't get to do that. I get to sit in the dark, drinking myself blind, and watching a girl who still sits beside my gift like it's a lighthouse keeping her from the edge.

"I am the monster under her bed," I murmur to no one, "and she will always leave the light on to banish me."

I hate her for it. I ache for her because of it. Because of this fucking tether that I have no explanation.

My fingers curl into fists, nails biting into my palms. I'm the

Prince of Hell. And this girl—this mortal girl—has reduced me to a shadow that lurks in her corner, begging for scraps of her warmth.

I swear to myself that I'll stop, but my soul tugs me here every night to watch the mortal who flipped my entire life upside down.

CHAPTER 21
DAISY

January third hits like a slap to the face.

My alarm clock blares, cruelly reminding me it was time to get back to reality. As lonely as it was over the Christmas break, hiding away from my friends, it was nice to just be by myself. No college, no work, no cheer, just me and my wine.

I drag myself out of bed, wrapping myself up in the ridiculous hoodie Ezra had bought me, and the bright yellow fuzzy socks Talia had given me. I should probably wash them, but it's nothing a few sprays of perfume can't fix. I pad into the bathroom, grimacing at my reflection. Those bottles of wine really weren't doing the bags under my eyes any favours. I pile on the concealer under my eyes, looking slightly less tired than I had five minutes ago, and brush the mascara onto my lashes for the first time in forever. It was time to get back to normal.

Ezra and Talia meet me by the campus gates, Ezra's hair like a beacon of orange light against the grey sky, puffy with clouds that threaten to pour snow down on us at any given moment. He's practically bouncing, wearing the jacket I'd thrifted and upcycled for him for Christmas. It was a jean jacket with the word 'Swiftie' hand-stitched on the back in glittering gold thread. He wore it proudly over his hoodie, grinning when he caught me staring at him. Talia stands shivering, wearing her hair in a low, messy bun, the little sun-and-moon necklace I got her twinkling against her throat. They both smile at me, each pulling me into a tight hug, telling me how much they had missed me over Christmas break.

We enter the campus to the sound of Ezra absolutely losing his mind over Taylor Swift's new album. Again.

"I swear to gods," I mumble, pulling the strings of my hoodie tighter, "she's got like a hundred albums now. Are we sure she's not some immortal witch?"

"She's just a talented queen," Ezra replies, deadly serious. "You just don't understand art."

Talia rolls her eyes so hard I'm worried she might dislocate them, if that's at all possible. My shoes crunch along the frosted path, the laughter from my friends fading into a dull hum as an unsettling feeling slides down my spine. Like a thread being pulled, a warning I can't quite place. It starts as just a little prickle, but it quickly turns into a heavyweight. The air turns too thick, like something's pressing heavily on my chest—and that's when I realise it. Eyes. Staring. Not just one or two. Dozens, maybe more.

I scan the courtyard and notice heads are turned, and whispers are passing like currents through the air. A girl in a pink beanie mutters something to her friend and, immediately, they look at me. Their expressions twist into curiosity, then something like pity, but even that quickly shifts to a judgemental, almost disgusted look. My stomach sinks.

"Am I going insane," I mutter, folding my arms tightly over my chest, "or are people actually staring at me?"

Talia and Ezra freeze in their tracks, sharing a guilty look between them. One I do not like in the slightest.

Ezra clears his throat, shifting awkwardly. "So, uh... Daze. Something happened."

I stop walking, my breath catching like a hook in my throat. "What?"

Talia bites her lip, her eyes soft, but I can see the panic in them. "The police report about Ethan... it got leaked."

"What?" I gasp. "What do you mean leaked?"

Ezra shoves his hands into his pockets, clearly bracing himself. "It's in the paper. Online. It says he died not long after... after sexually assaulting his girlfriend at the time. It named you, Daze."

The ground disappears, the sky presses in. My blood drains so fast I think I might actually pass out. My ears ring with the kind of high-pitched noise that usually comes before total collapse.

My name. My name, plastered on headlines, linked with Ethan, linked with violence, with pain. With everything. I didn't want the world to know. Not like this, not ever.

"How... how are they even allowed to release that information?" I whisper, my voice thin and shaky.

"I don't know," Talia answers, stepping closer and placing a firm hand on my shoulder. "I'm so sorry. Are you okay?"

No. No, I'm not okay. I'm not even close to okay. I feel exposed, picked apart, like someone reached into my ribcage and flipped everything inside out for the world to examine. But I can't let them see that; nobody can see that.

I breathe, deep and slow. Let my spine straighten and pull out the mask I've worn since I was a kid. The sunshine mask, the one that makes people believe I'm fine, even when I'm absolutely, completely unravelling.

"Yeah," I lie with a smile so fake it feels like broken glass. "It's good that people know he was a piece of shit."

Ezra gasps dramatically, pressing a hand to his chest like I just shot him. "Did our little Daisy Duke just swear?"

I force a laugh and elbow him in the ribs. "Shut up."

We start walking again, the whispers sticking to me like static. I smile through all of it, because I have to. I've come too far, survived too much, to let Ethan win. He's already taken enough; I won't give him more.

"See you at practice later," Ezra calls, blowing a kiss.

"Love you!" Talia echoes, linking arms with him as they veer off toward their class.

Unluckily for me, thanks to needing to catch up, Talia isn't in this class with me. I wave, watching them disappear. Once they're out of sight, I pull my hood up and lower my head. I keep it lowered as I walk through the main doors of the psychology building, trying to ignore the faces that glance at me and then quickly look away. Some faces I catch glimpses of try to offer fake smiles, but most don't bother.

Typically, my class is on the second floor, right at the back of the building. I move as fast as I can, my shoes echoing on the polished linoleum. My thoughts spiral with every step. Do they think I'm lying? Do they pity me, hate me? Do they think that I killed him?

I shove through the classroom door and spot an empty seat in the back, slipping into it like a shadow. Professor Doyle starts the class without acknowledging me. No forced "welcome back," no questions, no eye contact. I wonder if he saw the article. I wonder if he knows. Part of me is grateful nobody has said anything directly, but the other part of me wants to scream. I want someone to say it, to ask me what they're all so desperate to know. But I also just want to disappear, to melt into the floor and never be looked at again. Funny isn't it, the human brain. How it can want two things that are polar opposite to each other.

I sit through the whole lecture in silence. My notes are messy, my handwriting barely legible. The words just blur on the page, my pulse thrumming through me like a warning drum. I don't want to be the story people whisper about. But I'll continue to smile and shine. Because if I stop pretending I'm okay, I'm not sure I'll ever find my way back.

~

Cheer practice that afternoon was brutal.

Not physically—though the burn in my legs was ungodly—but emotionally. The kind of brutal that crawled beneath your skin and sat heavy on your chest. Every beat of the music felt too loud, every clap and stop and cheer a mockery of who I used to be. I went through the motions like a wind-up doll, arms raised, legs kicking, mouth forming the right words at the right times. But there was no soul in it, not anymore. Because who the hell were we cheering for? The football team? The one without the captain? The one whose former star player raped me, then died?

The pitch looked the same—fresh-cut grass, white lines bright in the low winter sun—but I wasn't the same girl standing on it. I felt like a ghost among the living, stuck in some alternate version of my life that I couldn't crawl out of, no matter how frantically I tried.

When practice finally ends, I collapse onto the bleachers next to Ezra and Talia, gulping down water like my life depended on it. My lungs sting, my thighs tremble, and my chest is unbearably tight. Sweat glistens at my temples, and I can't tell if I want to scream or run. But I don't have time to figure it out, regardless. Because Jason Mahoney is walking directly my way. Swaggering like he's the star of something shitty teen drama, with a malicious glint to his grey-blue eyes.

"Hey, Daisy," he says, loud enough that it makes my stomach drop. He wants attention for this, his predatory smirk confirming it. I brace myself, my heart pounding erratically.

"Uh... hey, Jason?" I manage, confusion in my tone laced with a hint of dread.

He steps closer, tilting his head like he's about to offer me a compliment. But the words that come out of his mouth make my blood turn to ice. "Listen, I heard you're not a virgin anymore. You know, after putting out for Ethan." He shrugs nonchalantly. "So, I was wondering if you'd consider me next. I've never had a bigger girl before. Or are you gonna scream rape if we fuck too?"

Everything freezes. The air, the people around us... Me. I feel my soul leave my body, hovering somewhere above the bleachers, watching myself sit there and take the vile words being thrown at me.

Ezra's voice cuts through the haze in my mind. "What the actual fuck?"

Talia doesn't wait to respond. She launches herself over the row in front of us and punches him—hard. There's a satisfying crunch as Jason stumbles backward, blood pouring from his nose. I watch as he wipes it with the back of his hand, glaring at me, despite Talia being the one who sucker punched him.

"You're a liar, Daisy," he spits. "Everyone knows Ethan wouldn't do that to you. You just regretted putting out, and now you're dragging a dead man's name through the mud." He angles his head towards Talia, still keeping his eyes firmly pinned on me. "You're just as much of a slut as your best friend now, though. Congrats."

He winks, like this is just one big joke to him. Like my life is nothing more than a joke. He walks away laughing before I can muster up the courage to respond, rejoining his pack of wolves. Their cackles echo across the field as they throw glares in my direction. My ears ring, my face is hot, and my chest hurts. The shame crashes into me as my palms begin to sweat, my hands trembling. Everyone's staring now, absolutely everyone., even the football coach and the cheer coach. This is never going to end, is it?

Ezra kneels beside me, gentle and tender as ever as he strokes a hand up my arm. "Daisy?"

Talia's seething, pacing back and forth in front of me. "I'm going to kill him." She tries to run after Jason, but Ezra catches her first, wrapping his arms around her waist, physically lifting her off the ground. Her legs kick furiously as she screams at him to let go.

"He's not worth it," he growls, his usually cheery voice cracking under the weight of his own rage. "He's not fucking worth it, Talia."

My skin continues to prickle with the weight of a hundred eyes pinned to me. My throat feels unbearably tight. "I… I have to go to work," I whisper.

"Daze—" Talia starts, reaching for me.

"I'm fine," I say, gently shaking my head with a smile suddenly plastered across my face as I frantically blink away the tears forming. "Honestly, I have to go."

I leave, not daring to run in case it draws any more attention to me—if that was at all possible. I grab my stuff, ignoring the looks in the locker room, deciding not to change out of my uniform. I'll deal with that at work. I just need to get out. I need to disappear before the sob building in my chest explodes out of me.

The coffee shop is quiet when I arrive, and the moment I step into the staff bathroom, I collapse down onto the closed toilet lid, my bag falling to the floor, pens scattering everywhere. I sit, shoulders shaking, tears tracking down my cheeks, painting wet trails on my skin. I curl in on myself, elbows to knees, hands covering my face. How is this still happening, haven't I suffered enough? I choke on a sob, the world feeling a little too heavy for me to handle all over again.

I'M FALLING APART.

Thirty minutes into my shift, and I've burned myself three times on the milk steamer—my wrists are literally blistering—I dropped a coffee cup during a rush, and I've had to remake two orders. I'm clumsy, I'm distracted, and I'm absolutely unravelling at the seams.

An hour into my shift, I'm slowly managing to get my shit together enough to make orders correctly, thinking maybe I'll make it through the rest of the night without messing up, when *she* walks in. Phoebe and her army of clones who think giggling louder than necessary makes them relevant and not just annoying as hell. I glance up, hearing their annoying screeches echoing through the cafe, and it suddenly feels like the air is thick. She stops dead in her tracks, arm shooting out to halt the girls behind her.

"Ew. I'm not being served by that lying whore," she says, loud enough that every head in the cafe turns to look at her, then me. Silence settles in quickly as the leeches surrounding me soak in the drama. "Let's go somewhere else."

My heart plummets into my stomach. The one place I thought I could just get on with life without drama. How naive of me. I force a shaky inhale, closing my eyes and running a hand down my face. Just as I reopen them, my manager appears beside me, his mouth in a sharp line. Shit.

"Daisy," he says, pulling me gently to the back, out of sight of the customers. "I believe you, what you went through. I do. Ethan was an asshole. But..." He sighs, dragging his fingers through his hair. "I can't have this kind of drama in the cafe. Customers are leaving. Not to mention you've been flaky, missing a lot of shifts. And now this." He gestures to where Phoebe was standing just moments ago.

"No, please—" My voice cracks. "That wasn't my fault. I'll fix it. I'll do double shifts. I'll—"

"I'm sorry." He says, shaking his head. "I have to let you go."

It hits like a punch, straight to the chest, knocking the wind out of me. It wasn't my fault. It wasn't my fault that my police report had been leaked. It wasn't my fault I was raped. It wasn't my fault that people were choosing to side with a dead rapist over me. So why am I being punished?

I nod. I don't argue any further; there's no point. I grab my bag, my limbs moving on autopilot as I hang up my apron for the last time. By the time I manage to burst out of the cafe door, I'm already sobbing. The snow outside is falling in heavy, wet clumps, instantly soaking through my hoodie. The wind slices through me as I begin to run, as fast as I possibly can. My feet pound the pavement, my chest heaving as staring faces pass by in a blur.

I stumble through my apartment door and slam it shut, my breath coming out of me in broken, sobbing pants. My bag crashes to the floor, and I finally break. I scream. It's raw and guttural, my soul seeming to tear in two at the sound that pours out of me. The kind of scream that rips through your chest, that leaves your throat shredded. I grab the nearest thing to me and throw it as hard as I can. I watch as my sunshine mug flies and smashes into the wall, exploding into a thousand tiny pieces.

"KORITHAX!" I shriek, my voice cracking. "KORITHAX, I FUCKING SUMMON YOU!"

Nothing. Of course, when I actually want him to turn up, he doesn't come.

I spin, tears blurring my vision as I desperately grab my phone from my bag with frantic fingers. I begin searching the internet like a madwoman. I pace back and forth as I read creepy forums, shady websites, anything and everything I can find that has Korithax's name attached to it. I don't care, I just need to find something. Anything that will make him appear.

Eventually, I find a method that swears to work. One that didn't need candles or incantations or fancy herbs and spices. Just blood, his sigil, and a summoning circle. Perfect.

I shove my rug aside and dash into the kitchen to grab the sharpest knife I can find. I move back into the tiny space in my living room and, without hesitating, I drop to my knees and drag the knife down my arm, whimpering at the pain as the blood wells thick and bright, dripping down to my wrist. I steady myself as I go light-headed from the adrenaline, then dip my fingers into the crimson fluid, drawing the shaky summoning circle the best I can onto the wooden floor, his sigil in the centre. I glance at the image on my phone, then slowly move my bloodied fingers. An inverted triangle with thorned tendrils curling around the edges of the shape. A spiralled serpent in the middle, consuming its own tail. Above the triangle sits a crescent moon, with a vertical slash through it and one across it. The bottom, a blood drop. I squeeze at the cut on my forearm, draining more blood from my body as I sketch out the image as perfectly as I possibly can. My fingers burn as I finish the last of the sigil, shaking as I look down at the bloodied mess on my floor. I take a slow, deep inhale, anger still vibrating through my core as I grit my teeth. This better work.

“Korithax!” I whisper. “I summon you!” Nothing again. “Korithax!” I cry louder, voice utterly broken.

I sit there, bleeding, panting through gritted teeth as my chest heaves, waiting. Hoping that the Prince of Hell will answer my broken, bleeding call.

CHAPTER 22
KORITHAX

I feel it the second it happens.

Blood magic. Her blood. My sigil burns across the veils between our realms, yanking at my very soul like a fucking leash. I roar from behind my desk, the force of it shaking the walls around me, shattering the delicate glass decanter I hadn't even touched. The walls pulse with my fury. I stand abruptly, wings snapping wide behind me, hitting the shelves surrounding me, sending their contents flying. My fists clench so tight my nails pierce my palms. Her blood—she's used her fucking blood to call me.

I vanish mid-snarl, the force of the magic pulling me through to the mortal realm like I've been hooked through the heart and dragged behind a chariot. Her apartment materialises around me, my body still vibrating with fury and residual magic. I stagger slightly from the potency of the summons, the sickening sweetness of mortal blood in the air hitting me like a drug. The scent is thick, intoxicating—her blood, coppery and warm, still wet on the floorboards. The summoning circle is shaky, but it's fucking perfect because it's been made from her, by her.

She's knelt in the middle of it, her hair sticking to her tear-streaked face, her arm bleeding freely as her trembling fingers hover near the sigil she carved in blood. I blink at the sight of it, the shock of it all making my stomach twist.

"What the fuck do you think you're doing?" I snarl, storming toward her.

She lifts her head, her wild eyes red-rimmed, glassy with rage and grief. Her lip trembles just once before she hardens her expression into something almost deadly.

"I accept," she bites out, rage lacing every syllable. Her breaths are sharp and erratic, like she's on the edge of falling apart entirely. "I accept your stupid fucking proposal."

The room is too small to hold her pain. It pulses around her like a second aura, hot and suffocating. My nostrils flare as I inhale the storm of emotions she's barely keeping contained. I can hear her heartbeat pounding erratically. It's too fast, like a cornered animal that's about to be slaughtered. Something's happened. Something monstrous.

"You said I could have anything I wanted in return, right?" She demands. Her voice cracks near the end, but she straightens her spine like the stubborn mortal I know, and looks me right in the eye without a hint of fear.

"Yes," I answer warily, my smoke flicking around me, betraying my calm exterior.

She rises, and my gaze is instantly drawn back to her arm. Her blood drips steadily from the open cut, falling from her fingers and splashing fat crimson droplets that stain the floor like roses blooming in reverse.

"I will marry you, Korithax," she declares. "Because you're clearly not going to let me die," she scowls at me but lifts her chin, "I will marry you if I can live in Hell. If I can leave this horrible place behind forever."

The demand hits me hard, entirely unexpected. She doesn't just want out of this world; she wants in on mine. My Hell. The one I have spent centuries protecting, ruling without a crown. The desperation in her eyes is unmistakable. Her voice isn't shaking anymore either, despite her body trembling. She's holding herself upright on the crumbling bones of her own strength. And gods help me, I should say no. I should tell her she's out of her damned mind. But I don't. Because I'm a fucking selfish, self-serving asshole who needs this.

A scroll unfurls in the air, the parchment dark as ash, glowing faintly with silver veins of contract binding magic. The black feathered quill floats beside it, awaiting her.

"Read it. Sign it. Then add a drop of your blood," I say, voice stripped of any emotion, marking this as nothing more than a business transaction.

I step closer, lowering my wings slightly, letting her see the slight tension in my body due to how serious this is. "But once you sign this, little flower, there is no going back."

"Fine."

She doesn't hesitate, snatching the quill and contract out of the air with shaking hands, carrying it over to her coffee table. She signs her name, then uses her finger to take blood from her arm before smearing it across the page. The once unseen runes blaze to life, my sigil in the centre of the parchment, thrumming with power.

I step forward and pick up her knife, slicing my own palm open without hesitation. I squeeze my hand into a fist and let my blood fall across the contract, the action sealing it with a low, vibrating rumble that echoes into the cosmos. The contract smoulders for a second, then vanishes back to my realm, back to my office.

"When does the contract start?" She asks through a tired, broken voice as her ocean eyes meet mine.

"Now." I grab her hand and teleport us instantly back to Hell.

SHE STUMBLES SLIGHTLY, blinking at her surroundings. I watch her closely as she looks around, searching for any sign of regret, any hesitation—something to confirm this was all just a moment of madness. But it doesn't come. Not even a trace.

"This isn't the usual room you bring me to?" She mutters, her voice raspy.

I smirk, the twist of my mouth sharp and cruel. "These are the Queen's chambers. Since you're to be my wife, this is where you'll stay."

She nods, her gaze shifting to the towering bed draped in obsidian sheets and velvet throws. She steps toward it, fingers grazing the fabric with that careful, soft touch of hers that doesn't belong in a place like this. Doesn't belong in a place anywhere near me.

"I'll have a healer come and clean up your arm," I say stiffly, turning to leave. At the door, I pause, casting a final glance over my shoulder. She looks so small in here. So breakable. "Welcome home, Daisy." I don't wait for her response before I exit.

I STRIDE DOWN through the hallway, tension riding every step. My boots echo like gunshots against the stone, my wings twitching with a need to tear something apart. I should feel utterly victorious. I got what I wanted. I've found a way to shut the Divine Six the fuck up. I have my bride, the throne is safe. This should be a win. But it's her. A mortal, a pathetic, broken mortal.

I rake my fingers through my hair, growling low. Gods, what has my life become? I took her at her lowest, claimed her in her ruin, and sealed it with blood. She'll never be free of me now. And maybe I should care. Maybe the old me—who still gave half a shit about honour and pride—would've hesitated. But that version of me died a long, long time ago. I've been a selfish, ruthless bastard for most of my life, and this just truly confirms that for me. But I'd do it all again if I had to.

A FEW HOURS pass before I return to her chambers.

She's curled on the edge of the massive bed, tracing the patterns in the obsidian headboard like they hold answers to all the questions I know she's too stubborn to ask. She doesn't look up when I enter, not until I speak.

"So, you've seen the castle," I say, voice low, "but you haven't seen Zeriavoss."

She blinks, then mutters as she continues tracing the patterns. "Aran showed me already."

I shake my head, even though she's not looking at me. "No. Aran showed you the castle and its gardens and pointed out things from the safety of my castle. Zeriavoss stretches far beyond these walls. Come, let me show you."

I don't wait for her answer as I stroll forward and offer her my hand. She hesitates for a heartbeat before slipping her small fingers into mine. I don't warn her as I teleport us to the outer path just beyond the castle cliffs. We arrive with the wind in our hair, the waterfalls falling from my home at our backs, the sky flickering with the flashes of red lightning. The cobbled path beneath our feet winds towards the heart of the valley, lined with wildflowers and fields upon fields of crops. The village sprawls ahead, rooftops of polished obsidian, smoke curling from the forge, and faint laughter echoing through the streets.

We walk, entering the village where demons pass us. Some with bark-like skin, some with translucent wings, all of them in varying shades of every colour known. Some look nearly human, others not at all. Every single one lingers their sight on Daisy, each with varying expressions across their faces—confusion, curiosity, disgust. She stiffens at first, then relaxes when we keep walking, painting the cool, calm expression across her face I've come to know quite well as her mask.

We pass the schoolhouse, and the sounds of giggling children ring through the air as they run about carefree. One small demon, his horns nothing more than little spikes protruding from his head, crashes right into my leg.

He stumbles back, falling to the floor, his eyes wide. "I... I'm so sorry, Your Highness."

I'm about to growl my annoyance when Daisy crouches down beside him, her voice soft and warm. "There you go," she says, brushing dust from his tunic as she helps him up. "Are you okay?"

He nods, staring at her with wide, inhuman eyes. "Who are you? You look different."

She falters, a blush creeping across her cheeks as she looks up at me. "This is Daisy," I say simply. "She is going to be your queen."

The child's mouth drops, then, without hesitation, he bows low, almost tipping forward. "Thank you for helping me up, Your Highness."

"Please," she chuckles. "Call me Daisy."

The child giggles and glances at me nervously. I lift a brow, angling my head towards the school. "Go on now, back to your teacher."

He scampers off, chanting about how he was helped by a "beautiful queen."

"You have children here?" She asks as we continue walking.

"We do. A lot of them. My father believes in drafting them young—too young. Many are trained to fight before their horns are even grown."

She falls quiet, but I don't explain further. There's only so much of my father's sins I can package into a sentence, and I don't plan on telling her that it will be one of the first rules I change when I officially become king. She thinks of me as a monster; no point trying to change her mind.

A scent hits the air, causing her to pause, her eyes fluttering.

"What is that smell?" She mumbles.

"That would be the bakery," I say, nodding to the stone building, its crooked chimney puffing out smoke. "Run by Marta."

Daisy's stomach growls audibly, and she groans, crossing her arms over it with embarrassment.

"Come," I say with a faint smirk. "I'll get you one of my favourites."

WE ENTER THE BAKERY, the door creaking with the sound of old iron hinges. The scent of emberfruit, burnt sugar, and spiced flour wraps hits us immediately. The heat from the ovens kisses my skin, wrapping around me like a familiar embrace. Daisy's breath catches beside me, her eyes wide as she takes it in: shelves lined with charred-black loaves dusted in powdered frost, twisted sweetbreads glazed in honey, and tiny cakes that glitter with what looks like stardust. Marta looks up from behind the counter. She's ancient—white braids twisted back from a stern face, her eyes sharp as obsidian blades behind her glasses.

She squints. "Well, well," she mutters. "Didn't think I'd ever see the day you brought company, Korithax."

I grunt in response, rolling my eyes. "Don't start."

Her eyes scan Daisy from top to toe with such intensity that even I feel slightly nervous. "Who's this?"

"She's to be my bride," I say flatly. "Your queen."

Marta blinks. For half a second, she's silent, and I brace for impact. Then she lets out a sound between a scoff and a gasp and flings herself around the counter with surprising speed. Before Daisy can even flinch, she's wrapped tightly in the kind of hug that could crush ribs.

"Blessed skies," Marta breathes into her shoulder. "You poor, poor girl."

Daisy snickers, the corner of her mouth tilting up. "I know."

Marta pulls back just enough to cup Daisy's face between her rough, flour-dusted hands, examining her like a jeweller examining a rare stone. Her expression softens—not something I often see from her between her scoldings.

"She's never hugged me like that," I mutter under my breath.

"Because you're not lovable, boy," Marta snaps without missing a beat, flapping her dishtowel at me. She turns her back to us as she returns to the counter to grab a tart. "You've got all the warmth of a frozen corpse."

She hands a tart to Daisy—golden crust, glistening with crystallised sugar and filled with ember fruit. She accepts it with both hands, eyes wide with awe. I watch her as she takes a cautious bite, curious to see what she'll think of the treat. Her eyes practically roll back into her head. "Oh my gods," she moans. "This is insane."

Marta beams like the freaking angels just came down from the sky to greet her. "She can stay."

"Uh, where's mine?" I grumble, crossing my arms.

Marta tsks and tosses me one with a roll of her eyes. "Always so needy. Go on, eat that before your sulking curdles my icing."

I roll my eyes and lean against the counter, biting into my tart as the two of them chat. It's surreal, the way Daisy talks to Marta like they've known each other for years. The way Marta already looks at her like she's something precious. The warmth between them is something incredible to behold and I find myself watching the sunshine girl in my world, and not wanting to look away.

EVENTUALLY, we leave Marta's, weaving back through the winding stone paths through the village. The smoky-sweet scent of the bakery still lingers faintly on our clothes. She's gone quiet again, her arms folded as her eyes scan the unfamiliar realm as if she's trying to memorise every detail. We're nearing the same fields we arrived in when she suddenly gasps and stumbles back with a sharp intake of breath.

"What?" I snap, hand already going for one of my blades as I instinctively step in front of her.

She points, her face a shade paler than it was a second ago. "What the hell is that?"

I follow her gaze, preparing for an ambush. Instead, my eyes land on a flamebeast descending from the cloudless blue sky, its wings stretched wide. The crops in the field ripple from the impact of its landing as its wings fold with a slow, deliberate grace. Its crimson scales shimmer under the light of the sun—iridescent like a thousand shimmering embers. The beast is twice the size of a mortal steed, with a long, serpentine tail swaying side to side and horns that curl back, sharper than blades. Its eyes glow molten gold, narrowed in a suspicious gaze.

It moves slowly towards us, and I tense, watching every movement, ready to strike if it so much as bares its teeth.

Daisy grabs my arm, her fingers trembling slightly. "Is it safe?"

"They're not usually interested in people," I mutter, more to myself than to her.

It pauses in front of her, tilting its head with a curious noise that rumbles deep in its chest. Daisy freezes, her hand twitching as if she's unsure whether to reach out or run. My eyes flicker between the beast and my future queen as the creature snorts softly—an exhale of steam curling in the air—-and lowers its massive head until it's level with her chest.

"I—What do I do?" She whispers.

"Don't move," I say lowly. Though, I'm not actually sure what she should do. I have never seen such an event occur.

Despite telling her not to move, she hesitantly raises a hand, her palm trembling as she presses it lightly against the flamebeast's snout. It closes its eyes and presses its head further into her palm, almost like a pet nuzzling into her. After a few seconds, it pulls away, lowering its head to her as if in a bow. It gives one last chuff of breath, then turns and strides away back into the fields.

My mouth opens slightly, then closes again. "What the fuck?" I breathe.

Daisy turns to look at me, her brows drawn together in panic and disbelief. "What?"

"They never approach anyone," I say slowly, my voice laced in shock. "In twenty thousand years, Daisy, I've never seen one act like this. They bow to no one. Not even me. The only time they approach their handlers is when they're being fed or if they are injured."

She gives a nervous little laugh, but her expression is pure wonder as she flips the hand over that the beast nuzzled. "So I really am the princess of Hell. Whispering to the freaking dragons."

"It's not funny," I mutter.

Because it isn't. I'm not sure what unnerves me more—what I just witnessed, or how calm she seems. This realm just continues to welcome her, and there she is, glowing brighter with each passing moment, fitting into a world she was never meant for.

~

We arrive back at the castle, Daisy vanishing into her rooms as I head toward mine. Today was good, nice even. We had both been civil as I'd shown her around the village, and she saw a fragment of my life... of what was to be her life.

As if summoned by my sense of peace, the pull of another damn summons grips my spine. I roll my eyes, exhaling with pure irritation. "Here we fucking go."

I rip through the realms, arriving in my least favourite place in the universe; the chamber of the Divine Six. As per usual, they're already seated, but instead of slight irritation marring their faces, they all look absolutely furious. The tension in the air is so thick that it even has me faltering for a moment before I regain my composure and stride forward with arrogance radiating from me.

"You have defied us." Seraphiel hisses, her crystal wings flaring behind her.

"Correction," I growl. "You said I needed a bride, and now I have one."

"You cannot marry a mortal!" Calrix bellows, the ground trembling with the force of it, making me stumble forward slightly.

"Funny, I don't remember you specifying that little detail." I sneer. "You said bride. You got a bride."

"It does not matter," Elaron says, his voice sickly sweet despite the venom dripping from his words. "If you marry a mortal, we will burn your kingdom to the ground, as we have promised."

I stare at him, the fury in my eyes not going unnoticed as his gaze falters.

Amarithe tilts her head, golden eyes gleaming. "Do not defy us again, Korithax."

Velentha watches me silently, her time runes flaring, her face unreadable beneath her hood. Mal'Thariel's presence looms heavier than ever, the air around him feeling cold, icy even.

I bare my teeth in a snarl, smoke curling off of me with my rising anger. "Try it," I say, voice deathly low. "See what happens."

I turn on my heel and vanish without warning, the clash of our power still rattling the realms behind me.

I storm through the door of my chambers, slamming it behind me, the barrier I had placed not long ago preventing me from teleporting directly into my rooms to ensure absolute protection. I didn't need any assholes appearing from thin air into my personal space. I look up, seeing Aran standing by my fireplace, arms neatly folded behind his back.

"Clearly, I need another barrier placed on my room to stop you entering whenever you fucking please," I growl.

He ignores my remark. "So," he says, arching a brow. "She agreed to the proposal."

"Yes," I grunt, dragging a hand through my hair. "Under the condition she gets to live in Hell."

His deep emerald eyes widen, tension rippling through him. "But, sire... the Divine Six. They made it abundantly clear that she was not welcome here."

"It was her condition," I snap through gritted teeth. "I wasn't about to say no and risk having to marry one of the other three fucking wretched souls. Besides, they're more angry about the fact that I'm marrying a mortal. Apparently, they forgot to mention in their little fucking rule book that my bride had to be immortal."

Aran stares at me before carefully asking, "What will you do?"

I smirk, cold and humourless. "Fuck them. I did exactly as they asked. They said I needed a bride, and I have one. If they didn't deign to specify the fine print, that's on them. They threatened to burn my kingdom down if I married a mortal," I scoff, "but they would not dare."

The words barely leave my mouth before a deafening boom shakes the entire castle. The walls shudder, dust falling from the high ceilings as the fire in the hearth sputters out. I freeze, Aran's head whipping to the door.

"What the fuck was that?" I yell.

A frantic pounding echoes from the hallway, and I yank the door open to see one of my soldiers, armour dented and covered in ash, running in the hallway.

"My king!" He shouts, panting. "The southern side of the castle, the guest wing, has been destroyed!"

I teleport without hesitation, Aran arriving right behind me as he steps through his own portal. The ruins stretch out before me, smoke curling into the air like the fingers of a dead god coming to claim the destruction. The south wing, where Daisy had once stayed, is now reduced to blackened stone and ash. Fire crackles weakly, licking at the bones of what was once polished marble and obsidian. Only celestial fire can burn through such stone easily. In the centre of the rubble, something glints.

I stride through the destruction, ignoring the heat and the wreckage as I bend down, picking up the scrap of golden parchment, seemingly unaffected by the blaze. The words are scrawled in divine ink:

This is a warning, Korithax.

You cannot marry a mortal.

Find another.

Or next time, your entire kingdom will be desecrated.

Do not take our threats as a bluff.

. . .

Aran appears at my side, his face pale as he reads over my shoulder.

"Sire?" He croaks.

"It was the Divine Six," I snarl, crumpling the note in my fist until it disintegrates into black ash under my burning touch. "Sending a message about Daisy."

He stares at the ruins, horror etched into every line of his face. "What will you do?"

I stare into the smoke, rage rising inside of me like a storm I can't contain. My fists clench so tightly I feel my nails pierce through my skin. "I have no fucking idea."

CHAPTER 23
DAISY

The chambers are absolutely breathtaking.

The bed alone is a masterpiece. A massive four-poster bed, carved from some dark, burnished wood with a canopy draped over it in crimson silk with an engraved headboard. The mattress is plush and larger than any I think I have ever seen, buried beneath velvet and satin darker than the night itself. It already feels homely as I settle down after the tour of Zeriavoss Korithax had given me. It was such a strange and wonderful day; the valley and the village were beautiful. And the way that creature had just approached me like we'd known each other our entire lives was surreal. A flamebeast. Such a thing existed. And it existed in the realm I now called my home.

The walls in the room are lined with towering windows that display the endless expanse of the realm in the distance, the flashes of red lightning skittering across the cloudless sky. Heavy embroidered drapes hang on either side of each window, patterned with sigils and symbols that feel familiar, but ones I don't recognise. Every inch of the room exudes dark, powerful, impossible beauty.

I sit on the edge of the bed, taking it all in as disbelief washes over me in slow, crashing waves. I live in Hell now. I'm going to be the queen of this beautiful kingdom, and there's no going back. I don't know a single thing about being a queen. I was studying to be a psychologist, not a freaking ruler of an ancient kingdom.

Panic begins to wash over me at the realisation of what I've signed up for. I take slow, deep breaths, reminding myself that being a queen in an ancient realm can't be any harder than being regular old Daisy back on Earth. Right?

I think of Talia and Ezra, and my chest tightens. I've abandoned them, again. Left them behind in a world I deemed insufferable enough to give up, to reign beside a demon who can't stand me. The tightening in my chest eases slightly when I begin to think of the freedom I've enabled myself. I don't have to go back to my old life, back to the pain, the stares, the whispers. I don't have to carry on trying to pay off my father's debt, or have to continue struggling to survive. Here, I can breathe. Here, I am something more than a victim.

I can't stop the laughter that bubbles up out of me. A freaking queen. Of Hell. Daisy Sandoval is about to become Mrs... Mrs what? Mrs Korithax? Did he have a last name? Crap. Not only am I marrying the future King of Hell, I don't know a damn thing about him, other than the fact that he's a grumpy asshole who thinks I'm a pathetic, weak mortal. I let out a long sigh. Still better than my life back on Earth, I guess.

Guards arrived at my door around half an hour ago, under Korithax's orders. Apparently, there was an attack on the southern side of the castle, with the worst of the damage aimed at the guest chamber I used to stay in. A chill crawls up my spine, my thoughts spiralling with an uneasy feeling that it wasn't just coincidental that those chambers were the ones most brutalised. What if it was the Divine Six, believing I was in there once again, trying to kill me? I jump down from the impossibly large bed and begin panic pacing up and down whilst nervously chewing my thumbnail. What if it was meant to kill me? What if they've figured out where I am? No.

Korithax wouldn't let anything happen to me. I'm his ticket to the throne, after all.

A knock on the door pulls me out of my panic, and it opens gently to reveal a small woman with a warm smile standing there. "Come in," I say softly, forcing a polite smile as I gesture toward the room.

"Your Majesty," she says with a tiny curtsy, her voice lilting and sweet.

Oh wow. I'd have to get used to that, and fast, apparently.

She's delicate and pale, almost translucent, with flowing lavender hair cascading down her back and small white horns curling back from her temples. Her wide, pale violet eyes meet my ocean-blue ones, offering me probably one of the kindest looks I've received in this realm, besides Marta. A strange ache flutters in my ribs at the thought of her. Marta had been one of the only people in this whole twisted realm who made me feel like I wasn't something to sneer at. She'd hugged me like I was her family, scolding Korithax like I was hers to protect. Her embrace had smelled like spiced flour and smoked wood; and her presence had felt like a warm kitchen on a winter day. Something truly good, calming.

This woman's smile doesn't have the same fierce spark Marta had—but the softness in her eyes carries a similar kindness.

"I'm Lyvia. I'll be your maid."

"Lyvia," I echo, trying not to gawk. She's so ethereal, like a ghost spun from mist. "Wait... maid? Like, actual maid? Am I that fancy now?"

"Yes, your Majesty—"

"Okay, hard pass on that," I cut her off with a small wave of my hand. "Call me Daisy. 'Majesty' makes me sound like I should be wearing a powdered wig and yelling at people."

She blinks, then smiles, her too white teeth catching in the candlelight. "Daisy."

"Much better." I smile back.

"Your dresses will arrive in the morning," she says, gliding across the room with a grace that makes me instantly self-conscious about my tendency to trip over air. "But for now, I have brought you a nightgown." She hands the beautiful piece to me, its fabric caressing my fingers.

"It's woven from the silk of the Lumispires," she explains, "a sacred creature from Luminaria, the realm of light magic."

"Of course it is," I murmur, running my fingers over the impossibly soft material. "I've been here five minutes, and even my pyjamas have lore." It's softer than anything I have ever felt, shimmering faintly even in the dim light of the room. Lyvia laughs gently, the sound like wind chimes in a breeze. "Thank you, Lyvia," I say softly.

She tilts her head in a bow. "Is there anything else I can get you, your Ma... Daisy?"

The way she fumbles the correction makes me giggle. "Nope, I think I'm good for now, thank you, Lyvia."

She smiles again and curtsies, disappearing just as quietly as she appeared.

THE HEALERS ARRIVED NOT long after Lyvia left, only a thin, silvery scar trailing down where the blade had kissed my skin in desperation. I marvel at the work. Healing magic was incredible. Apparently, the healer who fixed my arm was also in the room the day I was brought in after my overdose. I couldn't stop the blush that crept over my face from the embarrassment when she told me, and I think she noticed. Because in the next breath, she told me she was glad that I was okay, and was proud to serve the new Queen of Hell. I couldn't quite tell if she was being sincere or not, but the healing work she did on my arm was good enough for me to not really care, regardless.

My eyes catch on the beautiful black-wood desk by one of the windows, and I stroll over, perching down on the red velvet stool. Dipping a quill into the ink pot, I pull two pieces of parchment towards myself and begin writing letters to both Talia and Ezra, explaining as much as I can without putting them at any risk. I promise them I'll find a way to see them soon and finish the letter telling them both how much I love them. I hand them to the guards at my door, asking that they ensure they're delivered as soon as possible, only to be met with a nod and a grunt as a response. Guess they've not warmed up to me just yet.

LATER THAT NIGHT, I slip into the nightgown, the silk clinging delicately to my skin, which outlines my curves and the softness of my belly. I curl under the heavy covers, feeling lost in such a large bed, and stare up at the canopy. Exhaustion pulls at me almost instantly, making my eyes heavy and my body melt into the soft mattress beneath. When sleep lulls me in, it isn't the usual fitful dreams of ash or Ethan that consume me.

Velentha is there, standing among drifting veils of mist, her hood concealing most of her face. She slowly lifts her head, the hood slipping back to reveal raven-black hair and silver eyes that seem to forever be filled with glowing rivers of water. Her face remains cold as her eyes meet mine, her words making the hairs on my arms rise.

"Become immortal," she whispers, her voice threading through the mist, sounding like it's everywhere around me. "Rise again. Go to Maelkar."

She takes a step forward, grabbing onto my shoulders with an icy grip before shoving me down to the endless abyss behind me. I hear her voice calling after me as I fall endlessly, "Tell Korithax. Tell him now."

I jolt awake with a gasp, heart hammering in my chest. I scan the room, ensuring I'm safe and not falling to my doom in a never-ending nightmare, then shove back the covers and bolt to the large, heavy door of my room. I pull it open, startling the guards on duty, and demand they take me to Korithax instantly.

My bare feet slap against the cold flooring of the castle hall as I follow the guards to Korithax's rooms, the panic not easing for a single second as I pass door after door, praying the next one I reach is his. The guard outside of Korithax's chambers hesitates, looking at me with confusion and something else glinting in his eyes that I can't quite decipher.

"Let me in, now! I am to be your Queen." I didn't expect to have to pull the Queen card any time soon, but when desperation calls, I guess.

He knocks once before I usher him aside and push open the door myself. I step inside and almost choke. Korithax is standing in the centre of his room, wearing nothing but a pair of dark satin sleep pants, his sculpted chest on full display. Every line of muscle, every inhuman curve, every swirling tattoo across his torso, chest, and arms on display. My mouth goes bone dry at how overwhelming he is.

Korithax strides over, his jaw tight, fury practically radiating off of him. Without warning, he grabs my wrist and yanks me further inside.

"Sorry," I mutter, breathlessly. "I didn't mean to wake you."

"You didn't wake me," he growls.

I frown in confusion. "Then why are you being an ass?"

He lifts my chin with a single finger, forcing me to meet his dark, molten stare. Goosebumps pebble over my entire body at the contact.

"Because my bride is wandering my castle in a fucking silk nightgown," he says slowly, using his other hand to pull at the hem of the material, "with your nipples poking through the fabric for every guard to see."

I feel my cheeks flame. Frick. I should've probably put a dressing gown on or something. But this was the only thing I had been given to sleep in, and I didn't think to get dressed before rushing over here.

His eyes narrow as he looks past me. "Do you like what you see?" He asks the poor guard behind me, his voice lethal.

I spin around, mortified. The guard pales instantly, his eyes practically bugging out of his skull with fear.

"I was not looking, sire," he stammers. "She is to be my queen."

"Do not lie to me," Korithax snarls. Without hesitation, Korithax steps forward and rips the guard's eyes from his head. Blood spurts everywhere. I freeze on the spot, my eyes widening as I watch him proceed to snap his neck like a toothpick, his body crumpling to the ground.

"Korithax!" I shriek. "What the hell is wrong with you?!"

He barks at the other guards to drag the corpse away, then slams the door shut. When he turns to me, his eyes are almost entirely black. "Do not raise your voice at me."

"You just murdered someone!" I retort.

"He looked at what's mine," he hisses, stepping toward me. I backpedal until my knees hit the bed, making me stumble.

"What's wrong, little flower?" He purrs, placing his finger back under my chin, lifting it slightly. "Were you enjoying their attention?"

"You're insane," I breathe, the words catching in my throat.

"Maybe." His lips twitch into somewhat of a smirk. "Why are you here, Daisy?"

I swallow hard, trying to ignore my thundering heartbeat. "Right. Uh. This is going to sound crazy..."

I TELL HIM EVERYTHING—ABOUT the dream, about Velentha's words, and how she pushed me into an endless void. By the time I finish, he's sitting on a chair across from me, his brow furrowed. I perch myself on the edge of his bed, watching him stew.

"What the fuck is she up to?" He mutters to himself.

"What do you mean? It didn't make any sense to me."

"It does to me." He exhales sharply. "She's telling me to take you to Noxthrallia. To Maelkar Vyre. She wants you to be turned immortal."

I blink. "Immortal? Like... live forever?"

"Well, not forever. But yes." He says flatly. "The Divine Six threatened to destroy my kingdom if I married a mortal. They blew up the guest chambers to make their point."

My stomach twists. So it was them, and it was because of me. "So turning immortal would fix it?"

He pauses for a moment. "It's a loophole. If you're immortal, technically, you're no longer a mortal bride."

We sit in heavy silence, both of us pondering Velentha's words. Surely if she were so against him marrying me, she wouldn't be telling him to turn me immortal. But I guess, she wasn't against him marrying me... just mortal me?

"Then let's do it," I breathe.

He snaps his gaze to mine. "What?"

"I said, let's do it. I'll become immortal."

He scoffs. "You tried to end your life not long ago; now you want it to last for an eternity?"

The words cut me deeper than they should. I stand quickly, attempting to brush past him toward the door. "I was just trying to help. Forget it."

He grabs my wrist and pulls me between his legs, locking me there with his hands on my hips. Even through the silk nightgown, his touch is scorching, leaving more goosebumps in its wake.

"Why?" He asks, his voice laced with suspicion.

"Why what?" I reply, fighting the shiver crawling up my spine. Even sitting, he's eye level with me. He's a literal tower of a man.

"Why are you trying to help me?"

I hesitate before sighing. "Because you helped me. Twice. And... even though sometimes I wish you hadn't... You did. I also kind of like it here. Aran's nice, and I don't want to go back home."

He tilts his head, staring at me like I'm a puzzle that he's struggling to solve. "So, you're returning a favour?"

I smirk, raising a shoulder in a shrug. "Or maybe I'm secretly plotting to kill you and rule Hell myself."

To my absolute shock, Korithax laughs. A deep, rich sound that sets my body alight. Holy hell, he's gorgeous when he laughs. His fangs flash in the light, and his jet-black eyes gently gleam. I feel the blush on my cheeks as I watch him. He notices. Of course, he notices.

"Why are you blushing, little flower?" He teases, brushing a piece of hair behind my ear.

"You... you're just beautiful, when you're not scowling all the time." I whisper.

He looks directly into my eyes, his hand lingering on the strand he'd moved out of my face. I softly bite my lip, and he clears his throat sharply, pushing away and standing from the chair. It startles me, the tension between us evaporating entirely.

"You should go back to your chambers. I'll speak to Aran about Noxthrallia. Get some sleep."

I nod, silently kicking myself for hoping that moment would last a little longer. He walks me to the door, pausing just before it.

"Wait." He stops me from reaching for the handle, making my heart begin to pound. He walks to the other side of the room, exiting through a door before returning a moment later with a robe. "Put this on," he mutters. "I don't want to have to replace any more guards for staring at you."

I laugh despite the situation and put on the robe. It buries me completely, and it smells just like him, spice and smoke invading my senses. "Goodnight, Korithax."

He leans against the doorframe, watching me go. "Goodnight, my queen."

Tomorrow, everything could change. Forever.

CHAPTER 24
KORITHAX

I slam the door shut behind me when she's gone, the echo rattling through the chamber.

My breathing is ragged, and my chest is tight. What the fuck is wrong with me? I rake both hands through my hair, pacing like a caged beast.

The image of her is seared into my mind—branded into my skull with fucking fire. That gods-damned nightgown. That whisper of silk clinging to every curve like it was fucking painted onto her. Lush hips, full breasts, and a soft belly I wanted to sink my fucking teeth into like some depraved animal. She looked like desire itself made flesh.

And when she stood between my legs, my hands holding onto her hips, feeling the softness of her through the silk...

Fuck.

My cock had hardened so fast it was almost painful. I am so fucking glad she hadn't realised. I'm still hard, the fabric of my trousers biting into me like a punishment, and gods do I deserve it. I snarl and drive my fist into the nearest wall. The obsidian cracks, the stone spiderwebbing.

Pathetic. She's a mortal. A broken mortal who has barely recovered from nearly putting herself into a grave. She's supposed to be a pawn, a tool, nothing more than a contract written with blood. The Divine Six demanded a bride, and I gave them one. And that should be the end of it. But it's not. Because I keep thinking about the way she looked at me. Like she truly saw me, not the monster that clawed itself out from the depths of Hell.

I don't care that her laughter is comparable to sunlight. I don't care that she's one of the few beings alive who doesn't flinch when I touch her. I don't care that the colour of her blush reminds me of a summer morning.

It does not matter.

I let out another growl that borders on a roar and slam my fist into the stone again. Pain blooms across my knuckles, and I welcome the sting. Maybe if I break the bones in my hand, my brain will focus on something other than her. Because she truly is nothing more than a bargaining chip in a political game I've spent lifetimes playing. I don't want her, I don't need her, and I sure as fuck don't feel anything for her.

I take a deep inhale, shoving the thoughts aside and shift my attention to a much bigger problem than the mortal who is to be my bride. Velentha.

What the fuck is she playing at? Why push Daisy to seek out Maelkar Vyre, the ruler of Noxthrallia? Velentha has always dealt in riddles, but interfering this openly feels dangerous, even for her. Not to mention, I now have an incredibly big journey to plan thanks to her meddling.

Noxthrallia is the furthest realm from Hell that allows open travel. I can't just tear through the veils the way I normally would. Each jump will drain me the further I go. I need time to replenish between realms, and there are only five other realms with open travel for me to go through, which means I need a plan.

. . .

Aran is already awaiting me when I storm into the war room.

"Sire," he says calmly, nodding his head. "I got your summons."

"I am to travel to Noxthrallia with Daisy. First to Fjellheim Heights, then Auroras Veil. Solara, Stormravan, Luminaria, and finally... Noxthrallia."

He pauses, looking at me with weary eyes. "May I ask why, sire?"

"Daisy is going to become immortal. The only person capable of such an act is Maelkar."

"I assume the Queen is ready to depart?" He asks, not questioning the plan or the idea to turn Daisy immortal.

I frown at him for a beat before responding. "We leave tomorrow."

Aran whistles low under his breath. "That is no easy trek."

"I am well aware," I snap. "Each jump will take its toll. We'll have to rest between most of the jumps for several hours, maybe even a day."

Aran nods. "I'll prepare an endless pack. Clothing, supplies, and currencies for realms. Information too. You've not visited some of them in centuries."

"And the Divine Six?" I ask.

He smirks. "I'll tell them you went to negotiate a trade deal with Luminaria. That should keep them distracted for a few days."

I grunt my approval, but my suspicion rises. Why is he not shocked by the quest to turn Daisy immortal? And how did he come up with a plan so quickly to distract the Uppers?

"Also," Aran says carefully, "I suggest you allow me to send a few soldiers to accompany—"

"No," I cut him off. "I need every soldier here in case those celestial bastards try something whilst I'm gone."

Aran bows slightly. "Understood."

I exhale heavily. "Prepare the bag. Ensure everything is ready."

"It will be, sire," Aran says. He hesitates for a moment, then continues, "And for what it's worth... I think you're doing the right thing. Velentha has clearly seen something. Perhaps you should trust that."

I grunt again but say nothing. Did I tell him that this was Velentha's idea? I'm almost certain I hadn't. But with the lack of sleep, and a certain mortal running through my mind, I couldn't be sure. I eye him suspiciously as he leaves the war room. No. I trust Aran with my entire life. I must have slipped it in when I was distracted by the maps that were now strewn across the large table, mapping out each realm and how to navigate them.

~

THE NEXT AFTERNOON arrives far too quickly.

I stand outside Daisy's chambers, trying not to scowl. The door opens—and every thought, every shred of anger I've clung to—evaporates.

Fuck. Me.

Daisy stands there in a deep grey dress that's tailored to absolute perfection. The corset is pulled so tightly it showcases every curve—the swell of her hips, the full, perfect shape of her breasts. The dress ends mid shin, delicate silver ribbons lacing up her calves from the silk flat shoes she wears. Her bright blonde hair is styled in an ancient Grecian braid, half gathered at the back of her head in small, intricate plaits wound together. A small silver sword—a hairpin—sits stabbed through the knot, gleaming. Her ocean eyes are lined lightly, her pouty lips slicked with gloss.

A fucking vision.

Lyvia curtsies beside her, beaming. "Doesn't she look beautiful, sire?"

I clear my throat harshly. "You may leave, Lyvia."

She dips another curtsy and vanishes with a mischievous smile. Little devil knows exactly what she has done.

Daisy fidgets under my stare. "I know it's too much... Lyvia insisted I look more queenly. I can go change if—"

I take her hand and spin her lightly to face me. "You look radiant, little flower," I murmur, my voice rough as I stare down at her. "I see why you are known as the sun by your mortal friends."

Her cheeks flame, and it makes a feeling I'm unfamiliar with twist inside me. I release her abruptly, stepping back, the distance between us feeling cold and wrong. I can't afford distractions, despite how much I want to tear that dress from her body. There are many other women I can fuck, and she will not be one of them. Bride or not, I refuse to lie with a mortal woman, even once she's immortal. It's a line I can't cross with her.

"Here," I say, pulling a ring from my jacket. An onyx band crowned with a gleaming ruby, cradled between two serpent heads —each set with tiny, glinting diamond eyes. "This was my mother's," I mutter. "You will wear it while we travel. We must appear as any devoted couple would."

She gasps, staring at the ring. "Korithax... It's beautiful."

"Yes. It's yours now. Put it on. We leave immediately."

She slides the ring onto her finger, and I can't help but stare, for one dangerous heartbeat, at how perfectly it fits her. Her small, delicate hands wear the ring so perfectly, it almost takes my breath away.

My Queen.

Gods help me.

CHAPTER 25
DAISY

Korithax looks every inch the demon king.

He stands tall and menacing in a tailored black jacket that fits his broad shoulders perfectly, the collar lined in crimson velvet. His obsidian horns curve back from his head like a crown of living stone, his black silken hair falling in loose waves over his shoulders. His dark trousers tuck into boots that are polished to a subtle shine. His presence feels almost too large for the room, power thrumming from him like a living thing.

He stares at the slightly shaking hand I've slid the ring onto. It's absolutely breathtaking, the oversized ruby in the centre glinting in the sun that shines in from the large windows of my room.

"Come," he says, holding out his arm.

I step into his embrace without a moment of hesitation. His hands tighten around my waist, and a heartbeat later, with no further warning, the world lurches. The dizzying pull of teleportation grips me, making my stomach churn. The delicious breakfast of pyreloaf and emberfruit preserve almost comes straight back up out of me as everything whips and whirls around. Lyvia had brought it to me this morning with a beaming smile. The pyreloaf was a thickly sliced bread with a blackened crust, with small ashberries baked in. Lyvia said that they were small berries that grew near Hell's lava. It had a thick, sticky substance on top called emberfruit preserve, which was a rich honey colour and made from crushed emberfruit that gets cooked down into a sticky jam. It was sweet and delicious with a slight spice aftertaste, mixing beautifully with the sweet taste of the loaf. I practically groaned when I took a bite. Lyvia had described each part of the breakfast in incredible detail as I devoured it. Now, however, I was deeply regretting it.

When the ground steadies beneath my feet, I blink into a dream. We stand on a small stone landing platform, suspended in the middle of an endless sky. Floating islands drift lazily around us, interconnected by shimmering rainbow bridges that glitter and seem to ripple like water. Soft mist clings to everything, turning the air cool and making the skin on my arms pebble with goosebumps. Floating just above our heads, close enough to touch, clouds of silver and white dance across the endless blue sky. Waterfalls spill off the edges of the islands, their tinkling sounds filling the air like a symphony of bells. Flowers bloom in impossibly bright colours along the edges of the bridges, looking like peonies—but much more delicate and breathtaking.

"Welcome to Fjellheim Heights," Korithax says, his voice laced with amusement.

I gape openly, turning in a slow circle to take it all in. If Heaven were real, this is truly how I imagined it would appear.

"This realm," he continues, "is the realm of rain and mist. It's here that your world's rain and mists are born. Virena, otherwise known as the Mother of Mists, rules here."

I listen, utterly breathless as we begin the walk across one of the rainbow bridges. Korithax points toward a distant shimmering palace that appears to be carved from glass and mist itself.

"Virena is an ancient being," Korithax says. "When she cries, it floods down in the lower realms. When she sings, clouds bloom, fluffy and white. Children born during a lightning storm here are considered to be her chosen ones." He glances at me. "Tread carefully around her."

As we walk through the dreamy realm, mythical creatures move all around us. Enormous stags that look like they're made of cloud, bound between the floating islands, leaving trails of mist behind them as they gallop along. Serpentine water creatures swim beneath the rainbow bridges like fish, their scales iridescent, catching the sun like beautiful opals. The people of this realm have skin that's comparable to liquid silver, shimmering under the light like they've been doused in the world's brightest highlighter, their eyes glowing faintly in a variety of pale colours. Their clothing flows around them like pieces of clouds themselves, looking like one gust of wind will disintegrate the intricate clothing instantly.

"Hell trades with Fjhellheim Heights," Korithax adds. "We provide weapons imbued with flame. It's not as strong as Hell's weaponry, but strong enough to defend this realm against outside threats. In return, we receive rare mists and elemental waters for rituals, magic, and help with the growth of our crops."

I nod absentmindedly, trying to memorise every sound, every smell. The earthy, musky scent smells like a spring shower. Is this what it felt like to take psychedelics? Because I genuinely felt like I was tripping right now.

We near the citadel, a grand palace of transparent towers and flowing waterfalls. Guards stand at the entrance—tall beings with translucent skin, armoured in pale silver plates etched with what Korithax has told me are water runes. Their weapons are long, elegant spears that end in a sharp point that looks like a glimmering diamond.

One steps forward. "His Majesty Korithax," he says with a formal bow. "Her Grace, Virena, awaits you."

We follow the guard through the vast hallways of intricate carved glass that shimmers in the light until we reach an enormous chamber where Virena sits upon her throne. It's a large seat that looks like it's been carved from diamond and opal, and drifting clouds surround the base of the beautiful chair.

"Ah, Korithax," Virena says, her voice like a sigh of wind. "It has been a while."

"Virena." Korithax nods stiffly, hands clasped at his front.

Virena's eyes shift to me, one storm-grey, the other opal-white, surrounded by pale blue lashes. "And who is this beautiful woman beside you?"

Blushing furiously, I drop into a curtsy. "My name is Daisy, Your Highness."

"My soon-to-be queen," Korithax adds, his voice a low rumble that seems so out of place in a palace with such serenity.

Virena smiles, the sight of it making me uncomfortable. It looks almost predatory as she says, "Ah, Daisy. Please. One queen does not bow to another."

I rise, cheeks burning at the mistake I'd made.

"What can I do for you, Korithax?" She asks, her piercing eyes landing back on him.

"We're just passing through on our journey," he says, voice guarded. "As you know, realm jumping depletes magic the farther one travels. I don't require long to replenish with your realm being as close as it is, but we would be grateful for a night's hospitality."

Virena eyes him with suspicion. "And where might you be travelling to?"

"That is of no concern to you, Virena. I simply ask for your hospitality."

Tension thickens between them, the clouds darkening at her feet and shifting more erratically to match the scowl on her face. I watch carefully, silently praying that she doesn't mean any harm to either of us. Finally, after what feels like an eternity, she smiles again, slow and sly.

"Daisy, sweet child. Come here."

I feel Korithax stiffen beside me at her summons. I glance at him, and he offers me a small nod of approval, despite his jaw being tense. I step forward toward the throne, and Virena's eyes widen as she takes my hand. Her touch is warm despite her gaze turning icy.

"A mortal," she breathes. Her eyes snap to Korithax, "You bring a mortal as your bride?"

"Yes," Korithax growls.

Virena leans forward, her silver-blue hair floating on a phantom breeze. "Sweet child, has he captured you against your will? Speak truthfully. I can save you from this beastly man."

"Rude," Korithax mutters.

"Shush, demon," she snarls.

Remembering Korithax's words of being a unified front, I smile warmly, trying to put on the most queenly voice possible. "No, Your Highness. I'm to marry him of my own free will. I love him dearly, and I'm extremely excited to become his wife. No mortal man could ever compare to my Kori."

Virena stares at me for a long, unsettling moment, trying to read the truth in my eyes. Her unwavering gaze has my palms starting to sweat like I'm under interrogation.

Finally, she nods. "Very well. You may stay until morning, Korithax, as thanks for your continued trade with Fjellheim Heights. I shall have your room prepared by one of my servants and ensure you are comfortable."

"Room, as in, singular?" Korithax asks, narrowing his eyes.

"Well, yes. As a soon-to-be married couple, I do not see why you would need separate rooms. I know you have not had problems in the past sharing your chambers, Korithax."

I quickly step in, ignoring her last comment despite the sting in my chest. "That's very kind of you. Thank you, Virena."

WITH A FLICK OF HER HAND, we're dismissed and escorted back outside the citadel into the royal gardens. The second we're out of earshot, Korithax grabs me by the waist, yanking me close. To any poor soul watching, we probably just look like a passionate couple in a lovers' quarrel. In reality, his grip's just shy of bruising.

"Why did you just agree to one room?" He hisses against my ear.

I bat my lashes innocently. "You said we had to look like a real couple. And shocker—real couples tend to sleep in the same bed." I gasp as his grip tigthens. "She was suspicious. I did what I had to."

He studies me for a long moment before nodding and loosening his grip. "You did well. She's not easy to deal with."

I beam, borderline smug. "Aw, look at that. My first interdimensional diplomacy session and I didn't get turned into stone. Gold star for me."

He raises a brow, ignoring my sarcasm entirely. "Kori?"

I shrug, feigning nonchalance. "Sorry. I figured 'Korithax, Prince of Screaming Death and Suffering' might sound a little too formal. Just trying to make us seem more couple-y y'know?"

A smirk curves his mouth, which is annoyingly attractive. "I like it."

"Of course you do," I mutter, rolling my eyes.

We spend the rest of the afternoon wandering the floating islands. I marvel at the creatures that inhabit the realm, so alike Earth's animals, yet made entirely out of something new. Delicate air sprites zoom by, one landing with a soft giggle on one of Korithax's horns. He swats it away with a scowl, making the sprite laugh even more before three of them float towards me. They weave in and out of my hair, whispering quietly when they whizz past my ears.

A plump sprite floats over, landing on my shoulder to whisper into my ear. "She who was lost is not lost at all."

The sprites suddenly shimmer and vanish with laughter, my brow furrowing.

"What's wrong?" Korithax asks.

"That sprite just whispered something odd into my ear," I respond in confusion.

"Ignore them. Sprites are known for being a little... crazy."

We continue to walk hand in hand—for show, I remind myself—as the sky shifts to the soft colours of dusk, the realm quietening enough that the sound of tinkling water fills my ears. I close my eyes, inhaling slowly and letting the sounds and smells truly ground me. This place is magical. I can't believe something like this exists, and people back at home have absolutely no idea. I had no idea, before today.

When we return to the citadel, we're escorted to a sprawling suite of glass and rippling silk canopies. A large floating bed sits in the middle of the room that looks as soft as a cloud.

Dinner is brought to us, strange and wondrous foods filling the table. Silver-fleshed fruits that taste like honeyed rain, sparkling wines that smell like fresh blooms, and meats seasoned with something spicy that make my tongue feel like it's been zapped with electricity.

After eating and drinking, filling the meal with small, awkward conversation, Korithax stands, muscles flexing under his black shirt.

"I'm going to go shower, make yourself comfortable." He says, vanishing through a door at the other side of the room.

I walk over to one of the large glass windows, looking out at the realm in front of me. It truly was a sight to be seen. Ezra would love it here; Talia, however, would think it's pretentious and would make some form of back-handed compliment about Virena. I smile despite the lingering ache in my chest. I wonder if they've got my letters yet. I hope they weren't angry at me. I hope they understood why I left, and that they were happy for me that I had an escape from my messed-up reality.

Korithax returns sometime later, a towel slung low across his hips, droplets of water clinging to his skin. I stare, wide-eyed, unable to look away at his immaculate body. The way his muscles move as he walks, my eyes snagging on the deep V that disappears beneath the towel. Holy demon.

"Go shower," he says gruffly. "We have a long day tomorrow. There's a pack in the bathroom that's enchanted. Call out what you need."

I nod, darting into the bathroom, feeling my cheeks blazing from seeing him in just a towel. He looked utterly divine, his wet hair hanging by his ridiculously large shoulders. The way the water droplets trickled their way down the grooves of his abs. God's, even his horns looked sexy wet. Clearly, I needed a cold shower.

The bathroom is a fantasy in itself. Floors of smooth sapphire stone that glisten under the natural light of the room, with a huge waterfall shower that takes up most of the space. I strip down and step under the warm water, sighing as it hits my skin. The soaps smell like summer rain, and the shampoo makes my hair feel like silk between my fingers.

When I'm finished, I wrap myself in possibly the softest towel I've ever felt, and approach the pack that's been left on the vanity. He said to call out what I need, like that made any freaking sense.

"Uhhh, nightgown?" I whisper, crinkling my nose. I feel like an absolute fool.

My eyes widen as the bag glows faintly. Hesitantly I reach inside, and my hand lands on something soft. I pull it out, revealing a bundle of delicate white silk. It's a short, lace trimmed gown with matching lace panties.

My face flames, holding out the thin piece of fabric in front of me. "Lyvia, I'm going to strangle you when I see you," I mutter under my breath.

CHAPTER 26
KORITHAX

I dry myself off quickly, tugging on a fresh pair of black silk pants, not bothering with a shirt.

A very, very small part of me enjoyed the way Daisy reacted when my body was on show. Her little mortal heart probably isn't used to seeing many seven-foot, muscled, tattooed men. And despite the fact that there's something extremely different about my little flower, she is but a woman with eyes. I wasn't stupid; I knew I was what the mortals would call 'hot', and even though I had large horns curling from my skull, and eyes blacker than night, clearly, I was attractive in her eyes too.

I'm picking at some of the leftover food on the tray when I hear the soft creak of the bathroom door. She slowly walks in, muttering to herself quietly enough that even I can't hear what she's saying. I look up to see what's wrong and pause mid-bite.

Gods above and below.

She's wrapped in a white nightgown that stops mid-thigh, delicate lace tracing the V of her neckline. Her damp blonde hair clings to her skin, tiny beads of water running down her collarbone. Her cheeks are flushed, and she's nervously biting her lower, full blush-pink lip.

"Apparently, Lyvia thinks that this is appropriate bed attire." She mutters, blushing as she tries to dry her hair off with a towel.

I stare, frozen in place, my hands dropping the bread to curl into tight fists at my side. I can't seem to tear my eyes away from her. She looks up at me, noticing my lack of response, and I quickly offer a frown and clear my throat.

"Here," I manage, walking toward her and taking the towel from her hands. My voice comes out rough. "Let me dry your hair. My hands will be quicker than the towel. Go sit on that chair over there."

She hesitates, her eyes trailing slowly up my body. I internally scoff at the obvious way she's eying my body. She obeys my demand, padding across the room to the chair by the window. I watch her go, the back of the night gown swaying on a phantom breeze with each step, barely covering the curve of her ass. I bite my knuckles as I watch every single step she takes towards the chair.

"I'm going to kill you, Lyvia," I mutter under my breath.

She perches on the edge of the chair, the nightgown riding up her thighs, giving me a torturous glimpse of soft, thick creamy flesh and a hint of matching lace panties. I bite down on my lip to suppress a groan, whilst discreetly adjusting the now growing cock in my pants. I move, stopping behind her and placing my hands gently into her damp hair. I summon a low heat into my palms, ensuring I don't burn her, and rake my fingers softly down her scalp, drying the silky, soft strands with careful precision.

"You did well today," I say gruffly, distracting myself from the throb in my pants. "Tomorrow, we leave for Aurora's Veil."

My hands continue to comb slowly through her hair, drying it section by section, and she lets out a soft moan, the sound making me close my eyes and quietly inhale.

"Oh my god, I'm so sorry. That just felt so good. I love head scratches." She giggles, trying to hide how mortified she is.

I chuckle under my breath, ignoring the way the sound made me feel. Gods, what the fuck is wrong with me, getting pleasure from the sight and sounds of a mere mortal.

I spend the next five minutes finishing drying her hair and then step back slightly. "I'm all done," I announce, stepping in front of her.

She jolts slightly, blinking up at me with dazed eyes. "I must've drifted off," she murmurs, running her fingers through her hair. "Thank you, Korithax."

"I thought it was Kori now?" I tease, tilting my head.

"Ah, that's just for show, remember?" She says in a mocking tone.

My smile vanishes, my features instantly hardening as I turn to walk away from her. "Right," I mutter coldly. Just for show. Of course it was, fool. "You can take the bed," I continue, "I'll sleep on the floor."

"You don't have to do that," she protests.

"It's fine. Goodnight, Daisy."

She hesitantly climbs into the bed as I lie down on the cold marble floor, hating every second of it. The chill seeps into my bones instantly, despite my continuous heat. I'm so glad I can vanish my wings whenever I please, because it would be painfully uncomfortable laying with them spread out beneath me down here. I stare at the large glass ceiling, the stars above shimmering softly as I listen to her rustle about the covers, her teeth chattering softly.

"Can you stop that?" I snap.

"Stop what?" She mumbles.

"Chattering your teeth. It's very annoying when my hearing is considerably a lot stronger than yours."

"It is?" She squeaks. "I'm sorry. It's freaking cold in here."

I sigh, returning my focus to the night sky above. I manage to endure it for a few minutes longer, gritting my teeth against the sound. Finally, with an exasperated sigh, I push myself up off the ground and stride to the edge of the bed. I yank back the covers, making her yelp and sit up in surprise, and slide in beside her.

"Come here," I grumble. "If I have to listen to that all night, I might just bash my head off of these shiny fucking floors until my skull caves in." She scoots over hesitantly, shuffling close to me. Her body brushes mine—and holy fucking shit, she's freezing. "Gods above Daisy," I mutter.

"I told you!" She softly shouts as I squirm at the touch of her freezing body on mine. She presses her ice-cold feet against my legs, and I hiss, making her giggle. "Thank you," she whispers.

I don't respond, feeling her body slowly warm up with my body pressed against hers, her head resting gently on my arm. I lay there stiffly until her breathing evens out, and I dare a glance at her. Her lips are slightly parted, her hair falling over her face as she softly snores. I feel the tug between our souls pull gently as I watch her, the sensation so strange it makes me twitch

"Goodnight, little flower," I whisper, gently wrapping my arm around her to pull her closer into me.

~

I AWAKEN to find her still curled into my chest, my arm still wrapped protectively around her as if she were mine to keep safe. I guess she is now. My future wife, my future queen. This small, breakable mortal, her golden hair spilling across me like a river of light. She's still asleep, her chest rising and falling steadily, her soft little snores barely audible.

I watch her, unmoving. Her face is peaceful, relaxed in a way I've never seen before. The morning light makes the soft freckles on her pale skin stand out even more, each one like a smattering of the cosmos across her little button nose.

Gods, she's infuriatingly beautiful.

I stroke a hand gently down her back, feeling the delicate curve of her body beneath my fingers, savouring how nice it felt to have contact like this. This was not something I did at all in my world. I either had quick fucks or nights of long, filthy sex that would make any mortal blush. But afterward, they would be kicked out of my chambers, and I would lie alone. That's the way I like it, the way I have always liked it. I'm not a physical contact type of man, I'm the —I will destroy your body in the best of ways, then tell you to fuck off—kind of man. Yet here, right now, the feel of her soft body pressed against mine felt indescribable.

Her eyes flutter open, meeting mine in sleepy confusion. Fuck. I clear my throat and untangle myself from her immediately, standing to grab a shirt that I threw over a nearby chair.

"I'll go collect us breakfast," I say, my voice still gruff from sleep. "Is there anything you would like?"

She yawns, sitting up against the pillows. "Do they have coffee?"

"I shall find out," I reply. "A maid will assist you in dressing. Your clothing is in the pack."

Before she can respond, I stride from the room, needing a moment away from her. I need to create distance, instantly. That's the first and last time I will lay with her beside me. She was cold, and I couldn't handle listening to her stupid teeth chattering all night. I need my sleep.

I'M HALFWAY down the glass-lined corridor, the sunrise streaming in and painting the hallway in bright orange and pink hues, when one of Virena's guards steps into my path.

"Her grace requests your presence in the throne room, immediately." He says stiffly, his spear glittering in the soft light.

I grind my teeth, forcing my irritation down. I'm not even in my own realm, and I'm still constantly being summoned by someone who thinks they're better than me. "Fine," I mutter, changing the direction I was heading in to follow the guard.

The throne room is quieter this morning, the mist now swirling around the entire floor, giving the illusion that we're walking on clouds. Virena lounges on her diamond throne, her pale, mismatched eyes fixing on me the moment I step into the room.

"You captured that mortal girl," she says, voice sharp, yet smooth. Like a knife, but hidden in silk.

I bristle, the accusation instantly pissing me off. "I did not capture anyone."

"I heard of your little predicament with the Divine Six," she continues, "they forced you to find a bride." I say nothing, raising a brow whilst crossing my arms across my chest. "You have your pick of any woman in your realm," she says, slowly rising from her throne, her tone dropping. "Not to mention many women from many other realms. And you choose a mortal girl?"

I clench my jaw, keeping my face stony as she glares at me. "What are you getting at, Virena?"

She steps down from her throne, gliding closer, her bare feet whispering against the mist. "It's suspicious, Korithax. A mortal bride? Not to mention, you seem to be on some secret mission through the realms. Do not insult me by pretending your journey and the impending marriage to a mortal are mere coincidences."

"None of this is any of your business," I growl, stepping closer to her, deep black smoke slowly coiling around my shoulders as my anger heightens.

The action makes her guards move, angling their spears at me from every direction. I smirk, looking each one in the eye, ensuring they understand that I don't see them as a threat. I could burn their entire realm to ash if I wanted to. I could incinerate them from the inside out without so much as breaking a sweat, yet they think their pointy sticks are intimidating. I scoff, turning my attention back to Virena.

"Now, if you don't mind, said mortal needs coffee." I smile, ensuring the insincerity of it shines through. I add in a mocking bow for good measure before I turn on my heel, striding away from her.

Virena's voice slices through the air again, "Her soul is strange, Prince of Hell. Different. You feel it too, I know you do."

I stop dead in my tracks, my fists clenching. Does she know about the tug between our souls? I can't ask, because what if she isn't talking about that, and I reveal something for her to hold over me?

"I have no idea what you're talking about," I say over my shoulder.

Virena's misty form floats a few feet closer. "I'm not entirely sure what I'm talking about either," she murmurs. "But there is something... unnatural about the girl. Tread carefully, demon prince. Not everything that shines is harmless."

I frown at her. Does she seriously think that a mortal could be a threat to me? A laugh bubbles up out of me, causing her to frown.

"Despite the fact that you have enslaved her as your bride, she may not be as weak as she seems."

I whirl to face her fully. "For the last fucking time," I snarl, "she is doing this of her own free will. We are in love!"

"I do not hesitate that you love her, Korithax," she says softly. "But it is strange. All of this is strange. Mark my words." She turns, floating back to her throne, her misty robes fluttering. "I hope you have found your stay here pleasurable. I look forward to our next trade."

She gestures to a guard standing near the exit. A slender male, with pale silver skin and hair the colour of moonlight. His spear is placed across his back with the tip pointing out just past his head.

"Veyric will guide you to where your mortal's coffee can be found. Until next time, Korithax."

I grunt, nodding my head to her slightly. Despite the fact that she has pissed me off, I need to keep the peace, for trade's sake. Her blessed water is essential for some of the demons' spell work, especially the healers.

I follow the guard out of the room, Virena's words gnawing at me like a splinter under the skin. At least she believes I love Daisy, that makes things easier. But fuck me, if every realm we visit accuses me of stealing a mortal bride, this trip was going to get real tedious, real fucking fast. Even as the Prince of Hell, I have standards. I don't take mortal slaves, despite what my father might have wished during his reign. Even the Divine Six, hypocritical bastards that they are, drew the line at mortal slavery.

I shake off the simmering anger as Veyric leads me towards the kitchens to grab the coffee. I immediately notice a plate of fluffy-looking pastries that look like little shimmery clouds, and I swipe it up for her too. She's going to need all the energy she can get for the next realm jump. Despite her trying to hide it, I saw how her skin paled and the way she slightly swayed on her feet when we arrived here. Realm jumping was as taxing for her as it was for me, despite it being for entirely different reasons. Transporting through veils and realms depleted my magic; the bigger the jump, the bigger the hit on my reserves. And for her, it completely messed with her body, her mortal fragility struggling with such disorientation. I'd have to find a way to make it easier on her, maybe ask in Aurora's Veil if their healers have anything to make it easier on her. Even if it means knocking her out.

I RETURN to the suite with a tray in my hands—a cup of rich-smelling coffee and the little pastries. "I have your coffee and breakfast, Daisy—"

She stands by the window, bathed in the soft light of Fjellheim Heights. She's wearing a dusky blue gown, the fabric shimmering with tiny threads of moving starlight. It hugs her curvy body perfectly, the flowy sleeves fluttering slightly as she shifts. A delicate necklace strung with tiny diamonds, forming a constellation that looks like the fucking cosmos, is wrapped around her throat. Her hair falls in soft waves down her back, a glimmering silver hairpiece crowning her head, catching every stray glint of light. Her makeup is soft but radiant—a faint sprinkle of stardust sparkling across her eyelids, making her ocean eyes glow like twin nebulas. A thin midnight blue cloak is tied carefully around her shoulders, its flowing train speckled with pinpricks of silver light, mimicking the night sky itself. And in the centre of the cape—stitched in a faintly glowing thread—is my sigil.

She looks like a living, breathing goddess. A vision that's far too beautiful for mortal standards.

"I'm sensing Lyvia has my outfits match the realm we are going to?" She says, a nervous laugh escaping her as she anxiously smooths the endless folds of her dress with her hands.

I snap myself out of the trance, feigning disinterest. "Yes, apparently so," I say shortly, setting the tray down onto the nearby table. "It's a little over the top, but it'll do."

That was a lie. It wasn't over the top; it was perfect. She looks like the embodiment of the night sky. Divine and entirely untouchable. And that's exactly what I needed to remember—untouchable.

Distance. I need distance. Last night was too much. The closeness, the softness of her body against mine. It can't happen again.

"Drink and eat," I command, gesturing to the tray. "I'm going to go change, and then we leave for Aurora's Veil."

I stride toward the bathroom without looking back—but at the door, I hesitate. I glance over my shoulder, finding her seated neatly at the table, her small fingers cradling the coffee cup as she softly blows on the steam, her entire body wrapped in that ridiculous, perfect vision of starlight.

A bitter, ugly thing rises in my chest, and I can't help but grab onto it and project it onto her. I turn back to Daisy fully, my voice harsh. "Virena believes that I love you," I say coldly. "I appear to be a greater actor than I initially thought, for her to believe that I could truly love such a weak, fragile thing like yourself."

I walk away before I can see the way her light dims at my words.

CHAPTER 27
DAISY

The pastries taste like sugar-dusted clouds.

Soft, pillowy, melt-on-your-tongue perfection with a tiny zing of citrus at the end. I chew slowly, not to savour it, but because my appetite packed its bags and left somewhere between "I appear to be a greater actor than I initially thought" and "such a weak, fragile thing like yourself." Wow. Oscar-worthy, truly. Someone get him a little gold statue of a middle finger engraved with my name.

It shouldn't sting—he's a demon, he's cruel, it's literally his whole thing—but it does. Because last night didn't feel like acting. It felt soft. Gentle. The way he dried my hair, the way he climbed into bed behind me to keep me warm. I slept better than I had in months. Then this morning, his hand stroking softly down my back when he thought I was still sleeping. But he just had to go open his stupid, perfect mouth.

Whiplash. That's what it's like being around Korithax. Hot and cold, kind then cruel. It was genuinely a guessing game as to how he was going to treat me next, and it was becoming real tiring real quick.

I sip my coffee, still deep in thought about his behaviour, when he strides back into the room. "Finished?"

I nod, not missing the tone in his voice. Guess we're sticking with grumpy asshat today. Great.

"Let's go."

I rise to my feet, and before I can brace myself, his arm wraps around me, the horrible sensation of realm travel shredding through my body again. The moment we land, my legs give out. The ground lurches, the world around me spinning violently as black spots speckle my vision. Jesus, I hate teleporting.

"Holy—" I mumble, disoriented.

Korithax catches me before I hit the ground, strong arms wrapping around me, his heat enveloping me.

"Breathe, Daisy," he whispers against my hair.

I do as he says, his spicy scent invading my nose as I breathe in deeply. Slowly, my vision returns, the spinning dulling enough to register how tightly his grip is around my waist. When I finally blink fully back to awareness, we're face to face, his onyx eyes staring down into mine. There's concern etched into the furrow between his brows as he slowly looks me over. He sets me straight gently, keeping his hands braced on my arms as I find my footing, ensuring I don't fall over again.

"I'll ask if the healers here have anything to help you with realm travelling. The further we get from Earth, the worse it's going to get."

"Great." I mutter sarcastically, testing out my balance as he releases my arms. When he steps out of my line of sight, the realm comes into view, making my breath stall in my chest.

We're standing on the edge of a cliff overlooking a world straight out of a fantasy novel. The sky is dusky, cast in purples and deep indigos. The northern lights ripple overhead in shifting hues of greens, pinks, and violets, moving through the atmosphere like ethereal silk. The air is crisp and smoky, scented like pine and distant bonfires. I can hear the soft sound of chimes drifting through the breeze, echoing through the mountains.

"Wow," I breathe.

"This is Aurora's Veil. A realm of perpetual night and dusk." Korithax says beside me.

He points toward a distant structure across the expanse of land that is dotted with little glowing lights that look like cosy log cabins. A large castle carved from stone and glowing crystal, like the northern lights were trapped in its walls, sits nestled deep in the mountains. Towering spires reach into the sky, each glowing faintly, their outlines blurred by bright starlight and drifting mist.

"Kaelith, otherwise known as the Duskwalker, rules here. He is not a cruel man... unless you are afraid of the dark, then you should maybe watch your back. He likes to terrorise those who fear the night." I look at him for any sign of him joking, but his face is as serious as ever. My eyes widen at the thought. I'm not afraid of the dark... I don't think.

"This realm provides dusk and night to Earth." He says, looking back out to the realm in front of us. He starts walking without uttering another word, and I follow along behind him.

After a few minutes, his voice pulls me out of my mindless gawking, "We need to be at his castle, but my magic is almost fully depleted now. Even flying with my wings won't work because of my lack of energy."

"So, what do we do?" I ask.

He scans the treeline, "We try to find a Nyveryian."

"What's that?"

"It's like a horse, but... not. If we can tame one, we can ride it to the castle and arrive much quicker."

This was all so much to take in, my head reeling from everything I've seen and learnt in the last twenty-four hours alone. Would I get used to seeing such different and beautiful places, with such weird and wonderful creatures? So far, it feels like I'm stuck in a permanent dream, but I don't think even my brain could conjure up places so beautiful. Here I was, a regular girl, travelling realms with a seven-foot demon prince as my companion and soon-to-be husband. I'm still not entirely convinced I haven't been drugged, and I'm just tripping absolute balls in some hole back at home. I wish I could bring Talia and Ezra here, especially to one of the log cabins. We could drink hot chocolate and watch the aurora above for hours on end, whilst forgetting all of our worries. Maybe one day I'll ask Korithax if I can bring them here. Maybe.

We begin our descent down the mountain, each step careful on the uneven trail. Since the night doesn't lift here, I find myself tripping every other step, huffing with irritation.

"Daisy, look," Korithax says, pulling me from my momentary tantrum.

I look up from where my eyes have been focused on the ground and gasp. Glowing moths drift lazily through the air, their bodies dusted with what looks like stardust. It falls from them as they flutter through the sky, leaving a beautiful trail of shimmer behind them as they dance and weave through the night sky.

"It's absolutely beautiful here," I whisper in awe.

He nods, continuing on the path. I hear him occasionally sigh when he hears me stumble over something else that lies unseen on the floor. I hope my eyesight improves when I turn immortal because I am getting really sick of this. I trip on another part of the uneven path, and I swear I hear him growl.

"What?" I snap.

"I just don't understand why you can't watch where you're going. You're really slowing us down with your constant tripping."

I halt, making him stop in his tracks and turn to face me, his jaw ticking slightly. "Because I'm clearly doing it on purpose," I reply with a snark, crossing my arms.

He huffs a breath through his nose and just shakes his head, turning back around to continue stomping down the mountainside.

"Insufferable ass," I mutter under my breath, following behind him.

"I heard that," he responds.

Of course, he heard it; his ears are large and pointy. I bet he had the hearing of a bat. "Stupid bat ears." I whisper. I see his shoulders moving like he's silently laughing to himself, and I flip him off behind his back. Ass.

After a long stretch of silence, I decide to try and ignore my growing irritation by bombarding Korithax with questions.

"Sooooo... What about you?" I ask.

He quirks a brow, looking over his shoulder at me. "What about me?"

"Well, we're getting married, and I don't even really know you. Other than the fact you're going to be the King of Hell, and you're kind of an ass."

He scoffs. "What do you want to know?"

I grin, catching up to him to walk by his side. "We'll start with the basics."

He doesn't look at me, but I see a smirk tug at the corner of his mouth. "Go on."

"Favourite colour?"

"Really?" He frowns, slightly turning his head to look at me, the colours of the aurora above flickering in his jet-black eyes.

"Just answer it. You don't always have to be moody," I reply, rolling my eyes.

He sighs, "Uh... black?"

"That's not a colour, it's a shade. But sure. Black. Mine's yellow."

"Didn't ask."

I roll my eyes again, ignoring the way it makes the corner of his mouth twitch up. Evidentially he just likes to irritate me. "Favourite movie?"

"I don't watch movies. There isn't exactly electricity or televisions in Hell."

"Oh. Yeah. Wow, no TV, no internet? I think I'm changing my mind about all of this."

"What? You can't. You signed the—"

"Korithax," I cut him off, grinning. "I'm kidding. We can always visit Earth, right? Maybe we can watch movies together there. No horrors, though, please."

He looks at me for a moment, his brows furrowing. "You may come and go as you please. I'll remain in Hell."

Right. Because why would he want to come to Earth and watch movies with me? I nod, quieting again, deciding it was best for me to just shut up. He doesn't try and continue the game either; he just occasionally frowns as if he's lost in thought. I debate asking him what he's thinking about, but he'd probably just say it was none of my business and huff at me again.

An hour of silence later, he suddenly throws out his arm, stopping me dead in my tracks as I collide with the thick muscle of his bicep. "Wha—"

"Shh," he whispers, putting a finger to his lips. He points to a thick line of trees to the side of us with his other hand.

"I can't see anything," I whisper, looking to where he's pointing.

"Fucking mortals and your shit eyesight." He mutters.

I scowl at him just as a sharp crack—a breaking of a twig or a branch—sounds from the trees. "Is it one of those horse thingies?" I mumble.

He shakes his head, emphasising the finger on his lips to remind me to shut the hell up. He slowly raises his arm, reaching behind his head. A quiet noise sounds as he draws an onyx sword from beneath his cloak, the metal gleaming dully in the twilight.

"When I tell you to run, you run. Do you understand me?"

"What?" I breathe, panic instantly coursing through my veins.

"Daisy, listen to me. Run when I say so, straight down the mountain." The seriousness of his tone has me stiffening. "I'll catch up to you. Stay still until I tell you to move."

At that, the creature steps into view. A hulking wolf-like beast, its body made entirely of smoke and shadow, with eyes glowing an unnatural amber colour. Its paws are the size of my head, the claws on the end alarmingly long and glinting. They look like sharp blades poking out from the mists of its toes. Its snarl is guttural, saliva dripping down its maw from jagged fangs. My heart thunders in my chest as I watch the beast slowly prowl towards us.

"What the shit is that?" I ask between panicked pants.

"A Nyxmaw," he whispers.

Its nostrils flare as it begins to sniff, amber eyes landing directly on me. My entire body freezes as our eyes clash, terror taking over as it throws its head back and howls—a sound so piercing my ears ring.

"NOW, DAISY!" Korithax barks.

Fight or flight takes over, and I burst into a fast sprint, my eyes just catching a glimpse of Korithax's sword blazing to life with a bright blue flame. I don't look back, focusing on each step as my lungs burn. I keep running, hearing more creatures howl in the distance.

He'll be okay, he's the Prince of Hell. He can handle himself. My feet don't falter as I run faster than I ever have before, straight down the pathway. My breaths come in heavy and fast as my cloak billows behind me.

Suddenly, something slams into the side of me, knocking me onto my back with a whoosh of air forcing out of my lungs at the impact. A scream rips out of me as I'm pinned to the floor, the male-looking creature above me both beautiful and terrifying. Its skin a pale, grey tone stretched across a beautiful face with eyes like glinting steel. Sharp canines protrude from its mouth, curled into an insidious smile. He tilts his head, stroking fingers that end in deadly sharp claws down my face in a caress.

"Well, well," he hisses into my ear as he leans down, inhaling the scent of my hair. "What do we have here? "The creature leans back, tilting his head side to side like a serpent ready to strike as terror claws down my spine. He inhales slowly, eyes glinting in the starlight as they widen at my smell. "The king will pay handsomely for you," he says in a guttural voice that makes the hairs on my arms stand up.

He laughs, cold and cruel, before grabbing me in his tight grip with one hand, his claws digging into my side so tightly that it causes me to scream in agony. The creature launches into the air, dark tattered leather wings beating furiously as I struggle to try to get out of his grip, the wind ripping at my hair. I try to scream for Korithax, but the sound doesn't come as a hand clamps over my mouth, cold and sharp as he digs his fingers into my cheek. Tears blur my vision as I feel warm blood beginning to trickle down my frozen face. This definitely wasn't a dream anymore; it was a nightmare.

After what feels like an eternity of being pulled through the sky by piercing claws, I'm suddenly dropped from mid-air. A scream tears from me as I fall, painfully hitting the ground hard on my knees, agony jolting up my legs. I whimper, trying to scramble to my feet. I look around desperately, praying there's no more creatures surrounding me as I push my hair from my face. A shadowed figure stands nearby, voice crackling like a low-burning fire.

"Well, what do we have here?"

CHAPTER 28
KORITHAX

I wait until she's gone.

Until the soft thud of her footsteps has vanished down the path, and the scent of fear that's wrapped around her begins to fade from the air—only then do I raise my blade.

The beast growls low, a sound that vibrates the ground beneath my feet. Nyxmaw's are creatures of ancient nightmares, conjured of shadow and smoke, created by the dark magic that still lingers in this realm's darkest corners.

It lunges, and I meet it mid-air, blade slashing across its chest. Its howl tears through the now pitch-black sky as blue flame sears through the flesh that hides underneath its tendrils of shadow. It lashes out, claws like daggers scraping against my ribs. I hiss, the sting from its swipe searing my skin. Before giving it another moment to attack, I twist, slamming my elbow into its snout before driving my blade into the side of its neck. Thick, black blood spurts out, coating my chest, the smell vile enough to make me gag. The Nyxmaw collapses to the ground, twitching before it evaporates into a pile of ash in the powdery snow.

"Fucking disgusting," I snarl, spitting onto its remains.

I lean over, heavily breathing, trying to ignore the pain in my ribs when her scream cuts through the realm. I don't give myself a moment to think before taking off and sprinting down the mountain, the terrain blurring beneath my feet. The terror in her scream rings through me as I run furiously. If a Nyxmaw has found her, she doesn't stand a chance.

I skid to a halt, five of them suddenly surrounding me, seeming to step out of the shadows themselves. "For fuck's sake," I mutter, lifting my blade again. "I really don't need this shit right now."

One steps forward, snarling at me with saliva dripping from its jaws. I snarl in return, not letting it have an ounce of my fear. I don't fear creatures like this, not when the monsters that lurk in my realms are over forty feet tall.

"Here, kitty, kitty," I taunt, waving my sword back and forth between my hands. "Hold on, Daisy. I'm coming."

They attack all at once. One lunges for my throat, and I dodge it just in time, slicing its underbelly open in one swift stroke. Another snaps at my shoulder, teeth grazing my flesh and ripping through skin.

"Motherfucker." I roar, spinning and slamming my fist into its skull with a crunch. I feel my knuckles crack on the impact, but I won't stop. I lose myself to the carnage, another beast trying to tackle me from behind. I spin, my sword trailing through the air, cleaving off its head in one clean, flaming arc. Its corpse turns to ash mid-collapse. Now would be a really nice time to have more than a drop of magic coursing through me. I could incinerate every one of them with a flick of my wrist.

The last two come from either side, snarling and snapping. They both pounce at the same time, the one on my left sinking its teeth into my forearm whilst I focus on the one on the right, driving my sword straight through its eye. The pain is sharp, searing through me like acid. I growl, yanking my arm free, blood pouring down my skin. My healing magic is painfully slow, eating away at the base of my reserve. I turn to face the final beast, my blood coating its teeth before gripping a dagger from the sheath at my thigh and launching it straight into its throat. It falls with a thud, disintegrating into an ash pile with the rest of its pack. I stride over and pluck my blade from the snowy ground, placing it back at my thigh before sheathing my sword.

I stagger forward, heart hammering against my ribs. I can smell her scent, and a familiar smell I never wanted to have invading my senses again. Her blood. I find her cloak first, torn and tangled in a pile on the floor, smattered with dark crimson. I snatch it up, my fingers curling tightly around the fabric until my knuckles turn white. My entire body trembles as I release a roar of fury, the sound splitting the air. It's a sound that promises death to whoever fucking took her, a sound I hope the entire realm heard.

I conjure my wings, unfurling them slowly. The strain of it has me nearly dropping to my knees. I take a slow, deep inhale and force them open, grimacing through the agony wracking through my body, the sheer amount of power and energy it took just to make them appear battering me. The dark span of them snaps wide, catching the wind. I roll my shoulders, the pain ripping through me thanks to the fucking hideous thing that sliced its teeth across me. But it doesn't matter, not when her life is at risk. I launch into the air, my teeth gritted and her cloak dangling from my tight grip.

"I'm coming, little flower," I growl into the night sky.

And I swear to every god that ever existed—I will burn this entire fucking realm down if they have hurt her.

CHAPTER 29
DAISY

Terror roots me to the spot.

I'm sitting on a large stone platform that juts out at the mouth of a cave carved into the mountain, my body aching and blood growing sticky on my face. I press a hand to where the creature dug his claws into my waist, my fingers instantly coated with the warm crimson that seeps through my dress.

Pale crystal columns line the platform edge like signalling lights, each one flickering, casting iridescent light into the darkness.

A figure steps forward from the shadows, and my mouth gapes. His skin is the colour of burnt ember, a dark, ashy grey flecked with silver. His eyes, gods above, his eyes contain the entire night sky, constellations shifting and rippling within them. From his temples, faint aurora-like wisps drift like smoke from a dying flame. His long, obsidian hair that has streaks of metallic silver almost seems to float gently down his back. And a circlet with a shining opalite crescent moon rests upon his brow. He's tall, lean, carved like stone with veins that seem to glow faintly in shades of purple and green. A cloak made of galaxies and starlight billows around him, the sight of it utterly breathtaking. Beneath the cloak, he's layered in wool, leather, and fur. I can't seem to peel my eyes away from him. He's beautiful in an ancient evil kind of way, breathtaking to look at, but at the same time, terror rakes through me at the sight of him now starting to tower over me.

"Kaelith?" I whisper, pain making my voice wobble as my blood continues to trickle onto the stone flooring beneath me.

He pauses mid-step, genuine shock flashing across his stony features. "And how would a mortal like yourself know a man like me?"

His accent is strange, almost British-sounding. He strides closer, kneeling before me whilst placing a single finger under my chin to tilt it up. The touch is so light it catches me off guard, making my breath catch at the eerie stillness in him. It's like the entire realm holds its breath when he's present.

"You are a pretty little thing, aren't you?" He smiles, the sight utterly devastating. "Tell me, what's your name?"

I swallow hard, lifting my chin even higher, pulling away from his touch, despite the tears gathering in my lashes. "Daisy," I say, trying my best to hide the quiver in my words. "The future Queen of Hell."

Kaelith's entire facade fractures, his eyes widening. I swear the stars inside them stutter as the colour drains from his face. He whirls towards the creature that dragged me here, so fast his hair whips me in the face. The anger pouring from him is so intense I can physically feel it.

"You fucking fool," he yells, storming toward him, his voice echoing throughout the cave. "Do you understand who you have brought to me?"

The creature stammers, shrinking into himself. "She is no future Queen of Hell, your majesty. She is but a mortal."

"And yet," Kaelith seethes, "have the whispers not told us of Korithax preparing to marry a mortal, you insolent prick?"

The creature no longer looks like the arrogant beast that stole me into the night. Instead, he looks like a quivering servant, terrified of the man in front of him. What kind of man was Kaelith if a creature as vile as that feared him?

Kaelith's eyes flick back to me, panic rushing into his voice. "My dear, I am—"

He stumbles where he's stood, a thunderous boom shaking the mountain, causing the platform beneath us to tremble. Several of the crystal lights lining the platform shatter as a form crashes down like a meteor from the sky. Cracks web across the stone around him as he lands in a crouch, one knee touching the floor. His wings are flared out and still twitching, the curved spikes at the end of them glinting under the light.

"Korithax," I breathe, so quietly I barely even hear myself say it.

He lifts his head slowly, his chest heaving, sweat lining his brow. The look in his eyes steals the breath from my lungs. They're entirely black, utterly devoid of any of the white that used to reside there. Raw fury rolls from him in waves, the heat that emanates from him hitting me even from the other side of the platform. He's covered in a black substance that's mixed with dried, flaking blood. His hair hangs limply around his face, slicked with sweat and gods knows what else. He looks like he's just torn through an entire army. The creature that took me tries to flee, scrambling backward with a gaping mouth.

"Not so fucking fast," Korithax snarls. In a blur, he grabs the creature by the throat and lifts him into the air with one hand. I see his nostrils flare slightly, his jaw clenching so tightly the veins on his neck bulge.

"You took something that belongs to me," he growls, "and you smell an awful lot like her blood."

"I... I am so sorry, Prince—"

The creature's words cut off in a scream as black fire explodes from Korithax's fingers, burning his throat under his touch. The smell of his scorching flesh makes me gag, and I push my hand over my nose to evade the smell.

"You're very lucky that I don't possess my full magic," he hisses, before crushing the creature's neck in his grip. Korithax holds the lifeless body in his hand for a few more moments, his chest heaving before letting go. The creature's body hits the ground in a crumpled heap, smoke still wafting from the fresh corpse.

I've never seen Korithax use any other power except teleporting. He's utterly terrifying, the true embodiment of a demon King. My king. My soon-to-be-husband. Gods above.

He turns to Kaelith next, prowling forward with an animalistic look on his beautiful face.

"Ah, Prince Korithax," Kaelith begins, hands slightly raised in a defensive position.

Korithax punches him clean in the face without hesitation, not even deigning to speak to him as he pushes past the stunned ruler. His eyes are set solely on me as he drops to his knees in front of me. Korithax's hands are gentle as he wraps the torn cloak around my shoulders. He scans me from head to toe, nostrils flaring at each cut and bruise he spies across my body.

"Little flower," he breathes, cupping my face in his hands. "Are you alright?"

I nod, the tears now spilling over at the sound of his voice, the warmth of his touch against my frozen skin. I fling myself forward without thinking, arms wrapping around his neck as I collapse into his chest.

He grunts slightly, and I pull back on a gasp. "I'm so sorry. Are you hurt?"

He gives me the softest smile I've ever seen grace his face, the sight making my heart flutter. "It's okay. I'm okay," he whispers.

He glances once more at my wounds, then, without another

word, scoops me effortlessly into his arms. He turns to Kaelith, his voice deadly, "I suggest you find us one of your finest rooms immediately. I want your best godsdamn healers there before we arrive. And maybe, if they heal her to absolute perfection, I'll consider not reducing your realm to a pile of ash. Do you understand me?"

Kaelith nods his head once in obedience, not bothering to wipe the violet blood that trickles down from his nose. "Please, follow me."

THE ROOM they bring us into is unlike anything I've ever seen before.

It's carved into the side of the mountain, the walls smooth and gleaming with veins of crystal that pulse softly with light. Massive windows stretch across the far side, revealing the endless stretch of night sky with the northern lights dancing to a symphony only they can hear. The glass is curved and pristine, giving the illusion that the stars and galaxies are within arm's reach. A roaring fireplace of black stone crackles gently on the side wall, casting a soft golden glow that flickers across the ceiling like fireflies.

The bed is enormous, sitting beneath an arch of natural stone that's carved into the wall. The blankets look impossibly plush, layered with furs and deep violet silks that look heavenly. Everything seems to glow faintly, as if enchanted by the very magic of the realm. And by the bed stand several healers, already waiting just like Korithax demanded.

Korithax gently places me atop the soft furs on the bed, my cloak being peeled away by one of the younger looking helpers. A gasp escapes me when they begin cutting the dress away from my body, revealing my black laced bra and matching panties beneath. I burn with embarrassment, but Korithax doesn't look away. Instead, his eyes track down my body slowly, his jaw tightening visibly, a muscle jumping beneath the surface.

"Is she allowed no modesty?" He growls.

"Sorry, sire. We need to access the wounds," a healer responds.

. . .

I SCREAM when the healing begins, gripping the bed sheets as my back arches off the mattress. The pain is excruciating, my ribs feeling like they're splintering, the gashes along my side igniting with searing heat.

"What are you doing to her?" Korithax bellows, storming forward and grabbing a male healer by his robes.

Another one of the healers raises their hands in a calming gesture. "Sir, we are healing her. Our methods are different from those in your realm. We fix everything with our hands, not healing tonics. She has a broken rib and deep wounds along her waist. We are making the bones and wounds knit themselves back together."

"Can't you do it in a way that doesn't hurt her?" He asks, concern lacing his tone as he drops the young male.

"Unfortunately, we do not have the time to sedate her. The wounds are serious and must be addressed immediately. It shouldn't take much longer."

I listen intently, whimpering as they continue to move their hands over the wounds on my body. My eyes fill with tears as I feel my bones physically moving inside of me. The sensation is so horrible that I lurch forward, vomiting over the side of the bed and coating the dark stone flooring.

I look up to see Korithax dragging a chair over, placing it beside the bed where I just threw up. I cringe at how close he is to it, but he just ignores the pile of vomit, taking my trembling hand in his as he sits. With his other hand, he gently brushes the damp hair from my face. I lay my head back on the cool silk pillow, scrunching my eyes closed as the pain continues to wrack my body.

"Look at me, little flower." He whispers. I keep my eyes shut tight, trying to breathe through the agony. "Daisy, darling. Look at me."

His voice is so soft that it makes me open my eyes. I turn my head slightly to meet his gaze, his eyes boring into mine.

"Good girl," he whispers, looking into my eyes, keeping a tight hold on my hand. "Tell me your favourite movie."

"What?" I croak.

"Tell me your favourite movie."

"Um... Me Before You." I pant out through gritted teeth

"What's it about?" He asks.

I scream again, Korithax gripping my hand in his as I dig my nails into his skin. A loud crack sounds across the room, and I know one of my ribs has just fully crunched back into position.

"Focus, sweetheart. What's it about?" He murmurs, stroking his thumb over mine.

I take a small breath, trying to focus on what he asked me. "There's this girl, and she looks after a man who's disabled. He's a bit of a grumpy ass. Kinda like you." I laugh weakly, then hiss from the pain.

He frowns, living up to the grumpy ass label. "I'll let that one slide. Continue."

"They fall in love. But he still chooses to die because he's unhappy. It breaks her heart, but she supports him."

"That sounds... fucking awful." He replies, scrunching up his face.

"Oh, it is. I cry every time." I smile despite the agony I'm in.

"So, why do you love it so much?" He asks, confused.

"Because it's a beautiful story."

He stares at me for a long moment, something unreadable in his gaze. "Then, when this is all over," he says quietly, "we'll watch it together."

"I thought you didn't want to watch movies with me, Kori."

He flinches slightly when the nickname passes my lips, but the soft smile that follows is unmistakable. He likes it when I call him that.

"I think you've earned the right to torture me with one of your mortal movies after today, little flower."

A gentle smile plays on my lips as my eyes begin to flutter closed, the pain slowly dissipating. “I’m tired, Korithax.”

“I know, my queen. You can rest now, they have finished.”

I realise that he’d just distracted me entirely through the last of the pain as I let myself drift, my body already feeling lighter. My eyes close fully, and sleep takes me.

CHAPTER 30
KORITHAX

I remain seated at her side, just like I have the times before. This was starting to become something we did often, and it wasn't something I wanted to continue doing. But at least this time, she wasn't dying. She's okay, she's healing and breathing. And for that, I'm grateful. But that doesn't mean I'm not thinking about ripping that bastard back from the dead just so I could kill him all over again.

Narethyx's were Kaelith's servants. Horrible creatures who would do anything just to please the Duskwalker, including snatching up my little flower and making her fucking bleed. Gods, if I had a second chance at murdering him, I'd make it slow and painful. I would peel the flesh from his bones inch by inch, listen to every scream, and watch as the terror built in his eyes whilst I tore off his wings. I'd happily spend my time burning him alive over and over again for daring to touch what belonged to me.

I glance over at Daisy. She lies peacefully now, her chest rising and falling in a gentle rhythm. I pull a plush blanket up over her, careful not to jostle her newly healed body. I should be content knowing she's safe... but I'm not. Because the image of her, half-naked and bloody on that bed, is seared into my mind. When the healers removed her gown and revealed that black lace set that she was wearing... Fuck. I nearly lost control. Even bruised and broken, she looked like a goddess. Every lush curve, the soft roundness of her stomach, the thick thighs that I wanted to bruise with my fingerprints. Her breasts, perfectly framed by the dark lace, rose and fell with each pained breath that she took. It took everything I had not to kill the healers just for looking at her in her lingerie. I tried to be a gentleman, I really did. But the demon in me came out seeing her in such attire, especially covered in blood. She's turning into everything I want to devour but can never have.

I drag a hand down my face, standing from the chair. Maybe marrying her isn't a good idea. This was beginning to get complicated. I can't touch her the way I want to, and I have a strong fucking feeling it's going to start becoming painful to resist.

I check her one more time, brushing a strand of hair from her forehead, then I turn to leave the room. I don't want to leave her side, but I have a king to see. And he'll be one lucky son of a bitch if he makes it through the rest of the night alive.

~

I STRIDE into the throne room, ignoring the protests of the guards stationed outside the towering crystal-veined doors carved from stone. I slam them open, the sound echoing through the chamber.

Kaelith lounges lazily on his throne, the arrogant prick looking every bit relaxed and not at all like one of his fucking men hurt my queen. A VeliNymph—an ethereal, delicate creature tied to dream magic—is on her knees before him, her mouth wrapped around his cock as he groans.

I clear my throat as I stride towards him.

"Oh shit," Kaelith mutters, shoving the girl back onto her ass.

She lets out a pained whimper before turning to look at the reason she's just been discarded like trash onto the floor. Her eyes widen in horror as she sees me prowling towards them. Her bare breasts are on display, a small shimmer of fabric the only thing covering her lower half. She bows her head instantly, keeping her gaze aimed at the floor, not daring to move.

"Leave," I tell her, keeping my voice as calm as possible. She nods quickly, pushing to her feet. She bows her head once to Kaelith before scurrying out of the room.

"So not only do you kidnap my queen," I growl, stalking forward, "you have girls who are barely adults sucking your cock? She's practically a child, Kaelith."

He straightens, still half-dressed, tucking himself back into his pants. "She's an adult, Korithax. A consenting one at that."

"Hmm, I doubt that somehow. However, I'm not here to discuss whoever it is you decide to fuck."

He swallows hard. "I truly didn't know who she was, Prince. The second she told me, I scolded that fool Dravik and tried to help her up. But then you arrived, creating an absolute shit storm."

He rolls his eyes at me, and it takes every ounce of strength not to snap his fucking neck and leave him to decay on his throne.

I tilt my head, looking straight into his star-flecked eyes. "How else would a fucking mortal end up in your realm, you idiot?"

"I don't know. I was surprised. I wasn't thinking straight. Please—"

I step forward and grab his open shirt, yanking him off of his pretentious fucking seat until his feet dangle.

"Let us get one thing straight, Duskwalker. The only reason you're still breathing is because it's considered treason to kill another royal. And the Divine Six are already too far up my ass right now for me to give them another reason to be pissed at me. But don't mistake that as a bluff. If any more harm comes to my queen, I'll enjoy murdering you, consequences be damned." I pull him closer, his feet desperately kicking. “Consider any weaponry deliveries from Zeriavoss postponed until Daisy herself deems you worthy. Understood?”

He nods furiously, and I drop him back onto his throne.

“Why are you here anyway, Korithax?” He asks, dusting down his shirt like something filthy touched him. Dickhead.

“I require your hospitality whilst my magic replenishes so we can move on to the next realm.”

Kaelith eyes me cautiously, running his tongue over his teeth like he’s trying to suss out if I’m bullshitting or not. “You’re travelling far from home, Prince. For what reason?”

“One that doesn’t concern you, Kaelith. So I suggest you mind your godsdamned business. I want double the supply of shadowleaf resin for the next millennia to make up for your foolishness. Do you understand?”

Their resin was absolutely incredible. The perfect sealant for any woodwork on weaponry, ensuring it never splinters.

“Yes. But do not get it twisted, Korithax. You may soon be king in your realm, but you are in mine now. I do not take kindly to threats, and I will not tolerate much more of your brutality, no matter the circumstances of what happened to your queen.”

I step closer, lowering my voice to a deathly growl, placing a hand on either side of his throne and smirking as he shrinks backwards into the pretentious seat. “And you must not get these next words twisted. I don’t care what realm I’m in, and I don’t care who rules it. If anybody else dares hurt what belongs to me, there will be no realm left for you to rule.”

He flares his nostrils, the only sign of his annoyance. I outpower him in every sense, and he knows it. He dips his chin in a subtle nod. I take it as a sign of obedience before turning to leave, not bothering to show my respect by bowing.

Just as I reach the doors, I turn slightly to face him. “Oh, and Kaelith?”

He looks up warily. “Yes?”

“If I hear that you’re having sexual relations with any female who is not of age or unwilling. I will cut off your cock.”

I give him a wide, demonic smile and slam the door behind me as I leave.

CHAPTER 31
DAISY

When I wake up, the room is quiet.

The only light in the room comes from the soft, shimmering glow of the crystal sconces embedded in the cave walls.

Korithax is slumped in a chair beside the bed. His hair's damp, and he's dressed in only those loose black sleep pants that I've become embarrassingly addicted to seeing him in. He must've showered while I was asleep. A blanket's been draped over me, an act of surprising tenderness that makes my chest ache. On the wall above the fireplace, an intricate device of crystal and metal with soft runes encircling it, reads three thirty-three a.m. Gods. I've been asleep for hours.

I feel absolutely disgusting, the now dried blood feeling itchy against my skin. Carefully, I slip out from under the blanket and climb out of the bed, tiptoeing to avoid waking Korithax. I pad softly towards the door that's connected to the bedroom in search of a bathroom.

When I find it, I let out a low whistle in admiration. Smooth jet-black floors and quartz walls reflect the northern lights pouring in from the domed skylight overhead. There's a grand waterfall shower made of sculpted moonstone, trickling streams of glowing water that cascade down from high above. Silver fixtures shaped like vines curl along the stone wall outside the shower, holding fluffy towels. Bowls of fragrant oils and shimmering soaps line the edges of a carved-out ledge that sits deep within the wall.

I peel off my underwear and bra and step under the cascading water. The moment it touches my skin, I groan in relief. I close my eyes, letting the water flow down my body, appreciating the feel of the blood leaving my skin. But as the waters soak me, the memories start to creep in.

The creature tackling me to the floor, its long claws and insidious smile. The way it sniffed at me like I was defenceless prey. Because that's exactly what I was, even back home. I was weak, pathetic, and utterly incapable of defending myself.

My chest tightens as my breathing comes in quick and sharp. It feels like I'm suffocating, my chest burning as I fight to breathe. But I can't. I can't breathe. My heart pounds, thudding violently as panic sets in, my entire body igniting with fear. I grip my hair with my hands, sobs wracking through me as I fight for oxygen. My knees wobble as my head starts spinning and my ears begin to ring. Suddenly, hands grip my shoulders, making my panic rise to whole new levels.

"NO. GET OFF ME. NOT AGAIN!" I scream, the image of the creature flashing through my head over and over like a strobe light.

"Shhhh, little flower. It's okay."

He pulls me gently against his bare chest, my back pressed against him as he pulls my hands from my hair and wraps his arms round me. His voice is low and soothing, lips brushing my ear softly.

"Breathe, Daisy. You're safe. It's me," Korithax whispers.

I sag into him, my body instantly relaxing. I decide to ignore how easily I managed to relax in the arms of a demon prince, that's a whole other problem for another day. His arms loosen slightly, and I turn slowly to face him. He looks down at me, those onyx eyes dark but soft. I place my hands on his biceps, letting the feel of him ground me. I slow my breathing down, basking in the feel of oxygen filling my lungs, and blink away the tears that line my eyes, not moving my sight from his for even a second.

"I'm sorry," I whisper. "I thought you were that thing. The thing that took me."

"I'm deeply offended. I'm much sexier."

I snort, a borderline hysterical laugh escaping me. "We'll agree to disagree."

His lips tug into a faint smirk. We stand, staring at each other as the water continues to cascade behind me, filling the silence with a gentle patter. I slowly release my grip from his arms.

"Uhm... why are you in my shower?" I ask, suddenly extremely aware of my very naked body. I cross my arms over myself, trying to cover myself.

"I heard you panicking and came to make sure you were okay. I'll leave you to your shower."

He turns, but without thinking, I reach out and grab his wrist. "I'm still a little sore. Could you, um, maybe help me with my hair?"

Lie. I feel fine, physically. But I don't want him to leave me. Not yet. He hesitates for a minute, and I brace myself for him to tell me to stop being so pathetic. But instead, he nods silently, motioning for me to turn around. A bottle cap snaps open, and then his fingers are in my hair, lathering the shampoo. It smells divine—like honey with a gentle undertone of smokiness. I groan softly. His fingers feel like absolute heaven on my scalp. He rinses it out gently, then applies conditioner to my ends. Never, ever, did I think a man would consider conditioner after shampoo. I'm pretty sure every man I knew back home used those freaking ten-in-one shampoos.

"The bottle says let it sit for a few minutes," he says, his voice low.

I turn to face him again, still keeping my arms crossed.

He glances down at me, his brow furrowing. "Why are you hiding your body, Daisy?"

"I... is it appropriate to have my naked body on display?"

"You are to be my wife. My queen."

"Yeah, but that's just for convenience, right?" I mumble, staring at the floor. "I'm sure Hell's full of hotter, skinnier options."

The words sting more than I want to admit. The idea of him with someone else is irrationally annoying. Even if this whole thing is just mutually convenient, the thought of him touching another woman has me yet again questioning my sanity.

"And I'm sure you'll have men visiting your chamber also." He replies, grinding out the words.

I glance up, startled by his tone. I fight back my smile as I see how much his jaw's clenched. "I don't think so." I say, shaking my head.

"No? And why's that?"

"Because... well, before Ethan I was—"

"A virgin. Yes. I'm aware." He responds, cutting me off.

A blush creeps up my cheeks. "Yeah. I was waiting to have sex. I'm not sure what I was waiting for, maybe I just didn't want my first time to be with him. But I guess that choice was taken away from me."

I look down, chewing my lip in shame. He gently places his thumb under my chin, lifting my gaze as his forefinger rests just below my lower lip.

"He may have taken your virginity, Daisy. But that doesn't mean he's taken away your first time."

"What do you mean? Of course he has." I say, tears welling as I try to tear away my gaze. He doesn't let me, instead he grips my chin harder, forcing me to stay looking at him.

"No. He raped you... But rape isn't your first time making love. You still have your chance to do that. It also wasn't your first time having filthy, pleasurable sex. You still have your chance to do that too. He may have taken your virginity, little flower, but he didn't take away your first time for everything."

I smile softly through the warm tears sliding down my cheeks.

His words sink in, healing a part of me I'd grown used to feeling cracked.

"I wouldn't know what to do anyway. The idea of it all scares me for some stupid reason. He was even my first kiss."

I don't know why I'm admitting this. But the way Korithax is currently looking at me makes me feel safe.

He raises a brow. "Gods. So you've probably not even been kissed properly."

"What? Of course I have." I frown.

He tilts my chin up, lowering his face until our lips almost touch and his smoky scent invades my senses. My breath catches, a warmth pooling low in my belly.

"Are you sure?" He whispers.

"I... I don't know," I stammer.

"Would you like to know, Daisy?"

Is the Prince of Hell asking if I'd like him to kiss me? Do I? The butterflies hammering through my stomach right now seem to want me to. The sensation building between my thighs that has me instinctively rubbing them together also seems to want me to.

I nod gently, biting my lip as nerves surge through my body.

He groans softly. "I need words, darling."

"Yes," I whisper.

His mouth brushes mine, tender and warm. I lean in, placing myself on my tiptoes and bracing my hands on his chest as he deepens the kiss. A low growl rumbles in his throat, his tongue parting my lips, exploring me with such intensity it makes the low heat in my stomach turn to bubbling lava. One hand fists my hair gently whilst the other glides down to my hip, gripping tightly. He tastes like whiskey and sin, like fire and spice. A soft moan escapes me as he pulls back, both of us softly panting. I instantly miss the warmth of his mouth against mine. Gods, he was right. I haven't been kissed properly. Not like that.

Ethan used to just give me quick pecks on the mouth, or the occasionally sloppy kiss making our teeth clash if he was trying to push me to have sex with him. But that kiss was full of passion and an unspoken desperation from both of us. I stare up at him, the need in his eyes so apparent I nearly stumble as I notice they're blown. Entirely black, utterly void of any white.

"Tell me, little flower. Is that how he kissed you?" He breathes, his chest still rising and falling quickly.

I shake my head, my thumb instinctively brushing over my swollen lips.

"Words, Daisy."

"No," I mumble, utterly flustered.

He smirks, tongue gliding along his bottom lip as his gaze drops to my now exposed breasts. "Simply exquisite," he murmurs.

"I... I think it's time to rinse the conditioner out now," I stutter, doing anything I can to break the indescribable tension that sits between us. He chuckles softly, telling me to turn around.

~

When I wake up again, Korithax is gone.

The room is quiet, still bathed in the ever-present dusky glow of the realm. The strange clock on the wall now reads nine a.m.. I honestly don't know how I managed to fall back to sleep this morning. Korithax had climbed into bed beside me after once again drying my hair, no chattering teeth needed this time. However, instead of wrapping me in his arms, he simply said goodnight and turned over, leaving me to stare at his large, tattooed back, his wings vanishing once more. I studied him for a while, not being able to drift off easily after the way he had kissed me in the shower. The second we left the bathroom, it was like everything went back to normal, like he was barely tolerating my existence. His constant personality flips had me thinking I'd agreed to marry Hell's version of Dr Jekyll.

I laid awake for what felt like hours, wondering if his body filled with butterflies the moments our lips touched like mine did, or if he was simply just showing me how it felt to truly be kissed.

• • •

A SOFT KNOCK taps against the door.

"Yes?" I call gently, sitting up in the large bed, pulling the covers up to my chin.

The door pushes open, and a tall, willowy woman enters, her skin a pale silver hue, kissed with violet undertones. Her long dark hair sits braided with threads of glowing crystal strands. Her eyes are utterly mesmerising, flickering like candlelight trapped in glass. She's wearing a robe of midnight blue, the fabric billowing like mist as she bows her head politely.

"I'm Serya, one of Lord Kaelith's chambermaidens. I have been asked to assist you in preparing for your next journey."

I blink at her, enthralled by how ethereal she is. She's as captivating as the sky outside. Her aura radiates in a soft green glow around her. I wasn't entirely self-conscious about my looks, but the women in these realms were of a whole other level. I looked as plain as paper compared to them all. Hopefully, immortality makes me look slightly more interesting.

She steps further into the room, smiling softly at me. "Lord Korithax asked me to inform you that he is awaiting you in the throne room with King Kaelith. I believe you have your outfit in your pack, yes?"

"Right," I murmur, brushing the sleep from my eyes. "Let me just go get it."

SERYA HELPS ME DRESS, and I can't help but be flawed yet again by Lyvia's choices. The outfit is absolutely stunning.

A sundress in gold and soft yellow, milkmaid style, cinched at the waist with a corset bodice and straps over my shoulders lined with sunstone crystals. The skirt ends just above my knees, swaying as I move. Tiny golden vines twine along my calves, all the way up to my thighs, attached to the golden shoes on my feet—simple, yet beautiful. Serya carefully braids my hair into two long French plaits, weaving delicate golden threads through them to accentuate my already sunshine coloured hair. My eyes are dusted with shimmering gold eyeshadow, and my lips painted with a luminous, clear gloss that has specks of gold leaf in. She slides a metal cuff up my arm to sit in the middle of my bicep. The piece is gold, vines poking from the band in all directions before meeting in the middle with Korithax's sigil.

This is the most I've looked like myself since agreeing to be queen, yet at the same time, so far from myself that it makes my head ache. These were the types of dresses I would wear in summer, and the yellows and golds screamed Daisy Sandoval. But this dress, this makeup, was far more elegant than anything I would've worn back home.

"You look radiant," Serya says softly, blowing a handful of golden dust over me that clings to my skin, making my pale complexion shimmer.

"Thank you." I blush, offering her a small smile.

SHE ESCORTS me down the twisting corridors of the mountain palace until we arrive at the towering door of the throne room. The air feels colder here, making goosebumps prickle along my arms. Serya bows and leaves me at the threshold, wishing me a safe journey as she saunters away.

I step inside, my eyes scanning the vast room. It's impressive, yet cold. Whereas Fjellheim Heights' throne room was radiant, this room truly lacked any personality other than a few shimmery crystals. It's also empty—save for Kaelith.

"Ahh, Daisy," he says smoothly, rising from his throne. "Please, come in."

I hesitate, glancing around nervously. "Where's Korithax?"

He waves a hand casually. "He said he was on his way to you. You must have just missed each other."

That feels... unlikely. Still, I step forward slowly despite my apprehension. I didn't want to come across as rude, even though I didn't have the kindest of welcomes when I arrived.

"Please, sit." He gestures to a plush velvet seat placed beside his glowing throne.

I move reluctantly toward it, perching on the edge of the cushion, not daring to make myself too comfortable. Something about this feels very wrong.

"I am so unbelievably sorry about what happened when you arrived in my realm," Kaelith says, folding his hands in his lap. "I am truly appalled at the way you were treated."

"You didn't look so appalled when I was bleeding on your floors," I say quietly. "Not until you knew who I was."

"Yes. My mistake." His smile tightens, irritation flickering across his features.

Something about that look made me realise that Kaelith probably wasn't used to having people talk back. I saw the way that creature had reacted when Kaelith was angry. I was starting to see through his facade of warm smiles, calming British-like accent, and cosmic eyes.

"I do hope my healers did a good job. I see they did wonders on that beautiful face of yours. Not a scratch remains."

He reaches over and strokes a thumb over my cheek where the creature had sliced my face. I flinch at the sudden contact, pulling away whilst forcing myself to smile. What the hell did he think he was doing? Was it a weird custom here that they felt like they could touch whoever they pleased, whenever they pleased?

"They did fine," I mutter.

"You know," he continues, clearly ignoring my discomfort as his star-kissed eyes slowly drift down my body. "I had wondered what could have possessed Korithax to take a mortal as his bride. But now, I fear I understand. You are... lovely to look at."

He inhales deep, and I suppress a shudder. "And you smell absolutely divine. Fruit, lavender, with a hint of spice." He slowly licks his lips.

"Thank you," I mutter, rising from the chair. "I think I'll go find Korithax now. Thank you for your hospitality, Kaelith."

I bow my head slightly and turn, but as I go to take a step, his hand lashes out, grabbing my wrist and tugging me back. The sudden force causes me to stumble backwards, causing me to awkwardly fall into his lap. I instantly try to stand back up, but he wraps an arm around my waist, holding me securely to him.

"You, my dear," he murmurs against my ear, trailing a hand up my thigh, "are a prize I am not so sure I want to return. Would you prefer to stay here and be my queen instead? I can give you anything. Power. Wealth." He drops his voice an octave, his voice almost rumbling. "Incredible sex," he mutters against my ear, placing a cold, soft kiss beneath my lobe. "I bet I could make you scream so loud they'd hear it across the cosmos."

I suppress a shudder from the feel of his cold lips against my skin. His hand pushes under my skirt, slowly trailing higher and higher until I feel his fingers brush against my panties. I squirm against him, trying to release myself from his grip.

"I strongly suggest you take your hands off my wife before I cut them off and burn them to ash, Duskwalker."

Kaelith jolts, and I lift my head to see Korithax standing in the entryway, his face an unreadable mask of fury. He releases his grip on me, quickly shoving me to my feet. I stumble forward, just catching myself before I land straight on my face.

"Korithax, it's not what it looks like. She came on to me."

My head whips to him as my mouth drops open in disbelief, but I can't get a word out fast enough.

"She kept saying she wanted my realm, not yours," Kaelith adds hastily.

Korithax laughs, the sound booming through the chamber, cold and sharp.

"Kaelith, I know my queen. And I know that despite how pretty your realm is, she loves the dark and corruption that comes with Hell. Not pretty stars and obnoxious rulers. And most importantly," his eyes travel to me, "she loves me."

A scream tears through the air, and I turn my head back around to Kaelith. My eyes go wide as I watch as fire crawls up his legs, a black flame lashing up his body.

"Since a verbal warning did not suffice," Korithax says coldly, "I hope this does. Next time, I will kill you, Kaelith. I warned you not to take my words as a bluff." He steps forward, extending a large hand to me. "Come, Daisy. It's time we took our leave."

I place my hand in his, his grip punishingly tight as he escorts me from the throne room, Kaelith's screams following us on the way out.

CHAPTER 32
KORITHAX

I'm seething, dragging Daisy through the corridors of Kaelith's cursed palace, my grip ruthless on her hand.

Fury rolls through me like a storm, thunderous and unrelenting. Her otherworldly golden attire glows faintly in the dim light of the realm, but I can barely look at her without seeing red.

“Korithax, you're hurting me,” she whimpers, trying to pull away from my grip.

I ignore her, my jaw clenched so tightly it aches. When we reach our suite, I throw open the door and practically shove her inside. She stumbles, nearly falling over.

“What the hell, Korithax?” She snaps.

I don't answer. I storm into the bathing chamber and grab our pack, slinging it over my shoulder. When I return, I reach for her again, but she evades my grip, stepping back once, then twice.

“Daisy,” I snarl, “it's time to leave.”

She shakes her head. “No. That wasn't okay.”

I laugh bitterly, my rage officially boiling over. “Oh, I'm very fucking sorry that I set your lover on fire.” I step forward, "Now come on, we need to go.”

She takes another step back, sending a whole new wave of fury through me. "Daisy," I growl her name as a warning.

"My lover? Oh my god." She's suddenly storming toward me, her voice rising with every word. "You believe him, don't you? You think I came on to him."

She's nearly a foot and a half shorter than me, but she shoves a finger into my chest like she could knock me off my feet. Her eyes blaze in a way I've never seen.

"How dare you, Korithax?" she screams, voice cracking. "How fucking dare you!"

A growl tears from my throat, and the little restraint I had snaps. I grab her by the throat and throw her down onto the bed. She gasps as I pin her arms above her head with one hand. I place my other hand against her hip tightly, holding her still. My chest heaves as I stare down at her, baring my teeth.

"I don't give a fuck if you came onto him," I growl into her face. "But I won't tolerate being disrespected. I'm tired of these fools not holding our relationship in esteem because we're not yet wed. We will marry. Tomorrow. In Solara. Understood?"

She stares up at me, and her fury is like fire in her veins, matching my own. This isn't a side I've seen of her, and I can't tell if I like it or hate it.

"No," she spits. "Absolutely not. If you seriously think I'd throw myself at someone else, then congrats—I'm not going to be your wife." She glares up at me, seething. "And don't act like this is about honour or betrayal or whatever dramatic nonsense you've cooked up in that demon brain of yours. You were pissed because he touched me. I saw it. The way you zeroed in on his hands like you were ready to murder him. Just admit it."

I release her hands and grip her face, my thumb pressing hard against her jaw, my nose brushing hers as my control teeters on the edge of destruction. The way she's speaking to me, looking at me. I can't tell if I want to fuck her or kill her. Nobody has ever spoken to me with such fury, such disrespect. Yet this small mortal woman thinks she can defy me and not suffer any consequences.

"You will marry me, Daisy. You signed a fucking contract. And as for him touching you—I don't care. Anybody can touch you in any way they fucking like once we are married."

The flicker of pain in her expression is a punch to my chest, but I force my face into ice. Cold and ruthless. I push away from her, standing at the foot of the bed. She props herself up on her elbows, the neckline of her dress threatening to spill out her breasts. My eyes flick away, not letting her body distract me, tempting as it was.

"So what kiss last night—that was—"

"It was nothing," I interrupt. "It was me showing you what a real kiss felt like, like you asked. You are nothing, just a means to an end, Daisy."

She says nothing. Just a single, slow nod with a harsh swallow. Her entire demeanour changes as a cold calm settles over her. She stands, smoothing the fabric of her dress, and pulls her braids over her shoulder.

"Great," she says, voice flat and emotionless. "Let's just get this over with then, yeah? That way, you can go back to pretending I don't exist while we live out our happily never after in Zeriavoss. Pretty sure your realm's big enough for us to avoid each other forever."

I grab her wrist, and without another word, teleport us to Solara.

~

WE LAND, the brightness instantly burning my eyes after almost twenty hours in that fucking realm of perpetual bullshit. So much has happened in so little time, I feel like I'm cracking under the weight of it all. Daisy's attack, the betrayal, Kaelith's hands on her. I'm about ready to be done with this entire mission to turn her immortal if each realm keeps presenting a new way to piss me off.

Not to mention, I now had a fucking wedding to plan because it was clear nobody was going to respect whatever the Hell this was between Daisy and me. Not until I had her securely placed in wedlock. And now, I've got to smile and bow and play the proper prince in front of a goddess who radiates joy and sunlight.

I don't bother telling Daisy anything about the realm this time. I just begin walking the moment I know she's not about to pass out or fall over. The healers had given her something to help with realm travel, but they said she would still feel some effects from it. Thankfully, this time we land basically at the palace. Aran sent letters to the rest of the realms on our journey to let them know in advance of our arrival, allowing us to be approved to teleport in much closer than the outer borders. The only realm that wouldn't be possible was Noxthrallia. But I knew from the start, Noxthrallia was going to be a challenge.

We stand outside tall, golden gates that stretch high above us, their delicate carvings reflecting the golden light that shimmers in the air. The warmth here is incredible, sinking into my skin like a balm, though it does absolutely nothing to melt away the icy storm brewing inside of me.

I remain silent as the gates begin to creak open, pulled by invisible magic. The path ahead is lined with white sandstone, the road blinding in the golden light. Towers of gleaming citrine and polished marble rise in the distance, spires tall in the sky, crowned with golden fire. The smell of sun-warmed flowers and sweet citrus fills the air, and the gentle hum of magic dances in the breeze. The entire royal grounds are open to the sky, sprawling courtyards layered in gold-veined stone. Birds with jewel-bright feathers flit between flowering citrus trees, chirping a song so melodic they sound like harps. If any realm reminded me of Daisy, it was this one.

I begin walking again, not checking if Daisy is following. I know she is. I can sense her aura whenever it's near me, a warm, delicate feeling that follows her wherever she goes. She's been quiet since I threw those words at her like fucking weapons. I hear her footsteps fall into rhythm behind mine as I continue strolling up the long path.

The sun here never truly sets. It goes through sunrise, golden hour, and sunset, never dusk or darkness. Solara, the realm of light and beauty, that provides sun, dawn, and sunset to Earth. The place where Aran got the orb I'd gifted her at Christmas.

And in less than twenty-four hours, I was going to marry a woman here who now probably hated me. Perfect.

We're escorted through wide halls of glimmering sandstone and silk canopies, to where the throne 'room' should be. But of course, it's not a room at all. The throne is nestled in an open glade of light. Circular, column-lined, and filled with soft grass and blooming flowers. Petals drift down from the sky, swirling on the warm breeze. And in the centre, sits a carved throne of peach coloured sunstone, surrounded by benches, water features, and canopies of glowing linen that sway above our heads. Sitting on the throne is Sariya, Goddess of the sun, vibrant as ever.

"Ah, my dear Korithax," she beams, rising to her feet. She glides towards me, and the world seems to brighten with every step. "It has been centuries, my child. How are you?"

She throws her arms around me before I can respond, pressing soft kisses to each cheek. Her scent is golden: warm grass, citrus, and summer air.

"Very well, thank you, Sariya. And you?" I murmur, politely.

"Well, as always, Prince of Hell." She grins, her smile is light itself.

Her eyes fall on Daisy. "And who is this absolute ray of sunshine?" She asks, delight curling into her voice.

She takes Daisy's hands, not waiting for an introduction. "My dear, you look exquisite. Like you were made by my realm itself."

Daisy blushes hard, lowering her head slightly. "Daisy, Your Highness. Future Queen of Hell."

Sariya's eyes sparkle like twin suns. "So this is the poor soul who gets shackled to Mr. Grumpy over here."

I scowl as she grins at me. "I only joke, Korithax. Lighten up." She laughs, a bell-like chime that makes the flowers in her large afro bloom in vibrant oranges and reds.

"Nice pun," I deadpan, rolling my eyes.

"To what do I owe the pleasure of having the future King and Queen of Hell in my realm?" She asks, guiding us towards one of the stone benches that sits by her throne.

"We simply require your hospitality for a day or two while I restore my strength," I reply, taking a seat by Daisy's side.

Sariya tilts her head, her deep bronze skin shimmering with a golden glow under the rays of the sun. Her tight dark curls, streaked with glowing threads of yellow and rose gold, bounce around her haloed crown. More flowers tumble from her hair like confetti.

"You are travelling far, Prince."

"Please, Sariya, I don't wish to discuss it. I do, however, have a more... significant favour to ask, if you'll allow it."

Her smile softens, "Of course, I will. You and your beautiful queen are always welcome here. Just as your incredible mother was. I do miss her dearly."

She places a delicate hand over her heart, golden bangles softly clinking against each other as she moves. Beside me, I feel Daisy stiffen. I glance at her, but she says nothing.

"I was wondering," I begin, the words catching in my throat for a second. "If you would do us the honour of having us married here."

Sariya blinks, her golden irises gleaming.

"You see," I continue, turning to look at Daisy, who's cast in sunlight so warm and soft she may as well be carved from it. "My bride is the embodiment of sunshine. Like a summer's day born into a woman. I could think of no better place to make her my wife than in your kingdom."

Daisy whips around to face me, blue eyes wide and stunned. The sunlight paints her in gold, her freckles like tiny kisses from the sun. For one brief second, I forget the anger. The pain. I only see her, my heart aching slightly at the sight.

Sariya squeals, clapping her hands. "Oh my suns, I would be honoured! I shall have my best staff begin preparations immediately. Oh, this will be wonderful!"

"Please," I add quickly, dragging my gaze away from Daisy. "Something small. She gets shy."

Sariya nods with understanding. "Of course. Now shoo! I'll have a guard escort you to your room. I have a wedding to organise!"

She starts to call for a steward, but Daisy speaks up, voice soft.

"If it's not too much to ask... could we have separate rooms?"

I freeze. That sentence felt like a fucking punch to the gut, all the air in my lungs depleting entirely.

"In my world," she continues, her voice even but distant, "it's traditional to have the bride and groom sleep apart the night before they get married."

Sariya tilts her head with a small, graceful nod. "Of course, my dear. I will ensure you both have your own rooms."

I clench my jaw so hard I'm pretty sure one of my teeth cracks. Tradition... sure. Or maybe she just doesn't want to be near me. Not after what I said. Not after what I did. The burn in my chest intensifies, but I offer no protest. I simply nod as the guards arrive to escort us to our rooms—separate doors, separate wings.

I watch her enter her room, softly clicking the door behind her as she goes. I lower my head, continuing to my own room, feeling like a large part of me is suddenly missing. It feels like we've never been further apart.

CHAPTER 33
DAISY

Solara is... stunning.

And so is its queen. Sariya shimmered like her skin was made of molten gold, her golden eyes ringed with copper so warm they made me feel safe just looking at her. Her whole aura radiated kindness—soft and warm, the total opposite of what I felt in Aurora's Veil. She wasn't just royalty, she was divinity. You could feel it. You could tell the sun was born from her.

My mom would've loved it here. She was sunshine, too. I bet Sariya would've adored her, just like she once adored Korithax's mother. Hearing her speak about his parents reminded me, yet again, how little I actually know about the man I'm about to marry. His past, his family, his anything. And yet here I am, marrying him tomorrow.

I still couldn't wrap my head around it. Korithax hadn't said a single word to me since we got to Solara—not after dragging me through Kaelith's halls, barking at me like a beast, then tossing me onto that bed just to spit venom in my face. 'Just a means to an end.' And yet... He spoke to Sariya like I were sacred. Like I was his. He called me his bride. His sunshine. Said he wanted to marry me here because I was the embodiment of the sun. It made my stupid heart skip like a stone across a lake.

Confusing bastard.

I wasn't even the type to curse, but ever since Korithax stormed into my life, it had become a daily habit. He was infuriating, exhausting, and I was done with the whiplash. So when he pinned me to the bed and spat his venom, I made a choice—no more playing nice.

I'd wear the gowns. Smile when I had to. And be the perfect little bride in public. But in private? I was done trying. The separate rooms weren't about tradition. They were about survival. I needed space, any space I could get, just to breathe. And maybe it was childish, maybe I was running away from it all. But my heart physically hurts.

After that kiss in the shower, I thought something was changing. That maybe this wasn't just duty anymore. The way he groaned, the way he held me, the way he panted like it hurt him to pull away? It hadn't felt like nothing. But clearly, it was. Gods, I'm an idiot. I don't even know why I want him to care. Maybe I am just a pathetic mortal who is clearly desperate for some form of love.

I STEPPED into the room I'd been given for the night and immediately decided I was never leaving. Like, ever. If someone wanted me out of here, they were gonna have to drag me kicking and screaming.

The place was stupidly beautiful. Glowing sandstone walls with massive arched windows that filtered in soft golden light, the silk curtains billowing. Outside, wildflowers exploded across the gardens in endless vibrant blooms. Birds flitted around with golden wings and gemstone-coloured feathers, dipping into glittering pools of crystal-clear water.

The canopy bed stood in the centre of the room, wrapped in gauzy fabrics that shimmered like magic in the sunlight. The white marble floors gleamed, and vines climbed up the walls, blooming with soft, glowing blossoms.

It was all soft, radiant beauty. Everything here was beautiful.

The realm, the people, the queen. Every person I'd passed glowed with rich skin tones kissed in gold and rose. They were truly stunning.

I SAT AT THE VANITY, staring at myself in the mirror. I glowed here. Even though I felt heavy on the inside, like my heart was wading through wet concrete, I was glowing on the outside. Here, in Solara... I could be the sun.

A soft knock interrupts my thoughts. Before I can call out, Sariya sweeps gracefully into the room.

"Daisy," Her voice is so sultry, like sunlight whispering into my ear. "Forgive me for entering without your approval."

"Please," I reply, rising slightly. "This is your kingdom."

She smiles. "It may be my kingdom, sweet child... but you are about to be a queen. A mortal queen, with a demon husband." She perches elegantly on the edge of the bed, folding her robes beneath her. "Do tell me how that came about."

I smile, turning on the vanity stool to face her. "My father had made a soul trade with Korithax. He's... not a very good man. Not anymore. My father offered my soul because it was worth more than his own, apparently." I scoff.

Sariya's eyes widen slightly, the only crack in her graceful composure. "Oh, wow."

"Yeah. Imagine my shock, as a regular college student, when I come home to find a seven-foot demon with horns and a jacked body standing in my tiny apartment."

We both laugh, the sound making something in my chest lift. There was something about Sariya that made me want to talk, to be honest about everything. Still, I didn't mention the marriage contract or the immortality. Some things had to stay mine.

"Anyway," I continued, "it turns out, we just kind of get along. The whole opposites attract, I guess. He's saved me—more than once. And the fact that the ruthless Prince of Hell was so gentle, just for me. Well, it made me fall in love." I smile again, unsure if the words leaving my mouth were still pretend.

Sariya returns the expression, warm and full of such love. "What a beautiful story. But, Daisy, I believe you are not the only one who has been saved."

I blink, my smile falling as I'm entirely caught off guard.

"Korithax has had a troubled life," she continues softly. "Being the future King of Hell could never come without pain. But even for a creature born of fire and fury... he deserved a little light in his life. And now, he has been gifted the brightest light of all."

Her words hit something tender in me, causing my eyes to well up and a lump to form in my throat. "Thank you, Sariya. Your words mean a lot."

"Of course." She stands, extending a hand. "Come. Walk with me?" I nod, looping my arm through hers as she leads me towards the door. "Let me show you my realm, little flower."

WE'VE BEEN WALKING for about an hour, Sariya guiding me through the glowing heart of her kingdom. Every step is filled with wonder, every corner a burst of colour and life. The streets are lined with open stalls displaying woven silks in the hues of sunrise, baked breads glistening with honey, and jewellery made from the finest gold that glints in the sunlight. She loops through cobbled alleys where dancers spin in ribbons of amber cloth, their laughter rising with the chime of bells and the hum of music that sounds like nothing I've ever heard before.

Sariya greets everyone she passes with radiant warmth, a true goddess in her element. Her round, pouty lips never falter from the smile she always has on her face. She lifts giggling babies into her arms, placing kisses on their foreheads. She crouches to the height of shy toddlers, plucking flowers from her beautiful curls to tuck behind their ears.

The way the people look at her—with devotion, joy, comfort—it's no wonder she feels like the sun itself.

We stop at a small stall where an elderly man hands us two cone-shaped pastries wrapped in thin golden paper.

"Try these," Sariya grins. "They're called Solpetas. Flaky pastry filled with citrus cream and dusted in powdered sugar."

I bite into the pastry, and my eyes flutter closed, a groan escaping me. The outside crackles like sugar-glazed pie crust, while the filling is silky and light.

"Oh my goddess. This is heaven," I murmur through a full mouth. Not very queenly of me, but oh well.

She laughs, her smile beaming at my compliment as she continues on, leading me on until we reach the beach that borders the edge of her realm. We sink onto the soft golden sand, and I slip my shoes off, feeling the warmth of it as I wiggle my toes in the soft grains. We watch the sun slowly dip towards the horizon—except here, it never fully sets. The sky remains a hazy blend of amber and rose, locked in eternal golden hour. The waves shimmer under the light and my chest aches at the thought of my two best friends who would love it here.

I can't remember the last time I was at a beach other than the one time I went with Talia and her family. Even Ezra tagged along, and we ended up taking one of my favourite photos of us as a trio. I didn't live near a beach back home, but every summer, we'd rent a little house on the coast—me, Mom, and Dad. Two weeks of sea, sandcastles, and grilled hot dogs. Every night, my mom would count the freckles on my cheeks, her fingers brushing gently over my face. I'd fall asleep to the sound of the ocean and their soft laughter filtering in from the decking that wrapped around the little home. It was the safest I had ever felt, and I would give just about anything to go back. To have the chance to sit beside them just once more, all of us happy, all of us whole.

Sariya waves her hand softly, golden light gleaming at her fingertips as she conjures a glass from the air and hands it to me. I stare in awe at the pale pink liquid sloshing softly, making the ice cubes clink against the glass.

"This is called Blytrine. It's made from the blossom fruit trees that I created entirely myself. A fruit tree that only grows under Solara's light. Please, try. It's delicious."

She watches intently as I sip from the straw, and the first taste lights up my mouth. Like pink lemonade kissed by the sunshine itself. It's refreshing, tangy, sweet, and floral.

"Wow," I whisper, blinking in admiration. "That's incredible."

She smiles proudly. "Thank you, it's my absolute favourite. I'm glad you approve."

We sit a while longer, talking about Earth and Solara as I mindlessly run the soft sand through my fingers, watching it slip through my hands, back onto the golden beach.

"Ah, yes, Earth," she muses, her tone tinged with sadness. "That realm I pour sunshine into."

"I don't miss it much," I admit quietly. "Just my friends."

She nods, understanding in her golden eyes. "It isn't like it used to be. It's so full of misery now, it's a shame."

I hum in agreement, resting my chin on my knees to watch as the waves flow in and out, softly glimmering under the light of the sky.

"There is one last place I would like to show you before the day ends. Will you come?"

I look up to see her already standing, a hand outstretched. I rise, brushing sand from my dress before placing my hand in hers. "Of course."

WE RETURN TOWARD THE PALACE, the streets much quieter than they were before, but instead of turning down the main path, she veers left. We continue walking until we appear in front of an archway nestled in between blushing rose bushes. She gestures for me to walk through, and magic prickles over my skin as we cross its threshold.

"Oh... wow," I breathe.

We've stepped into a hidden garden, birds singing a harmony so delicate it feels like the wind itself is joining in. Water features trickle around the edges, their pools reflecting light like scattered diamonds. In the centre stands a marble pavilion, draped in hanging vines and surrounded by weeping willows that cast shadows in soft arcs across the stone.

"I would live here," I giggle. "No hesitation."

Sariya smiles, but her gaze shifts towards the pavilion, eyes soft. "I have someone who would love to see you. Delilah."

My heart skips at the name, my giggle vanishing entirely. My head whips towards the pavilion, a figure stepping slowly into view.

She's tall, wearing a yellow sundress not unlike my own. Her long blonde hair falls in soft waves to her waist, and she walks with a grace I would know anywhere.

I stumble forward, then another step before falling to my knees. A sob wracks through me so violently that I gasp out the only word I can say.

"Mom?"

CHAPTER 34
DAISY

"Hello, my little sunshine."

I sob, unable to stop the sounds that escape me. My mom is here. In Solara.

No... this can't be real. It can't be real. She died thirteen years ago. But she looks exactly like how I remember—long blonde hair, warm honey-coloured eyes, her smile so full of love.

"How?" I whisper.

"Your mother visits my realm often," Sariya says gently. "Since I'm not only a queen, but also a goddess who harnesses the power of light, spirits from the realm you mortals call Heaven often come by here every now and then. The moment I saw you, I knew exactly who you were, and I called for her."

I look at Sariya, tears pooling in my eyes. "You called her here?"

She nods, smiling softly. "Take it as a wedding gift from me. Now go, speak with your mother. She cannot stay long, unfortunately."

I stand on wobbly legs and run into my mother's arms, sobbing into her shoulder as she wraps me in her embrace. She feels real. Solid. Warm. Her sweet comforting scent wraps around me and I break all over again.

"I've missed you so much, Mom," I cry.

"And I've missed you, my little sunshine. I've been watching when I can, I promise." She pulls back, cupping my face with both hands. "What is this I hear of marriage?"

"About that..."

WE SIT BENEATH THE PAVILION, the sunlight casting a halo around her as if she truly were an angel. I tell her everything—my dad's soul bargain, Korithax, our deal, and the fact I'm going to become immortal. She listens without interrupting, her eyes pinned on me.

"So... you're marrying for a business transaction?" She asks, her eyebrow quirked.

"I guess you could call it that," I say with a weak smile.

She exhales slowly. "Daisy Duke, I swear if I could, I'd strangle your father right now."

I laugh softly, keeping her hand firmly in mine, afraid that if I let go, she'll vanish. "It's okay. I suppose in a strange way if all of this hadn't happened, I wouldn't have gotten to see you again. That alone makes every bit of suffering I've endured worth it."

Her eyes shimmer with emotion. "I would've waited on the other side for as long as it took so I could greet you when it was time. I guess I'll be waiting quite a bit longer now." She laughs gently.

I smile through fresh tears. "If you can visit here, can you visit me in Hell?"

She shakes her head, sorrow flickering across her features. "No, my love. Korithax isn't a God of light, and it takes a tremendous amount of energy to leave the other side. I come sometimes when I want a change of scenery, but I have to rest for so long afterwards. But when Sariya called, I knew it was important. I never imagined I'd see you here. It's strange, isn't it? How all of this exists, and most mortals never know until they die."

"What's it like... on the other side?"

She smiles wistfully. "That, I can't tell you. But it's beautiful. Peaceful."

"And you're happy?" I ask, my lip trembling.

"As happy as I can be without my baby girl. But the cancer's gone, and I'm not in pain."

I laugh gently through a sob. "I see you got your hair back."

She grins, running her fingers through her thick waves. "Came back the moment I crossed over. Like it had never even fallen out."

The weight in my chest lifts just a little. I'm so glad that she wasn't suffering anymore and that her golden locks had returned. She looked exactly like she had before the cancer took over. Her radiance was a rival to Sariya's. Even when she was alive, she was so angelic, so bright.

"I have to go soon, Daisy," she says softly, pulling me into another hug. "But please, try to be happy. For me. I know life has been hard for you since I left, and I'm so sorry. But you are so incredible, and you deserve the world. I hope Korithax treats you like the queen you are."

I scoff. "Fat chance of that happening. He can't stand me."

"That's not true, sweet girl. You'll see in time how he truly feels. He hides behind anger and fear, but there are big things coming your way. You are more than you ever imagined. You're going to change everything, my little sunshine, and I am so excited to watch."

"What do you mean?" I ask.

She smiles, pressing a kiss to my forehead. "You'll see, my darling girl."

She looks up to where she had initially entered the pavilion, a soft glow now pulsing there. "I have to go. But remember—I'm always watching. And if you return to Solara, I'll find a way to say hello."

"Wait. But if you knew everything, why did you ask?" I ask, confusion wracking my brain.

"You looked like you needed to just get everything off your chest." She smiles, stepping away from me.

Typical Mom. Taking my burdens from me, even now. I don't understand how I've survived so long without her. Because I really did need to just get it all off my chest. And now I feel so much lighter.

"I promise I'll come back," I whisper.

"I love you, Daisy Duke."

"I love you too, Mom. So much."

Fat tears stream down my face as I watch her turn and walk away, the soft golden glow swallowing her until nothing but the faint smell of her remains behind. A sob breaks from my chest, but this time it's not one of pain. She's okay, she's happy, she's radiant. And she's still with me—even if I can't always see her. Something inside me shifts, a crack I'd grown used to carrying feels like sunshine is slowly filtering through.

"Daisy?" I turn to see Sariya smiling at me from the garden arch. I rise from the seat I'd been sitting on with my mother and walk toward her, wiping away the tears from my cheeks.

"Can I hug you?" I sniffle.

She doesn't hesitate. She pulls me into her embrace, stroking my hair with a tenderness that feels like home.

"Death is painful for mortals," she whispers. "I hope seeing your mother and knowing she is well has lightened the burden of your grief. You are welcome to return here any time you wish."

"Thank you," I whisper. "You have no idea how much that healed a part of me I thought was gone forever."

She pulls back, her smile kind. "Come now, it's getting late. You need rest before your wedding tomorrow."

My stomach knots. The word wedding slamming me back into reality. I nod quietly, following her out of the garden.

I'm lying in bed, staring at the ceiling. It shifts faintly, mimicking the sky outside. The realm of Solara never truly darkens, but it feels dark tonight. Maybe it's the silence, or the heavy weight on my chest. The shifting light reminds me of the orb Korithax got me for Christmas, which now sits in an abandoned apartment I'm not sure I'll ever see again. I wonder if it's already been emptied out by the landlord since I didn't get a chance to pay my rent before being whisked away.

Seeing my mom felt like a fever dream. Part of me still doesn't believe it really happened. But she was there. I felt her, and I can still feel her touch on my skin, her lingering scent still clinging to me. The soft vanilla and honey smell. A comfort I'd long forgotten.

Tomorrow, everything changes. A part of my life—my freedom, my identity—is going to shift forever. And that scares the shit out of me. I don't have a choice anymore; I signed a contract. And I doubt Korithax would let me go back on it now. In fact, I know he wouldn't; he made that very clear when he pinned me down to the bed, his voice cold and cruel. My mind trails back to my mother's words:

"That's not true, sweet girl. You'll see."

"Things are coming."

"You're going to change everything."

Cryptic as ever. What had she seen? What could I do that would change everything so drastically?

I'm so tired of confusion, of the grumpy, towering demon whose every word seems to undo me. Could I ever have a happy ending with Korithax? Could I love him?

I think maybe I could. At least a part of me does. That kiss in the shower lit something inside of me. I let myself imagine being happy with him in that moment, let myself imagine a long lifetime of being by his side. How naive of me.

The door creaks open, making me jolt upright with a gasp.

Framed in the doorway, backlit by the hues of the sunset outside, stands Korithax. He doesn't speak, he doesn't move. He just stares at me, his face unreadable as he sways gently where he's standing.

"Korithax?" I mumble.

He swallows so loudly I can hear it. Still, he says nothing. A silent, unmoving force that seems to be radiating an energy I can't quite decipher. I slowly climb out of bed, my silk nightgown clinging to my skin. It barely covers anything, but I don't care. Something feels off.

"Korithax... talk to me."

He steps into the room, shutting the door behind him. Then another step. Is he... stumbling? I blink, taking in the mess of his appearance. His hair's tousled, some of it half-wrapped around one of his curved horns. His eyes look exhausted.

"Are you drunk?"

"Well..." He gives me a crooked grin. "Gotta have a bachelor party, right?"

"Sure." I sigh, watching him sway. "Go sit down. I'll get you some water."

He stumbles to the bed, kicks off his boots, and flops backward like a starfish—legs dangling off the edge. Not quite sure what I meant, but sure.

I return with water to find him sitting up, head in his hands. I hold the glass out in front of him. "Here."

He lifts his gaze to mine and takes the glass, draining it in one gulp before handing it back. "Do you want more?" I ask with an arched brow.

He shakes his head, and I place the glass down on the nightstand before stepping back in front of him. "Why are you here, Korithax?"

He looks up, eyes bleary but soft. "I like it when you say my name."

I blink, heat creeping across my cheeks.

"And when you blush," he adds with a soft smile. "You look like a pretty flower. My pretty little flower," he slurs to himself.

My brows furrow. Yeah, he's definitely wasted. His hands grip my hips, pulling me closer between his knees. His thumbs stroke softly across the silk of my nightgown.

"You don't have to marry me, Daisy," he murmurs, eyes trained on the floor.

"What?" I gasp.

He looks up from the floor, yet still he has to look down at me. Even sitting, he's still towering.

"I said, you don't have to marry me. I'll void the contract. I'll even let you stay in Zeriavoss so you don't have to go back to that miserable world."

I pull away from his grip, pacing across the room, biting the nail of my thumb. A mixture of emotions runs through me, but not a single one of them is relief.

"You hate me that much?" I snap, anger forcing its way to the surface. "You'd rather void the contract than marry me?"

"What?" His head snaps to me sharply. "No. That's not what I—"

"You show up here at nearly midnight, slurring words, drunk off your ass after a full day of ignoring me, and now you're saying you don't want to marry me?"

"I didn't say that." His voice grows sharper.

"You basically did!" I yell.

He stands, crossing the room in two strides, backing me against the door. His chest heaves with every breath as he braces his hands at either side of my head.

"I said you don't have to marry me. Not that I don't want to," he growls.

I stare up into those endless black eyes, his shadow draping over me like a blanket of night. "Then why are you offering me a way out?" My voice trembles. "You literally pinned me down this morning and told me I had no choice."

"Because I don't want to force you." His voice softens, breaking just slightly. "I want you to—" He sighs, "I want you to choose me."

My breath catches at his confession. "What?"

He turns away from me, walking back toward the bed. "Forget it. I'm giving you a choice. That's all."

I follow, grabbing his arm—my hand barely spanning his wrist. God, this man was huge.

"You seem to forget... I did choose to marry you, Korithax."

"You did it out of desperation," he mutters. "To escape your old life."

"I wanted to be tied to you!" I almost scream. But I don't. I can't. Not when he's looking at me like this. Not after how he treated me this morning. I can't allow myself to be vulnerable with him again because it never ends well.

"I'll still marry you," I say instead, keeping my face passive. "I made a deal."

He exhales sharply, jaw clenching like he's frustrated with that answer. "Okay. I'll see you at the wedding tomorrow."

"I look forward to it," I say, every inch of the words dripping with forced sarcasm.

He chuckles under his breath. "Me too, little flower. Me too."

And just like that, he's gone. The door softly clicks shut, leaving me in silence—my heart pounding and my mind more tangled than ever. His words and his actions continuously contradict themselves, and I was starting to believe that maybe Korithax wasn't being entirely honest with me, just as I wasn't with him.

CHAPTER 35
KORITHAX

A knock at the door jerks me awake.

Fuck. My head is splitting. I blink at the ceiling, trying to piece together where I am. I'm sprawled sideways across the bed, my shirt wrinkled, boots missing.

Oh. Fuck.

I left them in Daisy's room after I drunkenly stumbled there last night like some godsdamned lunatic. I'd spent the entire day after we'd been separated drinking myself stupid on anything I could get my hands on. I'd needed to just numb everything whirling around in my brain. I'd needed the company of the intoxicating liquids. The separation from her had gotten right under my skin the second she'd closed the door to her room.

I groan, rubbing a hand down my face. What a mess. I had made the decision two bottles deep not to force her into being shackled to me, but she still said she'd go through with the marriage anyway.

"I made a deal."

Her words still slam into me like a blade to the chest. I don't know why I wanted her to want to marry me. I don't know why I expected her to choose me—not after everything I've done. The way I treat her, I'm lucky she doesn't stab me in my sleep. I was just so angry, and I'd taken it out on her.

But I wasn't angry at her; I knew she hadn't made a move on Kaelith. Daisy isn't like that. She's too sweet, too soft. Too good. I saw the way our kiss shook her to her core. Her blushing cheeks, her glassy eyes—gods, if that was her reaction to a kiss, I can't even imagine how she'd react if I—

Another knock cuts through my thoughts, saving me from what was about to be another completely inappropriate fantasy of the golden-haired girl who haunted my dreams.

"What?" I bark, my voice raspy.

"Sire, I am here to assist you with your morning preparations for the wedding."

Right. My fucking wedding.

"Come in," I mumble, rising out of the bed.

Two attendants enter—a tall, androgynous male with dark bronze skin, and a female with radiant brown skin, her eyes molten gold. The male carries a large garment bag; the female balances a tray of food with practiced ease.

"Your suit, shoes, and breakfast, Lord Korithax." The male says with a respectful nod.

"Do you require assistance dressing, sire?" The girl asks, her cheeks flushing a soft rose gold as her gaze lingers far too long.

I scowl. "No. Get out. I'm perfectly capable of getting myself ready." She lowers her head in embarrassment.

"How long do I have?" I grumble, praying to whatever god that's listening that it's at least a few hours.

"An hour, my lord. I will knock again when it is time to leave and escort you to the ceremony."

I internally groan and watch as they bow and exit. The girl's lingering look irritated me more than it should. I'm used to flirtation; hell, normally I'd return it. Maybe even take it further. But lately... I haven't even looked at another woman, never mind considered fucking one.

I EAT the breakfast they left behind—a plate of Solaran sunfruit slices drizzled with honey, spiced flatbread with a golden glaze, and a warm drink that tastes like cinnamon. It's pleasant, but not enough. I reach for the glass bottle of nectarwine—amber-hued, thick like syrup, and sweet enough to burn the throat. I shoot it back in one gulp, but I know it won't help the emotional turmoil swirling inside my gut and head.

I sigh, stepping over to where the garment bag is draped over a chair next to a large, leaning mirror. I dress quickly, ignoring the uneasy feeling flitting in my chest. The suit is a tailored black ensemble with subtle red undertones. The collar is edged in blood red; my sigil is stitched into the lining in crimson silk. My shirt is fitted and is as black as night, a matching coloured thin tie hugs my throat. My pocket square is a soft yellow, embroidered around its edges with glowing golden thread. The boutonnière is a bundle of wild daisies and golden wheat, intertwined with sprigs of solthera—a fragrant green plant native to Solara, similar to eucalyptus, but with sunlight-kissed leaves that shimmer faintly.

My boots may be gone, but the shoes they brought are polished to a mirror shine. Gods, I hate them. I tie my hair back into a knot at the back of my head in the middle. I didn't like it in a low knot; I looked like a pretentious asshole. A few loose strands hang at the side of my face. I stare into the mirror, deeply inhaling.

"This is it, Korithax," I murmur on an exhale. "No going back. You're about to marry the mortal girl who flipped your entire world upside down."

A knock at the door interrupts my self-loathing. The male attendant, standing on the other side, clears his throat.

"It is time, my lord."

My palms are sweating, and I don't know why. This is just a

formality. Just a contract. So why the fuck does my heart feel like it's about to crack open in my chest?

~

SARIYA HAS TRULY OUTDONE HERSELF.

Despite it being bright as fuck—and nothing like what I'd ever imagined my wedding would look like—it's beautiful. Painfully so. And exactly what Daisy would choose.

The ceremony is set outside, under the endless Solaran sky that bathes everything in golden light. The aisle is a soft path of ivory stone, flanked by swaying grass and wildflowers that bloom in riotous colours—sunset orange, soft blush, buttery yellow. Canopies of sheer fabric ripple gently overhead, strung between tall white columns. The altar is a small sunstone podium nestled beneath a golden arch woven with vines and hanging blossoms. Pale pinks and golds, brilliant oranges and warm reds, all layered like fire caught mid-bloom.

Sariya stands beneath it all, glowing as always, wearing a long golden gown that drapes across one shoulder like a sash, a small book resting in her hands. There's no crowd, no audience. Just me, her, and soon, Daisy. Thank the gods.

I stride down the aisle, my shiny fucking shoes crunching lightly over scattered petals. When I reach the arch, Sariya greets me with a kiss to each cheek, her perfume warm and floral.

"This is beautiful," I murmur. "Exactly to her taste. Thank you for all your hard work, Sariya."

She waves a dismissive hand, smiling. "Ah, it was just my idea. My incredible staff are the true hands behind it all. How are you feeling, sweet child?"

"Fine," I reply, too quickly.

Not fine. Absolutely not fine. Was I... nervous? Was that what this was? My hands are sweating, my jaw won't unclench, and I swear my pulse is racing fast enough to rival a battle drum. I don't get nervous.

I'm the heir to Hell, the most feared ruler of all the realms. I have battled beasts, witnessed centuries of torment and pain—and somehow, the idea of marrying this soft, stubborn mortal girl has my heart clawing at my ribs.

"You're sweating, Korithax. And I don't think it's the heat," Sariya teases.

I laugh under my breath. "Okay. Maybe I'm a little nervous."

"That's understandable," she says, smoothing out her dress with one hand. "Daisy is a beautiful woman. You're a very lucky devil."

"Again with the puns," I mutter, my face deadpan as I pick at a piece of invisible lint.

She grins. "I hope you don't mind," she adds, lifting the golden-edged book in her hands, "but I've designated myself officiant of this wedding."

I smile softly at her, truly grateful for everything she's done. "I couldn't think of a better person."

WE STAND THERE in silence for a moment, and I crack my neck to release the tension coiling through my body. My hands itch, and my heart slams over and over as I wait for what feels like an eternity.

"It's time to see your bride, Korithax," Sariya says gently.

I glance toward her, her radiant face beaming at me. Soft harp music begins to play from somewhere unseen, the notes drifting through the warm air. I turn my gaze from Sariya and watch the end of the aisle, my eyes unblinking. Then I see her.

She turns the corner, standing at the end of the aisle, her arm laced through someone's whom I immediately recognise. Standing there, arms linked with hers in a black form-fitting suit and a bowtie, is Aran. Of course, it's Aran. The soft bastard adores her, just like everyone who meets her instantly adores her.

Gods... my mouth goes dry. She's not just beautiful. She's not just radiant. She is sunlight—wrapped in silk and hellfire, spun into flesh and flame. And she's walking toward me, toward forever, toward damnation. And she's doing it like she was born to be a queen of Hell.

If I live to be fifty thousand years old, I'll spend the entire time never understanding how the stars bent so violently in my favour as to place her in my path.

For the first time in my long, wretched life... I feel unworthy.

CHAPTER 36
DAISY

I'm standing at the end of the aisle, heart hammering, palms sweating, legs trembling as I stare at the man who's about to become my husband.

This morning felt like a fever dream. I woke up to two sweet, glowing servants who brought in breakfast, my shoes, and my wedding dress. I couldn't eat a thing. My stomach felt like a stormy sea, churning so violently I was sure I'd vomit.

One of the girls, Maren, helped me into the gown. She was tall and soft-spoken. Her skin shimmered with undertones of gold, her hair braided into a crown woven with glinting ribbons. She had a gentleness to her that eased my nerves, even as her fingers fastened each delicate button up my spine.

The dress itself was breathtaking. Pure white, with a lace bodice and a sweetheart neckline that hugged me in all the right places. The skirt flowed in soft layers with delicate petals in blush pink and ivory scattered across the fabric. Around my neck sat a necklace of diamonds and rubies, perfectly matching the stones in my engagement ring.

My hair was done up with soft curls twisted back into a messy low bun, woven through with tiny flowers, with stray curls framing my face. My makeup was soft, accentuating the freckles that had bloomed across my skin since arriving in Solara.

The shoes were perfect—white heels, with delicate daisies scattered across the strap that sat just above my white-painted toes. A thin ankle strap sparkled with faint yellow sunstone. I hope I didn't puke on them like I felt like I was about to.

A KNOCK SOUNDED at my door, and I gasped when Aran walked in—dressed to perfection, holding a bouquet of daisies, wheat, and something he said was called Solthera.

"Aran?" I breathed, rushing into his arms.

"I thought I'd walk you down the aisle," he said, voice thick with more emotion than I'd ever heard from him. "If you'll allow me to do the honours, of course."

Tears welled in my eyes as I hugged him tighter. "I'd love that."

He handed me a small box, and inside were the most beautiful teardrop ruby earrings I'd ever seen.

"For you, little sunshine."

AND NOW HERE I STAND, about to walk toward the demon prince who has turned my life upside down. The soft harp music plays in my ears, and Aran gently guides me down the aisle. Sariya has outdone herself; the space is nothing short of magical. A golden arch wrapped in flowers and glowing silk sits at the end of the aisle, where Korithax waits beneath like a shadow caught in sunlight.

I wonder what Ezra and Talia would say if they saw this. I'm pretty sure Ezra would faint. Gods, I miss them so much.

We reach the altar, and Aran kisses my cheek, gently taking my bouquet before stepping aside. I turn to Korithax, his hand held out for me. I place mine in his, walking up to meet him. Is he... sweating?

"Today," Sariya says, smiling warmly. "I have the absolute pleasure of joining Miss Daisy Sandoval and Lord Korithax in marriage."

"You really don't have a last name?" I whisper.

He smirks. "That's kind of a mortal thing."

"Oh." Huh. That's... weird.

"Korithax," Sariya begins, her voice rich. "Do you take Daisy as your wife, your queen, your love, and your equal—from now until the old gods claim your soul?"

"Until the old gods claim my soul," he repeats, voice quiet but firm. He lifts my left hand, a subtle tremble in his grasp.

"And Daisy, do you take Korithax as your husband, your king, your love, and your equal—from now until the old gods claim your soul?"

I look up at him, his pitch-dark eyes catching the gold of the sun.

"Until the old gods claim my soul," I repeat his words.

"Perfect!" Sariya beams. "Daisy, would you like to share your vows first?"

Oh shit. A speech. Of course, there's a speech.

I clear my throat. "Um. Sure." I take a small breath, voice trembling slightly.

"Korithax, you came into my life when I least expected it—grumpy as ever—and flipped it completely upside down." A small, nervous laugh leaves me. "You've saved me more times than you realise. You became my comfort... a part of my life I never want to lose. And for that, I am grateful." I force myself to keep going. "Despite our journey not being conventional, I'm thankful to the gods for what my father did. Because without his selfish actions... I never would've met you. So... thank you, Dad, for accidentally giving me the first man who's ever made me feel safe as an adult."

Korithax stares at me so intently that I glance away, cheeks flushed.

Sariya dabs at her eyes with a tissue. "Just... beautiful. Korithax?"

He clears his throat, taking both of my hands in his.

"Daisy," he begins, his voice deep and steady. "I never expected the day I broke into your apartment would be the day a mortal girl would break into my life. You've changed everything—surprised me in ways I didn't think possible."

His grip tightens ever so slightly.

"I've lived twenty thousand years in darkness. And never once did I crave the sun... until you. You make me wish I had lived a gentle life, just so I had cleaner hands to hold you with. But I promise to spend the rest of our lives keeping you safe, loved, and worshipped."

I stare at him, mouth slightly open in shock. His words burn through me like fire, even though I know they're not true.

Sariya lets out a sniffle. "Oh, Korithax, you love-struck fool. You speak such beauty."

And lies, I remind myself silently.

She steps forward, handing Korithax a curved ceremonial blade with a ruby-red handle. My eyes widen.

"Uh... what's that?" I whisper.

"In Hell, we don't exchange wedding rings," Korithax murmurs. "The bride keeps the engagement ring, but the husband wears none. Instead, we merge blood."

I grimace. "Of course we do."

He slices his palm, red blooming along the cut, then passes the blade to me. I hesitate, then follow suit. A sting shoots across my palm, followed by a line of blood.

"Place your palms together when you're ready."

I press mine to his, and his hand closes around mine gently. A shock of heat zips through the wound, pulling a gasp from us both simultaneously.

"What was that?" I breathe.

"I don't know," he murmurs, confusion etched across his face.

Sariya just smiles, like she knows something we don't.

"By the power of light and love," she declares, her voice ringing clear, "I now pronounce you husband and wife. Korithax, you may kiss your bride."

He pulls me in with an arm around my waist, the other rising to cup my cheek, his wound already healed. My breath hitches as I watch him lean forward. He kisses me softly, reverently. I melt into him, my hand brushing his jaw as I kiss him back. A low growl rumbles from his chest.

For a moment... I let myself believe it's real. That maybe, just maybe, this isn't all an act.

THE FOUR OF US—SARIYA, Korithax, Aran, and I—sit at a round candlelit table outside, golden hour wrapping everything in soft light. The air carries the sound of soft music, delicate notes from invisible instruments playing like a gentle tune as we dine on tender roasted meats, golden-crusted breads, and wine that sparkles in our glasses in the sunlight.

Aran and Korithax talk like brothers reunited, their laughter easy and relaxed. I don't think I've ever seen Korithax smile that much. Sariya and I talk quietly, the goddess's presence as soothing as ever.

"Thank you for today," I say softly. "It's been truly beautiful."

She smiles, her copper ringed eyes gleaming. "Anything for a fellow queen and goddess."

I laugh, shaking my head. "Future queen, sure. But certainly no goddess."

"I said what I said, sweet girl." She hums, and I swear there's something in her tone that makes my skin prickle.

Before I can ask, Aran stands and taps his glass.

"A toast," he says, lifting his wine, "to my brother, and the woman who seems to be taming him. May your rule be long, and your love... tolerable."

I snort. Sariya grins. We all raise our glasses.

"To the future King and Queen of Hell," Sariya says, voice full of warmth.

The wine is sweet, the moment sweeter. For a second, I almost feel content.

"Do people dance here?" I ask, half joking.

His brow arches. "You want to dance?"

"Not particularly," I deadpan. "But I figured we should get at least one awkward, wedding-style shuffle out of the way before I'm stuck with you forever. Following tradition and all."

That should cover up the fact that last night wasn't just about avoiding him.

He smirks. "Very well, wife."

He pulls me close, one hand on my waist, the other holding my hand like we've done this a thousand times before. We sway in small circles, and I almost step on his feet twice. He doesn't laugh, but I don't miss the way the corners of his mouth twitch.

"You're terrible at this," he murmurs.

"I never claimed to be good."

We finish the dance and pulled apart awkwardly, Sariya applauding us as I blush.

She turns to us with a sly grin. "The honeymoon suite is ready. I hope it's to both of your liking, so you can enjoy the rest of your beautiful day in peace... or not." She winks.

Heat blooms across my cheeks. "Thank you," I say, my voice shy and full of gratitude. I turn to Aran and pull him into a tight hug. "Thank you for being here."

"I shall see you when you return, Your Highness." He teases gently.

"I'm not a queen yet, Aran. And please, call me Daisy."

"Yet," he says with a smile. "But of course, Daisy."

Korithax turns to me, offering his hand. "Shall we?"

I hesitate, but place my hand in his and nod, and together we follow Maren toward the suite we would share for the first time as a married couple.

Gods help me... I was about to spend the night with my seven-foot demon husband.

CHAPTER 37

KORITHAX

She was my bride. My wife. My Queen.

And now she walked hand in hand with me to our honeymoon suite, wearing the most beautiful gown I'd ever seen on any woman. She looked like a living, breathing goddess.

And she was mine. Theoretically speaking. I knew she didn't actually belong to me. She couldn't stand me. But for now, I was going to let myself stay in the illusion of being happily married, just for tonight.

Maren escorts us to the large citrine doors, bows once, then takes her leave. Daisy steps forward to open the door, but I place a hand on her shoulder to stop her.

"Well, since you're so adamant about keeping up tradition—like you were last night—" I mutter sarcastically, "let's continue the mortal customs, shall we?"

"What do you mean—"

Her shriek cuts off her words as I scoop her up into my arms and kick open the door, carrying her over the threshold like mortals do for good luck... or for some other dumb shit. She giggles, slapping at my chest lightly.

"Put me down, you idiot."

I place her gently on the floor—but keep her in my arms just a moment longer.

"I like that sound," I murmur.

She doesn't respond, instead she averts her eyes and starts looking around the room in awe. I know I should be colder and keep my distance. But something about her laugh unravels all the edges I've spent centuries sharpening. And gods, it pisses me off. I don't want to feel that way, but regardless, that feeling sits there, clawing at my chest. It's not softness I feel towards her. But I feel the need to be less of a monster around her, even if I'm not entirely sure how.

The room's large—palatial, even. A massive four-poster bed sits in the centre, draped in sheer canopies that release a soft rain of petals, though none ever touch the sheets. Floor-to-ceiling folding doors stand wide open, letting in the warm breeze and the gentle sound of waves rolling in from the ocean. Pink and coral hues from the sun bathe the room in soft light, and golden butterflies flutter around us, leaving shimmering trails behind them. A wraparound balcony surrounds the suite, white gleaming marble that reflects the sun.

She steps outside, resting her hands on the marbled railing, and tilts her face toward the sun. She closes her eyes, inhaling deeply, looking so utterly at peace. I pad up behind her and stop at her back.

"Happy wedding day, little flower," I mumble.

"I saw my mom yesterday," she responds, ignoring me yet again.

So that was Sariya's surprise. She'd been glowing with excitement all morning, refusing to tell me why. I had no idea she even knew who Daisy's mother was—but of course she did. If anyone could bring her here, it would be Sariya.

"That's... incredible," I manage, unsure what else to say. "How was it?"

She turns to face me, eyes glistening. "Amazing," she breathes.

"She looked exactly like how I remembered. I've missed her so much."

A tear escapes, running down her cheek. Without thinking, I reach up and brush it away with my thumb. She doesn't flinch; instead, she leans into my hand with her eyes closed and exhales slowly.

"She also said something about you."

I stiffen. Fuck. "What did she say?" I ask quietly, still stroking her cheek. Her skin is so soft. Untouched by war, by centuries of rage. So unlike my own.

Her eyes slowly open and I swear they burn straight through to my soul. "She... she said it wasn't true. When I told her you can't stand me."

I look into her eyes. Those fucking eyes. She asked me my favourite colour back in Aurora's Veil. I told her black. It wasn't the truth—but I didn't know that at the time. No one had ever asked me something so... simple. But that, I thought about it. Really thought about it. And I realised, my favourite colour isn't black. It's the ocean. The sky. The exact shade of a perfect summer's day. Because all of them? They live in her eyes.

"Right," I murmur. "And you believe that? That I can't stand you?"

She nods and pulls away from my touch. "Can you blame me, Korithax?"

She tries to move past me, but I cage her in against the balcony railing, hands braced on either side.

"You're correct," I say. "I can't stand you."

Her brows furrow, and she pushes against my chest. "I thought so. Move, Korithax. I don't want to listen to you spitting any more hatred at me. You've done that enough."

"Stop and listen to me, Daisy," I growl.

She storms past me into the room, struggling to remove her gown with the endless row of buttons down her spine. She huffs, throwing the skirt like it's going to help.

"Please," I bite out through gritted teeth.

Manners weren't exactly in my repertoire. I was used to getting what I wanted—no questions, no niceties. But this girl? She pushed every button I had, tested every limit without even trying. Still… I told myself I'd try. For her. So if saying please is what it takes—then fine. So be it.

She freezes and turns slowly, staring at me in shock. "Did you just say please?"

I roll my eyes. "Don't be so dramatic about it."

She snorts a quiet laugh, then turns so her back is facing me once again. I step behind her, placing my fingers against the top button.

"Let me help."

She stiffens for a brief moment, then nods, and I let my fingers graze her skin as I begin undoing each button one by one.

"I can't fucking stand you," I murmur, voice low. "Because somehow… you, a mortal girl with too much light and too much mouth, has more power over me than any god ever has."

I trace my thumb along her spine, just to feel her again. I hate how much I crave her.

"You think if I didn't care, I'd have stayed by your side after you tried to kill yourself?" I pause, clenching my jaw. "You think I set Kaelith on fire for fun?" I snort, dark amusement curling at the edges of my annoyance. "Though I'll admit, his screaming was satisfying."

I lean in, my lips brushing the shell of her ear. She shudders, and I swear I feel it in my bones.

"When I saw his hands on you, Daisy, I wanted to rip his realm from existence. I would've, if you'd told me to."

Her breath catches, her body going rigid under my hands. I know I'm scaring her. But it's the truth, and I refuse to sugar-coat the storm inside me.

"I might rule Hell," I whisper, "but you rule me."

I undo the final button and pull my hands away. She turns to face me instantly, clutching the dress to her chest, her eyes wide with disbelief. I know words won't fix this. Not after what I've done, what

I've said. So I step forward without another word and lift her into my arms. I carry her across the room and lower her onto the cushioned chair by the window. She looks like a queen already. My queen.

I lower to my knees in front of her.

"What are you doing?" She whispers.

I look up, locking onto her eyes. I want her to see me. All of me. Not the demon prince. I want her to see the broken, furious, hollow thing that she's somehow managed to crawl inside and set ablaze.

"Daisy," I breathe, "I've been cruel. Arrogant. A fucking bastard. But I swear to you—I'll spend the rest of eternity making up for it." I press my hand to her knee to steady myself. "A king of Hell doesn't kneel for anyone. But for you? I'll kneel. I'll worship. I'll fucking burn the realms."

Her lips tremble as tears fall silently down her cheeks. Her eyes look into mine, like she's seeing something worthy. I'm not. But gods —I want to be. I hope she can see that maybe, under all the power and wrath, there's still something inside of me that deserves her.

"Say something, Daisy." I breathe.

She sniffles. "So... that kiss?" She asks quietly.

The one I told her meant nothing. I hold her gaze and tear down what's left of my walls to let her see inside.

"That kiss?" I say hoarsely. "Meant everything."

CHAPTER 38
DAISY

There he was.

On his damn knees, saying all the things I swore I'd never hear from him. The way his suit clung to his body, his dark hair falling into those stupidly intense eyes. Eyes that were somehow soft now and not full of hatred. The future King of Hell was on his on knees for me. Gods help me, the heat curling in my stomach at the sight. Low and traitorous, making my thighs press together to alleviate the pressure building between them. My body was all in at the sight of him. My heart? Hesitating. My brain? Screaming.

He'd been awful to me. Awful. He'd thrown words like daggers, made me feel like I was nothing, and treat me like some annoying little insect he was being forced to endure. And now here he was, kneeling and being vulnerable. Saying I ruled him, like that wasn't the most insanely confusing thing to hear.

I wanted to shove him as much as I wanted to kiss him. I wanted to scream in his face and then maybe let him tear my dress off me right here on this freaking chair.

Could I forgive him? Hell no. Not right now. But could I stop myself from wanting him? Even a little? Also no. And I think I hated that the most.

I WIPE MY FACE, trying to hold myself together. "I don't know what to say," I whisper, my voice shaking more than I want it to.

He nods once, like he expected that. Then he rises, slow and tense, dragging a hand through his hair. He growls, ripping out the band holding his hair and letting those dark waves fall around his face. Gods, he looked good with it tied back. But loose like this? Perfect. It framed his sharp jaw, those lips I couldn't stop thinking about since the last time they were on mine.

"I understand," he says softly. "I don't deserve your forgiveness. But I'll earn it, Daisy."

And just like that, my traitorous heart starts thumping again, louder than my common sense. I bite my lip, unsure of what the hell to say.

"Stop that," he says immediately.

I blink. "Stop what?"

"Biting your lip."

I do it again without thinking. Nervous habit, clearly.

"Daisy." His voice drops into a deep growl.

"Sorry," I mutter, cheeks burning. I'm mortified and also... weirdly smug about it?

"You have no idea what the sight of you biting your lip does to me."

Butterflies. There they go. Fluttering like idiots inside my chest. Traitors, every last one.

"What does it do?" I ask, this time biting my lip on purpose.

Everything seems to shift. His eyes darken, and his head tilts in a predatory way.

Oh. Shit.

He shrugs off his suit jacket and tosses it over the velvet bench at the foot of the bed. His eyes never leave mine as he unbuttons the cuffs on his midnight black shirt and rolls his sleeves up to the elbows—exposing his veined forearms. His tattoos seem to pulse like molten ink beneath his skin. I clench my thighs even tighter at the sight of him. I can feel myself practically panting as I watch him.

He steps forward and grips my chin, forcing me to look up at him, "Daisy," he says, his voice like thunder restrained. "I'm trying. Gods help me, I'm trying to be a better man for you. But if you keep looking at me like that..." his hand tightens ever so slightly. "I won't be able to hold back."

I should stop. Be logical about this. He's an ass. A demonic ass who has been nothing but a bastard to me. But is that going to stop me? Of course it isn't.

So instead of telling him to shove it, I whisper, "What happens if you don't?"

His eyes flutter closed for a second, like he's holding himself together. The tension rolls off him in waves, and I can feel each one crash into me violently as I continue to clench my thighs together to alleviate the growing pressure between them.

"Daisy, sweetheart," he grits out, "I can smell your arousal."

"You can WHAT?" I shriek, slapping a hand over my mouth in pure horror.

He chuckles darkly, and the sound skitters down my spine, igniting goosebumps all over my skin. His eyes open again, and the man I'd come to know is gone. What's looking at me now is something primal. Feral. Something crying to be unleashed.

"I'm giving you one chance," he says, his voice like silk. "Tell me to get the fuck out of this room. But if you don't, Daisy... I won't hold back. Not tonight."

I try to form a logical thought. But all I can focus on is the way he's looking at me.

"Why would I tell you to leave?" I ask, breathless.

"Because, little flower," he says, stepping even closer into me, his voice pure sin. "I want to put you on your knees. I want your mouth around me. I want you trembling and begging, and I don't have it in me to be soft tonight. If that's what you need, I'm not your man. Not tonight."

He leans in, his forehead against mine, his voice trembling with restraint. "But I promise you, when I'm done, you'll look at me like I hung the stars."

My mouth is dry. My body is not. I can feel how badly I want him. And I hate it. Hate that I want someone who's been such an asshole. Hate that I ache for him like he hasn't broken me over and over.

I don't know what I'm doing. I don't have the experience. But I know what I want. And right now, I want him. This.

"Stop overthinking," he says sharply. "You don't need to worry, I'll be in full control."

His hand is still on my chin, and my body is burning under his touch. Every nerve is on high alert.

He stares down at me, deadly serious. "Tell me to leave. Or give me permission."

I should tell him to go. I really should. But my body is a traitor, so instead, I lean forward and press a soft, hesitant kiss to his lips.

He growls, deep and guttural. The next thing I know, I'm in his arms, my legs around his waist, his mouth on mine like he's starving. My back presses into the soft silk of the bed as he sets me down with my legs still wrapped tightly around his waist. He doesn't break the kiss—not even for breath.

I moan into his mouth, which earns me a feral growl against my lips in response.

"Fuck, Daisy," he groans, "you have no idea what you do to me."

His hands skim up my sides, barely gentle. I can tell he's trying to hold on to that tiny bit of restraint. I can feel it in the way he breathes, in the way he trembles, his muscles twitching beneath my touch.

"I'm barely holding on here," he breathes.

"Then don't," I whisper, my voice trembling. "Don't hold back."

He pulls back just enough to look at me. Those pitch-black eyes wild, his jaw clenched, his chest rising and falling with sharp, hungry breaths.

"I could ruin you," he says softly. "I could destroy you, little flower. Mark you so deeply you'll never recover."

"I don't want to recover," I breathe.

That's all it takes.

One violent rip, and the fabric splits like paper, baring me to the warm air. I'm swallowed by the fire in his eyes. He's staying true to his word, not gentle at all.

"Look at you," he mutters, dark and possessive. "Laid out like an offering for the devil himself."

His thumbs drag across my nipples, slow and deliberate, sending lightning straight through my spine. I clutch at his forearms—thick, veined, unrelenting—needing something solid while the rest of me feels like it's about to disintegrate.

"You were made for this," he says through panting breaths. "Made to be ruined by me."

He lowers his mouth to me, devouring my breast with hot, relentless strokes. His tongue circles the sensitive peak before he latches on, sucking hard enough to make my back arch off the mattress.

"Korithax—" I breathe, arching into him.

He growls against my skin, the sound vibrating through me and setting every nerve on fire. He bites down with his pointed canines digging into my flesh, just shy of pain, causing me to whimper as the sharp heat flashes between my legs. My thighs clench, desperate for friction. For him.

"Fucking perfection," he mumbles between licks and bites. "Every inch of you. Every. Fucking. Inch."

My thoughts scatter like stardust as his mouth continues its descent down my body, nipping and marking my skin. By the time he reaches my hips, I'm trembling, nails digging into the sheets, gasping for air as I look down at him.

"Lie back," he commands, voice thick with need.

I don't even think; I just obey. Because I want to, no, I need to. I sink into the mattress, my dress hanging in tatters around my waist. He rips it the rest of the way off, panties included, tossing them aside. Then he just stares.

His gaze rakes over every inch, slow and unflinching. I squirm under it, suddenly aware of how exposed I am, how utterly at his mercy I am. I try to close my legs, but his hands clamp down on my thighs and force them to remain open.

"Don't you fucking dare hide from me," he snarls, eye burning into mine. "You are mine. Mine to touch. Mine to taste. Mine to fucking ruin."

I'm shaking. From fear? Maybe. From need? Absolutely.

He lowers himself between my legs, his breath hot against my thigh. I know what's coming, but nothing could prepare me for the first drag of his tongue.

"Oh—Gods—Korithax—"

His tongue strokes through me, slow and deliberate, and I swear the world tilts sideways. One hand pins my hip to the bed, the other wraps under my thigh, keeping me wide open for his mouth.

"You taste like sin," he murmurs against my heat, his voice rough. "You taste like salvation."

I cry out again when he sucks on my clit, gently, then harder. My fingers fly to his hair, gripping desperately, and he groans like the sound of my moan is feeding him.

"That's it," he growls. "Let me hear you, Daisy. Louder."

He devours me like he's starving and I'm his favourite meal. My thighs tremble around his head; every flick of his tongue, every growled breath, sends me spiralling faster. I'm close—so close—and I've never felt anything like this in my entire life.

"Oh, God—"

His mouth rips away from me for a single, furious second. "No. There are no gods here, only the devil, princess. Now say my fucking name."

I whimper, hips jerking, my breath stuttering in my lungs.

"Say it," he snarls, diving back in without any mercy, sliding a large finger inside me to accompany his mouth. "Say my fucking name while I make you come."

"K-Korithax—" I cry out, the sound half-sob, half-moan, too overwhelmed to breathe.

"That's right," he grits out, adding another finger, stretching me to the point of pain. "Now come for me. Be a good girl and fall apart for your king."

His fingers drive into me whilst his mouth devours my clit. I shatter as the orgasm crashes through me like a tidal wave. It's violent. Beautiful. All-consuming.

So this is what it felt like. To be worshipped. Consumed. Ruined.

I'M STILL GASPING, blinking up at the ceiling in complete disbelief, when he crawls up over me—his mouth slick with my arousal, his eyes still blazing. He kisses me, slower this time, letting me taste myself on his lips.

I watch as he rises to his knees and slowly undoes every button of his shirt, dragging it over his large shoulders, revealing every inch of veined muscle and tanned skin inked with curling ancient tattoos. I can't look away as he lowers his hands to where the deep V falls into hidden territory, his large, veiny hands beginning to undo his belt. It falls to the floor, and my pulse beings to race as he slowly drags his pants lower.

When his cock springs free, I think I forget how to breathe. My stomach clenches at the size of him. There was no way, no gods-damned way, that was going to fit anywhere in me.

"Korithax..."

"I warned you," he says, stroking himself lazily. "You didn't tell me to stop."

He leans over me again, dragging the thick head of his cock slowly through my arousal, raking it against my clit in slow, teasing circles. My whole body tenses.

"Are you scared?" He asks.

"No," I whisper, surprising myself.

"Good."

He thrusts into me in one long, brutal thrust that knocks the breath from my lungs. My back arches, hands clutching at anything I can reach. I'm stretched wide, so full it burns, making me hiss. Every inch, every ridge and vein, stretching me way past my limit.

"Gods," I scream.

"Wrong. Name," He growls in my ear.

"Korithax," I whimper.

"That's better."

He doesn't give me a chance to adjust. He pulls out and flips me onto my stomach. He drags my hips up until I'm on my knees, face pressed into the mattress. He grabs my thighs and pulls them apart, his grip bruising. A loud slap sounds through the air, the stinging sensation following straight after. I yelp, burying my face into the mattress.

"That was for biting your lip when I told you not to."

Another loud slap followed by a sting so painful it brings tears to my eyes.

"That one?" He says lowly. "Was just because I wanted to."

He drives back into me with such force I'm pushed forward into the mattress, the pain unbearable. But he doesn't stop. Instead, he grips my hair with his hand, using the force to pull me back into him. His other hand snakes around my throat, forcing my head back to look up at him, his large frame towering over mine. He forces two fingers deep into my mouth as he relentlessly pounds into me, the slapping of flesh and my desperate whimpers filling the air. Tears are streaming down my face from a mixture of pain and pleasure, and he pulls my head further back, a sinister grin on his face, before he spits into my mouth, using his fingers to smear it across my lips.

"That's my good fucking girl." Another thrust. "You take me so well, little flower." Another. "Your little cunt is barely bleeding."

Bleeding... What?

I don't have a chance to dwell on it before he removes his fingers and wraps them underneath me, stroking against my clit. I scream, the sensation so overwhelming it makes my entire body tremble.

"Say it," he pants. "Say you're mine."

"I'm yours," I gasp.

"Again."

"I'm yours, Kori. Fuck, I'm yours—"

And when I break apart beneath him for the second time, he follows—burying himself deep, his growl turning into a desperate moan as he fills me with his cum.

We collapse into the sheets, sweaty and breathless, clinging to each other. My body hurts, my pussy throbs, and my entire soul has been shattered. And even though the King of Hell just ruined me in every sense of the word... I feel alive.

"Say it again," he murmurs against my temple.

"What?"

"That you're mine."

"I'm yours, Kori," I whisper.

He wraps his arms tightly around me, chest rising and falling in time with my own. "And I'll spend eternity making sure you never forget it."

CHAPTER 39
KORITHAX

I shouldn't have crossed that line.

Daisy's asleep soundly beside me, her head resting on my chest, her naked body pressed against mine. After we had sex, we showered together, and I called for healing fruit to ease the soreness I knew she'd feel.

I took little mercy on her once I had her. Every ounce of restraint I'd been holding back since the day I met her came undone. And while I kept it to just fucking, the thoughts wouldn't stop. Tying her up. Teasing her. Punishing her for hours. I wanted it all. I couldn't be as gentle as she probably needed for her first consensual time, but I didn't care. I needed her. And now... I regret it. I shouldn't have touched her, shouldn't have kissed her days ago. But I was a selfish man, and I had to have her.

But this is becoming dangerous. More dangerous than I'd ever anticipated. Daisy was no longer just the woman I'd married to shut up the Divine Six. She was becoming something else entirely. And that's a problem. Because I could never offer her the kind of love or life she deserves.

She needs warmth, softness, and care. The things I was never built for. I was born into a realm of hate, death, and ruin, and was to be the King of Hell, ruler of chaos and destruction. She's light, sunshine incarnate, and I'm cold, sharp steel. Those two things don't go together; they shouldn't go together. I fucked up by taking her to bed, but I wouldn't keep fucking up. She deserved better, and I had to put the distance between us before it was too late.

I SLOWLY SLIDE out from under her, careful not to wake her. She shifts but doesn't stir. I throw on my clothes and boots and step into the hallway. The sunrise floods the corridor in a blaze of gold and orange. Birds chirp cheerfully in the background, the sound irritating the shit out of me. Everything here seems to be grating on me. The brightness, the flowers, the warmth. This entire realm is everything Daisy is—and everything I'll never be.

"Korithax?"

I turn to see Sariya approaching, radiant as ever. Her ebony skin glows under the light of her realm.

"Good morning," I mutter. "I never got a chance to thank you for yesterday."

She smiles. "Please, it was nothing. Come, have breakfast with me. We need to talk."

I raise a brow but follow her to a shaded table on a balcony framed by trees. Warm wind stirs the petals scattered across the stone flooring, the breeze doing nothing to cool the irritation bubbling inside me.

"What is it, Sariya?"

"Drink?" She offers.

"No."

She sighs, setting her teacup down, brushing at her skirts with both hands. "I know you think you're not meant for her, Korithax. But—"

"What are you talking about?" I cut her off sharply.

"Daisy. I see the way you look at her, I feel the way you feel about her."

"You feel it?" I ask, frowning.

"Yes. And I feel the way she feels about you, too. Don't push her away, Korithax. Things are about to change drastically. She is more like you than you realise."

"What aren't you telling me?" I ask, voice dropping low.

"I can't say," she says gently. "For your safety as well as mine. But when the time comes—you will need me, you will need my soldiers." She lowers her voice. "And I promise you—we will answer."

"You're not making any sense," I huff, already standing. "I don't have time for this cryptic bullshit."

She reaches out, grabbing my hand. Her amber eyes lock with mine, her expression unreadable.

"Just remember my words, Korithax. I won't be able to say goodbye before your departure. Please... give Daisy my love. She's a wonderful girl, and she will make a wonderful queen again."

"Again?"

Before I can ask more, she rises and walks away. I stare after her, my jaw tight. I'm so tired of riddles.

I grab a few pieces of sweet bread and a jug of pale pink fluid and head back to our room.

Back inside, she's still asleep—peaceful and unaware. Sariya's words claw at my skull. She's wrong. I don't deserve Daisy. And it's about time she understood. "Daisy," I bark her name.

She jolts upright, blinking blearily. "Wha—?"

"Get up. We leave in an hour."

She rubs at her eyes, frowning.

"Are you okay?"

Of course, she asks if I'm okay. Even when I'm a bastard, she cares. Like an absolute idiotic puppy.

"I'm fine. Just move your ass."

"Okay... can you pass me that robe?"

I toss it at her without looking and sit at the table, tearing into a chunk of honeyed bread.

She pads over, robe tied around her waist, and sits across from me. She's still sleepy-eyed, her hair in messy waves, and absolutely beautiful.

"Oooh! You brought Blytrine," she says brightly. "Sariya told me it comes from a tree that only grows under Solara's light; it's delicious. Want to try it?"

She holds her glass out to me, smiling.

"No." I don't even glance at it.

Her smile drops. "... Right. Okay."

"Just eat."

"Has something happened?"

"No." I snap. "And I don't want to do the whole awkward morning-after thing. Just because we fucked doesn't mean we're friends now."

She flinched like I slapped her. "Wow. Really?"

I shove my chair back and stand, the legs scraping loudly against the floor. "We leave soon. Hurry up."

"You really think that'll work?" Her voice rises as she follows me. "That if you're enough of an asshole, I'll just pretend last night didn't happen?"

"Nothing did happen, Daisy. It was sex. That's it. No feelings. No promises. No delusions."

She storms after me, absolutely furious. "So I was just convenient? A warm body?"

"You're reading into it."

Her face twists. "Was I not good enough? That it?"

"Don't be dramatic."

She storms into the bathroom and slams the door shut behind her.

Fuck. FUCK.

I follow and try the handle, but it's locked. "Daisy, open the door."

"I don't like swearing, but fuck you, Korithax!"

I snarl and kick the door open. She screams, backing into the corner.

"GET OUT!" She yells, throwing a bottle at me.

I let it hit me, barely feeling it. "Was that supposed to hurt?"

"No, you idiot. I don't want to hurt you. I just want you to go away."

"It's not about last night." I snap, stepping closer.

She stares at the floor, hands wringing in front of her.

"Daisy," I sigh, reaching out and forcing her to look at me. "You were perfect. The way you sounded, the way you felt... gods, I could lose myself in you for eternity."

Her face turns pink, and despite everything, my cock twitches at the memory of her flushed face as I was buried between her thighs.

"Then why are you being such an ass?"

I steel my voice, pulling away my gaze. "You deserve better."

"What?"

"I'm not soft. I don't love. I can't. I was made to break things. You were made to be worshipped. I don't worship, I burn things down."

She snorts. "You don't get to decide what I want."

"I'm telling you what's best for you."

"You think I want someone gentle, someone safe? Korithax, I stopped being gentle a long time ago. You're the first person who's seen the ugly parts of me and didn't look away."

"There's nothing ugly about you," I respond, a little too quickly.

She chews her bottom lip, and I growl, using my thumb to tug it free from her teeth. "Stop that."

She looks up and smiles at me, her face entirely too smug. "Why are you smiling at me?"

"Because you're full of shit," she says sweetly. "And I see through it. You're not pushing me away because I'm not enough—you're pushing me away because you think you're not enough."

My jaw clenches at her words. Am I truly that readable?

"I'm honoured to stand by your side, even if it's just as a business transaction."

She smiles again—but it doesn't reach her eyes. She still doesn't get it. All I hear are my father's mocking words that nothing I touch survives. Not even my mother.

"Exactly," I say coldly. "A business transaction. So let's not confuse it."

I turn to leave, and she doesn't stop me. But her quiet voice hits me from behind. "I see what you're doing, Korithax. But I am still yours."

Her words gut me.

"Daisy," I growl, gripping the doorframe until it cracks.

"I'm yours, Kori."

I squeeze my eyes shut, my knuckles turning white. I want to believe her. But the thought of belonging to her terrifies me more than anything I've ever faced before.

CHAPTER 40
DAISY

He thought I was stupid.

And maybe a few days ago, I would've believed his words.

But the way he looked at me, the way he spoke to me, the way he dropped to his knees before taking me to bed? That couldn't be faked, and I was no business transaction. Not anymore.

Korithax might be a grumpy bastard at the best of times, but he was a horrible liar.

Apparently, Sariya knew this would happen, because the outfit I just pulled from the pack was from her, with a note attached that read:

Don't let him fool you, sweet girl. If he wants to play hard to get, you play harder. Enjoy the rest of your journey. Love, S.

SHE'D GIFTED me an outfit to die for. I didn't know much about the realm we were heading to next, but just like Lyvia, Sariya clearly had a theme. The dress was flawless—tight, black, with a deep plunging neckline that barely contained my breasts. The long skirt flowed to my ankles, high slits slicing up both thighs. Thin straps adorned with black diamonds held it in place, and the low back exposed my back dimples. Simple, yet jaw-dropping. Shock painted my face as I caught my reflection and watched lightning strikes dance across the fabric like flickers of a storm.

Alongside the dress, she'd packed a black circlet—delicate and powerful. It sat across my forehead, a teardrop ruby in the centre flanked by thorned bands embedded with more black diamonds. A matching black lace thigh sheath held a dagger with a ruby-encrusted hilt. Paired with all of it were elegant black heels, sparkling with stardust and streaked with lightning that crackled faintly across the surface of the shoes.

A knock at the door pulled me from the mirror.

"Good morning, your Highness. I'm here to assist with your hair and makeup."

"Come in. And please, call me Daisy."

The girl who entered had rich bronze skin and long, beautifully styled dreadlocks woven with golden thread. Her eyes were warm brown, and her presence—like everyone else here—was calm and gentle.

"What's your name?" I ask, smiling at her.

"Naema, Daisy," she replies with a blush. "I was told to make you look so breathless your husband won't be able to stop himself from falling to his knees."

Her blush deepens, rose-gold spreading across her cheeks. I can't help the laugh that bubbles out of me as I nod my head.

When she finishes, I barely recognised myself. It was the heaviest makeup I'd ever worn. Dark, smoky eyes with winged liner that made my blue eyes electric. My lips were painted a blood-red so deep it made my skin look nearly porcelain. My golden hair was in loose, cascading waves down my back. And for the first time in my life, I felt powerful. Dangerous. Sexy even.

If Korithax wanted to play hard to get, I'd play harder—looking like a Queen of Hell, apparently.

I thanked Naema, then stepped out of the bathroom. Korithax sat at the table, aimlessly turning over a piece of the sweet bread he'd brought in.

"Gods, finally—"

He looks up, his mouth agape, crushing the bread in his large fist. I can't help but smirk when a low groan escapes his lips. "Are you ready to go, my king?" I ask, letting my voice turn smooth as silk.

He clears his throat, dropping the bread and rising slowly before closing the distance between us in two long strides.

"You're going to be the fucking death of me."

Before I can respond, he grips me in his arms, and the horrible feeling of teleportation rips through my body. That gut-twisting, stomach-lurching sensation yanking me from Solara. We land, and I gasp. My vision flickers as the nausea rises up my throat.

"Gods, I'll never get used to that." I whimper, stumbling into Korithax.

He catches me easily, holding me steady.

"You look absolutely divine, Daisy."

I smile up at him, my vision clearing. "You don't look so bad yourself, Kori."

He wore a loose black shirt tucked into equally loose black pants and his usual boots. The sleeves were rolled up, exposing those veined, muscled forearms. The shirt was unbuttoned just enough to tease a glimpse of his chest. His hair was down, some of it caught in his horns as the wind whipped through it, the sky above crackling. The ground trembles a second later.

I gasp again, falling slightly forward into him. I straighten myself, looking around, and for the first time, I wasn't sure I'd enjoy the realm we'd arrived in. Dark clouds loomed overhead, thunder roaring in the distance, and streaks of lightning danced across the sky. I see where Sariya got her inspiration. The air smelled of rain and fire, thick and charged. The ground beneath my heels was cracked and unsteady, as if at any moment the Earth beneath us might split open.

"Welcome to Stormravan," Korithax whispers in my ear, tucking a strand of hair behind it. "The realm that provides storms and natural disasters to Earth."

"This is... definitely different from the other realms," I say, shivering.

"Yes. It would appear Sariya didn't think her little plan through when she chose your outfit."

I laugh. "Clearly, she was too focused on how much of an idiot you are."

He frowns. "Yes. I am."

Another tremble shakes the ground, causing me to yelp in surpise.

Korithax huffs a laugh. "Come on, little flower. Let's go meet our host. He's... not like the other rulers you've met. Brace yourself."

WE WALK ACROSS THE DARK, cracked path toward the looming castle ahead. It matches the realm perfectly—towering and jagged, as though it had been carved straight from a volcano mid-eruption. Thunderclouds circled above the spires, lightning cracking across the sky with violent flashes. Lava flows down grooves etched into the stone walls, pooling into glowing channels that disappear into the ground. At the entrance, tall gargoyle-like soldiers stand guard. Massive, winged, and stone-skinned, with glowing eyes and molten veins beneath their obsidian armour. They bow as we approached.

"These are the creatures born from Hell," Korithax explains quietly. "They were sent here to help protect Vor'Khar's realm. Because he's such a powerful and destructive ruler, his lands often come under scrutiny and attack. Vor'Khar isn't evil—just chaotic. He doesn't destroy for pleasure; it's simply in his nature. Like lightning striking a tree... it just happens."

I nod, absorbing it all.

"Every natural disaster you can think of—from earthquakes to hurricanes, to volcanic eruptions—is his doing. Not many people live here; most choose to relocate to Hell, where it's at least less unpredictable. We have an open connection between our realms—his people and mine can travel freely if they can make the journey, as long as they behave accordingly."

He gives my hand a soft squeeze.

"Due to the nature of this realm and its magic, I can recharge quickly here. We'll only need to stay for a few hours."

"Good," I murmur with a shiver. "I already miss the peace and sun of Solara."

The guards lead us inside, where a massive, cracked stone door slowly groans open. The throne room is large and terrifying. Lava pours in steady streams down the walls into glowing cracks in the floor. Lightning crackles across the ceiling like a pulse. And at the far end, upon a throne made of jagged rock and molten lava, sits the King. Vor'Khar.

He's enormous. A towering, inhuman man, carved like a mountain struck by meteors. He has skin like obsidian rock, cracked with glowing veins of red, blue, and gold, each vein pulsing with an element: fire, lightning, and molten earth. His wings look like storm clouds torn into shape, and his eyes are a blinding white, like lightning frozen mid-blink. His smile reveals jagged teeth, the action making the sky above the castle crack and roar.

"Don't stand on the cracks, little flower," Korithax mumbles. "They'll burn."

I nod, training my eyes on the stone as we move.

"Vor'Khar. It's been a while." Korithax says, nodding his head.

Vor'Khar nods once in return.

"Still a man of many words, I see. I hope you don't mind my beautiful wife and me stopping by to recharge before we move on to the next realm."

He nods again, another smile revealing those horrific teeth. Again, the sky outside lights up, thousands of lightning flashes blinding the clouds. Thunder booms so loud I slap my hands over my ears, grimacing.

"Thank you," Korithax says, unfazed. "Is there a room in which we can rest?"

Vor'Khar grunts, the sound making the entire room shake.

"This way, Your Highness." One of the guards rasps, his voice like gravel.

"Well, that was brief," I whisper as we follow.

"Yeah, he's not a man of many words. He just sits and causes chaos. What a life to have."

I nudge him, laughing. "But if you had his life, you wouldn't have me."

He looks at me, and I give him a wink. He barks a laugh, the sound rich and beautiful.

We're led to a smaller room, the walls made of cracked stone with glowing lava veins. The room is bare, save for a stone slab shaped like a bed—no mattress, no covers.

"Well. I'm glad we're not sleeping here." I say, wrinkling my nose.

"Yeah. He doesn't get many guests, as you can imagine." The guard leaves as Korithax sits on the edge of the stone bed, pulling me between his legs.

"But I don't need a mattress to make you scream, little flower." He whispers, stroking a hand down my bare back.

I pull away, watching as his brows furrow. "Oh no. I'm just a business transaction. And I don't recall seeing anything in the contract about sexual relations, Korithax."

He runs his tongue over his teeth, making a low sucking noise.

"Really, Daisy?" He asks, irritated.

"Really," I say, crossing my arms. "If you want to play those games, then so do I."

"I'm not playing any fucking games," he snaps.

"So, I'm just a business transaction then?" I ask.

"No. That's not what I meant, and you know it." He growls.

"So, what do you mean, Kori? Because I'm tired of your bullshit now."

He raises a brow. "Such a foul mouth, my little flower. I'm really rubbing off on you."

I roll my eyes. "Maybe you are."

He sighs, running a hand through his tousled hair. "And that's exactly what I don't want. You're too pure for a man like me, Daisy. I don't know how to navigate this." He gestures between us. "I don't love. I don't do gentle. I'm a beast, a man built to destroy, born from darkness."

I step between his legs again and cup his cheek. He closes his eyes at the contact, inhaling deeply.

"Look at me, Korithax," I murmur.

His obsidian eyes meet mine, and I take a deep inhale, trying to calm my nerves. "I told you; I'm yours. And if you don't want me, that's fine. But I'm only going to say this once, because I'm not going to beg you to feel the same way. I want you, Korithax. I see who you are, what you are, and where you came from. And I still choose you."

My heart thunders in my chest, the fear of rejection almost too much as he stares at me in utter silence. He exhales sharply, dropping his head and shaking it.

I sigh, lowering my hand. I take a step back, "Okay," I whisper, my voice trembling as I feel my heart crack—fracturing just like the stone all around us.

~

We sit in silence for an hour.

Korithax hasn't moved from the bed, and I alternate between the windows in the room, looking out over the realm before me. It's terrifying here. Nothing but broken rock, rivers of lava, and storm-filled skies. I really can't wait to leave.

If I'm right, we only have one more realm before we arrive in Noxthrallia, where I'll say goodbye to my mortal life and spend thousands of years with a man who sees me as nothing more than a contract.

I suck my bottom lip between my teeth to stop it from trembling, and discreetly wipe away the tear that escapes my eyes. How did I let myself begin to feel this way for him when I knew from the start he only wanted a bride to silence the celestial asshats who controlled the realms? He'd done nothing but treat me like dirt, and my traitorous heart still decided she wanted him. Evidentially, I'm living up to the 'weak, pathetic mortal,' brand he gave me. Clearly I just have issues with caring about asshole men. My dad, Ethan, now Korithax. Lucky me.

A KNOCK at the door pulls me from my thoughts. I turn and watch as Korithax strides over and opens it. He nods once, takes something from the guard, and shuts the door behind him.

He's holding a scroll, sealed with his sigil pressed into ruby-coloured wax. He breaks it open and reads it as I bite the side of my thumb, waiting patiently.

"FUCK!" He roars, slamming his fist into the wall. Lava trickles over his hand before he jerks away with a hiss, chunks of stone crumbling to the floor.

I startle. "What is it?" I ask, walking toward him.

He turns to face me, his eyes feral. "Those fucking assholes, who think they're so high and mighty. That's what's wrong."

He paces, dragging a hand through his hair.

"Calm down," I say gently, reaching out. He shrugs me off, still pacing. I sigh and sink onto the edge of the stone bed, finally giving my aching feet relief from those god forsaken heels.

"What happened?" I ask.

"They summoned Aran, demanding to know where I am. They know I'm with you—and they're threatening consequences if we don't return soon."

I frown. "But that's not possible. It took us five days just to get here."

Of course, we spent an extra night in Solara, but even so, four days without an extra stay is crazy.

"I know. Aran says he's dealing with it, but they're pissed. They've given us three days to return."

My eyes widen. "What happens if we don't?"

He shakes his head, his jaw clenched. "I don't know."

"So what do we do?" I ask nervously.

He exhales sharply, rubbing a hand down his face. "Looks like I'll have to ass-kiss Elyistria and hope she'll help us with her magic."

"Who's Elyistria?"

"The goddess of Luminaria, which is the next realm we go to. She rules over light magic and mercy. She's extremely powerful, probably more powerful than the Divine Six. How they haven't tried to destroy her like they did the First Queen, I don't know."

"The First Queen?" I echo, nervous that all my questions are going to further piss him off.

"The first Queen of Hell. Rumour has it, the Divine Six destroyed her to preserve their rule. She was beloved—strong, powerful, fair, and loving. All of that combined made her very dangerous to them."

He lowers himself to the floor in front of me, pushing my thighs apart to move closer.

"Your birthmark," he murmurs, brushing his thumb over it. My skin pebbles under his touch. "It looks oddly like her symbol."

I smile faintly. "My mother always said it looked like a little flame."

He nods, studying it. "Her symbol is a flame—within a crackled circle of thorns."

"Well, mine's just a weird-looking flame. So not that similar."

He pulls his gaze from the mark, nodding. "Maybe. Either way, we need to convince Elyistria to help us return faster."

I stiffen. "Wait... so we're not turning me immortal?"

He smirks, brushing a lock of hair from my face. "Oh, my little flower. Of course we are. When we return—with you as my immortal bride—I'll finally shut those bastards up about the throne."

I offer him a tight-lipped smile, nodding. "Right. The business transaction in all of this."

He groans, tipping his head forward to rest his forehead on my shoulder. "Can we not do this right now, Daisy?"

"Sorry," I whisper, my voice cracking.

He looks at me, his expression almost softening as he lifts my face to look at him. "I'm not frustrated with you. I'm frustrated with them. Because..." He growls in frustration and blows out a breath whilst staring into my eyes. "Because you are the first thing in existence that's ever made me care about whether or not I die. And if they could wipe out the strongest Queen in history... what could they do to me?"

I stare at him, stunned.

"Whilst you're still mortal, I won't claim you. I can't. You're too easy for everyone else to hurt. But as an immortal, it'll be much harder. Although, if anyone even tries, I'll tear them apart and burn what's left." His onyx eyes stare into mine, holding so much emotion it makes my heart stutter. "For the first time in my life, Daisy, I'm fearful. When they took you in Aurora's Veil, I felt something I've never known. I've lost friends on the battlefields; I've watched that many people die it no longer means anything. But when they took you? All I felt was rage, desperation, and a soul-deep panic that you'd be lost to me."

His voice drops. "Your soul calls to mine, Daisy. It tugs. And when it's safe, I'll answer that fucking call. But right now, I have to keep you alive. I won't lose you. I can't lose you."

I STARE at him in absolute awe, a tear rolling down my cheek. I lean in slowly, truly testing the boundaries to see if I'm reading between the lines correctly. I'm done with hot and cold. I'm done with confusion. Right here, right now, I need to know where I stand with this infuriating creature.

"Kiss me, Korithax," I whisper.

He hesitates, and I feel my heart begin to ache. I nod once and move away from his touch, accepting that he's set in his decision.

He grips my chin and pulls me back towards him, his eyes alight. "Fuck it."

His lips crash into mine with such ferocity that I collapse into his lap on the floor. I thread my hands into his hair, moaning with a mixture of pleasure and relief as he groans into my mouth.

He pulls back, panting. "Fuck," he breathes. "I'll never tire of your lips. Especially when you're moaning into my mouth."

I smile and kiss him again, tongues exploring as I grind against him. I feel him harden beneath me and release another breathy moan.

"Daisy," he growls. "Stop it."

I pull back just slightly, pushing myself up onto my knees. "You want me to stop?" I lean in, kissing under his jaw, feather light and teasing.

His hands clamp down on my hips to hold me still. "Yes!"

I continue my trail of kisses, moving my lips across his chest since his grip is stopping me from reaching his neck with our height difference. "Are you sure?"

He swallows hard, his composure cracking. "Yes."

"Okay," I whisper, suddenly standing. My dress slips from my shoulders slightly, exposing my breasts and my peaked nipples.

A growl rips from him before he lunges, lifting me so fast I shriek. He moves to pin me to the wall. I wrap my arms around his neck as he slides his hands beneath the skirt of my dress, whilst his teeth graze my throat.

He pauses as his hands reach my backside, pulling his head back to stare me dead in the eyes. "Are you... not wearing panties?"

I giggle, blushing slightly. "Nope."

A sharp slap hits my ass, and I yelp, clinging to him. He frees his cock in one swift movement, the head pushing against my soaking entrance.

"This is mine," he growls, rubbing the head of his cock up and down my clit.

"Yours," I gasp as he suddenly thrusts into me, filling me to the hilt. The sting brings tears to my eyes as he fucks me against the stone wall, and I find myself not caring about the burning lava pouring through the cracks surrounding my body.

His breath is hot in my ear. "Fuck, Daisy. Your little cunt is so wet for me."

"Is this part of the business transaction?" I mutter between moans, clinging tighter as he slams into me.

The question makes him relentlessly pound into me, and I feel myself struggling to accommodate him as he pulls all the way out to the tip and slams back into me.

"Strictly. Business," He grounds out between thrusts.

It doesn't take long for the pain to melt into pleasure, and I feel myself building and building until the ecstasy of an orgasm is tearing through my body. My entire body shakes as he buries himself so deep in me, my inner walls gripping him through the waves of pleasure.

"That's my good girl," he growls. "Coming all over my cock."

He grins, sliding himself out of me with a grunt. He walks over to the stone bed with me in his arms and lays me down gently, the cold concrete making goosebumps erupt all over my body.

"Head off the edge, princess."

I obey, letting my circlet fall as I dangle my head off the bed.

"Let's see how well that pretty mouth takes me."

He drops to his knees, and I gasp at the sight of him from this angle. His thick, veined cock is positioned above my face, slicked with my arousal and pulsing with need. I hesitate at the size of him before opening my mouth wide. He slides the head past my lips, slowly pushing himself in until my mouth is filled entirely. He hits the back of my throat in a punishing thrust that makes me gag, my eyes streaming with tears. There's still so much left of him that won't fit, so I wrap my hand around the rest of him and move in time with his thrusts.

"Fuuuuuuck, Daisy. That's it, good girl," he groans as he leans forward to play with my hardened nipples.

I hum, hollowing out my cheeks as he continues to assault my throat with his cock, my jaw aching from the size of him.

"Fuck. That's it." He grunts, upping his pace as he nears his release. "Swallow me, baby."

He groans loudly, emptying his hot cum into my throat, the salty liquid sliding down. He releases my nipples and pulls out of my mouth, panting.

"Fuck. You're incredible." He grins from above me.

I wipe my face to clean up the spit and cum I didn't manage to swallow, and sit up. "Was that... good?" I nervously ask.

"Daisy," he says, crouching down to hold my face in his hands. "That was fucking incredible."

I blush as he leans forward and places a kiss on my forehead.

He tucks himself back in and then holds out a hand for me, "Ready to go to Luminaria?"

I glance at my dress. "I think it's customary that I wear a new outfit for each realm, to match the vibe. Let me get changed." I point to my face. "I should probably clean up whatever mess you've made of my face, too."

He groans. "Fine. I fucking love that dress though. And wear panties, for gods' sake. You're going to be the death of me otherwise."

I giggle, slipping into the bathroom, excited to see what the hell Lyivia has planned for me next.

CHAPTER 41

KORITHAX

There are days I wish I could tear away the crown and cast it into the void between the realms.

From the moment I took my first breath, I've been a symbol, a weapon, a looming heir carved from brutality and expectation. The Divine Six have watched me like hawks watching a serpent, waiting for the day I'd either snap the neck of fate, or fall beneath it. I was raised not as a son, not as a boy—but as the future ruler of Hell. And Hell, in all its brutal honesty, never offered me the luxury of weakness.

Each of the Divine Six has shaped my life in one way or another.

Seraphiel—the Voice of Judgement. Silver-plated justice with blind, glowing eyes and a tongue sharp enough to cleave empires in two. She never looked at me once without disdain. To her, I was a ticking time bomb, a creature born of violence. 'Mercy is weakness,' she once said, 'and the King of Hell must never kneel for anyone.' I've hated her since that day. How would she feel now, knowing I've not only knelt, but it was for a mortal girl who holds my blackened heart in her delicate hands.

Amarithe—the Bloom of Light. She smiles when she lies and

twists affection like a blade. With hair like liquid gold and a voice dipped in honey, she's the most dangerous of them all. She called my mother unworthy behind silken smiles. I remember hearing her whisper it, "A flower rooted in ash cannot grow and be strong." My mother had heard it too. She just smiled, knowing they had cast her fate long before she got a chance to prove herself worthy. She was worthy; they were the ones who weren't.

Calrix—the Spear of Order. The militant bastard. His every breath is flame, every movement a declaration of war. He used to spar with me when I was barely tall enough to lift a blade, and every time he knocked me down, he would whisper that I was unfit, unworthy. His eyes lit with glee when I bled, the smile that would break across his face each time he carved a new scar into my skin would haunt my dreams as a boy. When I finally bested him, he said nothing. Just left a sword at my door, as if to say: You've earned this. Finally. Arrogant prick couldn't even hand me it himself.

Elaron—the Whispering Star. Quiet, terrifying. His power isn't brute force, but control. Controller of dreams, of memory, of thought. I never trusted him. Once, I awoke with a memory that didn't belong to me—a garden of stars I had never seen, and a voice I had never known. I wonder if he'd planted it. I often wonder what manipulation he's planted, tucked away in the minds of gods.

Mal'Thariel—The Architect. Cold and inhuman. Logic without mercy. He's the one who reminds us all that we're dust and design. That fate is not a thing to be fought, but followed. His presence alone bends time. He's the creator of all, and his presence alone tells you he is not one to fuck with.

And then, there's Velentha. The Oracle of Time. She was the only one who had never raised her voice, who had never struck me. But her silence was somehow always worse. Because when she looked at me, she didn't see a boy. She saw the future... my future. She saw the 'Child of Ruin'. Though her tone was soft when she called me it, it carried with it a weight of doom. I've never forgotten that name, the way it makes my skin prickle whenever it's called.

They all treat my mother like she was never meant to sit beside my father. Almost like she was a placeholder, a fragile flower in a field of divine flame. Even as a child, I could see it. The looks, the snide remarks. Because she wasn't one born of royalty, she wasn't worthy. The way they erased her presence from the castle the second she passed. And when she had died, I saw no grief in them. Only relief.

If they dare treat Daisy that way—if they so much as look at her with that same contempt, I'll raze the heavens. I'll tear their temple down with my bare hands and drown the stars in their blood. She's mine. Not because she belongs to me, but because I would carve out my own ribcage just to keep her safe.

I fear for her. Even as I plot her immortality, I fear they'll never accept her. That they'll find a way to rip her from me, just like they did to the first Queen. If the stories are true—and I believe they are—the Divine Six destroyed her because she was too beloved, too strong. And that made her dangerous. They feared an uprising, that the people would follow her, only listen to her, not them. Their fragility truly shone through when they decided they could have no other that was respected, or should I say feared, in such a way. It was them, and nobody else.

Now, I have offered them a weakness. Because now, I have something to lose.

I never wanted to be king. I've said that only to myself. I never wanted the throne, the rituals, the heavy silence of the court, the mask I wear to keep Hell in order. I've always found joy in the battlefield—leading armies, protecting my realm. I should have been a soldier. A blade to wield, not a crown.

But when my father stepped back a millennium ago, I had no choice but to. Peace was fragile then, trade routes unstable. Tensions with the outer realms were high, almost at breaking point. But I fixed it, I forged alliances, opened gates, and offered our weapons in exchange for their magic, their ores, their scholars. And it worked.

For the last thousand years, there has been peace. I was handed responsibility at too young an age, but I made it work.

And yet, all of them—the rulers of the other realms—still dance to the strings pulled by the Divine Six.

Solara is the only realm that resists them openly. Sariya's warmth is a threat to them, and they know it. I've always admired her defiance, but even so, she obeys just like the rest of us, despite her resistance. The others? I'm not so sure. Virena plays her cards close to her chest, Kaelith is a coward, and Vor'Khar just does whatever. Elyistria is powerful, but secretive, I don't know where she stands at all. She knows she's a threat to the Divine Six, which is dangerous in itself. But neither have come to a blow as of yet. Noxthrallia is the only realm the Divine Six don't bother with at all, leaving it to its dark and dodgy ways. They gave up trying to police the realm a long time ago and seem to enjoy the chaos they bring upon Earth.

My mind flicks back to Sariya's words that have haunted me since we left her golden halls.

"When the time comes, you will need me, you will need my soldiers. And I will answer."

Why would I need her army? Is war coming? If it is... gods help us all. Especially now that I have Daisy. Would they use her against me? Would they come for her, to twist my strength into weakness? They've never had a way to wound me before. But now... now they do. And it terrifies me.

SHE STEPS out of the bathroom, and I forget how to breathe.

For a moment, everything stills—even the storm outside the walls of Stormravan seems to hold its breath. Daisy stands before me not just like a queen... but a myth come to life. The Queen of Hell cloaked in the grace of light itself.

Her gown is made of flowing silks spun by Lumispires, the rare creatures of Luminaria. The fabric is pearlescent white with an inner sheen of silver and soft blush, rippling with light magic that responds to her every breath. Embroidered along the hem and bodice are golden runes of fate, glowing faintly—some of which I recognise as blessings, others I'm not even entirely sure of myself.

The neckline plunges modestly, forming a delicate heart shape framed by curling golden vines that wrap around her shoulders like living jewellery. Her arms are wrapped in translucent sleeves—slitted from shoulder to wrist—lined with flickers of starlight and stitched with Hellfire thorns in black thread, barely visible unless the light hits just right.

Around her waist is a slim girdle of onyx and gold, inlaid with ruby shards shaped like broken hearts. From it falls a split overskirt of sheer obsidian silk, cascading over the shimmer of Luminaria's white fabric beneath—light and shadow dancing with every step she takes. At her thigh, a dagger rests in a black-lace sheath, the hilt wrapped in a velvet ribbon that bears my sigil. Her heels are delicate yet deadly—strapped sandals made of molten gold, the edges trailing soft wisps of smoke wherever she walks.

But it's her crown that ties it all together. A diadem of white gold rests against her brow, shaped like a twisted halo of light and fire—pearls softly glowing beside ruby tips shaped like demonic horns, merging heaven and hell in one perfect, blasphemous arc. From the centre hangs a teardrop gem—a piece of glowing Luminaria crystal kissed by demon blood—hovering just above her forehead, suspended by an enchantment.

Her hair is left long, wavy, and threaded with tiny crystal blossoms, and her lips are stained the colour of fresh pomegranate, bold but soft. Her freckles are in full bloom now, each one kissed to life by the sun in Solara. Thirty-six of them, scattered like constellations across her cheeks and nose. Most wouldn't have noticed them. But I did. I counted them every night as she slept. She's Luminaria's grace and Hell's fire, woven into a single breathtaking form. My wife. My queen. She's divine. Not in the way Elyistria is or Sariya, not in the way gods are born and celestials are made. But in the way a wildfire is divine—untamed, beautiful, inevitable.

"You're staring," she says softly.

"You're glowing."

She blushes as I step closer, closing the distance between us.

I brush my knuckles down her cheek softly. "Thirty-six freckles," I mumble.

Her brows lift. "You counted?"

"Every night."

The flush deepens. "Wow, you really are obsessed."

She giggles, pushing at me with a hand in a playful way, and I grab hold of it, pulling it up to my mouth to place a kiss against her knuckles. Her engagement ring sparkles, and I can't help the grin that takes over my face.

"You have no idea, little flower."

She exhales, smiling despite herself. "This is it, huh? The last realm before Noxthrallia."

I nod. "This one's different though. Luminaria isn't elemental like the others. Elyistria doesn't command storms or sea, or war. She is the source of magic itself. All light magic, all good fate—it flows from her hands. She's more powerful than any of us... though not more powerful than the Divine Six combined."

"And they just... let her exist?" She asks.

"They fear her," I say simply. "Because if Elyistria dies, magic dies. Every spell, every enchantment, every blessing, every good fate given. Gone."

Daisy huffs, arms crossing. "Well, maybe I'll have a few choice words for her about what the hell I did so wrong for her to not be on my side with fate."

I smirk, not being able to stop myself from being a sarcastic asshole. "There's a rumour that she always answers the pleas of the desperate. Maybe she heard yours and thought you needed a sexy seven-foot demon in your life." I lower my eyes to her plump lips. "And your mouth."

I flex, posing like some ridiculous Greek God statue just to make her laugh. It works, and she grins, giggling as I pull her in for a kiss.

Her voice softens. "Is this the end of hot-and-cold Korithax?"

I flatten my mouth into something almost like a smile, but shrouded with sadness. "I'm sorry." I breathe, "I was trying to keep you—keep this—at arm's length." I gesture between us, tilting my head. "But it turns out, no matter how hard I tried, I couldn't stay away."

"You stayed away long enough before Christmas," she whispers, a trace of hurt curling through her tone.

I shake my head. "Wrong."

She quirks an eyebrow at me, now her turn to tilt her head. "What?"

"I watched you. Every single night in the scrying mirror."

She gasps, pushing at my chest. "Stalker!"

"Mmhm." I kiss her temple. "And I saw how you stroked that pretty little pussy over me night after night."

She slaps my chest, her cheeks flaming red. "I did not!" She shrieks.

I chuckle, wrapping my arm around her lower back. "Come on. We've got a Goddess of Magic to meet."

~

For the first time, Daisy doesn't stumble when we land. In fact... she straightens, almost seeming to glow. I frown, looking over her, still holding onto her regardless of her steady posture.

"You alright?" I ask.

She blinks, a slow smile spreading across her face. "Yeah," she breathes. "I feel... wonderful."

I narrow my eyes, watching her rub at the birthmark that sits just below her shoulder. "Maybe it's because this is the realm of magic."

I watch her, both of us with confusion etched across our faces as I take her in. She seems more radiant than ever, and I swear her ocean blue eyes are shimmering. We begin walking, and I take her hand, walking together straight towards the palace of Luminaria. This felt strange; the way her small hand was placed in mine without the reasoning of trying to fool people. But she deserved to be treated with softness, and I was going to try my best to give her it. For her, I could be soft. I could save my ruthlessness for the bedroom.

My mind wandered back to the way she had taken me down her throat, the way her body jostled, her tits bounced as I fucked her mouth until I emptied into her. Fuck she was incredible. The feel of her was like nothing I'd ever known. And the soul pull when we fucked was so intense, the feel of it alone almost made me finish. She was truly spectacular, and I couldn't wait to tear her dress from her body later and taste every godsdamned inch of her.

The air here is warm, the skies the colour of soft dawn—pinks, peaches, creams, all melting together in hues that I've never seen exist anywhere else. Mountains stretch into the heavens, white as pearl, glowing softly under a sun that doesn't quite cast the same heat as Solara. The grass beneath our feet is iridescent white-gold, and gentle music floats through the air—harps, flutes, voices that sing hymns of welcome.

Creatures roam freely—winged deer with glowing antlers, white-furred lions with golden eyes, flocks of tiny glowing wisps trailing sparkles as they zip through the air. Pegasi fly overhead, their wings casting soft shadows across the path that lies just ahead.

The palace looks like it's carved from light itself. Pure white stone rises in soft spirals that reach the sky. Runes of good fate shimmer across every surface. Flowers bloom in places that shouldn't be possible—cracks in the marble, corners of windows, even the tips of the spires seem to sprout white florals. They all softly pulse with the realm's magic, as if they were truly alive and breathing.

As we approach, guards armoured in yellow and white gold drop to one knee, bowing their heads.

"Queen of Hell," they say in perfect unison.

I arch a brow. "Wow. News travels fast around here, huh?"

One of the guards straightens. "Prince of Hell, you and your Queen may follow me."

I scowl, acting more like a bratty teenager than a twenty-thousand-year-old. "Why does she get Queen and I get fucking Prince?"

Daisy giggles, and I glance down at her. "Glad you think it's funny."

I can't help but pout. Assholes.

We walk the grand corridors, passing beings that seem born of light—tall, graceful, and glowing softly. Some have wings, some wear halos, all of them exude calm. The inside of the palace hums with magic that softly kisses my skin as the scent of a thousand blooming flowers trails by me on a phantom breeze. The throne room doors appear at the end of the hallway, a large arch of gold-tipped vines that part like petals as they slowly peel open at our approach.

We step into the most radiant chamber I've ever seen, golden runes spiralling across the floor. Crystal spires rise like trees, blooming with their own source of light, and a gentle river of magic flows through the air, seeming to circle around Daisy as her hair softly flutters around her like golden waves.

At the far end of the throne room, seated upon a large, white throne that pulses soft, glowing light, is Elyistria. She rises slowly, robes flowing like water and wind, light trailing from her fingertips as she holds out her palms.

"She returns," Elyistria breathes, voice layered with harmony. So soft and gentle, a stark comparison to my home.

Daisy looks around, confused. "Me?"

Elyistria smiles, her gaze warm enough to melt the stars themselves. "Yes, my dear."

CHAPTER 42
DAISY

I stare at the radiant goddess in front of me, her palms outstretched as she glides towards me. I smile softly, taking a step forward.

"I don't believe I've been here before," I say gently. "I'm Daisy."

"I know who you are, my dear," she replies, "just as someone else."

My smile falters, and I glance sideways at Korithax, but his face mirrors my confusion.

"May I?" She asks, gesturing to my hands.

I nod and place my hands into hers. A gasp escapes me as her magic flows into my skin—warm and luminous like morning light through stained glass. Images flash behind my eyes, all moving way too quickly to decipher. Scene after scene blurs past, but each one pulses with power, and some deeper part of me seems to respond.

Elyistria releases my hands slowly, blinking as she smiles. "Yes. She truly has returned. Fascinating."

Her eyes—blinding silver-blue with golden flecks swirling through them—lock onto mine. The power in her gaze soothes every raw edge in me, like a balm poured over my fractured soul. I blink rapidly, blinking away the spell that her eyes seemed to place me under, and turn toward Korithax, hoping he can take the lead because I have absolutely no idea what's going on.

He reads my expression instantly and clears his throat.

"I don't believe we've officially met. Allow me to introduce myself and my wife. Korithax, Heir to the Throne of Hell. And this is my beautiful Queen, Daisy Sandoval."

Elyistria smiles softly, then turns and floats back toward her throne, each step trailing light like floating petals behind her. She's tall, statuesque, the very embodiment of divine serenity.

Her platinum-white hair cascades like silk over her luminous ivory skin. Her layered robes mirror the ones I wear—white silk and translucent gossamer embroidered with golden runes of fate. A crown of golden branches tipped with glowing pearls rests gently atop her head.

"I know your bride well, Korithax," she says, seating herself elegantly, looking like one of those Greek goddess carvings. "And I've heard many stories about you, Child of Ruin."

Korithax bristles beside me, his hands not so subtly curling into tight fists. "How can you know my bride," he growls, "if she's never set foot in your realm? And who told you that name?"

Oh gods. I widen my eyes at him. He was really using that tone with the literal Goddess of Magic. His rage makes my palms sweat, and my pulse quicken. But also... godsdamn, he looked hot doing it. He's the polar opposite of the realm surrounding us. A smudge of dark, terrifying power against such light. I can't help but stare at the behemoth of a man standing beside me. A pool of heat floods straight to my core as I watch the ruthless man I've come to know not give a damn about who he releases his anger on. As if he could read my thoughts, his gaze snaps to mine. His nostrils flare once, and a small smirk pulls at his lips.

Shit. Right. He can smell when I'm turned on.

Think of spiders.

Think of taxes.

Think of the time my tampon string snapped, and Ezra had to hold my hand whilst Talia went into my hooter all gloved up to retrieve it.

The heat in my belly simmers down, and I lower my head to hide the blush that's blooming across my cheeks.

"Answers will come in time, Heir of Hell," Elyistria says calmly. "But rest assured, when you return from Noxthrallia, you will need my aid. And I will offer it—if your queen remembers this..."

I lift my eyes to find her staring directly at me, her irises glowing faintly. "I failed to stand beside you the first time, and I will not repeat that mistake. I am with you now, Daisy. When your hour comes, I will be there."

I blink at her, smiling stiffly. Why is everyone in the celestial hierarchy always so damn cryptic? Is that part of the job description?

Essential Goddess Skills:

A) Be devastatingly beautiful.

B) Speak exclusively in vague riddles.

C) Offer help but never explain how or when.

Still, I manage a polite smile and bow my head. "Thank you, Elyistria."

"You do not yet understand," she says gently. "But you will. And when the sun rises from the ash, I will stand at her side."

"What is it with you divine types?" Korithax mutters under his breath. "Maybe the Divine Six should recruit you and make it a solid seven. You'd fit right in with the rest of the cryptic assholes."

I shoot him a look, my palms damp again. "I apologise for my husband," I say sweetly through clenched teeth. "Clearly, he needs a nap."

I watch as his face turns into a devilish grin, clearly unbothered by the way he's behaving. I scowl at his reaction, only making his grin grow wider.

"What?" He murmurs. "I just love hearing you call me husband. Say it again later, when I'm nine inches deep inside you."

My eyes go wide as my mouth goes bone dry. I whip my head toward Elyistria, praying to any higher being listening that she didn't hear that.

She tuts softly. Yup. She definitely heard it. I resist the urge to groan and instead imagine stabbing Korithax with the nearest ceremonial spear. Would a wooden stake work? No, that's for vampires. Holy water? Ezra already tried that. Didn't work.

Despite myself, I smile. Because I know what Ezra and Talia risked for me by summoning him that night. A pang shoots through my chest. It feels like forever since I saw them. I need to visit when this is over. But the thought of watching them age, knowing I'll live on for centuries? Another pang. I shove the grief aside like I always do. *Not now, Daisy. Later.*

"Well," Elyistria says gently, "since your husband seems eager to get you to bed, I'll have my guards show you to your room. Please, enjoy your stay, and feel free to explore the realm if you'd like. It is yours to walk freely."

We both nod our thanks and turn to follow the guard, the urge to stab my husband stronger than ever. Although, he'd probably like it.

"Oh, and Daisy?"

I pause and look back. "Yes?"

"I would like to speak with you before you leave tomorrow. Alone." She eyes Korithax. "Breakfast, perhaps?"

I nod. "Sounds perfect. I'll see you then. Thank you so much for your hospitality."

With that, we're escorted from the throne room, my heart pounding and my head spinning like a kaleidoscope of questions.

~

We're guided through endless hallways and flights of gleaming white stone stairs. My thighs are burning by the time we reach the room we've been given, located in one of the northern towers of the palace.

A guard opens the door for us, one arm outstretched in polite invitation. "Here are your rooms. I hope you find them to your liking. If there is anything you—"

"Yeah, got it. Thanks," Korithax cuts him off sharply, stepping inside and slamming the door behind us.

I spin on him with a glare. "Korithax, what on earth has gotten into you? You're being more of an ass than usual."

He just stares at me, a grin spreading across his face—dark and gleaming, bordering on sadistic. His obsidian eyes flicker as he watches me. Then I smell it. Burning fabric. I look down and shriek—flames are crawling up my gown, devouring the silken material.

I slap at them, panicking as I shriek, "Korithax! What the hell!"

"They won't hurt you," he says calmly, clearly amused with his shit eating grin.

"What?" I pant, my body stalling as the fire eats through the fabric... but leaves my skin entirely untouched. Unharmed.

"It's my Hellfire. I told you, it won't harm you."

I stop struggling entirely, standing still as the flames finish their work, dissolving my gown into ash and leaving me in nothing but the black lace lingerie I wore underneath.

"You thought I'd burn you?" He asks, his voice quieter now, but I don't miss the hint of hurt behind it. His gaze is molten as it travels slowly down my body.

"The way you've been lately—hot, cold, terrifying—I didn't know what to think." My voice trembles.

He growls low in his throat and storms towards me. I don't even have time to breathe before his hand is wrapped around my throat, tilting my chin up.

"I have not, nor will I ever, physically hurt you. Unless it's something you enjoy." His voice is gravel and heat. "And I promise you, from this moment until my last breath, I will make up for how I've treated you. I am trying, Daisy. I don't know love. I have only ever known pain and torture. But for you... I'm learning. I will worship you like a queen, and fuck you like I hate you. And you will love every fucking second."

His grip is firm but not cruel, and I can feel his chest rising and falling as he stares down at me. He's right. He's trying, and it's not fair that I keep throwing the past in his face. I was cruel to him, too, on Christmas Eve. Yet he's never once thrown that in my face.

"I believe you," I whisper. "I'm sorry. I should trust you more."

He loosens his hold slightly, brushing his thumb along my jaw. "I understand why you don't. And like I said; I can't give you all of me yet. I won't answer that soul call until you're safe. Immortal. But once you are... you'll never doubt me again. You'll see."

I turn my head slightly, pressing a kiss to his thumb that's resting near my mouth. Then I open my lips and suck it slowly in, swirling my tongue across the pad before releasing it with a soft pop.

A growl rips from his chest, and that's the only warning I get before he grabs me, one arm under each thigh, lifting me with ease as he strides across the room. He stops just before the wall, his eyes ravenous.

"Legs. Over my shoulders," he commands.

"What?" I gasp.

"Now, Daisy."

I obey, my heart pounding. I hook my legs over his broad shoulders, breath catching as he pushes me higher up and pins my back to the cold stone wall. A soft snap sounds, and I feel my panties fall away.

He growls, pressing a kiss to the inside of my thigh, then biting it gently, his extended canines scraping at the skin. "Your pussy is perfect."

I moan softly, flushed with heat, feeling utterly exposed and slightly terrified of how high up I am right now. Korithax is seven freaking feet tall, and he has me in the air against a wall. If he drops me, that's going to hurt. Bad.

He pulls me out of my thoughts as he drags his tongue from my entrance to my clit, sucking gently, then harder, his mouth moving like he's starving for me.

Remembering his words from the throne room, I look down at his face buried between my thighs and smirk.

"Husband," I breathe, and he groans against me like the word itself drives him insane. His grip tightens, and he pushes his face deeper between my legs, tongue plunging inside me before circling back to my clit, relentlessly.

My thighs shake as I fist my hands into his hair, one slipping slightly, my fingers grazing one of his curved horns.

He shivers violently, his wings snapping out behind him and destroying his shirt. I gasp, and he pulls back just enough to meet my gaze. His eyes are entirely black, a crazed expression across his face.

"Hold them," he growls. "Hold my fucking horns whilst I feast on your sweet little cunt."

I nod, dazed and desperate, curling my fingers around the smooth, deadly curve of his horns. The instant I do, a sound erupts from his throat—somewhere between a roar and a groan—and he dives back between my legs.

I grind against his face, trembling as my climax builds fast and hot. His tongue slides deep, curling just right, and I come undone. I shatter with a cry, my body convulsing as my vision flickers. But he doesn't stop. His tongue moves slower, drawing every ounce of pleasure from my over-sensitive clit as he drags out my orgasm. I whimper, twitching from the intensity. It's too much, yet I never want it to stop.

Finally, he unhooks my legs and slides me down his body, keeping a firm grip to hold me upright. Thank gods because I'm pretty sure my legs would give out if he even attempted to put me down.

"You taste fucking incredible," he murmurs, licking his lower lip.

Still trembling, I lift my mouth to his and kiss him, tasting myself on his tongue. I suck his bottom lip into my mouth and decide I'm going to push my luck with the devil in front of me. I softly bite down, pulling at his lip before releasing it.

"Is my little flower trying to be a bad girl?" He asks, raising a brow.

I nod, chewing on my lower lip. He tilts his head, his eyes lowering to my mouth before coming back up to stare into my eyes.

"Words, Daisy."

"In the shower, you said that he hadn't taken away my first time having filthy sex," I mumble, trying to hide my nerves.

"Mhmm," is his only response, his eyes gleaming with a predatory gaze.

"I want you to..." I clear my throat, trying to sound confident in myself despite feeling anything but confident. "I, erm."

"You want to be fucked like a filthy little slut, little flower?"

I nod, a blush creeping over my cheeks.

"Words," he growls, gripping my jaw.

"Yes," I breathe.

He searches my eyes, almost like he's looking to see if I know what I'm asking for.

"I know you've been holding back. I want you to fuck me how you like to fuck, Korithax."

I swallow hard, but I mean every word. Despite my inexperience, I found the rougher he was with me, the more my body responded. The more I enjoyed it. I wanted to see how far my body could go as a mortal before I was changed forever, and I wanted it now. With him.

He studies me for a long beat, then nods. "Hard limits?"

I blink in confusion. "What?"

"Things I can't do to you. Things you won't allow. Any?"

I shake my head. "I don't think so."

He smirks darkly. "Safe word?"

I blink again.

"A word that makes me stop. One word, and everything ends immediately."

I nod. "Okay. What is it?"

"Flower," he grins.

I smile nervously. "Got it. Flower."

He walks over to the bed with me in his arms, placing me down on the edge of it.

"Good. Now lie down in the middle of the bed, princess. I'll be back."

I do as he says, staring at the too-bright white ceiling, nerves and anticipation dancing through me. What the hell have I done? Who the hell did I think I was asking the freaking Heir of Hell to 'fuck me like a filthy little slut'? Gods help me. It hurts when he's not in full demon mode. I'm not entirely sure I'm going to be walking out of here with my body fully intact. Maybe Elyistria will be able to fix me with her magic.

I hear the sound of him walking back into the room, and when my eyes land on him, my breath hitches. He's holding a rope, a black tasselled whip... and a vial of healing tonic. Well, at least he's considerate.

"Just remember. Flower." He murmurs before moving to the side of the bed next to my head.

He binds my wrists above my head, securing them to the golden headboard. I watch him as he stands straight, finished with tying me down. Sweet Jesus, he's pure muscle and menace—tattoos swirling, horns gleaming, and his jaw flexing as he strokes himself through his pants. My bra slowly burns away, revealing my bare chest and extremely peaked nipples. I blush, entirely exposed under his hungry gaze. He moves to the end of the bed and slowly licks his bottom lip.

"Knees up. Now spread those pretty thighs for me, Daisy."

I obey, moving a little slower than necessary just to keep a tiny grip on what little control I had left of the situation.

"Good girl," he growls.

The praise hits me like lightning. Yep... I have a praise kink.

He picks up the whip, teasing my breasts with the tassels. Then he flicks it. The sting makes me gasp, heat pooling between my legs instantaneously. He does it again, harder, making my hips jerk, a small breathy moan leaving my lips.

"So, my little flower likes pain?" He smirks, the look in his eyes making a shiver run down my spine.

I don't answer, and he cocks an eyebrow, dragging the whip lower. The corner of his mouth lifting slightly is all the indication I have that he's about to do something before he strikes between my legs. I yelp, slamming my thighs closed.

"Open your legs, Daisy."

I take a shaky breath, obeying his demand. He strikes again, just brushing my clit. I keep my thighs open despite the urge to slam them shut again.

"You're learning," he chuckles.

Sadistic bastard.

He tosses the whip aside and crawls onto the bed, trailing kisses over every red mark he's left on my body. He groans as he reaches my breasts, softly teasing them with flicks of his tongue, electricity shooting down my body, straight between my thighs, with every lick. He unsheathes a dagger from his trousers, softly trailing the blade up my body. I gasp, my eyes going wide as he looks up at me with his onyx eyes fully blown.

"Don't worry, sweetheart. This isn't for you... yet."

He slices his palm without hesitation and watches intently as the blood wells across the open wound.

"I want to see how sexy you look covered in my blood, and not your own for a change."

I nod and watch as he lowers his palm to my chest, smearing his blood from my throat, across my breasts, and down my stomach, stopping at my hips. He leans back, groaning deeply as he takes in the work of art he's created.

"Fuck," he breathes. "You look fucking incredible covered in my blood." He leans forward and whispers in my ear, "I'd happily let you slit my throat so I could bleed all over you."

His low, husky voice makes the hair on the back of my neck

stand. He moves slightly and begins cutting the rope from my wrists. I use the opportunity to lift my head from the pillow and kiss over his pecs, biting down on one of them. He grabs my throat, pushing my head back into the pillow with so much force I gasp.

"Bad girl," he growls in my face as my wrists come loose, the rope falling away. "You weren't given permission to touch. And here I was, being nice, cutting you free from your bindings." He tuts at me, shaking his head.

He leans in close, using the blade to move my head to the side. I feel his breath tickle my ear, and I shudder beneath him.

"Don't touch again without permission, sweetheart. Understood?" He nips at my ear as he holds the blade firmly against my skin.

"Yes," I whisper, the cool steel of the blade pressing against my jaw, hard enough to sting.

Korithax lowers his mouth to my throat, and without warning, bites hard with his elongated, sharp canines. I hiss, gripping the headboard with my hands so hard my fingers ache. He groans against my skin as he releases me, giving a soft lick over the bite mark.

He pushes himself up, and my eyes widen at the sight of my blood on his lower lip. "Your blood tastes just as good as your cunt."

"What, are you a vampire now?" I ask through a breathy laugh.

"I might just become one. I could become very addicted to tasting that." He smirks, his tongue cleaning the blood from the corner of his mouth.

He leans back on his haunches and flips the blade in his hand so the handle is facing me. "Take it."

I take the handle in my hand and hold the knife so the blade is inches away from him.

"Cut me, Daisy."

"What?" I ask, shaking my head softly.

"From here," He points just below his throat, between his collarbones. "To here." He drags his finger slowly, all the way down his muscled, tattooed body, to just above the waistband of his pants, a line of hair trailing below the fabric.

"Korithax," I whisper, the hesitation clear in my voice.

"I like the pain, Daisy. I like blood play. If you can't do it, use your safe word. Otherwise, fucking drag that blade down my gods-damned body." He leans forward into the blade, the tip of it poking exactly where he pointed, just below his throat. "Now," he growls.

I swallow hard and look up into his eyes. If this is what he wanted, then fine. I was afraid to hurt him, but if he enjoyed the pain, then I could offer that to him, just as he did me. I push the blade harder against his skin, a bead of blood forming. He groans, slowly closing his eyes as his head falls back.

"Yes," he breathes.

I slowly drag the blade down his body, and he leans into it, causing the tip to push deeper into his tanned flesh. I watch as the blood trickles down his body, some of it splashing down onto my stomach. I reach the edge of his waistband and let out a shaky breath, pulling the knife away from his skin. He lowers his head to look at me, his eyes glinting, almost looking possessed.

"Fuck, that felt good. You're doing so good, baby."

The praise sends another searing jolt of heat straight between my thighs, and I instinctively move my hips to try and alleviate the building pressure. I needed him badly. He chuckles, running his fingers through the blood on my stomach, dragging them all the way down to between my legs.

"Gods, you're soaked."

I bite my lip and decide to hell with it all. If he wanted this filthy, I was going to do my very best to give it to him. I bring the blade to my mouth, keeping my eyes pinned on his as I slowly lick up the edge, coating my tongue with his blood.

He completely stills, watching with fascination as I clean every last drop from the weapon, the coppery taste of him overloading my senses. I moan softly at his taste, my body seeming to come alive from his blood. His chest starts rising and falling hard as he watches me, his eyes seeming to get impossibly darker. I smirk at him, steeling myself to be as brave as possible. I can do this.

"I want to ride you, my king," I breathe, voice sultry.

He swallows thickly, nodding slowly before flipping us so that I'm suddenly above him. I shriek with laughter, making sure the blade doesn't hurt either of us as he positioned himself beneath me.

"Eager?" I giggle.

"For you, princess? Always."

CHAPTER 43
KORITHAX

I stare up at the most divine creature I've ever seen as she straddles me, blade still in her hand—now entirely clean after licking every last drop of my blood from it.

The sight of her tongue dragging across the steel made my heart thunder. In all my long existence, I've never seen anything more fucking beautiful. Watching her taste my blood confirmed what I already suspected deep in my bones. This mortal girl was created for me. She's divine. She's *mine.*

Considering her lack of experience, she's blowing my gods-damned mind. Everything I've thrown at her, she's taken in her stride—hesitating only for a second when it came to cutting me. And yet... she still did it. And the sight of her coated in my blood? It made something primal snap inside me.

She starts grinding on my cock, the length of it still trapped behind my pants, her body moving so perfectly it drags a groan from deep within my chest. Even through the barrier of fabric, I can feel her arousal.

"Fuck, Daisy. You're incredible."

She blushes, smiling as she toys with the blade, dragging it lightly across my chest but not cutting. My restraint is hanging on by a fucking thread. I need to be inside her. Now.

I burn my pants away with a flick of a thought. She gasps, and I chuckle darkly as her eyes drop to where my cock now throbs, free—and soaked from how wet she is. "Gods, you're dripping, baby girl."

She giggles shyly. The sound is soft, sinful, and electrifying as she begins to slide her slick cunt along the length of my cock, dragging her clit over the head with every stroke. The friction makes her whimper, and she starts picking up her pace as she grinds harder.

"That's it, princess," I growl. "Grind on me until you come."

I grip her hips, guiding her rhythm, watching her tits bounce as she rocks herself against me. Her head falls back, mouth open as she pants my name.

"Oh gods... Korithax..."

My name on her lips like that nearly ruins me. My grip tightens, bruising her soft, plush hips as I feel her start to tremble. Her orgasm hits hard, her body shaking as she falls forward, planting her hands on my chest to steady herself. She pants, twitching with the aftershocks of her pleasure, but I don't wait. I line myself up and slam inside her in one brutal thrust. A scream rips from her lips as I fill her completely. Her eyes fly open, glassy with tears as her cunt clenches around me. I hiss as I start to move, and she whimpers, her senses overwhelmed.

My hand wraps around her throat as I drive into her. Her pale skin reddens, her tears falling freely now as her oxygen depletes beneath my grip. Just before her eyes flutter shut, I release her. She gasps, greedily sucking in air, her body shaking with each punishing thrust that I deliver.

"Let me," she pants, voice hoarse.

I use every bit of restraint I have and go still, watching her carefully. She pushes herself up slowly, planting her hands on my stomach, shifting to straddle me fully. She winces at the angle, feeling all of me buried deep inside her. Gods... she's fucking breathtaking.

Never have I let a woman take control. I was the controller; I was the one who held the power. But Daisy? I'd give her every ounce of power I possess. I'd let her use me, break me, own me. I was hers entirely. She could use and abuse me in any way she saw fit, as long as she remained mine.

She begins to move slowly, trying to adjust herself to accommodate me. I see the pain on her face, the tears still streaking her cheeks, but she doesn't stop. She takes every single inch of me with stubborn grace. She slowly rocks her hips, the sight of her utterly hypnotising as her blonde hair falls over her tits, her ocean blue eyes smudged with mascara, her soft, plush body coated in my blood. Had my soul been transferred to the other side? Because there was no way this could be real.

She rises, hands moving to her breasts, rolling her nipples between her fingers. She moans loudly as she lifts herself high enough that my cock is barely inside of her, then she slowly lowers herself back down. Every inch that she drops, my soul feels like it's being torn from my body.

"Fuuuuuuuck Daisy," I groan.

She rises again, this time dropping back down hard and fast.

"Gods," she hisses, repeating the action over and over again.

Each thrust inside her drives me closer to the edge of insanity. She's fucking torturing me. My entire body is alight with need, her pussy pulsing around me like she was made for me.

"Let me fuck you, Daisy." I beg.

She shakes her head, hips slamming down again.

"Please... fuck. Daisy, please..." I growl, hands gripping the sheets, my head thrown back. She's driving me fucking crazy.

"Say it again," she breathes, stilling above me.

"What?" I pant.

"Say please," she smirks, devilish.

Little fucking minx. "Please," I snarl.

She doesn't even have a chance to agree before I yank her forward, forcing her body flush against mine. I grab her wrists and pin them behind her back with one hand, my other wrapping tight around her throat. I plant my feet into the mattress, bringing up my knees so I can slam up into her with reckless, brutal force.

Her cries echo through the room as I drive into her mercilessly. Her orgasm crashes over her, a scream ripping from her throat as her inner walls convulse around me. But I don't stop. I fuck her harder, deeper, my body locked on hers like a predator.

"Korithax. My husband. My king!" She screams.

Those words send me over the edge. I slam her down onto me, burying myself as deep as I can go, roaring my release as I explode inside her. The power pours from me unchecked—so wild the silk curtains around the bed burst into flames.

She collapses against me as I release her throat, trembling but still full of my cock, both of us panting like we've just survived a battle.

"Holy gods," she breathes.

"What the fuck," I mutter, glancing at the flames eating through the curtains.

"Does that happen often?" She asks between soft laughter, pointing at the desecrated pile of ash.

"That's never happened," I say, frowning. My brows pull together as something tight curls in my chest.

That power—I've never lost control of it like that before. Not once in all my life. Not even during war. Not even during my worst wrath. Not to mention my reserves were practically empty from realm jumping.

What the fuck is she doing to me? This girl—this mortal, beautiful, devastating little flower—was changing everything. And for some godforsaken reason, I found myself not giving a single fuck.

~

SHE's asleep on my chest.

Her cheek rests just over my heart, soft breaths puffing against my skin, her leg hooked lazily over mine like she's always belonged there. My arm is propped under my head, my other hand drifting slowly up and down her bare back, tracing the curve of her spine with light strokes.

I should be sleeping. I want to. The exhaustion from the journey was truly hitting me now. Not to mention the way Daisy and I had just fucked each other like our lives depended on it. But I can't. The soul tether has grown so strong, it's bordering on painful. Like something deep inside me is pulling tight, demanding I acknowledge what's happening between us. And I'm starting to believe that this is more than just an obsession. More than lust. More than fate's cruel game.

This, whatever she is, feels like a bond I've only ever heard whispered about. A myth. A legend. A mate. I've never believed in them, considering I've never actually seen any. Most immortals die before they ever find theirs in my realm, if they exist. And a mortal with an immortal? Unheard of.

But the way her soul calls to mine? It's exactly how they describe it. Once two bonded souls come into contact, there's no resisting it. No denying. You can try to walk away, try to lie to yourself. Hell, you can even try to kill the connection. But it always comes back. Always finds you, always burns through. And gods, ever since I met her... I haven't even been able to stay away.

I don't want to stay away, I can admit that to myself now. Even before I met her physically, there was something strange, something that pulled at me. I rarely linger after a soul deal is made. I collect, I leave. That is how I've always done it. But the day her father summoned me, offering up her soul, something inside of me couldn't wait to go and tell her. I waited for her, I actually fucking waited. And when she appeared... everything changed. Her voice. Her eyes. The broken light that still glowed softly inside her, even when the world had tried its damned hardest to stamp it out. Her soul sang to mine instantly. Even then—especially then—I think I already knew. Like the universe had placed her right in my path, gift-wrapped in pain and defiance, just for me.

I never believed in fate, not really. The divine assholes had me convinced that everything was planned, made, and created. But this? This feels like fate handed me something precious. Something once-in-a-lifetime. And now that I have her, I'll never let her go. Not in this life. Not in the next. Even if I were reborn a thousand times, I'd choose her in every single life. I'd spend every lifetime carving through time and space to find her again. I've lived my entire existence as a weapon. As an heir. As a monster. But now... something inside me is alive, and it burns only for her. I'm more than just the heir to a broken throne. I'm hers.

I CLOSE MY EYES, resting my chin against her head. Her hair smells faintly of her lavender scent, and the familiar heat of her skin comforts me in a way nothing else ever has. She softly moves, a small sound escaping her lips. A whimper. Her fingers twitch against my ribs, and I glance down to see her brows furrowed. Her whole body begins to tremble, delicate muscles tensing against mine.

"Shhh... Daisy, you're okay." I whisper, brushing my lips to her temple. "You're safe. I've got you."

But she doesn't wake. She keeps shaking against me. I've never seen her have a nightmare before. She starts mumbling, words I don't understand. The language is ancient. Not demonic, not celestial or fae or anything I recognise. I strain to make sense of it, but whatever it is, it's older than any tongue I've ever heard spoken.

My heart lurches. Her skin starts heating beneath my hands rapidly. The warm, sleepy glow becomes something more volatile. Her body is radiating heat like a forge, sweat beading across her skin in seconds. The air around us thickens, and the scent of ash slams into me like a wall. My head jerks up, scanning the room. No flames. No hellfire or soulfire to be seen. My powers are under control. So why does it smell like smoke?

I glance down at her again. Her eyes are shut tight, tears spilling in steady streams from beneath her lashes. She's crying in her sleep, but not waking. Her breathing is ragged. Desperate.

"Daisy," I whisper again, voice sharper now. I cup her cheek. "Daisy, wake up." She doesn't. "Daisy," I growl.

Her lips part, another line of that ancient language slipping from them, soft and urgent. And then—

She goes still. Limp. The heat vanishes all at once, like a flame being snuffed out. The room cools, and the scent of ash fades. But still, she doesn't wake. The tears stop and her breathing evens, her body curling slightly closer into me.

I stare down at her in stunned silence for a moment.

"What the fuck was that?" I whisper.

I brush my fingers over her brow, pushing her damp hair away from her face, but her expression is calm now. Peaceful even. Like nothing happened at all. But it did, I felt it. I felt something ancient and fucking terrifying move through her just now.

I look around the room again, adrenaline coursing through me.

"What the fuck is going on in this realm?"

CHAPTER 44

The flames are everywhere.

They twist and roar like a storm made of fire, licking up the stone walls, swallowing the air until it tastes of soot and blood. The throne looms again—closer this time. I can almost reach it. Its spires rise from the scorched earth like jagged bones, blackened and cracked, glowing faintly at the seams. A crown lies at the foot of the throne, twisted, broken, melted. Like it's been ripped from someone's burning skull.

And there—just beyond the flames—I see them.

Seven silhouettes.

Seven beings cloaked in shadow, standing in a wide arc before the desecrated throne. They do not move. They do not speak. But their presence cleaves the dream in half. My soul recoils in recognition.

The one that stands broad, still as death, has a presence that makes my stomach twist. Something inside me knows—he is the betrayer.

The flames shift. Screams echo.

The throne is empty; but the ash around it is soaked with blood. My blood.

I try to scream, but my voice doesn't work. My hands are burnt, bones peeking through peeling skin, and still, I reach toward the throne.

I hear it now, for the first time. It is clear. The voice, hoarse, ancient, made of smoke and dust. It murmurs in a language I do not understand. Until I do.

"Vireth at'zul... e'kara sultan..."

Ash and betrayal...

"Kael'vireth a'sul... shetha'zai en'karan...

Thaloriren ez'rem, vae'shakar il'drun.

Na'kaziel vel'tharan... kael'rion et'shara.

Vireth kai'syl... elthea'nur az'shal.

Aelari su'nai vel'zur... il'saerin et'kal."

She was created from the ash.

She was destroyed in the ash.

Her soul chained, her name erased.

But she will rise as the sun—

And burn us all.

THE SHADOWS STEP BACK. The throne ignites in golden flame. And the ash coats my tongue once again.

CHAPTER 45
DAISY

The bright light of Luminaria streams through the tall windows, casting golden ribbons across the bed as I wake up.

My eyes flutter open slowly, my body aching in the best way. Every muscle hums with soreness—the kind that makes you blush just thinking about it. The healing tonic still sits untouched on the bedside table like an afterthought. Heat rushes to my cheeks as I remember how filthy it'd gotten. He was all demon—punishing, relentless, mine. And I'd loved every second of it.

The shower afterward had been tender. Gentle. He'd held me like I was breakable, like I was something precious and fragile. I think that part undid me more than anything else. I'm not sure anyone else has ever seen that side of him, and I relished in the fact that I got to see the tender side of the Heir of Hell. I just hope he doesn't go back to cold Kori today. I don't think I could handle the whiplash, not after last night. Not when I'm still riding the high of being fully his.

I lift my head from his chest, blinking up at him. He's already awake, watching me with his brows furrowed and his jaw tight, like he's in the middle of a war with himself.

"Good morning," I say softly, offering a small smile.

Please don't be an ass. Please don't be an ass.

He quirks his mouth up slightly and strokes his hand slowly up and down my spine. "Good morning, little flower."

I internally release a sigh of relief. Thank the gods. Not an ass. Not yet, at least.

"You okay?" I ask gently. "You were frowning when I looked up at you."

He nods and leans forward, pressing a kiss to my forehead. The tenderness of it hits me right in the chest, and the butterflies go feral.

"How did you sleep?" He asks, voice careful. His eyes look into mine like he's searching for something.

"Good, I think," I say, frowning slightly. "My body definitely hurts, though." I huff a laugh, heat blooming across my cheeks.

He stretches across me and grabs the healing tonic from the bedside table. He pops the cork and gently presses it to my lips.

"Drink up, princess. I need you strong for the last leg of our journey."

I tip my head back and swallow the cool, swirling liquid. It slips down my throat like silk, the magic tingling as it goes down. I feel the power of it slowly soothing the ache in my limbs. He pulls the bottle away, setting it down again, and uses the pad of his thumb to wipe the corner of my mouth.

"So..." he says, "no nightmares or anything?"

I blink. "Uh, I don't think so. Why?"

"No reason." He says, just a little too quickly. "Just asking."

My mouth parts to push him, but he cuts me off. "Any regrets?"

"Regrets?" I echo. "About what?"

"Last night," he says, almost too softly. He lays his head back on the pillow, eyes staring up at the ceiling like he's afraid of my answer.

I pause for a moment. Still naked, I climb over him and straddle his torso, pressing my palms into the pillow on either side of his head. I lean down until our foreheads touch, having to rise to my knees because of how freaking tall this man is. My golden hair falls like a curtain around us.

"Not a single one," I whisper. "Husband."

I press a soft kiss to the tip of his nose. His eyes flash, and he growls at me. The next second, I'm on my back, pinned beneath him. His hands trap mine above my head, his body pressing me into the mattress. I don't miss the feel of his cock pressing against me, solid and fucking huge.

"Don't say that word while straddling me naked," he growls, "unless you want me to fuck you until you're a whimpering mess, Daisy."

I consider my options:

Option A: Be a good girl and behave.

Option B: Whisper that word again and see if he follows through on that delicious threat.

I smirk, sucking my lower lip between my teeth. His nostrils flare, his eyes narrowing as he senses what I'm about to do. I feel the shift in energy, and a low, feral sound rumbles in his throat as he narrows his eyes at me.

"Husband," I whisper.

I LAY PANTING, the ache between my thighs blooming all over again in the most intoxicating way. Korithax lies beside me, his chest rising and falling heavily, sweat still glistening on his golden skin.

"I'll never, ever, tire of being inside you," he murmurs, voice low and rough with after-sex satisfaction.

I blush, giggling as I bury my face into his arm. I don't think I'll ever tire of it either. He was right about what Ethan did. Yes, he'd taken my virginity—but he didn't claim me. He didn't make love to me. He didn't have filthy sex with me. He just... took.

But Korithax? Korithax touched me like I was a living altar. He worshipped every inch of me. Maybe it wasn't gentle—maybe it never would be—but it was mine. Ours. I liked how he treated me in bed. I loved the way his hands explored me like he was memorising every curve. The way his mouth devoured me like I was his favourite meal. The sinful sounds he made when he tasted me, moaning like I was a prayer answered. Those sounds would echo in my head for a lifetime. This seven-foot god of a man, this demon prince, was entirely mine.

Maybe Elyistria had heard my quiet, desperate pleas and sent me the man of my godsdamn dreams.

A sharp knock breaks the silence, and Korithax snarls. He freaking snarled, like a wild animal being disturbed from its peace.

"Down boy," I giggle, swatting at his chest. In retaliation, he slaps my ass.

I yelp—just as a voice calls through the door.

"Your Majesty, Elyistria asked me to remind you of your breakfast arrangement. She would like to see you within the next half hour. I shall return to escort you shortly."

"Thank you," I call out, trying to suppress my laughter.

Korithax groans dramatically and wraps his arms around me, dragging me against him.

I snort, trying to wiggle away. "I have to get ready. I can't keep a literal magical goddess waiting."

"Of course you can. You're the future Queen of Hell." He grumbles against me.

"Future being the keyword," I mutter, rolling my eyes. "And I'm pretty sure you already pissed her off enough yesterday with your whole Child of Ruin tantrum. I'm not looking to add fuel to that particular fire."

He scowls but rolls out of bed with me, his hair tousled, wrapped around his horns. His elongated ears poke out from his onyx locks, and his dark eyes shine in the glowing light. I stand for a moment and just marvel at the sight of him, fresh out of bed with sex hair. I can't help the snort of laughter that escapes me.

"Why are you laughing?" He asks, tilting his head.

"Because I'm standing in a freaking magical realm, god knows how far away from earth, with my seven-foot demonic god of a freaking husband. Who, not to mention, is standing butt naked in front of me, with his sex hair wrapped around his horns. It's all so absurd, yet feels entirely right."

The grin that splits his face has those freaking butterflies going feral yet again. His too-white teeth shining, the sight of his elongated canines sends a shiver down my spine at the memory of them digging into my throat just a few hours ago.

"Me. Daisy Sandoval. A boring, twenty-year-old mortal girl, married to the most feared twenty-thousand-year-old demon in the universe." I laugh again, the sound echoing through the vast space.

He prowls towards me, holding either side of my face with his hands as his expression turns serious. "There is nothing boring about you, little flower. You are fucking divine. A prayer answered. The most magnificent creature I have ever laid my eyes on. And you are mine. In this life, and every life after." He presses his forehead to mine as I stare at him in shock. "If death takes me, I'll claw my way out of the grave. If the gods erase me, I'll set the universe ablaze to return to you. Across lifetimes, across worlds, I would crawl through ash and ruin just to touch your hand again."

I blink up at him, his words settling in every crack, every fracture of my soul, mending it in its own, tragically beautiful way. He places a soft kiss on my lips, a rumble sounding in his chest. He pulls me in tight, the kiss quickly turning heated as he trails his hands over my still naked flesh.

"I have to get ready." I breathe, pushing at him softly.

"Fine," he sighs. "But only because we're going to need her help to get back home once this is done."

Home.

The word sends a flutter through me. I'll be going home, to Zeriavoss. To the obsidian halls and the skies that flicker with never-ending blood-red lightning. Back to the demons I'd started seeing as my own people. I'd be going as an immortal, to become a queen. My life had taken a turn so sharp; I was still trying to catch my breath. Yet there was one thing holding me back from truly being happy.

"When do you think I'll get to see Talia and Ezra again?" I ask, gnawing at the inside of my cheek.

He gently brushes a thumb over my jaw before planting a soft kiss atop my head. "As soon as we return and it's safe, I'll take you back to the mortal realm. I swear it."

I nod, but it doesn't chase the anxiety away that's been eating at me since I agreed to this deal. We both knew it wouldn't be that easy. We didn't know how the Divine Six were going to respond to what we'd done.

I tried not to think about it too much, but it was becoming harder to ignore. What if they still tried to kill me? Immortality wasn't a shield, I could still be destroyed. And what if they destroyed Zeriavoss? All those people. The children. The families. Everything Korithax had fought to protect—gone. Because of me.

Panic creeps into my chest like cold fingers. Korithax senses it instantly, and he gently tilts my chin, forcing me to look up at him.

"Hey," he says firmly. "It's all going to be okay. I'll deal with the divine assholes. Nothing will happen to you."

"It's not me I'm worried about," I whisper. "It's your people. Your kingdom. What if they try to destroy Zeriavoss?"

He shakes his head. "Our people. Our kingdom. And I'll destroy them before they ever get the chance. I swear to you, Daisy, I won't let them lay a single finger on what's ours."

I stare into his eyes, searching for any signs of doubt. But there's none. Only steel and fire. Only the same ruthless determination I've seen in his eyes time and time again.

For the first time in days, the storm inside me quietens. Because I believe him. And gods help anyone who dares threaten what's his. I saw what he did to Kaelith. I know what this demon of mine is capable of.

I'm escorted through the luminous hallways of the palace, my footsteps echoing softly against the bright white marble beneath me. The walls shimmer faintly with embedded veins of crystal, casting refracted rainbows with every passing glint of light. Magical sconces pulse gently with warm light, and the air smells faintly of citrus blossoms.

The guard leading me wears an intricate gold uniform, his breastplate engraved with protective runes that shimmer with faint magic. His long, silken cape trails behind him, embroidered with a blazing crown set against rays of dawn. He doesn't speak, and I don't try to start a conversation. My stomach is too tightly knotted up for any form of pleasantries.

We turn a corner and enter a grand chamber. A long, gleaming white marble table sits at its centre like something out of a medieval TV show where a banquet would take place. At the head of the table sits Elyistria. Her serene gaze lifts to mine, and despite her ever-soothing aura, a strange anxiety coils in my gut. I don't know why, but something tells me I'm not going to enjoy whatever this is.

"Good morning, Daisy," she says softly, a warm smile on her face. "Please, take a seat."

I return her smile politely and walk to the single chair that's sat at the opposite end of the massive table. There's so much space between us, and I can't help but think that was done purposefully. I sit just as a beautiful elven-looking woman steps up beside me with a crystal jug of shimmering liquid.

"Good morning," I say softly, nodding to her.

She pours the drink, and it sparkles like liquid starlight. I hesitate just for a moment. Could it be poison? No... surely not. She doesn't seem like the murderous type, but isn't this exactly the kind of thing I should be worried about now?

"It is called eltherai," Elyistria says, noticing my hesitation. "A sparkling fruit juice harvested from solvine blooms. Everything grown here is born of my magic."

I don't want to appear rude, so I lift the glass. The scent hits me instantly—fresh, sweet, and so intoxicating my mouth waters. I take a sip. "Gods," I gasp. "This is divine."

She laughs softly, and I blink, startled by how beautiful the sound is. She looks every bit the angel you see depicted in art—flawless ivory skin, nearly white-blonde hair, and those piercing silver-blue eyes with flecks of gold that seem to see too much. Her hands fold calmly in her lap, but I can see it now—something in her posture is tight. Wound up to the point she looks like she may snap.

"So," I say, trying to sound neutral. "I'm guessing there's a reason I'm here this morning. Alone."

"Yes," she replies gently, "Especially without your king. I wanted to speak of who you are... and who you are becoming."

The anxiety claws higher. I say nothing, letting her continue. I just want this over with, I hate confrontation.

She exhales slowly. "I know you do not remember. But you will. And all I can do now is apologise for who I was before." I look at her in confusion, but she doesn't pay much attention to it as she continues. "While I am one of the oldest beings in the universe, it took me a very long time to trust in my power. In myself."

Her eyes glimmer, and I swear I see a tear form. But it's gone as quickly as it came.

"I am sorry, Daisy. When the truth comes to light, I only ask one thing—that you remember this moment. That I am here now. And that I will not fail you again."

I frown. "I have no idea what you're talking about. You seem... afraid of me. Elyistria, I promise, you don't need to be."

Is this what it was going to be like now that I was going to be Queen of Hell? People fearing me? I didn't want that. Not even in the slightest.

"I am afraid," she whispers. "But not of you. I am afraid of what's coming. Of the challenges you'll have to face. And I am afraid that you will forget that I am with you, because last time, I wasn't. And you died."

My breath catches, her words settling into my brain. *Died.*

I grit my teeth, anger coursing through me alongside confusion. "I'm getting really tired of the riddles and cryptic crap, Elyistria. Please forgive me if I sound rude, but either tell me what you mean, or I'm leaving."

She sighs and bows her head. "I cannot. Not yet. But remember this: I am with you, Queen of Hell. And when you need me most, I will answer your call."

I push my chair back with a loud scrape, frustration boiling over. "Thank you for your hospitality," I mutter, standing to leave.

I turn on my heel and head for the exit, tension crackling in my spine like lightning. What a freaking waste of time. Another vague speech. Another warning wrapped in a riddle. Why can't anyone just give me a straight answer?

I'm halfway down the corridor when I hear a scream. "DAISY!"

I whirl around just in time to see Elyistria sprinting toward me, her gown billowing behind her like a wave of moonlight, her guards not far behind.

Her face is paler than normal, a panicked expression etched across her beautiful face. "The Divine Six are here. Where is Korithax?"

My blood runs cold. "He's in our room."

She grabs my hand—her grip almost painful—and a blinding flash envelops us before I can scream. We appear in the bedroom not a moment later. I stumble slightly from the jolt of magic coursing through me, my heart thudding in my chest. Korithax is already on his feet, storming towards us. His eyes zero in on Elyistria's hand, still gripping mine painfully.

"Get your hands off her!" He snarls, yanking me away from her. His body moves in front of mine, full of rage and protection.

"Korithax, you need to leave. NOW!" She shouts.

"Excuse me?" He snaps.

"The Divine Six are here," I whisper, dread crawling up my spine. "They found us."

His face drains of colour. "What the fuck... did you tell them we were here?" He growls at Elyistria.

Her expression flashes with offence. "Of course not. If I had, I wouldn't have come running to your queen like this. You need to go. They want her dead."

Her words hit me like a blow to the chest. I knew it. I knew this would happen.

"But—" I begin, "maybe if we just explain that I'm becoming immortal. That was their problem, right? That I was mortal—"

"No!" They both bark in unison.

"It doesn't matter," Elyistria says. "They won't listen. They won't hesitate. The moment they see her, they will strike. You must leave. Now."

Korithax is already grabbing the pack from the bed, his movements sharp.

"Thank you," he says quickly. "I won't forget this."

"Go," she says. "When it's done, come straight to me. Do you understand?"

He nods once, then pulls me into his arms. Shouts erupt from the corridor outside, and Korithax doesn't wait a minute longer. With one last look at Elyistria, he teleports us out of the realm of light, straight into the unknown.

CHAPTER 46
KORITHAX

The second we land, I finally let myself breathe.

Not because we're safe—we aren't. But because we're no longer within arm's reach of the Divine Six. And that has to count for something.

I have no idea how the fuck they found us, but hopefully they have no idea where we're heading, and why. Even if they did, I didn't think they'd follow us here. This is the only realm they don't bother with. They gave up a long time ago on trying to police this realm, and I couldn't fault them.

"Are you okay?" I ask, catching Daisy before she stumbles. Her legs wobble from the sudden transition, but she steadies herself, clinging to me like I'm the only stable thing left in her world. She nods, taking a deep breath. But the second her eyes take in our surroundings, they widen. And unlike the other realms, it's not a pleasant look that follows after.

"This is Noxthrallia?" She whispers.

"Yes," I answer grimly. "Welcome to the final realm of our journey."

A shiver runs down her spine, and I feel it in my bones. The atmosphere here sinks into the skin like rot—thick, humid, and laced with something so heavy and dark it makes the hairs on my arms rise. It's a realm that doesn't just want to destroy you; it wants to know what you ache for first.

"Gods," she murmurs, eyes scanning the murky bogs and twisted trees. "This place makes Hell sound like a fairytale."

I can't help but smirk. "Well, it is, isn't it? After all, your Prince Charming came from there."

She scoffs and lightly pushes at my chest. "Prince? Sure. Charming? Not even a little."

"Rude." I scowl, and she just winks back at me.

I take her hand in mine as we start walking, the action just instinct now. Never in my twenty-thousand years of life did I think holding hands would be something I would enjoy, but the feel of her tiny palm in mine is a comfort I've grown to crave.

The ground beneath us is spongy with black moss that's coiled around ancient roots of gnarled trees. The air smells like wet earth and death. Whispers cling to every gust of wind, brushing against the backs of our necks like cold, dead fingers that we can't slap away.

"This is the realm of dark magic," I murmur. "Where corruption is currency, and desire is poison. The creatures here... they don't need to hunt you. They just wait until you want something badly enough to beg. Then they give it to you, for a price."

We follow the narrow, half-submerged path winding toward the northern swamplands, where Maelkar Vyre—the Shadowtongue—keeps his throne made of stolen souls and blackened bone. A palace sits there, built from the broken bodies of his victims. Some of them human, some of them creatures of the realms, some of them mine.

I grit my teeth at the thought of seeing him perched upon the bones of my people. This isn't about me though; it's about her. Turning her immortal. This is the place she becomes stronger, less fragile, less breakable. And I'll ensure that here, nothing hurts her. I will burn this entire fucking realm to nothing but blackened ash before I let it harm her.

We pass a bog that gurgles as something shifts beneath the surface, causing ripples to spread across the murky water. We're already being watched. The whispers seem to grow louder the further we walk, coming from the bogs and the bones beneath our feet.

Daisy flinches beside me. "What was that?" She gasps, pressing close to my side.

I follow her gaze. In the bog, just beneath the veil of darkness, a pair of eyes gleam—dead, glassy, and completely void of thought.

"That," I say grimly, "is a Vyreshade. Creatures made by Maelkar from corrupted beings—mortal, fae, demon, even gods. They come seeking desires, and when their deals run dry, he strips their souls and twists them into those things. Now they drag others into the dark and feast."

Her grip tightens on my hand as I feel her fear vibrating around her.

"They're not just here," I continue. "He sends some into other realms disguised as temptation. A perfect lover, a lost child, a promise of peace. They're all the same in the end—bait."

Her voice is small. "So... he's worse than you. No offence."

I nod once. "So much worse. I take souls in trade for their wants, with no trickery. He takes everything, the deals lasting as long as he wants them to. I await death before collecting. He collects whenever he likes."

A beat of silence. Then, quietly, she asks, "Was this really the only way to make me immortal?"

My jaw clenches. "Only dark magic can turn a person immortal from mortal. And Maelkar is the only dark magic wielder that I know of. Although I'm sure it won't come without a price."

Her swallow is so loud it's audible even above the whispers. I grip her close, hooking her chin up to look at me. "I'll keep you safe, Daisy. I won't fail you again."

She frowns. "You have never failed me, Korithax."

I look away from her gaze, knowing damn well that her words weren't true.

"Look at me," she says.

I look down at her again, her ocean-blue eyes glowing with purity, even here. "You saved me, Kori."

She chews her lip, like she's nervous for whatever she's about to say next. But before she gets a chance, a loud screech sounds from the sky, and I drag her back against my chest instinctively, my wings exploding from my back with a loud whoosh. My magic reserves are low—dangerously low—but I know exactly what's lurking above, and if I need a quick escape, by foot wasn't going to work.

"What the hell was that?" Daisy asks, eyes darting skyward.

"A Velgrithon," I mutter. "A flying predator that looks similar to a gargoyle with venom for blood. And no, it's not friendly."

She groans. "Of course it isn't."

"Nothing here is, little flower," I say. "Not even Maelkar. Especially not Maelkar. Remember that."

I don't put away my wings, even though they feel like they're carved from stone now. We walk deeper into the mire, the path ahead winding into shadow. Daisy presses close, and I feel her tremble. I wrap an arm around her, trying my best to make her feel as safe as possible.

"I won't let anything happen to you," I promise. "Even if I have to rip out my soul and hand it to Maelkar myself."

Just as I finish my sentence, the whispers halt, and the sudden silence feels so much worse. Because now we're being watched, but not by the dead—by something very, very alive. We've reached the edge of Maelkar's domain, the bones beneath our feet glowing faintly violet, like veins of corruption threading through the land. The Shadowtongue knows we're here. And he's waiting.

"FUCK" I breathe, frustration biting into every word.

"What? What is it?" Daisy asks, her voice laced with panic.

"He knows we're here." I clench my jaw. "I wanted time to build my reserves before facing him. But I guess we don't have that luxury today."

The whispers suddenly start again. This time, much louder, more frantic, and coming from every single direction. My heart pounds against my ribs as I brace myself, forcing my mental shields up. I lock every desire, every weakness, behind a wall of impenetrable stone in my mind.

Daisy throws her hands over her ears, her breathing turning rapid. Her eyes squeeze shut as she whimpers, stumbling into me to bury her face into my chest as she shakes her head violently. Shit. I should've prepared her better and taught her how to shield her mind before ever bringing her here. It's too easy to forget that she's mortal, that she's untrained. And this realm is poison to the unguarded mind.

I wrap my arms around her, then unfurl my wings, pulling them tight around us like a shield. We're wrapped entirely in me now—a cocoon of bone, leathery skin, and muscle.

"Shh, you're okay," I whisper, my mouth at her temple. "Daisy, listen to me. I need you to picture a door in your mind. A heavy one, okay? Put every want, every need behind that door and slam it shut. Hard!"

She shakes her head again, her entire body trembling as she whimpers softly against me.

"Try harder, Daisy. Slam that fucking door."

Her body stiffens, her whimpers turning more frantic as her breaths coming in fast and hard. I grip onto her tightly, my heart racing in panic, but slowly, she stills as a calmness takes over her. Her breathing begins to slow, and I watch her eyes screw tight as a faint furrow forms between her brows. I watch her intently, not wanting to break her concentration. Come on, little flower, you can do this. She slowly lifts her hands from her ears and blinks up at me, her face glistening with sweat.

"I did it," she whispers, her voice trembling slightly. "I slammed the door."

A slow, wicked smile curves my lips as I lower my mouth to hers. I kiss her gently, letting my wings begin to unfold. "Well done, my sunshine."

"WELL, WELL, WELL..." A smooth, velvet voice cuts through the air like a poisoned blade. "Look at what the cat dragged in."

I glance up, immediately placing the source. Maelkar Vyre.

He stands barefoot on the murky path, dark purple robes swirling around him like smoke. His shoulder-length inky waves glisten, drenched like he's just emerged from the bog himself. His skin is slick midnight, laced with glowing violet veins. Bone and silver trinkets sway from his ears and neck, clinking faintly with every movement. And his eyes—pitch black, with a thin glowing ring of violet—lock onto mine with amusement. A too-perfect, chilling smile stretches his lips. Warm yet wrong. Kind yet predatory.

"Keep your walls up," I murmur to Daisy. "Keep that door locked tight."

She nods once, stepping slightly behind me.

"Maelkar," I greet, voice cold.

"Child of Ruin," he croons with a grin. The title burns like a slap. "And this... must be your sunshine." His gaze slides over Daisy, slow and heavy, like he's imagining her without her clothing. "Aren't you a delicious sight?"

I pull her firmly to my side, shielding her with my body as undead shadows begin to slither closer, forming a tight-knit half circle around us.

"What's with the welcoming party, Shadowtongue? I pose no threat to you... yet."

Maelkar laughs, a low and sharp sound that has my spine stiffening, waving a hand. Instantly, the undead slink back—some vanishing into shadows, others dissolving into the mire.

"Just a precaution, princeling. Not every day royalty comes strolling through my rot. Or such tempting mortals." He licks his lips slowly, his gaze still locked on Daisy.

"I think you'll find there's nothing tempting about me," She says, chin lifting in defiance, even as her heartbeat thunders against my side.

Gods... I love her fire.

Maelkar's eyes spark with delight as he releases another laugh. "Your desires smell utterly divine, sunshine. Why don't you let me have a taste, and I'll be the judge of how tempting you really are."

A snarl rips from my chest. "Back the fuck off of my wife, Shadowtongue. Or I'll rip that silver tongue from your skull and mount it on my wall."

"Wife?" Maelkar purrs, his eyebrows raised in clear amusement. "The Child of Ruin marries a mortal? Oh, I'm sure the Divine Six fucking loved that."

"That's why we're here," I growl. "I need a favour."

His eyes flash with delight. "Now there's a proposition I'm dying to hear." He turns smoothly, gesturing toward the grotesque palace behind him. "Come. Let's not linger in the wastes too long. Even I can't control all of my creatures' thirsts."

I KEEP my body close to Daisy's as we follow Maelkar through the twisted paths of Noxthrallia. The swamp thickens around us, black water flowing beneath warped bridges of rotted wood and bone. Vines drip from twisted trees, slick with decay, and the air reeks of wet earth and something rancid beneath. The shadows never seem to stay still, and every step feels like we're walking deeper into a nightmare.

The Shadowtongue leads us to his palace—if you can call it that. It rises from the mire like a corpse clawing its way out of the earth. Made entirely of blackened bone and corrupted soul stone, it moans softly with the wind, the stolen souls woven into its walls still trying to scream out for help. Daisy clings tighter to me, her gaze darting around the decrepit courtyard. Even brave as she is, this place is a fucking nightmare; and we haven't even stepped inside yet.

"Welcome to my little home," Maelkar purrs, spinning on his heel with his arms stretched wide, facing us with a grin that makes my skin itch. "Forgive the decor. Bones are in fashion this century."

I don't respond, my jaw flexing as I watch him closely.

"And this," he gestures to the tall twisted doors behind him, "is where your salvation begins, or your doom. Depending on how well you negotiate."

He throws a wink in my direction, and it takes every ounce of strength I have not to punch his fucking face in.

"We didn't come for games," I growl.

"You came to bargain with temptation incarnate, princeling. Everything is a game to me." His eyes slide to Daisy again, his tongue slowly dragging along his lower lip. "Especially her."

Daisy narrows her eyes, lifting her chin. "I'm not some prize to be toyed with, Maelkar."

He tilts his head and grins wider, his sharp teeth glinting. "No, sunshine. You're the storm that'll drown kingdoms. But even the fiercest storms can be bottled... if you find the right vessel."

I place myself between them, letting what little of my power I have flare, thick black smoke coiling around my shoulders. Just enough to remind him that I'm not in the mood for riddles or flirtation.

He sighs dramatically in response. "Fine. Come in, come in," he mutters, sweeping the doors open with a wave of his hand. A low groan echoes from within, like the house is alive and reluctant to host us.

We step into the hall of bone and souls, the air thickening instantly. The walls pulse faintly, veins of violet corruption glowing beneath their surface. Maelkar walks ahead, the door groaning closed behind us as we follow him to a chamber that sits deep inside the palace. The floor is a circle of carved runes, black and slick with something that looks like oil... or blood. In the corner is a dark obsidian basin, smoking faintly.

"So, you wish to turn her immortal." He smirks.

"How—"

"The whispers, Korithax. Even your shields aren't strong enough to keep everything hidden."

I grit my teeth. My mental walls were fucking impenetrable; there was no way he could get through them, surely.

"This is where the rite will take place," Maelkar says, voice suddenly lower. "But first... payment."

"Name it," I snap.

Maelkar looks between us, then speaks slowly and deliberately. "I want a memory. One you treasure. One that hurts. One that burns."

I frown. "Okay, fine." I go to step toward him.

"No," he says softly. "Hers."

I feel Daisy freeze beside me, and I feel the fury bubble inside of me. As if sensing the growing rage inside of me, Maelkar turns his eyes to mine.

"No harm will come to her. No mark left behind. I only want to taste what made her who she is. To understand the fire I'm being asked to ignite."

"Absolutely not," I snarl.

"Then the rite does not happen," Maelkar replies with a shrug, as though we've just declined fucking tea. "Your choice."

I turn to Daisy, but she's already staring at him, unblinking. Her shoulders are squared, and her chin is raised. She stands at five feet five inches, but she currently faces the Shadowtongue as if she were also seven feet tall.

"You'll take a memory, but I'll still remember it, right?"

"Of course," he says sweetly. "It will merely taste... dimmer. A page half-burned. Still there, but harder to read."

She swallows hard, then nods. “Fine. Take it.”

My jaw drops as I grab a hold of her, turning her to face me. “Daisy—”

“I want to be strong, Korithax,” she says, cutting me off. “I want to be immortal, to stay with you for as long as possible. If giving a memory is the price, then I’ll pay it.”

Maelkar grins, his voice almost manic as he sing-songs. “Then let the ritual begin.”

CHAPTER 47
DAISY

I step into the darkened tub, the black gown I wear clinging to my body, the fabric floating in the water like spilled ink.

The liquid is warm, murky, and dense, clinging to my skin with the weight of something unnatural. The scent is overwhelming, like earth, ash, and ancient magic long since rotted. The tips of my hair brush the surface, steam curling around me like a living thing. I lower myself until the water reaches my neck, my breath hitching as anxiety claws at me.

"If you fucking hurt her," Korithax snarls, taking a step toward me. His voice is low, a lethal warning.

"Oh, please," Maelkar says, waving a lazy hand. "Like I'd be stupid enough to piss off the Heir of Hell. I'm not suicidal, Korithax." He smirks, gliding to my side. "Back up, princeling. Unless you want your own memories peeled from that pretty skull."

Korithax's jaw flexes, his eyes seeming to have a glowing ember behind them.

"It's okay, Korithax," I whisper, meeting his eyes. "I'll be okay."

Reluctantly, Korithax steps back, but the murderous energy radiating off of him could ignite the walls. Gods, if looks could kill, every inch of Noxthrallia would be ash.

"Alright, sunshine," Maelkar says, lowering his voice into a croon as he moves behind me. "Lay your head back and let the water hold you. Just relax for me."

I inhale sharply and do as he says. My head tips back against the curve of the tub, the warmth lapping at my throat. He gathers my hair with a reverent touch, letting it fall like a golden curtain over the outside edge of the basin. I look up and see Maelkar's eyes gleaming, those pitch-black irises circled by that eerie violet ring. His thumb strokes my bottom lip.

"Delicious," he murmurs.

His face is breathtaking. Beautiful in the way a predator can be—mesmerising, exquisite... and absolutely wrong. Korithax snarls from across the room, a guttural warning that shakes the very air.

Maelkar merely chuckles, drawing his hand back from my face. "Down, boy."

He leans in, his voice velvet, his murky scent invading my senses. "Now... let's open that little door in your mind, shall we?"

I nod, breathing through the knot in my chest. I find the door—the one I had slammed shut earlier just to stay sane—and I let it creak open. The memory waiting behind it slithers into the forefront of my mind like a venomous fog. It rises, threatening to choke me, but I don't fight it. I let it in. Maelkar's nostrils flare, his pupils dilating so much that the violet completely vanishes. His body trembles as he moans—low and guttural, like he's tasting something exquisite.

"Close your eyes, sweetheart."

I obey, and his hands slide to my temples, cool and firm. The world falls away, and I'm there again.

THE HOSPITAL ROOM IS WHITE.

Too white. It smells like bleach and sadness. Machines beep

softly behind me, counting down the seconds to a final breath. I'm seven years old, clutching my mother's hand in both of mine, my little fingers barely able to wrap around hers. Her skin is pale—almost translucent. Her lips are dry and cracked. She's bald beneath her bright yellow silk scarf, her once-glowing blonde hair now only a memory. Her honey eyes, sunken and rimmed in purple shadows, flicker slowly open. She smiles.

She always smiles. Even when the pain's unbearable. Even when the nurses whispered, and the doctors stopped offering words of hope.

"Sunshine..." she whispers, her voice so faint it could be mistaken for wind. "You're...so brave..."

Her hand twitches in mine, her thumb barely grazing my knuckles.

"I'm scared," I say through tears. My nose is running, my cheeks soaked. "Don't go."

She smiles again, weaker this time. Her chest rises with a shallow breath, then another. Then... stillness. The beeping slows. Then a long, solid tone fills the air.

"NO!" I scream, pushing to my feet. I shake her with as much force as my tiny body can manage. "No, mama! WAKE UP!"

I scream until my throat aches. I scream until my voice cracks. But she doesn't wake up. She never wakes up.

My father sits in the corner, head down, a single tear tracking down his cheek. He says nothing. Offers nothing. Just stands and walks out of the room, leaving me alone. Leaving me holding my mother's hand as her body slowly turns cold. After what feels like hours, my father returns, beckoning me to leave.

"No. I can't leave her here. She has to come home. She has to."

I scream and scream and scream as he tears me away from her. My little arms and legs kick furiously as he drags me away from my mama's cold, still body. Down the too-bright hallways, and back to a house that will never feel my mother's warmth again.

. . .

A SOB TEARS from my throat, and I jolt upward—but Maelkar's hands keep me still.

"It's done," he whispers, his voice hoarse with power.

I open my eyes, gasping. The tub feels colder now, the frigid water lapping at my skin. The memory fades like smoke, vanishing from the forefront of my mind, but the ache of it lingers, like a phantom limb that still tries to twitch. I blink up at Maelkar, my entire body trembling.

He smiles, looking almost drunk from the power of the memory he stole. "Such pain, so very young. Absolutely beautiful."

Korithax is instantly by my side, growling at Maelkar as he wraps his arms around me and scoops me out of the tub, the warmth of his magic drying me. His voice comes out as a low snarl. "Don't fucking touch her again."

Maelkar raises his hands. "I've taken what I wanted. Now let's give her what she came for."

He walks towards a slab of stone in the centre of the ritual chamber, his fingers trailing violet sparks in the air. Korithax helps me to my feet, holding me against him like I might shatter. I'm shaking, every nerve in my body buzzing from the emotional storm I just endured. But I'm still standing, I'm still me. And I'm about to become so much more.

THE WARMTH in Maelkar is gone, replaced by something cold, something almost sinister. The air around us thickens as he lifts his hands, sleeves swaying as he claps twice. A sudden gust of unnatural wind sweeps through the chamber, snuffing every flame in the room. The only light now pulses from the corrupted runes etched around the slab of stone. Maelkar gestures to the slab, and I hesitate for a moment, a voice in the back of my head screaming at me to run the other way.

"You don't have to do this if you don't want to, Daisy. It's okay," Korithax murmurs, pushing a strand of hair behind my ear.

I stare up into his depthless onyx eyes, knowing my mind is already made up. I wasn't leaving this place without my immortality secured. I wanted as long as possible with this man at my side, and there was only one way to do that. Besides, what were my other options? Go home, back to my miserable life, my miserable world. Or even worse, return and be killed by the Divine Six. Not a chance.

"I'm ready." I nod to Maelkar, placing a soft kiss on Korithax's lips before padding over to the dark stone in the centre of the room.

Maelkar gestures for me to lie down on the slab, and I position myself before lying back slowly, the cold of the stone seeping into my bones, making my body erupt with goosebumps. He slowly begins to circle me, his bare feet slapping against the flooring, his violet-glowing eyes fixated on mine.

"Sunshine," he croons, "be still. What I'm about to do is going to hurt. More than anything you've ever known. This is not magic that is kind to mortals. This is the shadow in the marrow of the gods. This is death rewritten. Prepare yourself."

I grip the edge of the stone, my nails aching with how tightly I hold on, like it'll make any damn difference.

"What do you want me to do?" I ask, my voice steady. Barely.

He smiles, stopping at the edge of the stone beside me. "Bleed."

He draws a long, curved blade from his robes—black metal veined with his violet light. It hums like it's alive, the entirety of it vibrating with power. More and more runes begin to glow around the room, seeming to pulse in time with my heartbeat.

"This blade is called Il'kethai. The Tongue of Undoing. It was forged from the bones of the first mortal ever turned immortal. It carves the soul from the flesh and then remakes it."

Korithax's wings rustle behind me. I can feel the tension radiating off of him, like a dam about to break. I swear I can feel a tug between us, one so taut it feels like it's going to snap. Maelkar places one hand gently on my forehead and presses the tip of the blade to my chest, just above my heart.

"Your blood is the ink. Your pain is the price. Your soul... is the canvas."

He begins to chant in a tongue I don't understand:

"Verev'ash kar talren.

Ilk's shoran ez'kai.

Velar na'kheth ai'sora..."

The blade cuts into me, and I scream. The sound tears out of my throat before I even know it's happening. It feels like fire—pure, liquid fire—spilling down from the blade into my flesh as it slices in a single, clean line. My blood hisses where it touches the runes, turning them a deep, shimmering red. Maelkar doesn't stop. He presses his hand to the wound, pushing into it—into me— and I feel my soul flinch.

My vision fractures, my breath catching in my lungs. This time, when the screaming begins again, it's not just mine. Voices. Memories. Too many. Not all mine.

I see myself in the mirror at seven years old, crying in a hospital.

I see myself as a teenager, bleeding alone on a bathroom floor.

I see Ethan. His eyes. His hands.

I see Korithax. His smile, his fury, his hands on my throat, on my heart.

I see a throne made of black stone and ash. I see fire licking at the stars.

I see my own face, but different. Older, crowned, terrifying.

"Vel'shakar, naevrith al'domai..." Maelkar chants louder, voice now echoing all around me.

The stone beneath me seems to burn. My back arches, my body thrashing as it's held down by an unseen force. Then, I can't move. I can't scream. I feel like my bones are shattering, reforming, and crashing open just to be rebuilt entirely wrong. My soul... it hurts. Not my body, not my mind—my soul is burning. Like it's being torn in half and sewn back together with needles of the purest flame. I feel everything. Every nerve, every inch of my body, screaming in pain. I see flashes of myself—but not myself. Other lives, other worlds. A woman with silver hair and black eyes standing in the middle of a battlefield, crowned in fire. Another sitting on a throne of ruin, lovers and enemies bowing at her feet. I see her mouth moving, words forming—

"From the ashes..."

My lungs seize. The room tilts. I feel the string of my being fray, unravel, twist into something new. And then—

Silence.

The pain vanishes, the stone beneath me cools, and I...

CHAPTER 48
KORITHAX

I watch her climb onto the slab, every muscle in my body coiled tight with panic I refuse to show.

She looks so small on that stone. So fucking breakable. The black gown clings to her, still slightly wet from the basin, despite my efforts at drying her off. Her golden hair spills behind her like a dying flame across the stone, and her chest rises with slow, even breaths that do nothing to show the anxiety I can feel radiating off of her.

I feel her fear, I feel it humming through the strange bond between us, a rope pulling taut, but not yet knotted. My palms ache from the restraint, my low amount of power itching beneath my skin, screaming to be used, screaming to tear this place apart and drag her out of it, away from it all.

Maelkar circles her silently. The flickering torches gutter out one by one as he moves, only until the pulsing runes light the chamber. They cast jagged shadows across the walls. I see things in those shadows—faces, malformed spirits, clawing behind the bone lattice that makes up the temple. Some whisper, some scream. The sounds are distant, like they're underwater. But I know all of them are real. They're watching, hungry and waiting.

Maelkar stops beside Daisy, raising the blade Il'kethai high above her chest, and the runes throb in time with her hammering heartbeat. She's afraid, but gods—she's brave. Braver than anyone I've ever known. He speaks low, an ancient language flowing from his tongue.

"Verev'ash kar talren. Ilk's shoran ez'kai..."

The blade touches her, and she screams, the sound ripping through the chamber. Blood hisses across the stone, and I feel something deep and primal snap inside of me. I step forward, nearly launching across the room, only to feel a burst of resistance from the stone itself—like the ritual is holding me back. Maelkar pushes his palm into her chest, fingers disappearing into the wound, and her small, fragile body jerks. Then, she goes silent. Her back arches, her lips part, and her eyes open, staring at something I can't see.

The tether between our souls snaps so violently into place with such a brutal force that it brings me to my knees. A blinding, excruciating pull tears through my chest like lightning. It's not pain, but something so raw it leaves me gasping. Like I've been stripped bare, branded, and claimed. I feel her. Not just her heartbeat or her breath, but her being. Her soul is latched onto mine, and it's not asking, it's taking. Binding and fusing so tightly to mine, it's becoming one.

I lift my head, my entire body shaking, and find Maelkar staring down at her with wide, terrified eyes. He takes a step back, like she's something unholy.

"What have you made me do, Child of Ruin?" He breathes, still not taking his eyes away from her.

My voice is gravelly as I pant, "Turn her immortal. You knew this."

"No..." he whispers, still frozen. "I have not turned her immortal. She has been reborn."

My heart lurches. "What?"

He whirls to face me, eyes wide, ringed with fear. "Who the fuck have you made me bring back, Korithax?"

Silence crashes over the room like thunder. Then he says it. So quietly I strain to hear it. "She is your mate, princeling."

"What?" I croak.

"Your one true love. Your souls match. Your destiny."

She is mine. I am hers. Forever. All along, that tether, that pull, that inability to stay away. It was because she was my mate.

Maelkar gasps, stepping forward toward Daisy. "Shit... shit. Shit."

I stagger upright, my wings spreading unconsciously. "What is it? What's wrong?"

He leans forward, staring at Daisy's unmoving body. His face goes pale—truly pale. I've never seen the bastard look afraid before.

"She is fleeting," he whispers. "Her body... It is not responding well."

My blood runs cold. "What the fuck does that mean?"

"She is dying," Maelkar says, and this time, even his voice breaks.

Rage erupts in me. I lunge forward, grabbing him by his robes and slamming him against the bone wall. "Then fucking help her!"

He doesn't fight back. His black eyes just meet mine with a terrifying expression.

"I can't. You need light to conquer the dark. Something was placed on her soul long ago. Something that does not want her back. Someone does not want her to return. Only the purest of light can heal this."

Panic drowns me. She's my mate. I can't fucking lose her now.

"No," I snarl. "No. My magic is too low—I can't open a gate." I punch the stone altar so hard it cracks straight down the centre. "HELP ME!" I'll give you anything. Anything!"

Maelkar stares, slowly nodding. "I don't want anything from you, Prince. But promise me this—if she survives, remind her who helped you."

If. There can't be an if, only a when. I can no longer imagine my life without Daisy. I don't know if that's the soul bond—the mate bond. I have no idea. But I don't think I could survive without her. I need her.

"Yes!" I roar. "Fine. Just fucking help me."

"I need a soul pact, Korithax. Now."

I snatch the curved blade and drag it across my palm, the cut deep and stinging. I thrust it at him, blood pouring from the wound, the dripping sound of my blood hitting stone, hammering against my skull. "Hurry the fuck up!"

Maelkar slices his own palm and slams it into mine. Our blood mixes, the light explodes—our magic colliding so loud the chamber rattles. The walls tremble, the bones seeming to moan as the trapped spirits shriek behind the walls.

"It is done," he pants. "Now take her. I'll open the gate to Luminaria, but you have to get her there. Fast."

I scoop Daisy into my arms, and gods, she's cold. Her once blush lips are pale, so fucking pale.

"Stay with me," I whisper, gripping her tighter. "Don't you fucking dare leave me. I will cleave you back from the heavens themselves if I have to. Nothing and nobody will survive if you do not stay with me."

Maelkar kneels beside the runes, letting his violet blood from our pact drip onto the sigil etched into the floor. It glows so violently I have to squint my eyes.

"Stand there. Hold onto her tight. If you let go, I cannot tell you where she will end up."

I step into the circle, holding her to my chest like my life depends on it. Because it does.

"Please, little flower," I whisper. "Please stay with me."

The air tears open. A wind so powerful it shreds the darkness, wraps around us, pulling, tearing, dragging me forward. My wings snap out, wrapping around us to shield her. Everything goes pitch black, the sensation of falling wracking my body as I grip Daisy with everything I have. Ahead, light, blinding and endless, pours towards us, and I feel a sense of hope filling me. But just as quickly as it comes, it leaves, just as I feel Daisy's heartbeat stutter.

"NO!" I scream as we're hurled into Luminaria.

THE LIGHT BLINDS ME.

We land in a thunderous quake, and I fall to my straight to my knees, still cradling her. I pant as I try and gather myself, the teleportation like nothing I've ever felt before. It felt like I'd travelled the entire universe, not just from one realm to another.

I glance around in confusion as my vision settles. My palace rises around us, the shimmering obsidian walls and floors, the scent of florals and sulphur. The throne looms just ahead, the obnoxious seat sitting at the centre of the empty room. Zeriavoss... we're home. But, we were heading to Luminaria... to Elyistria. I needed Elyistria to help me, she said so herself. How the fuck did I get here?

I blink rapidly, trying to figure out what just happened. I could see Luminaria. Maelkar opened the gate there for me, not Zeriavoss. Had I somehow managed to change the path accidentally?

I glance down, looking at her almost lifeless body in my arms.

"Daisy," I choke, my voice raw and broken. "Stay with me. Don't you fucking leave me now."

I brush a hand over her face, pushing away her golden hair so I can see her properly. Her skin is too cold, too pale. Where's her warmth? Where's her bright smile, her ocean eyes? Where is my beautiful, radiant queen?

Elyistria appears beside me in a burst of golden mist, her hair whipping around her in the force of her arrival. I hear footsteps barrelling towards me and look up to see Aran stumbling through the throne room doors, heading straight toward me, a knowing look on his face.

"She's slipping," Elyistria whispers, placing her glowing hands above Daisy's chest. "I don't know how long she has. You were right to come to me."

"I did?" I ask, confused.

"I felt you arriving and opened the gate straight to Zeriavoss. She needs to be here."

"She's not immortal," I stammer out, "He didn't make her immortal. He fucking rebuilt her. She... what is she?" I ask, hopelessly.

"She is something else entirely now," Elyistria murmurs.

My head spins as everything slams into me at once. The ritual, the runes, the portal. Zeriavoss. Elyistria, Aran... Daisy. What the fuck is happening? I didn't like this feeling. The lack of control, the lack of knowledge.

Aran looks to Elyistria and gives her a nod before turning his attention to the guards. "The Soul Chamber is opening. Guard the door, do not let anyone pass."

They all scramble as the floor beneath us begins to shift. Ancient runes glow red-hot as the obsidian tiles before my throne split open. A dark, spiralled stairwell unfurls, leading us down underneath the chair, right into the oldest part of Zeriavoss. A place I had heard whispers of, but had never seen. It was said the Soul Chamber was a place for the gods, a place of death, of rebirth.

I glance to Elyistria, confusion etched across my face. She knew something I didn't, something that meant Daisy needed to be taken into one of the most sacred places ever created. I didn't have time to question her; Daisy's heartbeat was still stuttering, like a candle in the wind. I lift her tightly into my arms, rising as her hair falls like golden threads against my forearms. Her head lolls against my shoulder, and I don't speak to anyone as I move. I can't. My throat is constricted, bone dry with fear.

Bits of stone crumble under my boots and fall into the vast crater below. The deeper we go, the heavier the air surrounding us gets, the scent of sulphur so strong my nose stings.

The chamber comes into view as I descend. The vast space is circular, carved into the blackened roots of the earth itself. Sconces spark to life as we move further inside, fuelled by magic so old it has the hairs on the back of my neck prickling, my wings trembling. A stone altar awaits in the centre, looking eerily like the one she was just laid upon in Noxthrallia. Images of her lying screaming and writhing flash through my head, making me stumble a step as the pain of it all crashes through me all over again.

Faded runes flicker to life the moment I step into the circle with her. A shiver runs down my spine that feels like a welcoming caress from the ancient magic that coats the atmosphere.

Elyistria halts beside the altar. "Lay her down."

I hesitate. My arms won't let her go. Not when the last time they did, she screamed, she—

"Korithax," Elyistria says gently. "You must. This place... it was once hers. She must return to it to survive."

I stare at her. "What do you mean, this was hers?"

She says nothing. She just places her hand onto mine, giving me a reassuring look. I inhale deeply, giving her a tight nod before lowering Daisy onto the stone, cradling the back of her head as I place her down, the runes flashing as her body connects with the altar.

I look down at her almost lifeless body, her radiance gone. Another flash of light pulses through the runes, and the presence in the room shifts entirely. The air grows still, humming with a power I've never felt before. Elyistria shudders, stepping back as the runes around the altar burn brighter, and I follow suit, stepping out of the circle.

A low, ancient chant begins to echo around the chamber, speaking in a tongue I don't understand. I glance at Elyistria and Aran, but they either don't hear the chants or they don't care enough about them as their eyes stay glued to Daisy.

The runes continue to pulse, low and slow, like an ancient heartbeat. They cast a glow across Daisy's skin, making her look even paler than she had moments ago. Still, she doesn't stir. I take a step forward—every inch of me screaming to pull her back into the safety of my arms—but Aran shifts in front of me, his palm braced against my chest.

"Don't," he says quietly, but I don't miss the firmness in his tone. "She needs to do this, Korithax. She's okay."

My jaw clenches. “She doesn’t look okay.”

“She is in between,” Elyistria whispers, her eyes unblinking, trained on my queen. “Between what was, and what will be. You must not interfere.”

I want to ignore them both. Gods, I want to. But something in Aran’s eyes, something unshakable, roots me to the spot. So I stand there, and I watch as I feel my heart slowly break. The longer we stand there, the heavier the air grows around us. I can feel magic weaving through the chamber, slithering across the runes, coiling around Daisy like a serpent.

Her chest suddenly jerks as she sucks in a sharp, loud breath. Then again, faster this time. Her entire body tenses as her chest rapidly rises and falls. Her eyes are still closed, but her lids flutter rapidly like she’s having a nightmare. Her breaths grow more ragged, causing panic to bloom in me like wildfire. I can see the pain in her face, see her eyes dancing beneath the lids like she’s reliving every horror she’s ever known.

I instinctively step forward again, but Aran yet again blocks me with nothing more than a stern look.

“She’s remembering.”

Those two words from Elyistria have me pausing in my stride. Remembering what? Because it looks like she’s remembering every painful thing she’s ever endured. My fists tighten at my sides. I’ve laid her on two altars in one fucking day, and both times I’ve been utterly powerless in stopping her pain.

Daisy lets out another gasp, choked and uneven. Her head twitches to the side, her lips parting in a silent cry. Tears slip from her closed eyes, trailing down her temples and disappearing into the runes.

“Please,” I whisper, the word torn from me before I can stop it. It felt like my soul was begging for her to be okay, begging for her to pull through this. Because without her, I was nothing. Not anymore. I watch as she suddenly goes still, the runes dimming and the entire chamber slamming into a silence so potent I can hear my own heartbeat.

"Daisy?" I rasp, stumbling forward.

She doesn't move. I can't see her breathing. I can't see any sign of life inside of her. I search desperately with my heightened senses for any sign of life, but I come up short. Even the soul bond seems muted.

"No—no, no no..." I'm already in the circle, dropping to my knees beside her, my hands shaking as I gather her face in my palms. "Please. Not like this. Don't go. Don't fucking leave me. I haven't had enough time."

I look up desperately to Aran and Elyistria. Both of them stare at her lifeless body with an expression I can only decipher as... grief.

CHAPTER 49
DAISY

Everything's black.

I can hear a distant voice. Korithax. He's begging me to stay with him. But I am with him, I just can't see him.

"I'm here," I try to say. But I can't seem to speak either.

Something's wrong, so very wrong. Where am I? Why is it dark? Am I dead? Am I hearing his voice just before my soul leaves forever? No. No, I can't die. But it doesn't feel like I have a choice as I suddenly begin to feel cold. I can feel something heavy wrapping around my body. Something ancient, calling to me like it's an old friend, beckoning me to come closer, to reach out.

I can faintly feel my body in this dark place. I feel my arm slowly reaching into the unknown—reaching for the source of whatever it is that's calling to me. Is it death calling, welcoming me with a heavy embrace? If it is... I don't want to go. I lower my arm, willing myself to ignore its pull.

"I won't go with you. I'm needed back in Zeriavoss."

A whisper surrounds me, wrapping around me like a warm, tight hug.

"Dasmyrin," it whispers against my ear like a welcoming caress.

"No." I whisper back. "You have the wrong person. I'm Daisy. I need to go back."

"I know who you are, Queen of Hell. But you do not know yourself," the ancient voice whispers back.

"Yes, I do. I'm Daisy Sandoval. Sunshine incarnate. Future Queen of Hell." I respond in a desperate shout.

"Future. Past. Present. All at once."

"What are you talking about? Who are you? Where am I?" I stutter the questions out one after the other, panic lacing my voice, desperation seeping through me. I need to get back. I need to go home.

"You need to see. You need to remember."

Before I have a chance to respond, I'm violently thrust forward like two hands pushed on my back as hard as they could. I'm suddenly falling, wind ripping by me as I screw my eyes shut, screaming as I descend further and further. I throw my arms out, trying to grip onto something. But there's nothing there, just wind rushing through my fingers as I desperately claw at the air.

"Open your eyes, Ashborn."

I do as the whisper says and gasp as I see hundreds of images fly past me one by one. I see my entire life flitting by me, scenes of being a child, my mother, my father, my friends. Tears fill my eyes as I see image after image of my life. The good, the bad, and the ugly. Images fly past me that I don't recognise, and I feel the sudden, overhwhelming urge to reach out and try to grab at one.

My soul seems to call to the strange places that flit by, seeing the same strange woman over and over again. I reach out, subconsciously willing the image to come to me as I try to wrap my fingers around it. I watch in awe as my hand goes straight through the image, then my wrist, my forearm, my entire body as it slowly sucks me inside.

I'm thrown onto hard ground, landing harshly in a vast space. Nothing but barren land stretches before me. Nothing but darkness in the sky, and a large crater sitting just a few feet ahead. I crawl to the hole on my hands and knees, peering over the edge. In the centre, right at the bottom, lies a girl around my age. Her hair lies around her like liquid silver, her skin's pale, and she's dressed in a black and red gown. She's lying on her side, and I can't tell if she's asleep or dead. Beside her, another girl lies, her hair is bright white, her skin a pale ivory with a slight golden hue.

"Elyistria?" I gasp, recognising her soft face, her ethereal features, and her bright white hair. She looks so young, so delicate. Both of their eyes crack open as they lie facing each other, recognition flitting over their features as they stare at one another. Was that Elyistria's sister? She hadn't mentioned having a sister when we met. Her words suddenly echo through my head:

"I apologise for who I was before."

"I will not fail you again."

I'm suddenly falling again, another image of Elyistria and the stranger she was lying next to, trying to flit by. I reach out as before, my body once again sucked into the image before me. I land in a field, surrounded by the wild blooms I instantly recognise from Zeriavoss. But this isn't the kingdom I know. The red lightning streaks the sky, the flowers bloom, but nothing else is here other than the two women standing just before me.

I rise to my feet, watching them as they talk. I strain my ears, but I can't hear them. It feels like I'm trapped in a soundless bubble, destined to watch but not listen. The woman I don't recognise raises her palms, and I watch as the familiar obsidian castle forms from nothing, rising from the ground to sit upon the piece of land that juts out of the mountains. The kingdom forms before my eyes. Then, Cinderspine, The Realm of Children, The Welcome Circle, Gehenna. Each and every part of Hell is sculpted like clay, brought to life by her hands. I was watching my home, my kingdom, be formed by the silver-haired woman with eyes as black as Korithax's.

I continue to watch as Elyistria raises her hands. Creatures rise from her palm, flamebeasts forming from glowing threads of light. They roar and fly, flames crackling across the sky as the other woman laughs beside her, awe filling their eyes. I realise I'm watching the very act of creation.

I take a step forward and fall straight through the flowers, back into the dark abyss, as more and more images fly past me. I see images of the two girls growing, creating realm after realm with just their hands. The silver-haired woman seems to create the worlds by hand, whilst Elyistria seems to create magic and life with hers. Creatures, humans, everything to ever exist, all coming from their very palms. I knew Elyistria was a goddess, and I knew she had magic. But I didn't know she had a hand in creating everything in existence. But I thought the Divine Six—

I'm pulled straight into another vision. I land on my feet, stumbling forward into a place I instantly recognise as the Six's realm. My body shudders in response, remembering how it had felt the last time I was here.

I look around the room, noticing the thrones they sit on aren't here. Nothing's here, apart from Elyistria and the silver-haired girl. This doesn't make any sense. I had been told the Six were the original creators. That everything that existed was due to them. But I'd just watched these two girls create realm after realm. Everything that had existed since the dawn of time had come from their hands. Which meant the Divine Six's version of history was a lie.

My head starts spinning with too many thoughts.

I stay standing at the far side of the room, watching with utter disbelief as one by one, each member of the Divine Six is formed. Voices suddenly sound around me, letting me finally hear for the first time since falling into these strange visions.

"You are to be known as the Divine Six," Elyistria says.

"You will help us with the realms and ensure they all run smoothly." The other woman continues.

"I am Elyistria. Goddess of Magic. Ruler of Luminaria. And this is my sister." She gestures to the silver-haired girl.

"I am Dasmyrin. Goddess of Creation. Queen of Hell."

I gasp. It was her. The first Queen of Hell, the one the whispers claim the Divine Six killed.

"We give you each a power, each a responsibility which will help us protect what we have created." Dasmyrin continues.

Elyistria steps forward, placing her hands on the forehead of the one I recognise as Seraphiel. "You are the voice of judgement. You have the power to pass judgement on any being."

She moves onto Amarithe, once again placing her hands on her forehead. "You are the bloom of light. A manipulator of perception."

I frown. Why would they need someone who can manipulate perception?

She places her hands on Velentha next. "The oracle of time. You can see all possible futures."

Velentha gasps as the magic is transferred into her, and her eyes dart to Dasmyrin, tears swimming in her eyes. But she doesn't speak.

Elyistria continues on to Calrix. "The spear of order. The master of divine warfare, the protector of realms."

He growls in response, his sword gleaming with fire.

She places her hands on Elaron, and Velentha lets out a small sob. I frown at her response, but Elyistria ignores her, continuing on.

"The whispering star. The manipulator of thought, memory, and dreams."

She moves on to the last of the Divine Six. Mal'Thariel. The one who I was told was the creator of everything we know.

"The architect." She whispers. "The one who will help structure and control the laws of the realms and its fates."

So, he helped with the laws. He didn't create shit. I feel anger rising in me as I stare at the pretentious assholes standing ahead of me. They lied. They had lied to everyone, erased history, and had it rewritten to make themselves appear as almighty gods. But why hadn't Elyistria corrected the lies? Why had she sat back and let them continue on to rule as they were, knowing her and her sister were the creators? It didn't make any sense.

I move forward, trying to scream, trying to warn Dasmyrin about their betrayal. But once again, the second I move forward, I fall. This time, the images don't return, just utter darkness, with the whispers flying all around me, speaking to me in a language I can't decipher.

"Vireth at'zul... e'kara sulan...
Kae;'vireth a'sul... shetha'zai en'karan...
Thaloriren ez'rem, vae'sharak il'drun.
Na'kaziel vel'tharan... kael'rion et'shara.
Vireth kai'syl... elthea'nur az'shal.
Aelari su'nai vel'zur... il'saerin et'kal."

"I DON'T UNDERSTAND," I sob. "What is happening?"

I land on my back with a thud, the impact so brutal the breath whooshes out of my lungs. I sit up, coughing while trying to catch my breath.

"I'm getting real tired of falling through shit now," I mutter.

"Creator of worlds. Queen of Hell. Risen from the ash."

I snap my head up, watching a man I've never seen stand towering over Dasmyrin. She's on the floor, bleeding, her silver hair coated in crimson.

"You were created from the ash. You will be destroyed in the ash."

He laughs, a wicked sound that makes the hair on my arms rise. He looks familiar. Those eyes, that smile. He looked like an older version of Korithax.

"How could you, Korran. You were my sword and shield. My brother in arms," Dasmyrin spits, blood pouring from her mouth.

He sneers at her, kicking her in the chest so hard she lands on her back.

"You are not worthy of the throne," Korran snarls. "You make a mockery of Hell with your laws. Your codex is bullshit. Your court is bullshit. You do not rule with fear, you rule with a kindness that does not work in a world like this."

"I built this godsdamn world," she growls. "It is mine to rule as I please."

"Well, now it is mine. Nobody will remember you, Ashborn. We will erase you, and if your sister tries to leave her pretty little realm, I will erase her too." Korran sneers down at her as he places a boot on her chest.

"You fucking touch her and I will burn you all."

He barks a laugh, the Divine Six following suit. All but Velentha, who just stares on, her expression vacant.

"You will do nothing. You will be nothing." He spits. "Your crown is gone. Your throne is burned. And now your soul will be erased, your body incinerated."

"You cannot," she breathes, trying to stand.

Elaron moves forward, and Dasmyrin raises her hands. Nothing happens, and she stares at her palms in disbelief as a mocking laugh breaks from Seraphiel.

"Disabling elixir," Amarithe purrs.

"You fucking bitch," Dasmyrin screams. "Fuck all of you. I created you, I can end you."

I watch as Elaron places a hand upon Dasmyrin's forehead, an unseen magic holding her still. "This will hurt." He smirks.

I watch in horror as a light shines briefly from his palm. Dasmyrin's screams tear through the space so loud I have to throw my hands over my ears. I try to run to her, but I run into an invisible barrier. I pound my fists against it, begging them to stop. But what good would it be? This happened over fifty thousand years ago. I was just watching as history played out right before my eyes.

A pain spears through my head as Elaron works at using his magic on her. It's so painful it burns. I drop to my knees, holding my head between my hands as my eyes screw shut. A scream tears from me, loud enough to match the goddess being torn apart in front of me.

"Stop. Please. Stop this," I beg of anybody who will listen. "STOP!"

. . .

Everything goes quiet, the pain vanishing instantly. Slowly, I open my eyes, blinking a few times to clear the stars that blur my vision. I lift my head, seeing a large mirror standing in front of me. The thick black frame is covered in runes and a sigil that feels so familiar it makes the skin near my shoulder itch. Right where my birthmark sits. A flame, carved into a cracked circle, wrapped in vines with tiny thorns. Dasmyrin's sigil.

I stand slowly and walk over to the mirror on wobbly legs. It's not me I see in the reflection. Dasmyrin stands there, her movements mimicking my own.

"I don't understand," I whisper at the same time she does.

I tilt my head, and she does the same. Taking another step closer to the glass, I watch as she copies my every move. I place my palm against the glass, her palm pressing against mine in the reflection.

"It is time." A voice whispers. "She will rise as the sun. And burn us all."

Dasmyrin reaches through the mirror and pushes me backwards with two strong hands, smiling softly at me as I begin falling once more. My golden hair whips around my face as I feel my soul tethering back to where I know my body lies.

I gasp hard, and my eyes fly open. My chest heaves as I breathe in my surroundings.

"Daisy," Korithax's voice wraps around me as he stares at me, my face in his palms. "Oh, thank the fucking gods." He breathes, pulling me into a kiss so fierce it steals my breath away. He pulls back, searching my eyes frantically.

"She has risen again." A voice sounds from behind me.

I turn to see Elyistria staring at me, tears brimming in her striking silver-blue eyes. She steps forward, her voice barely a breath.

"Hello, sister."

CHAPTER 50
DAISY

The silence after Elyistria's words is louder than any scream I've ever heard.

No one moves. No one breathes. My heart hammers like it's trying to claw its way out of my chest, as I stare at her like she's just stabbed me in the heart. *Sister.*

"No," I whisper, my voice trembling. "Don't call me that."

Elyistria steps forward, her movements slow and cautious; like I'm a wounded animal about to lash out at anybody that dares come near me. Maybe I'm exactly that. My body still trembles from whatever the hell I just climbed out of. My fingers twitch against the runes beneath me, still warm with a magic I don't understand.

I glance around the large space, realising I'm not where I last remember being. I was with Maelkar... in Noxthrallia. Gods knows where I was now.

I glance back at Elyistria, a look of hope swimming in her eyes. "I'm not her," I say, shaking my head. "I'm not... I'm not whatever you think I am. I'm not Dasmyrin."

Tears blur my vision as I scramble to sit upright on the altar, shoving Korithax's steadying hands away without meaning to. The cold rushes back in instantly without him. Gods, I didn't mean to do that. I need him. I don't know who I am without him right now. But I can't stop the shaking that's wracking my body.

"What's happening to me?" My voice breaks, ugly and raw. I look to Elyistria, then Aran, then finally to Korithax. "Please. Someone. Tell me this is a mistake. Tell me this is just a dream, that I'm still stuck on that fucking stone back in Noxthrallia. Tell me I'm not her."

Korithax looks like he's breaking apart. His eyes burn, his hands hover like he doesn't know whether to hold me or let me fall apart. He crouches beside me, his brows drawn in confusion and pain.

"Daisy," he murmurs, voice shaking. "What are you talking about?" He brushes my hair back from my face, his eyes flitting back and forth, searching mine like they might give him the answers. "Why are you saying these things?"

"I'm Daisy," I sob. "I'm Daisy Sandoval. I'm a psychology student. I drink way too much iced coffee, I hate small bugs, and I dance in the kitchen when no one's watching. I am not—"

"You are," Elyistria interrupts gently.

Korithax jerks his head toward her. "What the fuck do you mean, you are?" His voice is laced with panic now. "She's not some ancient being. She's my wife. She's just... Daisy."

I see the anguish in his eyes, the way his chest heaves like it physically hurts him not to understand. His hand trembles against my arm as he tries to steady me, and maybe himself.

Her voice cracks. "You are Daisy. But you are also Dasmyrin." She says softly. "You weren't supposed to remember yet. Not this soon."

"No!" I scream. The word echoes around the cavernous space. "No, no, no!"

"I don't care what she's supposed to remember," Korithax snaps. "She's breaking in front of me. Tell me what the fuck is happening to her."

The runes beneath me flicker with sudden force, glowing a deep, pulsing red. The air warps around me, making my skin pebble. Aran shifts, ready to step in, but Korithax raises a hand, stopping him.

"When you stepped into the Soul Chamber, the truth in your blood couldn't be hidden any longer. The runes... they recognised their queen." Elyistria murmurs.

"I'm not a queen," I sob. "I'm not a goddess. I'm not some ancient being who created worlds. I'm just a fucking girl who's had enough of being broken."

Korithax stares at me like I've become someone else entirely. And maybe I have.

"I don't understand," he says again, softer this time. Almost like he's pleading with the universe to figure out what's going on. "What did they do to you? What did you see?"

I try to climb down from the altar, but my legs give out the moment I touch the floor. Korithax catches me, kneeling beside me as I collapse against his chest, his arms wrapping around me like a shield. His heartbeat is like thunder beneath my cheek. I don't know how to answer him. I don't know how to tell him what I saw. Who I saw.

"I don't want this," I sob into him. "I don't want to be anyone else. I just want to be me. I just want to be with you."

His voice is low, broken. "You are. You are mine. Nothing changes that, Daisy."

"But it has. Everything has changed now," I cry.

"You saw it, didn't you?" Elyistria asks gently. "The past. You saw the truth."

I nod, trembling. "They killed her."

"Yes."

"They erased her." I grit out.

"Yes."

"And you let them," I say, a little harsher than intended.

It lands like a slap. Elyistria flinches, her eyes shimmering. "I tried to stop them. But I was too late. And then... I stayed quiet. Because I thought it was the only way to survive long enough to bring you back."

I stare at her. "You left her. You left me!"

The pain in her face answers for her. I turn my face into Korithax's chest, tears soaking his shirt. I feel like I'm cracking down the centre, like every piece of me is being ripped open, and I'm being forced to look at something I wasn't built to understand.

"I'm scared," I whisper.

He pulls me tighter. "I know, little flower. But I've got you. I've got you."

Elyistria approaches slowly, kneeling in front of us. "Daisy, you don't have to become her. Not yet."

"She keeps saying that name," Korithax says hoarsely. "Dasmyrin. Why does that name sound like it's splitting her in two?"

"She is both," Elyistria replies. "She always was."

Korithax's expression turns unreadable as I glance up at him. He holds me like I'm glass, like he's terrified he already lost me to the broken pieces, and he doesn't know how to put me back together.

"You're still you, Daisy. This is just the truth of where you came from, of what was stolen from you. But you choose who you become." Elyistria whispers, trying to offer me a reassuring smile.

My eyes sting. "And what if I don't want to become anyone but me?"

"Then we fight for that," Korithax says, his voice firm and reassuring. "We fight for your future, not your past."

The air settles around me, the runes dimming once more. Korithax's words settle in my chest. Maybe I have a choice. But to have a choice, I need to know it all.

I lift my head and look to Elyistria, my mind unsteady, unsure. "Tell me everything," I whisper. "Every lie. Every truth. I want to know it all."

She nods. "Then it is time you learn what it means to be born from ash."

Korithax doesn't speak, but I feel his hand close around mine like a silent vow. He's not letting go, even if the truth changes everything.

CHAPTER 51
KORITHAX

I follow them through the garden like a ghost.

Daisy walks beside Elyistria and Aran with her arms wrapped tightly around herself, the loose strands of her golden hair catching the late afternoon light like silk. Her bare feet brush against the soft grass, her movements slow and wary. Like every step forward might crack the ground beneath her.

I don't speak as I follow. I can't. My thoughts are a storm, and I'm trapped in the eye of it. The silence between us says more than I could ever voice aloud right now. She's my wife. My mate. My Daisy. But now she's something else too. Something ancient, something that was forgotten. She's something that rewrites everything that I thought I knew about this world. I took her to Noxthrallia to become immortal, and she's returned as someone else entirely.

She chooses the far edge of the gardens, near the blood blossom vines and the thorned fruit trees, where the air hums with quiet. Aran gestures to a nearby bench, but she shakes her head and continues to slowly pace, and I find myself pacing in time with her. Elyistria gives me a look that warns me to be still, that my confusion, anxiety, and irritation are all shining through too loudly. But I can't stay still. Every muscle in me is thrumming with tension, and my jaw aches from how hard it's clenched.

Finally, Daisy stops walking and speaks without turning to look at us. I stand still, listening to her words. "I saw everything," She says softly.

The fragility of her voice punches the air from my lungs.

"I saw her. Me. I saw how she died." Her voice wavers. "I saw the mirror. I saw him."

She turns then, her eyes glassy with tears as they find mine. "Your father, Korithax. Korran."

The name hits me like a blade to the gut, my skin crawling at the mere mention of him. "What?"

"He... he killed her," she whispers. "He burned her for three days in a pit of fire before her body gave out. He wasn't alone. The Divine Six helped. Then they stood by and watched as she suffered."

"No," I breathe. "No, that's not—he was... He told me..."

My thoughts fracture. I'd heard whispers. I'd heard he had some kind of hand in it. Part of me believed it. But another part of me, deep, deep down, thought it was bullshit. That the man who had sired me couldn't be such a heartless bastard.

I look to Elyistria. "Tell me she's wrong."

But of course, she doesn't deny it. She steps forward, her eyes dim with grief. "She's not wrong."

My hands ball into fists as the information goes from speculation to fact. He truly was a coward. A betrayer. A worthless piece of shit.

"He betrayed her," Elyistria continues. "He was her second. Her most trusted general. The Divine Six promised him the throne, and he snatched up the opportunity without a second thought. They feared what she was building."

"What was she building?" I ask.

Elyistria sighs. "Hope. Dasmyrin ruled with a sacred codex. A law that declared all souls must be judged with truth, not fear. Her court was called the Court of Embers. She didn't rule through terror; she ruled through reckoning. Through understanding. She offered sanctuary to fallen angels, and sinners were given the chance to change. She believed in evolution, in rehabilitation."

I stare at her like I've been struck. I'd heard the rumours of how she had ruled, how Hell once was. My father could never be like that. He loved the fear, the tyranny.

"And that made her dangerous?" I ask.

Elyistria nods slowly. "To those who profited from fear? Yes."

Daisy crosses her arms tightly across her chest. "I don't want this. I'm sorry. But I just want to be," she pauses, looking at me with tears in her eyes. "I just want to be yours."

Something inside me cracks at the sight of her. I walk to her slowly, closing the space between us until I'm just inches from her.

"You already are mine," I say, my voice rough. "No matter what else you become—who else you become. You're mine."

The tears glisten, one rolling down her cheek. "Are you saying that to me, or to her?"

I ignore the sting from her words and reach for her hand, placing it in mine. "You, Daisy. I've felt the pull to you since before we even met. To you. To my little flower. The sunshine who looked the Heir of Hell in the eye and cursed him out for getting smoke on her rug."

Her lips twitch with the ghost of a smile.

"I don't understand any of this," I admit. "The Divine Six. Elyistria. My father—my fucking father—being the one who killed Dasmyrin. I feel like everything I knew has been shattered. But I still know you. That hasn't changed."

Her eyes search mine. "Korithax... you said something. When Maelkar finished the ritual, before everything went dark. I heard you say that I... that I was your mate."

I nod, my throat tight. What if she rejected us being mates? Did she know she could do that? So much for her has changed, and maybe her being my mate is too much for her.

"Yes. You are," I murmur.

She blinks rapidly. "Mates are real?"

"Yes," I take her hands gently. "It's not common. It's ancient magic, older than I understand. When two souls are created to complete each other, they tether. Sometimes violently, sometimes gently. But when they find each other... It's like breathing for the first time."

"Are you mated to me, or Dasmyrin?" She asks, fear dancing in her eyes.

I don't hesitate. "To you, Daisy. I would burn the world for you. Not for who you once were. But for who you are. I knew from the moment your father offered me your soul. I felt the tug, the pull. And when it secured into place when you became immortal, the strength of it dropped me to my knees. You are my beginning and my end, Daisy."

I cup her face, using my thumb to brush away her tears. "Do you accept the bond?" I whisper, my voice shaking with fear. So many things have been taken from her or given to her without choice. She deserves to know she has a choice in this. "You can reject it if you don't want it." My heart hammers; the thought of her rejecting our bond makes a pain in my chest pulsate.

She shakes her head, and my heart plummets. I knew she wouldn't want me as her mate. I knew I wasn't good enough to be hers in marriage and soul. I lower my head, nodding just once.

"Of course I want it, Korithax. You are the only thing I'm sure of right now. You are the only thing that makes sense."

I lift my eyes to hers, her ocean blues staring into my soul. The soul that belongs entirely to her. I exhale a long breath and slam my mouth to hers, the force of it nearly knocking her backwards. I wrap an arm around her back to steady her and pull her in tight.

"Thank the fucking gods." I murmur between kisses.

Aran clears his throat from the pathway, and I break the kiss to turn and look at him.

"I need to speak to someone," he says carefully. "I'll be back soon."

"Place extra guards on duty. I want all of my best soldiers surrounding the kingdom grounds. If the Divine Six show up, I want to hear about it instantly." I respond.

He nods once and turns to leave without another word.

Silence settles between the three of us, and I watch as Daisy turns to look out over Hell from the edge of the garden. She looks so broken, and I feel utterly helpless. I don't know how to fix this. I've pieced her back together after being raped, after trying to take her own life. But this? I don't even know where to begin.

"You need to rest, Daisy," Elyistria says, breaking the silence. "Come, I'll walk with you back to your chambers."

We move together through the castle, quiet and exhausted. A servant escorts Elyistria to her own guarded quarters, and she offers a small smile as a goodbye to us both. This must be hard on her, too. Her sister, risen again after fifty thousand years, yet entirely different. But she wasn't my concern, my little flower was.

Daisy walks beside me, her arm looped through mine, but her steps are still hesitant, her body still tense. When we reach our room, Aran is standing outside the door.

I raise a brow. "Aran, what is it? I swear if there's another—"

He raises both hands. "Sire, I understand you probably want some alone time right now. But I think it's important that Daisy be around familiarity. When everything else feels foreign, she needs a constant."

My eyes narrow. "What have you done?"

He smiles sheepishly and pushes open the door.

"Talia. Ezra?" Daisy gasps.

Her voice breaks on their names, and they run to her, dragging her into a tight three-way hug. She sobs, clutching them like her lifeline as they all fall to the floor in a heap of tangled limbs. I glare at Aran, wondering what the fuck he's thinking, bringing two mortals to Hell after the uproar bringing Daisy here caused.

Talia pulls back first, holding her at arm's length. "Immortal? Daisy, what the fuck?!"

Ezra laughs through a tearful grin. "So that means you don't get wrinkles for like hundreds of years? You bitch."

Talia rises and whirls to me, marching into my space and jabbing a finger at my chest. "I don't know why she looks so traumatised. But if you've hurt her, I'll find a way to kill you, demon boy."

"Down, girl." Daisy laughs through tears. "I have a lot to tell you."

I step back. Despite wanting to be with her, I know she needs this right now. "I'll leave you to it. I'll be back soon. I'll have the help bring you food and drinks."

"Korithax," she says gently, like she wants me to stay.

"It's okay," I murmur. "You need time with your friends."

She gives me a soft smile and nods. I close the door behind me and walk to the war chamber. I need silence, strategy, a plan. I need something to make fucking sense. I push a hand through my hair as I enter the chamber, but a figure in the room stops me dead in my tracks.

"Korithax," a voice says from the shadows.

I draw my sword in a flash, hellfire erupting in bright blue flame.

"Velentha," I snarl.

She steps from the shadows with her hands raised. "Wait. Please."

"You have ten seconds," I growl.

"I knew she would rise, that she would burn the sky," she says breathlessly. "I bided my time, Child of Ruin. I had no part in what happened before, but the part I am yet to be involved in... I can only apologise for."

My grip tightens. "What the fuck are you talking about? Spit it out, Velentha."

She meets my eyes with sorrow. "I have been the enforcer of fate. I am the key."

And then she's gone, disappearing in a whisper of golden light before I can swing for her fucking head. I roar in fury, hurling my sword across the room. It embeds itself in the stone wall with a crack that echoes like thunder.

Everything is falling apart, and I don't know how to stop it.

I WATCH the sword quiver where it's lodged in the stone, its flames flicking upward, then dying entirely. Silence stretches in the chamber, broken only by the ragged sound of my breathing. My hands are shaking uncontrollably, the feeling so foreign it makes my anger flare even more. I press both palms against the table in the centre of the room, trying to steady myself.

The plan from before we left is still strewn across the surface, mapping out each realm, each ruler, each possibility. Never could I have planned to return with an immortal wife who was the resurrected version of the first Queen of Hell. I close my eyes, letting the bite of the cold obsidian seep into my hands. But it doesn't help. I still feel like I'm unravelling.

My father. My fucking father. He burned her. Three days in flame, and he stood there while her screams filled the sky. I grip the edge of the table harder, the veins in my arms straining as I lean forward, my breath coming in shallow pants as I grit my teeth. I want to scream. I want to tear the walls down. I want to—

The door creaks slightly, but I don't look up. I don't need to. I would know Aran's presence anywhere. The calmness of his aura has always been grounding for me. But right now, I'm not sure anything could help me.

"I need to be alone," I mutter.

"I know," Aran says quietly. "But I'm not choosing to listen." Stubborn bastard.

For a while, neither of us speaks. The silence hangs thick between us, pulsing with my magic and rage.

Without thinking, I speak the words I know I shouldn't. The

words that are boiling so hot under my skin that they're threatening to burn me alive. "I should kill him."

Aran shifts behind me. "Korithax..."

"I should carve his heart out and throw it to the flamebeasts." My voice is dangerously low. "He murdered her. Lied to me, denied the whispers and the rumours. He raised me like it didn't fucking happen. Let me, my people, my kingdom, worship him. Let us believe he took the throne because he deserved it. Because he was fit to rule."

"I know," Aran says gently.

I finally look at him, and I know my eyes are wild. "You knew?"

Something like panic flashes in his eyes, but it's gone before I can decipher it.

"I didn't know, I suspected. I heard whispers, but nobody could prove it. And the Divine Six... they've had their hands in every truth and lie for thousands of years." He steps closer. "But I never believed he was innocent."

I step away from the table, pacing up and down like a crazed animal. My wings snap out behind me, twitching with the need to take flight.

"I could do it. Right now. I could fly straight to his bed and shove a blade through his fucking chest. The court wouldn't stop me. Not if they knew—"

"Korithax." Aran's voice is stronger now. "If you kill the king, it's treason. You'll lose your claim. You'll lose everything. Including her."

My throat tightens at the thought of being ripped away from her. I've come too close to losing her too many times in such a short fucking amount of time.

"She needs you. She doesn't need vengeance. Not yet. She just needs you."

I let the words settle. Because they're true. And I hate to admit it, but Aran's right. Killing him won't change anything. His time will come.

I press the heels of my hands into my eyes, hard enough to see stars.

"I don't know who I am anymore, Aran," I whisper. "The world I've built in my head—my father, my legacy, the Divine Six, everything—it's all bullshit. And she's looking at me like I might shatter her without even meaning to. Because at the root of it all, this is my fault. I should've stayed away from her."

"You won't shatter her. And you couldn't stay away from her," Aran says. "Because, despite the mate bond pulling you together... You love her."

I look up sharply.

"Don't look at me like that. It's not a secret that you worship the ground she walks on. You'd kill a fucking god for her. Or six."

I sink into one of the chairs, leaning forward to place my forearms on my knees. My head drops into my hands as I let out a deep exhale. Even Aran was changing. I don't think I'd ever heard him swear before. What the fuck was going on?

"She doesn't even want to be who she is," I murmur. "She doesn't want to be a queen anymore. She just wants to be... Daisy."

Aran walks over and places a hand on my shoulder, the small gesture somehow calming. His reassurance washes over me, and I look up to face him.

"Then remind her she can be Daisy, and she can be so much more. She's already yours, and whatever crown she wears, whatever throne she's destined for... she's still the girl who stared a seven-foot demon in the face and told him to piss off."

I huff out a laugh. "She's everything," I whisper. "She's my mate, my little flower."

Aran squeezes my shoulder. "Then be her mate in every way that counts. But don't burn the world down before she asks you to."

I look up at him, and this time, I really see him. Not my advisor, not my assistant. Just my friend, my brother.

"Thank you," I say, voice hoarse.

He nods once, then pulls the sword from the wall and lays it on the table beside me. "Try not to throw this again. It's very old."

My lip tugs up at the corner as I offer him a small nod in response. He leaves the room, the door clicking quietly behind him.

I sit alone for a while, the sword beside me, my thoughts a battlefield. I don't know what tomorrow brings, but I know who I'm fighting for. And I know who I won't spare when the time comes. Not even my own blood.

CHAPTER 52
DAISY

I sit cross-legged on the rug, my fingers curled around a cup of honeyed tea I'm not actually bothering to drink.

The room is still glowing with the warmth of their laughter from their stories of what's been happening back home. But underneath it all, there's a tension I can't hide anymore.

Ezra leans forward, arms braced on his knees. "Okay, bitch. Spill everything. Like, everything. Start with the getting married part. Why the hell did you marry Satan?"

Talia elbows him, but he doesn't look away from me. She's quiet, and her eyes are full of worry, like she's trying to read me before I can even start speaking. She's always done that, read me like an open book. I'd trained myself over the years to hide the darkest parts of me from her, but she still mostly managed to figure me out.

I take a breath. "Technically, I didn't marry Satan. He's down in Gehenna," I force a laugh. "But, I married Korithax because I had to. It was part of a political agreement. He needed a wife to become king, and I..." my voice falters. "I needed somewhere to belong. Somewhere that didn't remind me of being broken."

Ezra's expression softens instantly. "You're not broken, Daze."

Talia says nothing, but her hand finds mine in a strong embrace, her thumb tracing softly over my knuckles.

"I was," I whisper. "After Ethan, after everything. I felt like I was splintering into pieces that I couldn't hold together anymore. Korithax showed up after I was raped, when I had whispered his name. He had shown up when I took the overdose, saving me even when I didn't want him to. And when I summoned him with my blood, I wasn't expecting him to actually care, not after I'd basically told him to go fuck himself on Christmas Eve."

I huff out a laugh, remembering how he'd come to me to ask for marriage. How I'd thought he'd lost the absolute plot, with his little glowing orb and his fake smile.

Talia's brows knit. "You summoned him?"

"Yeah," I nod. "After that day at college, when the report got released, and Jason came over to be a dick. Some of the players' girlfriends came into the cafe and started talking shit and got me fired... I'd just had enough." My throat catches, but I keep going. "I used my blood and his summoning circle and screamed at him to come. I agreed to marry him as soon as he arrived, signed the contract, and then well... here we are."

Ezra's eyes are wide now. "Jesus."

I TELL them all about the realms. About Fjellheim Heights, how it was a world in the clouds. Aurora's veil, and how I'd wanted to bring them there to one of the cabins under the ever-twinkling northern lights. Well I did, until one of the creepy ass people kidnapped me, and the literal king of the realm tried to seduce me. I told them about Solara, where the sky's always golden, and their goddess is perfection personified. But I left out the part about my mom, just wanting to keep some things to myself. I told them about Stormravan, where the wind screams through the mountains. About Luminaria, where light bends and breathes like it's alive. I can't bring myself to tell them that Luminaria's goddess is also my sister, because I still can't quite believe it myself. Then I tell them about Noxthrallia, how I'd rather die than ever return back to that godforsaken realm, and the ritual that was performed.

Finally, I tell them about Zeriavoss—where they are right freaking now—and how it felt like home the moment I stepped into the fields. I describe the way the blood blossoms bloom, and how the lakes reflect the blood-red lightning streaks like molten ruby in a vast blue sky. And I tell them why I agreed to become immortal, and with a quivering voice, exactly what happened when I had become immortal. And just who, or what, I had become.

"I JUST WANTED MORE TIME," I say, staring into my cup. "More time with him. More time to find out who I am. It felt like the only way to live without waiting for the clock to run out."

Talia leans back against the bed frame, arms crossed. "So let me get this straight. You got dragged into a soul bargain from the Heir of Hell, married him, became immortal, visited magical realms, and—oh yeah—you're apparently the reincarnated version of someone who created... everything?"

"That pretty much sums it up, yeah," I say, shrugging helplessly.

When she puts it like that, it really all does sound like some crazy, far-fetched dream. How had all of this happened in just the space of a few months? I'd gone from being a regular college girl to a long-lost Queen reborn.

Ezra sighs dramatically. "Ugh. When you created everything, you could've made me rich!"

I giggle. "I think you're about fifty thousand years too late for my help."

Typical Ezra. I've just told him things I don't even think my favourite fantasy books could conjure up, and he's concerned about the fact I didn't create him as a rich man.

Talia gives a slow, wary nod. Like she's slowly processing everything. "So... what are you going to do?"

"I don't know," I admit. "I'm exhausted. I left home to come here and be someone who wasn't broken. And now I'm a long-dead queen, a creator of realms, and Korithax is my mate."

Ezra nearly chokes on his tea. "Your what?"

"This is like your bullshit fae books you have at home," he cackles. "A fucking mate? You have a mate now?"

"I know," I groan. "It's crazy. But I feel it. It's like this tug toward him. I can't stand being away from him, my body, my heart, my soul—it aches for him."

"Okay, horny bitch, calm down." Talia laughs, throwing a pillow at me.

I roll my eyes, blushing. "He's also great in bed."

I smirk behind my tea as both of them gasp, letting out a soft giggle when Ezra slaps my arm.

"STOP. This is too much!" He fakes fainting onto the floor, and we all burst into laughter. That wild, unfiltered kind of laughter that comes when you're seconds from crumbling, but someone reminds you that joy still exists. It makes me feel lighter than I have since I woke up.

"Wait," I ask, frowning. "How the hell did you even get here?"

Talia and Ezra glance at each other before Talia speaks. "Aran came. He said you needed us, said you were lost and overwhelmed, and that you might not even remember yourself when we arrived."

"And of course, we didn't hesitate," Ezra adds. "We just came."

I stare at them, my chest aching. How was I going to do anything without them? Maybe I could have them turned immortal, too.

"So, uh," Ezra says, eyeing me carefully. "You really gonna be Queen of Hell?"

I shake my head. "I don't know. I was supposed to just be Korithax's wife, Queen of Hell. But now it's way more than that, and I don't know who I'm supposed to be anymore."

• • •

A KNOCK SOUNDS on the door, and we all look to it as it slowly creaks open, Aran's head popping in. I offer him a genuine smile of thanks, and he offers me a soft smile in return.

"Sorry to interrupt," He murmurs, "it's time for your friends to leave."

I nod, the ache in my chest instantly returning at the thought of them going home.

"We'll visit again soon," Talia says as she stands. "Or maybe you can come back to us for a little while. We'll have a sleepover."

"I'll bring the mint choc chip!" Ezra grins, bouncing like an excited puppy.

I feel the tears fill my eyes. "I'd love that."

They move in, wrapping their arms around me in another three-way hug, holding me like I'm something sacred as our heads touch together.

"I love you both so much," I whisper as the tears fall.

"We love you, Daisy Duke," Ezra says softly, his voice catching.

"Laters, queen bitch," Talia says, blowing me a kiss.

A FEW MOMENTS LATER, and they're gone, Aran included. The room that was so filled with joy and love just moments ago is now empty, and the silence feels like it has swallowed me whole. For the first time in what feels like forever, I'm all alone.

I FINISH the rest of my tea and move towards the bathroom. I hadn't even realised I was still in this dress—the one I'd been immortalised in until I'd zoned back in and had seen the black fabric pooled around me. The second I realised, it felt like it was suffocating me. I need it off. I need to wash away the last twenty-four hours from my skin.

I step into the quiet bathroom, basking in the peace and quiet, and strip the gown from my body, leaving it in a heap on the obsidian tiled floor. I step beneath the warm flow of water and brace my hands on the cool stone wall. Steam rises around me in thick coils. I close my eyes, and for a moment, I just allow myself to breathe. Everything I've endured in the last twenty-four hours whirls around my head, and before I can understand what's happening, the world shifts. Heat rushes up my spine, and my head feels blurry. The sound of running water fades, and my hands are no longer against the cool stone.

I open my eyes, and it's like I'm having an out-of-body experience. Except, the body isn't mine. The world around me is in flames. I'm standing in armour darker than night, obsidian etched with red runes glowing like embers. My silver hair is whipping behind me in a violent wind, stained with streaks of blood. My face is spattered with it too—demon blood, fae blood—I can't tell whose is whose. All I can hear is the sound of voices chanting.

Ashborn. Ashborn. Ashborn.

Thousands of soldiers stand behind me, all chanting that name. My name. The sword in my grip is engulfed in white flame, so bright it burns the colour from the world around me. Upon my head, a blazing wreath of fire is wrapped in spirals of molten gold to resemble a crown. I blink, and I'm suddenly no longer looking at myself, but out of my eyes. Before me, the battlefield smoulders. A massive beast lies dead at my feet, smoke rising from its split-open chest. All around are corpses, some demon, some fae, and other things I don't even recognise. And there, standing directly in front of me, is a large, fae warrior. His eyes burn violet, his ash coloured hair stuck to his skin, drenched in blood. One hand clutches at his ribs, right where a blade has pierced through. He sneers at me, canines longer than any I've ever seen.

"This is not over, Ashborn Queen," he growls. "They sent me to destroy you. I may not have won, but they will."

The vision shatters, causing me to stumble backwards. My palms grasp at air as I struggle to find my footing. I turn, slamming my back against the wall as I gasp for breath, the steam suffocating as I fight for oxygen. My heart is racing like I've just come off the battlefield for real. My body trembles, my skin freezing despite the warm water. The fear won't leave, it's deep in my bones. It felt so real.

"Daisy?"

His voice cuts through the haze. I turn my head, breath still catching in my throat. Korithax stands just outside the shower, eyes wide, concern carved into every sharp line of his face.

"What is it?" He asks, already moving to be by my side.

"I just had... I don't know. A vision?" I whisper. "A battlefield. Dasmyrin had just won a battle against a huge fae man. He was bleeding out, and he used his dying words to tell me something."

"What. What did he say?"

"This is not over, Ashborn. They sent me to destroy you. I may not have won... but they will." I whisper, repeating his words as my heart thunders.

Korithax's brow tightens as he steps fully into the room, scanning me, like he's making sure I'm whole and safe.

"The gates to other universes were sealed long before I was even born," he says, his voice low. "There were whispers that the fae had grown greedy. That they wanted more than their realm, that they wanted all of ours too. Every ruler in every realm joined together to close the borders." He moves to me, stroking my hair out of my face. "No one should be able to cross over again, Daisy."

I grip my arms, water pouring over the pair of us. "But what if they already did? What if the 'they' that sent him—what if that's the Divine Six?"

Korithax lets out a slow, cold breath. "It sounds like something they'd do. Manipulate someone else to do their dirty work. Someone they could cut ties with. Someone who'd be impossible to trace." I watch as his jaw pulses. "Universe travel is nearly impossible. It takes catastrophic power. God-tier magic."

"But there were fae in the realms we visited. What if they want blood?"

Korithax shakes his head. "They are the offspring of when the fae were welcomed here. They are not out to harm you, Daisy. They are more our creatures than theirs."

I shiver against the feeling of dread taking over my body. "This is too much. I don't even feel like I can breathe."

He steps closer to me, not caring that his clothes or boots are getting soaked through. He wraps his arms around me, lowering himself to press his forehead against mine.

"You don't have to carry this alone," he murmurs, pressing his lips to my soaked hair. "We'll face this together, my little flower. You and me. You are my wife, my mate, my Daisy."

My arms wrap around him tightly, fingers curling into the fabric of his wet shirt as it clings to every muscle that hones his body.

"I've got you, okay? You're not alone."

I let out a shuddering breath. He's right. I'm not alone. I have the strongest, fiercest man by my side. And I think with him, I'll just about be okay.

CHAPTER 53

KORITHAX

Zeriavoss was never quiet. But tonight, the silence felt like it was watching me.

The scent of her skin is still clinging to mine. That mixture of hers that is so indescribably addicting, but now has a hint of sulphur to it that makes her feel even more like home.

Daisy's asleep beside me, her breath even and shallow, her hair fanned out across the pillows like liquid gold. She looks peaceful for the first time since she returned from Noxthrallia. But I know it's only a pause. A single inhale between the shitstorm we're standing in.

I lay there with my hand on her waist, eyes fixed on the intricate carvings on the ceiling above us. I can feel the pressure in my chest building to an almost suffocating amount. I should be grateful. She's safe, she's breathing, and she's home—with me. But I can't lie here. I can't rest. My blood is thrumming too loud in my ears, and every heartbeat is laced with a fury so potent it feels like it's going to consume my very being. How had everything gone so wrong so fast?

• • •

Without a sound, I slip from the bed and dress quickly in all black. No armour, just my blade strapped to my thigh, and shadows of smoke coiled tightly around me. I softly press a kiss to Daisy's temple and whisper against her skin, "I'll be back soon, little flower."

The halls are still as I walk through them, my footsteps echoing off the stone, slicing through the kind of silence that feels almost sentient. The guards stationed near his royal wing straighten the moment they see me. One of them opens his mouth, as if to stop me, but I narrow my eyes, and he quickly closes it again before bowing and stepping aside. They know exactly where I'm going, and the look on my face is ensuring none of them are brave enough to attempt stopping me.

I reach the elder king's chambers and push the doors open with a quiet creak. There he lies, sleeping in silk and luxury, stretched out beneath furs and gold thread. He looks peaceful, as though the realm doesn't carry the weight of a million ghosts screaming his name. As though he didn't burn a queen alive.

I watch him for a moment, my fists curling at my sides. I could end it now. Slide my blade between his ribs and twist, ensuring he couldn't take another breath. But there's something I need more than revenge now, more than the need to satiate the bloodlust coursing through me. I need the truth.

"Korran," I speak, my voice devoid of any emotion.

His pitch-black eyes open slowly, locking onto mine. There's no fear in them, no surprise etched across his face. Just an infuriating smirk that has my hackles rising.

"Ah, my boy," he says, voice rough with sleep and the whisper of death. "You visit me at last."

"This isn't a visit," I growl, my ability to keep my emotions in check instantly obliterated by his idiocy. "This is reckoning. I need answers, and you're going to give them to me."

I pull a vial from my pocket—a twisted golden glass filled with a liquid the colour of fresh blood. The elixir gleams under the firelight. There wasn't a chance I was going to do this without the aid of an elixir. He was a manipulative fucking liar, and I didn't have the time or energy for his half-truths. Not today.

He narrows his eyes. "A truth elixir, Korithax? What is this, some dramatic ploy?" He scoffs, and it takes every inch of my willpower not to punch him in the throat. "I'll answer your questions. I don't need to drink that bullshit."

I move fast and grab his wrist, the sudden contact making him gasp so hard he starts to splutter. I use my thumb to pop the cork and slam the vial into his hand, forcing it up to his lips.

"Fucking drink it," I snarl.

He glares at me, defiance in his eyes. I bare my teeth, squeezing his hand hard enough that I know damn well it hurts. He drinks slowly, the potion hissing down his throat, smoke curling briefly from his nostrils as it enters his system. I release him and step back, drawing my dagger and letting my Hellfire flow into it. The black flame dances along the edge, casting menacing light across the chamber.

"Start talking."

He sits up, the potion fully taking hold as his jet-black eyes pulse in a faint red glow. "What is it that you want to know?"

"The Divine Six," I snap. "Tell me how it started. Tell me why you killed Dasmyrin."

He doesn't flinch, doesn't even blink. Like the news of him destroying the queen becoming public knowledge doesn't bother him at all. Of course it won't. He's on his fucking deathbed, his sins done and dusted.

My father always was a ruthless leader, never caring about the consequences of his actions. This was the only thing he seemed to have done that he hid shamefully. But was it really shame, or was it the fact that he knew Dasmyrin's people would cause an uprising against him? They'd see him destroyed if they knew the real truth of what happened to her. There were so many different versions of the story, all muddled over the centuries, that nobody really knew the truth of it all anymore. She was merely a myth to most; half of the people who lived under her rule had long since passed, and the other half were too young to remember. And any open followers remaining after her death were destroyed, executed, or exiled.

"They came to me in whispers," he says. "One by one. Pretending to seek counsel. Pretending they were concerned about how Dasmyrin ruled Hell. They said she was dangerous. That she was fracturing the natural order. That her vision would destroy everything we'd built."

"And you believed them?" I ask, tilting my head at him like he was nothing more than a stupid child.

"No," he says simply. "Not at first. But then they showed me what could be mine. A throne, power, obedience from realms that once spat at my name. I was her general, her second in command, but I was still beneath her." He meets my eyes. "And I didn't want to be beneath anyone anymore."

My hand tightens around the handle of my blade.

"They offered me the kingdom," he continues. "If I helped bring her down, I could have it. All I had to do was let them plan everything. They let the fae into the realm." He shrugs. "I didn't even have to do much. Not really. Just hold her still. Keep her from escaping. And I did."

So that's all it truly took to turn my father from a loyal second to a filthy fucking traitor. The promise of a throne that wasn't earned, and the ability to rule people who didn't choose him. That wouldn't choose him. Dasmyrin was loved. She ruled fairly, not like him, who chose corruption and fear.

I felt sick just looking at him. I was by no means a kind man. I've acted irrationally, without thinking, without caring. But to take a queen and destroy her, one who looked at him like a brother. He truly was scum.

"I knew what I was doing, I knew what would happen. And I did it anyway. I wanted the crown."

"You let the fae in?" I ask.

"The Divine Six did, they struck a deal. The fae would cross the realms—bring their magic, their beasts, their warriors. And in return, they'd be given a seat of influence here. A place in our realm." His lips twist. "But they failed. They couldn't kill her, even with all their power."

"So the Divine Six closed the door between our universe and theirs?" I ask, desperate for all the information I could get before the elixir wore off.

"Cut them off permanently," he confirms. "Left only the bloodlines behind. Some of them had already sired children here, others died on the battlefield."

I begin pacing up and down the room, combing a hand through my hair. "Were there others? Anybody else who helped you in your fucking desperate climb to the throne?"

He stills, and I watch as his face twists, sweat forming on his brow. He clamps his lips shut, fisting at the furs around him. The bastard is trying to withhold information. He's trying to fight the elixir.

I narrow my eyes, stopping dead in front of him. "Spit it out, Korran," I growl, raising my blade to him.

"The Særathi," he grits out, the sweat now dripping down his forehead.

I watch as his expression shifts. For the first time, I swear I see something like fear in his eyes.

"What's that?" I ask.

"They weren't part of the original deal," he says slowly, still trying to fight the words. "They weren't from the fae universe. They weren't from any realm we knew. The Divine Six didn't tell me much. But they said they found a door... one that wasn't supposed to exist."

"What door?" I push, my pulse rising with each word he mutters.

"The Aetherhollow," he whispers.

"What are they? What is that place?" I can feel my panic rising. I'd never heard any of this information before. Not even in whispers.

He shakes his head. "I don't know. Not truly. All I know is they aren't mortal, or divine, or anything in between. The Divine Six were terrified of them and utterly obsessed with them at the same time. Said they lived in the space between spaces. That they could rewrite memory, and that time bends for them like wind."

"And the Divine Six wanted their power?"

"They wanted it badly. Enough to slaughter them. Enough to steal their knowledge and bind it into a book."

I freeze. "What book?"

He looks away, his body shaking as he tries his hardest to fight the elixir coursing through him.

"Korran. What book?" I snarl.

"They called it the Grimoire of Shattered Threads. I never saw it. I only heard them whisper about it. But it holds everything they ever learned. Everything they took."

"Where is it?" I demand, grasping at his silken nightwear.

"I told you—I don't know."

I raise my blade, the flames licking the underside of his jaw.

"Korithax—"

"I should gut you where you sit. For her. For everything you've done."

"I don't regret it," he says, smiling faintly. "I would do it again. Because you wouldn't be here if I hadn't."

My vision blurs red, my hand shaking with the desperation to plunge the blade straight into his jugular. Fucking bastard. Of course, he didn't regret it. But how dare he use my existence for his reasoning behind that? How fucking dare he?

"Korithax..."

My eyes snap to him, my breath coming in quick pants.

"Fuck." I release him, stepping back as he flops back down onto his pillows. His eyes blink, slow and heavy as he looks up at me.

"It's time, isn't it?" He says, his voice low.

"What?"

"I feel it," he rasps. "In my body. Like something's leaving. Like... It's done."

His hand twitches at his side, and his face slackens.

"No," I growl, moving forward. "You don't get to fucking die yet. I need to know more."

His eyes meet mine one last time. "You'll make a better king than I ever was."

His eyes flutter closed, and I listen as I hear his heartbeat stop. He's gone. Korran, the Betrayer King, has died without a single fucking soul in the world to give a shit about it. The air shifts, and I can feel it in my bones, in the bloodline that coils through my veins. Korran is dead, which means I'm now King. It's finally time to start fixing every wrong that piece of shit did. Starting with the divine assholes who thought they could murder a queen and get away with it.

I PAUSE outside the doors to our chambers, the weight of the hour sinking deep into my bones.

I feel lighter somehow. My father is finally dead, a clean ending to a legacy built on ash and betrayal. But the relief is short-lived, because what he left behind is a trail of destruction that doesn't have a map. The Særathi, the Aetherhollow, the Grimoire. These aren't just well-kept secrets—they're weapons of mass destruction. And I don't know how to stop them from detonating.

I run a hand through my hair and lean against the door for a moment, closing my eyes. It's nearly four a.m., meaning it's currently too late... or too early, to do anything about it. I can't storm into Elyistria's room demanding answers. Not when her sister has just clawed her way back into existence after fifty thousand years of erasure. She's grieving all over again, processing everything that's happened, just like Daisy. And then there's me. I don't have the luxury of time on my side.

The throne is unclaimed now. Korran's death makes me the rightful ruler of Hell, but without a coronation, without formal ascension, the realm is left cracked open and weak. I can already feel it in the walls of Zeriavoss. Like the magic that runs through it is holding its breath, waiting for someone to sit their ass on the throne and tell it who to be.

I don't want to pressure Daisy. Gods, the last thing I want to do is add more weight onto her already bruised, breaking shoulders. But she's not just my wife, she's my mate, my queen. And not having her crowned at my side... it isn't an option.

I steel myself and push the door open slowly, the hinges quietly creaking in the silence. She's still curled up in the bed where I left her, her golden hair a halo on the pillow, the sheets twisted around her waist. I lean against the frame watching her, her breathing so steady and soft. She looks so peaceful, more peaceful than I've seen her since we returned. Her soft snores seem to be the only thing in this godsdamned palace that gives me a semblance of peace.

I strip silently, placing my blade on the table, discarding the black clothes that have my father's death clinging to them like a bad aura. The second I slip into the bed, I pull her close, unable to resist touching her. Her body instinctively melts into mine, her hand splaying across my chest. Like even in sleep, our bond can detect the other, like her soul knows exactly where it belongs. I hold her there for a moment, burying my nose into her hair, indulging myself in her scent. She's here, she's safe.

Despite everything—despite the burning truths, the weight of legacy, the terror of what might be coming—for a few seconds, it all feels worth it. Would I have her if Dasmyrin hadn't died? Would this soul... this fierce, broken, radiant girl, have found her way to me if the Divine Six hadn't shattered the world once before? The thought of it guts me. Because, as cruel and twisted and as wrong as it is... I wouldn't change a single thing that had happened if it meant I could keep her. I would set every realm on fire and never look back. Because without Daisy, without my little flower, none of this means a damn thing to me.

I slide my hand down to hers and interlace our fingers against my chest, feeling her warmth pulse through me. I never wanted a crown, I never wanted to rule. I just wanted to fight and protect. But if claiming the throne means giving her safety, power, and freedom, then I will sit on it proudly. For her, with her. And if she wants the throne for herself, I will gladly step aside. I will kneel before her, worship her in every way she'll let me, and guard her until my last breath. Hell doesn't need a king; it never did. It needs her. But whatever path she chooses, whatever version of herself she wants to be, I'll be beside her. If she decides to burn every kingdom that dared to forget her, if she desires to eradicate every soul who decided to stand by and accept Korran as king, I will be her sword and her shield. And if I die doing so, I will find her again in every future.

~

THE SUN WAS NOW BLEEDING through the windows, soft golden light catching in her hair, but I still hadn't slept. The thought of Daisy waking up and me having to tell her I needed to be crowned king within the next twenty-four hours made me feel physically ill. I didn't want to pressure her, not when she'd already survived so much. But time had ran the fuck out.

I slipped out of the bed and dragged on my pants, not bothering with a shirt. Popping my head out the door, I find the two guards stationed outside.

"Tell the help I want breakfast brought up. And coffee. Now."

They both dip their heads in unison with a firm, "Yes, Your Majesty," before one of them hurries away.

Majesty. Fuck. Guess the news was out about the old King's demise. Fan-fucking-tastic.

"Korithax?" Her voice is soft and sleepy, but it hits me like a punch to the gut. I turn, finding her propped up on one elbow, waves of golden hair tumbling around her. Daisy rubs her eyes, blinking blearily. She looked so at peace, and I was about to bring a fucking storm.

"Good morning, beautiful," I respond, my voice low and full of reverence.

She smiles back, but it falters into a frown. "What is it?"

"What's what?" My pulse kicks up. Fuck. Was I really that readable?

"I can feel it. Through the bond. You're anxious. Something's wrong." She responds, rubbing at her chest exactly where I know the bond pulls the hardest.

"Shit," I mutter under my breath.

"I heard that," she teases with a small smirk.

Of course she did, because she has immortal hearing now. I roll my eyes and click the door closed, moving to the edge of the bed, awkwardly looming as I try to string together the right words. How the fuck was I supposed to say this?

"It's... my father."

Her brows pinch together. "What's happened?"

She rises from the bed and pads towards me, sliding her arms around my waist as she pushes herself up onto her tiptoes. I lean down, placing a soft kiss against her perfectly pouty lips. I needed to taste her before I broke her world again.

She kisses me back with hunger, threading her fingers into my hair, making me groan into her mouth as my hands find their way to her waist to pull her in close. God's I fucking loved the feel of her mouth against mine. I lift her effortlessly, hands gripping under her thighs as she wraps her legs around my waist. I slide a palm to her ass and squeeze, pulling a breathy moan from her lips.

She pulls back, breathless and flushed, brushing a strand of hair from my face. "You're trying to distract me."

I smirk, nipping at her bottom lip. "Is that such a bad thing? We both need it."

Before she can argue, I kiss her hard, devouring her mouth with the desperation of a man clinging to the one thing anchoring him to sanity. I move forward, laying her down onto the bed, magic sparking in the air as I burn away her nightgown, revealing every inch of her to my greedy eyes. My breath catches at the sight of her. She's perfection. Curves made for sin, dusky nipples already peaked, and her soft stomach making her look like the fucking goddess she is. I slowly trail my eyes down her body, taking in the sight of her thick, creamy thighs that were just begging to have my face between them.

I trail slow kisses down her jaw, my stubble grazing her skin as I drag my teeth over her pulse at her throat before biting down to leave my mark on her like the possessive bastard I was. She lets out a small yelp, threading her hands through my hair as her thumbs softly caress my horns. I shudder at the sensation, the feel of her touch going straight to my already throbbing cock. I lower my mouth to her breast, sucking it into my mouth before biting down on her nipple gently, making her hips buck.

"Korithax," she moans, digging her nails into my scalp.

Gods, I love it when she moans my name. I trail my right hand slowly down her body, leaving goosebumps in its wake as it trails slowly down to between her thighs. I force my hand between them, pushing them open.

I lift my head, smiling at her darkly. "Your thighs are soaking baby. Is that what I do to you, do I make your little cunt drip?"

She nods, sucking her lower lip between her teeth. I bring my hand up from her thighs, slapping it across her cheek before gripping her chin. She gasps in surprise but her eyes spark with delight.

"Words, Daisy. You know the rules by now," I growl.

"Yes," She breathes. "Yes, you make me so wet, Korithax."

I groan in satisfaction, lowering my mouth back to her nipple and sucking hard as my hand finds her cunt. I run my middle finger through her slit, gathering her juices and rubbing it over her swollen clit in slow circles. Her hips buck again, and I force my weight onto her so she can't move as I suck at her nipple, flicking my tongue in time with my finger.

"Gods, Korithax. Please!" She moans, grasping onto my horns as I tease her body.

I don't deign to answer as I continue torturing her nipple and pussy whilst she writhes beneath me, desperate for release. But I don't want to give it to her, not yet. I want her begging. I want her soaking and needy and on the verge of tears before I give her what she wants. I need a release, and using her body is the perfect way to find it.

I pull away when her breaths start to come in little pants, and her thighs tremble. Pushing myself onto my haunches, I stare down at her, laughing sadistically.

"Whyyyyyy?" She whines, panting as she rubs her thighs together in desperate search of friction.

I push my middle finger into my mouth and groan at the taste of her. Gods, she tastes so fucking sweet, it's addictive.

"Spread your thighs, princess," I murmur around my finger.

A blush spreads across her pretty little face, but she does as I ask, moving her feet apart so I have the perfect view of her cunt. She has the most perfect pussy I'd ever seen, and I couldn't wait to be buried inside of her.

A knock sounds at the door, and I can't stop the furious growl that escapes me. "What?" I bark.

"Uh, breakfast, Your Highness." A servant's voice quakes from the other side of the door.

"Leave it outside and fuck off," I snap.

"Korithax!" Daisy scolds before shouting a thank you to the help.

"My breakfast is spread before me, and I don't like to be disturbed when I'm about to eat."

Her eyes go wide as I grin at her, lowering my head between her thighs. I place my arms under her legs, pulling them further apart and digging my fingers into her supple skin. I don't waste any more time and drag my tongue straight from her hole to her clit in one slow motion, savouring the taste of her. She throws her head back against the pillow, moaning loudly as I begin to devour her, lapping my tongue up and down her slit, flicking her clit with the tip of my tongue, and sucking it so hard she gasps.

She grips the sheets, writhing beneath me as I continue to eat her, not giving her a chance to catch her breath as I nip and suck at her swollen, sensitive clit. I take one of my hands and slide my middle and ring fingers inside her, stretching her tight hole as I move them in and out gently, curling them up towards that delicious, sensitive spot that has her screaming my name as I feast upon her. I feel her walls tightening around my fingers as she builds towards an orgasm, and I instantly pull away, making sure she doesn't have the chance to fall over the edge.

She screams in frustration at her second orgasm denial, and my eyes widen as I watch the curtain go up in bright white flames around us. I quickly extinguish them with my magic and look at her with shock etched onto my face.

"Did I do that?" She pants, her face red and sweaty.

I nod, then burst into laughter, the sound booming around the room as her cheeks go even redder from embarrassment.

"Looks like you've found a way to reach your power, princess," I smirk.

"Orgasm denial, apparently, you asshole," she growls, and I swear it sounds just as animalistic as when I do it.

"I like your feisty side, baby. What else you got?" I ask, quirking a brow.

She moves quickly, using her legs to flip me onto my back. Before I know what's happened, she's straddling me with a huge grin on her face.

"What the fuck?" I ask in utter shock.

"Turns out, I'm strong too." She says sassily, quirking her brow back at me.

Without giving me another second to think, she lowers herself onto my throbbing cock and slams herself down to the hilt with a scream of pain and pleasure.

"FUCK!" I roar, gripping her hips so hard I know it'll bruise.

She leans forward, placing her hands on my chest as her golden hair falls around her like a curtain. She stares down at me, her ocean eyes looking into my soul as she begins riding my cock. Each time she slams her hips down, a hiss of pain escapes her, but she doesn't stop. She continues to rise and lower herself, her nails digging so hard into my chest that blood begins to bead underneath her fingers.

"I'm gonna come." She moans loudly, thrusting her hips back and forth to grind her clit against me.

"Come for me, baby," I groan.

I feel her cunt tighten around me to a vice-like grip as her orgasm begins to tear through her body.

"That's it. Come all over my fucking cock, you filthy girl."

Her screams fill the room, the walls beginning to shake as the pleasure ripples through her body. I watch in awe as she rides out her high, the bed and floors now trembling along with her. She collapses onto my chest, but I'm still not done with her.

I grip her hands behind her back and pin her to me as I begin relentlessly thrusting into her, my cock soaked with her pleasure. She shakes against me as I ruthlessly use and abuse her body for my own high. She bites down on my chest, the pain taking my pleasure to a whole new level.

"Fuck, you feel so good, baby," I groan as I feel myself getting close to the edge.

She lifts her head to face me, and I stare into her eyes, the sight of her utterly devastating. "Fill me, Korithax. Please."

Those words unravel me, and I slam myself into her again, tearing another orgasm from her as I go still, my cock pulsing as I spill into her, filling her just as she asked. We ride through our orgasms together, panting hard as the pleasure ebbs through us both.

"Gods," I pant, dropping my head against the bed. "I will never, ever get tired of fucking you."

She giggles, pushing herself off of me and falling to my side. "I don't think I'll ever get tired of it either," she breathes.

I pull her to me, her head resting on my chest as she uses her thumb to swipe at the beads of blood she left behind. I pull her hand up to suck the blood off, but she beats me to it and places the thumb into her own mouth, sucking it clean herself.

"Fuck. That made me hard again," I mutter, watching as her tongue laps up the last of the blood.

"Tough," she laughs. "You've had your distraction. Now what's wrong?"

I SIGH, the ecstasy of what just happened vanishing like smoke. Her warmth is still on my skin, her scent thick in the air. Daisy rests her cheek against my shoulder, tracing lazy little circles across my sternum. But she's not stupid. She knows I'm stalling, and she's waiting. I tilt my head and press a kiss to her forehead.

"I'm not going to like this, am I?" She whispers.

"No," I rasp. "You're not."

She lifts her head and looks at me with those too-perceptive eyes—oceans kissed by shadow now. The black rings around her eyes are a part of Dasmyrin's immortality shining through her. She's so beautiful it hurts. And I know the second I open my mouth I'm going to watch the light dim in her eyes again.

I sit up slowly, pulling her with me until we're both sitting against the headboard. Her legs drape across mine, her arms curled around her knees. She looks so small, like she's trying to fold in on herself already.

I run a hand through my hair, exhaling hard. "My father is dead."

Her breath catches. "What?"

"I forced him to take a truth elixir earlier this morning, and after he told me everything, he just... died. It's like his soul was holding on to give me what I needed."

A moment of silence stretches between us. Daisy's lips part, her eyes going wide, but she stays silent, letting me continue on.

"The Divine Six opened the gates to the Fae universe and promised them power in exchange for helping them destroy Dasmyrin. When the Fae failed, they were cut off, and the door between universes was sealed, leaving only their offspring behind." I pause, watching as her expression darkens with every word, like she's slowly remembering too. "But that wasn't all. There's another universe, Daisy. One even fewer know about. And the Divine Six... they made contact. My father didn't know much, just a name."

She leans in, almost afraid to breathe. "What name?"

"The Særathi."

She blinks at me, a small frown forming in the crease of her brow. "I don't remember anything or anyone with a name like that."

"They made contact with a realm called Aetherhollow. There's something there. Something ancient. The Divine Six have been gathering secrets, magic, and power. Power beyond anything we know, even beyond Elyistria's reach. There's a Grimoire with records of every spell and secret the Divine Six learned. But it's hidden, and my father didn't know where."

Daisy swallows, her throat working hard. "Why tell me all this now?"

I take her hand in mine, pressing it against my heart. "Because the throne is empty. And the moment my father took his last breath, the crown became mine. I have to ascend, Daisy. Within the next twenty-four hours. If I don't, we leave Hell vulnerable. And that's a risk I can't afford. Not with the Six hunting us. Not with you here, knowing who and what you are. Not now."

She stares at me, her heartbeat thundering so loud I can hear it pulsing against my eardrums. "You want me by your side," she says softly.

"I need you by my side." My voice cracks. "But I'll never force it. You're my wife and my mate. That means more to me than a fucking crown. If all you want is to live here with me, far from politics and power—I'd give it to you. I'd burn every last inch of Hell to give it to you."

Her eyes fill with tears.

"But if you can be my queen..." I whisper. "Even just for the ceremony. Even just to anchor the realm. Then I'll give you everything, and no one will touch you. No one will command you, Daisy. Not even me. You'll be free. But I need your light to get through this darkness, little flower. I can't..." I swallow the lump forming in my throat. "I can't do it alone."

Her fingers tighten around mine as she blinks away stray tears. "I don't know how to be a queen," she says.

I kiss her hand softly. "You already are."

CHAPTER 54
DAISY

The chamber is silent as I sit on the bed, the soft hush of the morning light bleeding through the curtains to paint the dark stone room in brightness.

Korithax had left for a meeting with the realms' rulers after dropping the bomb on me that his coronation needed to happen ASAP. Of course it did. Because I didn't have enough on my plate, apparently. What's one more thing added onto the ever-growing pile of shit I have to carry?

I stretch slowly, my limbs aching in that dull, post sex satisfaction kind of way. But the heaviness in my chest is at a weight I'm struggling to bear. The truth presses down on me, feeling almost suffocating. I'm not just Daisy Sandoval anymore. I knew that the second I had agreed to marry Korithax. But gods, if I knew all of this was going to happen, would I have still agreed to it all?

I climb from the bed, still naked, and step into the steaming bath waiting for me that Korithax had ran before leaving. I sink down slowly, the water enveloping me like a warm hug as I close my eyes, letting out a long sigh. I lower myself slowly, letting my head sink under the water, submerging myself fully in an attempt to escape reality. I lie there, thoughts swimming through my head until my lungs burned and I burst my head through the water with a gasp for air.

"Good morning, Daisy."

I let out a small shriek, pushing the water from my eyes to see who the hell had entered the bathroom. My vision clears, and I see violet eyes so pale they almost look lavender staring at me with amusement.

"Sorry, didn't mean to frighten you," Lyvia says with a giggle.

"Lyvia!" I gasp, a smile spreading across my face. "I've missed you."

She smiles softly, a blush creeping across her cheeks as she brushes a strand of lavender hair away from her face.

"I missed you too. How was your journey?"

I quirk a brow at her. "I have a few bones to pick with you regarding some clothing, actually."

Lyvia slaps a hand over her mouth to hide her smile, a giggle escaping her, and I find myself giggling along with her.

"Was the nightwear really necessary?" I ask through a soft laugh.

"Aran said you both needed a little... push in the right direction," she replies, her blush deepening.

"Of course he did," I respond, rolling my eyes. "It's okay. I forgive you. Only because it worked." I look at her and wink, a blush creeping across my own cheeks, and we both fall into a fit of laughter.

"Would you like help getting ready this morning, Daisy?" Lyvia asks after we both calm down.

"I'd like that, thank you. I'll be right out."

She nods once before leaving, and I finish up my bath, washing my hair and body before stepping out and wrapping myself in a fluffy towel. When I re-enter the room, there's a gown on the velvet bench at the foot of the bed. It's stunning—midnight black silk threaded with silver. She helps me slide it on, the fabric clinging to my body like shadow and smoke. The sleeves hang off my shoulders, and a delicate pattern of flame embroidery licks across the hem. She helps me style my hair in soft waves down my back, and when I glance at my reflection when we're finished, I almost don't recognise the woman staring back. There's a strength in my eyes that I haven't seen in a long time.

We talk a little more, the desperation to tell her about everything on the tip of my tongue. But I can't yet. Not when there is still such a big threat looming over my head, and the pressure to become queen is still sitting on my shoulders. I pull her into a tight hug, and she returns it, wrapping her arms around me.

"I hope you understand that you're more than just my maid, Lyvia." I smile softly, holding her at arm's length.

"It's an honour to be your maid, and your friend, Daisy."

She leaves the room, and I find myself needing air and something to keep me busy.

My bare feet carry me through the corridors without thought, as if my body remembers a path my mind has long forgotten. And when I finally pause, I realise where I've come.

I press my hand to the door, pushing it open slightly and steel myself before stepping inside the large throne room. It's quiet. Still. Dust motes dance in the golden light cutting through the stained glass. And there, at the far end, is the obsidian throne. It's large, jagged, and so obnoxious it hurts to look at. I step toward it, each footfall echoing like a heartbeat.

A tremor races through me as I approach, my breath catching in my lungs as I take in the seat that had replaced the one I... Dasmyrin used to sit on. I run my fingers over the cold, solid arms of the chair, and my lungs falter as sudden images flash behind my eyes; violent and overwhelming.

I see myself—Dasmyrin—dragged from this very room, blood soaking the floor, her powers stripped from her as she screams to the high heavens. She's dragged by the Divine Six into the pit. They've burned her crown, her throne, and shattered her legacy.

I stumble forward, reaching out to steady myself, and my fingers grasp onto the curved edge of the throne. More visions. A memory. No... a reliving.

She's seated, proud and regal, a crown of flame settling on her head as the court roars in loyalty. Her eyes are black as coal, her hair gleams silver, her expression is made of justice and power.

I jolt back to myself, gasping for air. My head aches, and as I turn my focus to the pain, something begins to form, a heat searing across my scalp. I instinctively move my hands to my head and feel something solid forming. Rushing to a small diamond-shaped mirror that's placed on one of the walls, panic races through me. My reflection stares back at me, a crown of flame curling around my head. I stare at it, the heatless white flames flickering around the golden spires that protrude from the crown. It feels so familiar, so at one with me. It's the crown I'd seen on Dasmyrin, now sitting on my head, once again reunited with its owner.

"I guess fate is telling me it's time to be a queen again," I whisper, voice trembling as my fingers trace along the delicate golden spires.

STILL DAZED from the visions that had flown through my head, I wander the halls, fingers idly trailing the stone walls to try and anchor myself. I find myself wandering right up to the war room, the voices inside reaching me in the hallway. The two guards snap to attention, their heads bowing as they move aside to let me in.

I push the doors open, and silence falls. Every leader of every realm sits around the table, Korithax standing at the head, mid-sentence. When his eyes lock on me, his mouth parts, but no words come out. Every person turns to look at me, their expressions matching Korithax's when they take me in.

"Sorry, I..." I falter. "What? Why are you looking at me like that?" I ask, feeling my cheeks flame.

Korithax stares. "The crown. Your hair."

"My hair?" I ask, raising a hand to pull it forward. I catch a glimmer of silver streaks running through the golden strands. "Oh."

"It has started," Elyistria says softly. "Parts of her are shining through."

"Does she know?" Sariya asks, eyes wide.

Elyistria nods. "She does."

I turn to Sariya. "You knew?"

"I did, my sweet child. I am a goddess too, remember. I know you… Dasmyrin, as well as I know myself."

There's a tension in the air now as the other leaders in the room try silently piece together what's happening.

"What is going on?" Virena demands.

Korithax holds out his hand, beckoning me forward. "Come, little flower. We have news to share."

My fingers find his. His touch is warm and comforting as I step towards him, falling to his side.

"You ready?" He whispers, stroking a thumb across my knuckles.

I nod, chewing my lip slightly as the anxiety inside of me begins to make my body tremble.

Korithax clears his throat, silencing the murmuring throughout the room. I catch Aran's eye, and he gives me a soft smile to reassure me. "Daisy isn't just my wife. She's my mate." He pauses as the murmurs begin again. "And," he continues, demanding attention, "she is the reincarnation of the First Queen. Dasmyrin."

Gasps echo through the room, and I feel my heart on the verge of exploding.

"Bullshit," Kaelith hisses. "She's just a mortal."

I glare at him as Korithax tightens his grip on my hand.

"She's more than that," Korithax growls. "And if you insult her again, I'll show you exactly what I've become. This realm has a new king now, and I bow to no one who speaks against my Queen."

Korithax raises his free hand, flames sparking to life at his fingertips. "Or do you need a reminder of what happens when you try and fuck around, Duskwalker?"

Kaelith averts his gaze, his teeth clenched so hard his jaw pulses. I wonder if he managed to fully heal those burns after Korithax set him on fire. I try to hide my smirk at the memory of him setting him alight after he tried to turn me into his queen. Clearly, he's still bitter.

Maelkar lets out a low laugh. "So, I didn't just make her immortal. I brought back a legend."

I scoff a laugh, and he winks at me as he places his hands behind his head, leaning back in his chair, truly proud of himself. Idiot.

"Sorry for the whole memory thing, Queenie." He shrugs.

"No, you're not," I reply, smirking at him as he smirks back. Bastard wasn't sorry at all. But I can't be angry at him for taking what he wanted for his part of the deal. It could've been so much worse.

"She's more than a legend," Korithax says. "And more than a queen."

"May I?" Elyistria steps forward. With a nod from Korithax, she continues. "Dasmyrin was my sister," she says. "We were born in the beginning, created from the ash of the cosmos itself. She created the realms—the structures of everything you see. I am the magic behind it all. The creatures, the people, you, and your powers. Dasmyrin made the Divine Six, and I gave them their power to help us guide and rule the realms." She lowers her eyes, regret painting her beautiful face. "But they betrayed her. With Korithax's father, they burned her from history. But you cannot kill the creator. And now, she has risen."

The room is utterly silent for a beat, every pair of eyes wide.

"So this isn't Korithax's coronation. It's Daisy's or... Dasmyrin's?" Kaelith asks, venom lacing his tone.

"Please, I just want to be known as Daisy. And this is still his coronation." I mutter.

"Will you be by his side as his consort, or his queen?" Virena asks.

"My queen," Korithax responds without hesitation. "If she wants that."

Before I have a chance to respond, Elyistria moves to step in front of me and lowers herself to one knee, bowing her head slightly. "I vow to offer my protection, my armies, and my loyalty to the Queen."

I stare in utter shock at Elyistria on her knee before me. A chair scrapes, and Sariya steps forward to stand by Elyistria, lowering to one knee beside her, bowing her head.

"I vow to offer my protection, my armies, and my loyalty to the Queen."

One by one, the rulers move forward to kneel. Even Vor'Khar bows, grunting with his hand crackling with lightning against his chest. I glance to see Aran also on one knee, a proud smile plastered across his face, tears brimming in his emerald eyes.

Tears sting my eyes, my voice is shaky, but sure as I speak words that feel like they're from memory, as well as my heart. "I vow to rule with love, with fairness, and with strength." I turn to Korithax, gripping his hand tighter. "With my king, my mate, at my side. As equals."

The room erupts into applause, and I feel my heart swell with so much pride and love. Elyistria and Sariya pull me into a fierce embrace as we all smile, tears brimming our eyes.

"We have a coronation to prepare," Sariya laughs, her eyes gleaming with so much joy, it's contagious.

For the first time in what feels like a lifetime, I let myself bask in the love and laughter surrounding me, and smile and laugh too. I'm not just a girl anymore, I'm not just a queen. I'm the flame reignited, and with the love surrounding me, this time, I won't be the one to burn.

CHAPTER 55

KORITHAX

I watched Daisy disappear down the hall with Sariya and Elyistria, their voices fading into laughter as they whisked her away to prepare for the coronation.

I had watched in awe as Daisy had smiled like she believed it was finally allowed, and my chest ached at the sight. I turn toward the guards waiting by the still-open doors of the war room.

"Escort the realm leaders to their quarters and make sure they are seen to. I don't want anybody wandering the halls unescorted until the coronation. Understood?"

"Yes, my King," they reply in unison.

The title still felt foreign and too heavy. I wasn't even king yet, not officially. I wasn't even sure that I deserved to be king. But I'd made a promise to be the one to rule my people, and to stand by Daisy's side.

I lingered by the table, the map of the realms still unfurled in front of me. With a sigh, I roll it shut, still feeling the weight of the meeting lingering in the air. One by one, the rulers had voiced their support, not just for me, but for her. For us. For what was to come with the Divine Six. Elyistria's barrier around my realm and hers would hold for now, and I knew the others were already planning to place their own on their own realms, but I knew better than to underestimate the Six. They would find a way through eventually; they always did. And when they did... I needed every realm prepared and every ruler ready to fight.

When the room finally empties, Aran appears beside me like a shadow in the quiet. "Busy day," he says with a grin, hands placed casually in his trouser pockets.

"You think?" I mutter, dragging a hand down my face. "Gods, I feel like I've been hit by a Drekkar."

He chuckles and steps closer. "You pulled it off. I knew this would work out in the end."

I arch a brow at him. "And how exactly did you know that?"

Aran clears his throat, his emerald green eyes suddenly very interested in the wall behind me. "Just... had a feeling." He shrugs.

"Uh huh," I say, squinting my eyes at him. "Whatever you say."

I didn't have the time or the energy to question him on his weird ability to just know shit. But it was definitely something I'd been noticing a lot of lately, and I had a strong feeling my right hand man was hiding something important from me about himself.

He dropped the act and stepped forward, pulling me into a tight hug. And for once, I let him, because I didn't have it in me to pretend I didn't need the comfort. His grip is warm and steadying, something he had always been in my life.

"You ready for this?" He asks quietly as he leans back, knowing just how I felt about being a ruler.

"No," I reply honestly. "But I'll do it anyway. For her. For them." I nod to the window that faces the rest of my realm.

"That's what makes you a real king," he murmurs. "The ones who want the title for power's sake? They're the ones who ruin everything. But you? You never wanted this, Korithax. And that's exactly why you'll do it right."

I swallow the lump rising in my throat, clearly exhausted since such a thing like words from Aran were making me emotional. I give him a nod, my voice thick when I finally answer. "Thanks, Aran."

He steps back and claps me on the shoulder. "Now, I have one last thing to take care of before tonight."

"Oh?"

"I'm going to the mortal realm." He replies with a grin.

My heart stops in my chest. "No, you're fucking not." I growl.

"I am," he says casually. Like, defying my orders wasn't literal fucking treason. "You're going to want her friends here for this. You know that."

I clench my jaw, balling my fists at my side. "It's too dangerous. The Divine Six—"

"Don't give a rat's ass about me," he cuts in. "They're after her. I'm just the assistant. And besides, I'll be quick."

I eye him for a moment. He was right, they didn't care about anything or anyone except getting to her, and fucking me over. They'd not expect me—the heartless asshole—to give a shit about my assistant. I let out an exasperated breath through my nose, knowing damn well that if anybody was going to retrieve her friends, it would have to be him.

"Are you sure?" I ask.

He smiles at me in that charming way that's gotten him off my shit list several times in the last few thousand years. "Let me do this, Kori. I know it matters."

I sigh heavily, and nod once. "Be safe."

"Aren't I always?" He chuckles, winking at me before conjuring a portal and vanishing through it in a flash.

With him gone, I turn back to the room.

"Captain," I bark. The soldier steps in the second his title leaves my mouth.

"Yes, my Lord."

"Inform the realm. The coronation will happen tonight, midnight sharp. The feast for the leaders and rulers will begin at seven p.m. All are expected to attend."

"Including...?"

"Yes," I growl with an eye roll. "Even Lucifer."

His eyes widen, but he nods and sprints off to relay the command. I take a seat, throwing my legs up onto the table, my fingers gripping the arms of the stone chair. Soon. Soon, this kingdom will have a king and queen. And maybe—just maybe—Hell will finally have the chance to be what it once was before my asshole of a father. Before the Divine Six. But until then, all I can do is anxiously wait. And pray that when midnight strikes... she'll still be standing by my side and taking the oath to be queen.

THE HALLS of Zeriavoss are the polar opposite to what they were just hours ago.

Word spread like wildfire through the corridors. Servants were called from every wing, torches were lit, tapestries unfurled. The castle, built for darkness and war, was being reborn—if only for a night—into something that resembled a celebration. The coronation was to be held at midnight, but the feast with the rulers and leaders would begin far earlier. Yet Hell's people... they were already waiting.

The paths throughout the kingdom and beyond stirred with movement. Horns sounded from the watchtowers. Demons, fae, shapeshifters, and shadowfolk emerged from their homes and hide-outs. They were all whispering, wondering and wide-eyed. The King and Queen of Hell were to be crowned before the sun rose again.

I stand in the highest tower as the sun slipped behind the ash-draped peaks of the horizon, casting the sky in a fiery bronze glow, the crimson lightening skittering across the sky. Down below, the courtyard bustles with activity as guards formed rows, emissaries arranged rows of flaming braziers, and Hell itself came alive. Yet, there was still no sign of Aran. And I hated how much that twisted in my gut. Every moment he was gone, I imagined the worst. The Divine Six catching him in transit, Talia and Ezra lost to fate, Daisy broken when she realised they wouldn't make it. I couldn't let that happen.

I turn from the window and make my way down the stone stairwell, the soles of my boots echoing through the only current quiet space in my entire realm. The grand hall had already been transformed with banners of deepest black, and wine-red silk fell from the vaulted ceilings. A sea of torches glowed along every wall, their fire charmed to flicker white and gold in honour of Daisy.

Dozens of tables lined the marbled flooring, already laden with trays of roasted meats, fruits, and golden platters piled with pastries and desserts. I could smell wild citrus, spice-root, and the faint metallic bite of ceremonial wine.

Every ruler, every leader would be here soon, to celebrate us. My mate and I. Not just the rulers of the realms we had visited. Rulers of every realm across this universe were to arrive, leaders of places too small to be considered realms, some too large to be considered worlds. Sons, daughters, anyone of importance would be in this room, feasting with us, cheering for us.

I moved through the preparations silently, nodding to the guards and ignoring the stares of the palace servants who now greeted me with lowered eyes and murmured titles. "My King." "Lord Korithax." "Sire." I hated it. Not because I wasn't ready, but because I didn't want the crown to make me someone else. I wanted to be known as Korithax, fierce protector, loyal solider. And I sure as shit didn't want to be seen as a replacement for Korran either.

THE CORRIDOR CURVED toward the throne room, and each step I took toward it seemed to echo off the obsidian walls, my boots pounding like a war drum. Soldiers stood at attention as I passed, lined all along the corridor in full ceremonial armour—gleaming crimson and shadow-forged steel, their cloaks flowing like blood down their backs. Their helms bore my sigil now; an inverted triangle with thorned tendrils curling around the edges of the shape. A spiralled serpent in the middle, consuming its own tail. Above the triangle sits a crescent moon with a vertical slash through it and one across it. And sitting at the very bottom, a singular drop of blood.

As I reach the towering doors of the throne room, two guards step forward, pulling them open with a low groan. I step inside and halt. The throne room has been truly transformed. Gone was the bare, cavernous austerity I had grown used to. Tonight, it looked nothing like the room that belonged to a traitor. It had become a sacred chamber fit for gods.

Columns of black stone spiralled up into the vaulted ceilings inlaid with glowing red-gold veins of magma. Between each column, massive crimson and silver banners—one bearing my sigil, the other a blooming ash rose wreathed in white fire, with a half sun and its beaming rays sitting just above it. It was Daisy's newly chosen sigil —one that fit her and Dasmyrin together.

The walls flickered with torches that burned with magically imbued fire, alternating between white flame and red. It casts the whole chamber in a surreal glow, where shadow met brilliance and clashed together with a harmony only Hell could manage. At the far end of the room, raised high on a polished marble and obsidian dais, sat two thrones carved from the very bones of the realm itself. My breath caught when I saw them. My father's throne had disintegrated the second the news arose about his death. These were new. Reborn and forged, just for us.

Mine was carved from jagged obsidian, the black glass twisted into sharp, regal angles that reflected firelight. My black hellfire glowed faintly within the carved cracks along the arms and back, alive with my magic, pulsing faintly in time with my heart.

Hers... hers was something else entirely. Where mine was brutal, hers was beautiful. Sculpted from pale onyx streaked with silver, Daisy's throne glimmered with a sheen like pearl kissed by starlight—iridescent under the flames bouncing around the room. Carvings of ash roses and suns swept along its back. Wisps of white fire licked along the throne's spires, cool and ethereal, illuminating the dais in divine brilliance. Her flame. Together, they looked like the promise of a better world. Of a prophecy fulfilled. Light and shadow, fury and grace. And for the first time, I began to see this was not just a coronation. It was a resurrection.

Rows upon rows of seats lined the hall below the dais, stretching far back. Hundreds had already gathered, eager to see the ceremony even though it was hours away. Nobles, commoners, soldiers, merchants, scholars. They whisper, craning their necks, gasping, and bowing as I pass. I could feel the weight of every single stare; some curious, some afraid. But most seemed to be in awe. And they should be. Because tonight, their kingdom would not just rise. It would burn back to life.

I RETURN to the Great Hall, finding it one of the quieter places to be right now. I close my eyes and try to will the weight of everything to not crush me, letting out a loud, exasperated sigh.

"You always were dramatic."

I turn with a smirk as Aran strolls into the hall, a lopsided grin tugging at his lips, and two very familiar figures trailing behind him. Ezra's dressed in fitted black slacks and a dark pink button-up shirt with gold thread running along the seams, his usual sass tempered by disbelief. His mouth hangs open, his green eyes wide as he takes in the grand space. Talia wears a flowing gown of midnight blue that shimmers when she moves, her dark hair pinned up in soft coils, her tanned face illuminated by the torches. Their expressions look like they'd just walked into a fairytale.

"She's in her chambers," I say, almost nervously. "She doesn't know they're here."

"Good," Aran replies, patting Ezra's shoulder as if they'd been friends for years. "Let's give her the surprise of her afterlife."

I watch them take it all in, their mortal awe a reminder of how far Daisy had come. How far we had all come.

I gesture to the large table in the centre of the room. "Go sit at the table over there, it's where we'll be sitting."

Ezra leans in close and gives me a sly wink. "You clean up well, demon boy."

I snort. "Don't push it, sparkles."

He laughs as they wander off towards the table, arms linked together as they continue to look around the room, gasping at the most ridiculous things.

"You made it," I say to Aran, clapping him on the shoulder.

"Of course I did." His smile falters just a little. "I wouldn't miss tonight for anything."

A beat passed between us. We both knew what tonight meant. Not just for Daisy, not just for me, but for the future of Hell. After tonight, there would be no going back.

"Thank you," I say quietly, squeezing his shoulder once.

He nods once. "Always."

At exactly seven p.m., the doors to the grand hall open. A chorus of horns blow from the balconies surrounding the room, and the realm leaders begin making their entrance. Vor'Khar of Stormravan thunders in first, his cloak made of lightning. Queen Virena of Fjellheim Heights follows, her mismatched storm grey and opal eyes lined with kohl, her dark gown studded with raindrop-shaped diamonds. Kaelith, king of Aurora's Veil wanders in behind her, his black suit looking like a void beneath his cloak that billows behind him, shimmering with starlight and the colours of the northern lights. Beside him, Maelkar, king of Noxthrallia, strides in wearing a deep purple suit. His midnight skin shimmers, the glowing veins of violet beneath his skin pulsing. And lastly, Sariya, Goddess of Solara, enters the room, hand entwined with Elyistria, Goddess of Luminaria. They both looked absolutely ethereal. Sariya wears a golden gown, her large afro covered in blooming ash roses, her deep bronze skin shimmering under the light. Elyistria has on a pearlescent white gown, her platinum hair twisted into two braids, also adorned with ash roses.

I watch as they all take their seats, offering them all a nod of thanks for being here for the pre-ceremony feast. Just as I'm about to turn, a plume of flame appears in the doorway, announcing the arrival of none other than the pain in my ass, Lucifer himself, dressed in black robes that shimmer like ink. And at his side, Vailith, the ruler of the Realm of Children, wearing a pale pink gown that compliments her pale silver-blue hair.

"Thought you might skip it," I mutter as Lucifer approaches.

"Miss the coronation of the only demon in history who ever gave me a headache? Never." He grins.

I roll my eyes. "Take a seat."

He joins Vailith at one of the tables just as the music begins. It's ancient and vibrant, played on harp strings and bone drums. I take my seat at the table with Aran, Ezra, Talia, Sariya, and Elyistria, awaiting the arrival of my soon-to-be queen.

The doors push open once more, and Daisy appears through them in a black and silver gown that clings to every curve, her newly streaked hair tumbling in soft waves. The room silences as she enters, every eye turning to her, every breath caught. Her eyes find mine, then widen as she takes in who's sitting beside me, her hand flying to her mouth.

"Talia? Ez?" She whispers, hurrying towards us.

"Surprise, bitch," Ezra beams with tears in his eyes, already pushing back his chair to get to her.

Talia pushes her way to her first, flinging her arms around Daisy in a crushing hug. They both sob, laughing and crying in the middle of the hall as Ezra wraps his arms around them both. They saw each other just hours ago, yet act like it's been a millennia. The hall erupts into applause. Glasses are raised, and wine is poured as they take their seats together. Daisy looks at me, her eyes shimmering and her freckle-smattered cheeks flushing as she mouths, "Thank you."

. . .

THE FEAST ROARED on for hours. Toasts were made. Aran delivered an obnoxiously sentimental speech that made both Talia and Daisy tear up. Vor'Khar smashed a wine goblet onto his own head and howled, "TO CHAOS." Which was probably the most I've ever heard the gigantic bastard speak. Sariya clinked her fork against her glass and toasted, "To the flame reborn." Ezra tried to flirt with Maelkar and ended up screaming after he'd shown him his worst nightmares through his mind magic. Lucifer kissed Elyistria's hand and got punched in the gut by Sariya for even trying.

And I? I just watched her. Her laughter lit my nerve endings on fire; her presence made me feel whole.

As the final course is cleared, and the wine begins to run dry, I rise from my seat and clear my throat.

"My friends," I speak, my voice cutting through the celebration. "Tonight, when the moon hangs high, you will see something this realm has not witnessed in thousands of years. The crowning of a King. And the rise of a Queen."

The room quietens.

"She is more than legend, she is more than fire, flame, blood, or the crown. She is mine, and I am hers. Tonight, we rise together. Tonight... Hell remembers who it belongs to."

Applause erupts, and cheers ring out. My eyes find hers, and I give her a single nod, raising my glass to her. She raises hers back in understanding.

It was time.

CHAPTER 56
DAISY

The feast blurred in a haze of clinking glasses, roaring toasts, and stolen glances with my soon-to-be King.

I had laughed until my ribs ached, cried into Talia's shoulder, and held so tightly onto Ezra's hand under the table that I'm pretty sure I saw him wince more than once. I was grateful they were here for this. I was so upset they couldn't be there for the wedding, so them being here to see me become a queen—it was surreal. Seeing their faces at the grand hall with all of the different leaders had me chuckling. So quickly, all of this had become normal to me—these people with magical powers, who looked so ethereal and strange. I'd started to forget that this wasn't normal for people to witness, so seeing them so wide-eyed when glancing across the tables... It was a stark reminder of just how much my life truly had changed in such a short amount of time.

But now, as Sariya gently takes my hand and leads me from the grand hall, the weight of it all presses into my chest.

We slip into my chambers—Sariya, Elyistria, Talia, Ezra, and me. The room's softly lit by the sconces holding flickering candles, the midnight-black velvet canopy above the bed glittering with stardust, looking like a night sky. My body aches from tightly wound emotion and consuming too much wine, but my soul trembles from what's coming. I was about to become a queen. Again.

"Holy shit," Talia whispers, "this entire castle is insane."

Ezra flops dramatically onto the velvet bench at the end of the bed. "I want to live here. I want to die here. I want to be reincarnated as that throw pillow." He laughs.

Sariya giggles at him. "I'm sure you'll be welcome any time."

Talia sniffles, looking around the room. "This is all so fucked. You're all freaks, and I love you so much."

I burst into laughter, wiping away my tears before pulling her into a tight hug. "Thank you for being here."

As if summoned by the emotions in the room, Lyvia steps through the door. Her lavender hair braided back, her delicate hands clasped before her. She looks so small in this room of goddesses, but her presence fills something inside me.

"Lyvia," I breathe, hurrying to her. "I was hoping you'd come."

"I wasn't sure if I should," she whispers. "There are... more important people with you now."

I cup her face, making sure her pale violet eyes meet mine. "You are important, Lyvia. You're not just my maid, you're my friend. Be with me tonight, please."

Lyvia's cheeks flush, matching the colour of her hair. "Only if I can still help dress you. Let me help my queen ascend."

My throat constricts, a lump forming instantly at her words. I nod, hugging her tightly.

She takes my hand and leads me toward the dressing screen that's been put up in the corner of the room. And just to the side, next to the roaring fire, a mannequin stands, the gown draped over it. It's breathtaking. Midnight-black silk that shimmers with starlight, as if the cosmos had been dusted across the fabric itself. The embroidery around the hem dances with magical flame imbued into the design, curling in white, alive, and flickering like liquid silver. The corset bodice shimmers like obsidian armour, sculpted to my form with sharp edges, only to be softened by translucent black lace that falls like smoke down the arms.

"This..." I gasp. "This isn't mine."

Elyistria steps closer, her silver-blue eyes shining with unshed tears. "It was Dasmyrin's design. She sketched it centuries ago but never lived to wear it."

I turn to her in shock. I couldn't wear this. It was hers to wear, not mine. Even though technically I am her, but I'm also not. Gods, my heart's hammering.

"It will suit you well, sunshine queen." She whispers.

"I can't," I sniffle. "What if I'm not enough. What if I fail her legacy? To wear her dress, only to not live up to her name."

My breaths start coming in heavy, my pulse quickening as the anxiety and pressure threaten to shatter me entirely.

Elyistria moves closer, cupping my face, forcing my head to look up at her.

"You don't have to live up to her. You are her, and something more," she murmurs. "Reborn, rewritten, but still her. And you are enough as yourself, Daisy."

Sariya's hand softly brushes my hair from behind. "You were chosen by fate, little flower. A fate that even Elyistria couldn't choose. That kind of power does not make mistakes."

Ezra sniffles from across the room. "Is it weird that I'm crying? I'm literally ugly crying. You're going to look like a goddess, Daze. You're gonna be fucking amazing."

"I love you all," I say, my lower lip trembling.

THEY HELP ME DRESS SLOWLY. Lyvia laces the corset with steady hands, whispering words of reassurance as her fingers work. Talia fluffs the shimmering train, pride shining in her amber eyes. Sariya fastens a delicate chain across my collarbones, connecting to the points at each side of my corset, charms of sunshine and ashroses clinking along the silver metal.

When they finish, Elyistria steps back, her voice hushed. "Let them remember who and what has risen from the ash."

I stare at myself in the mirror, the reflection stunning me. I wasn't the broken girl in a cheer outfit anymore. I wasn't anything like her. I was a reborn queen, coming to reclaim her throne. My eyes are lined with dark-black kohl, my lips painted dark red. Even my cheekbones have been carved out with a subtle contour. My silver-streaked golden hair flows in waves, two strands pulled back and tied at the back with two long hairpins, one with my newly created sigil sitting on top, the other with Korithax's. I let out a steadying breath—and with one final glance at my reflection—I square my shoulders, ready to enter a brand new chapter of my life.

~

THE HALL outside the throne room hums with low voices, sconces lighting up the space with a delicate glow. Guards in ceremonial black stand rigid, their expressions unreadable. I walk between Sariya, Elyistria, Ezra, and Talia—each one a piece of my story, my strength. Lyvia clings to my hand until the very last second, our fingers trembling as they part.

The guards bow as we approach, and I spot Korithax waiting alone before the great gilded doors. Each of my friends give me a kiss on the cheek before slipping through the doors into the throne room, offering more words of reassurance.

I turn and face my future King. His armour is black and crimson, layered and sharp, like it was forged for the battlefield. His obsidian cloak hangs heavy behind him, clasped with twin silver serpent heads. But it's his eyes that steal my breath. His jaw goes slack, his shoulders drawing back like I'd hit him straight in the chest.

"Daisy..." he breathes, voice raspy. "You look like a goddess kissed by Hell and the stars."

My heart lurches. My throat is dry as brine, and I don't know why the words slip out, but they do. "Are you sure you want me as your queen?"

He doesn't hesitate. Two strides and he's in front of me, pressing his forehead gently to mine, our noses brushing.

"I've wanted you since the moment you looked at me in your apartment like I wasn't a monster," he says, voice barely audible. "You saw the worst in me. I tried to break you. I called you weak, fragile, gods I was awful... and yet, you stayed."

His words are deep, peeling back the final layers of doubt curled around my heart.

"I love you," He says softly. "I've loved you longer than I knew. And I'm sorry. I'm sorry I took so long to say it. I'm sorry I tried to protect you from myself, from this world, instead of just choosing you."

I lift a hand to his cheek, my thumb brushing the edge of his jaw. "I think I've loved you since the day you killed Ethan," I whisper. "I didn't know it then, but... my soul did."

His eyes flicker, obsidian shining faintly as he lowers his mouth to my forehead, pressing a tender kiss. For a moment, time stills. We just breathe. One last quiet moment before the world changes.

He pulls back, straightens, and extends his hand to me. "Let's go claim what's ours."

I slip my hand into his, and we turn together as one. As the guards open the doors to the throne room, I know everything ahead will test us. But I also know one thing for certain—he's mine, and I'm his. No gods, no fate, will ever take that from us.

THE THRONE ROOM stretches wide and endless, lined with hundreds of beings. Fae, demon, fallen angels, creatures I don't even have names for. A thousand eyes turn as Korithax and I walk down the aisle, hand in hand. My steps are slow but steady, my grip tight around his large hand. Whispers swirl around us, soft gasps echoing through the hall.

The thrones rise before us—his is jagged and regal, forged from the deepest obsidian and dark power. It pulses with magic, deep and endless. But mine... mine is something else entirely. Pale onyx streaked with silver, carved with ash roses and suns, white flame flickering gently along the edges. It's rage and beauty and legacy, all wrapped into one breathtaking seat of power.

Elyistria steps forward as we ascend the dais, radiant in a gown of pale gossamer. Her voice cuts through the murmurs with weight, silencing the room in an instant.

"To rule is to be bound. Blood to blood, magic to magic. This union is not just of flesh and crown, but of soul and flame."

Korithax holds out his left hand, and I follow. Elyistria slices our palms with a curved blade etched in ancient runes. I don't flinch as the blood blooms across my hand, waiting for the moment everything changes.

Korithax places his hand atop mine, our hands clasping and our blood mingling together. Magic erupts between our palms—black fire crashes into me as white flame lances into him. We both gasp as the power tears through our bodies. His flame doesn't burn; it hums, filling me with heat, making my skin feel alive. It makes my soul sing, and my breath come in soft, short pants.

I stare into Korithax's eyes, and in them I see everything: the power, the pull, the bond. Power pulses outward like a shockwave, causing flames to flicker, rippling across the room. Gasps echo around us as our joined magic floods the space.

We release our hands, and Elyistria turns to me. A crown of flame sits in her palms; white fire flickering across the golden spires. She lowers it to my head with a soft bow, the flame not burning at all. It feels right, like it has always belonged there.

Korithax drops to one knee, and the room collectively stills.

"A king never kneels," someone whispers from the crowd.

I glance down at him in confusion, but he only stares up at me with fire in his eyes.

"A king never traditionally kneels to his queen," he says, voice echoing through the room, loud and clear. "But I will spend the rest of my life bowing to you. Worshipping you like the queen you are."

The silence in the room breaks into a thunderous roar. "ASH BORN," they cry, "ASH BORN!"

He rises, a small smile tugging at the corner of his mouth as the room quietens once again for their king to be crowned. Elyistria crowns him with a circlet of black thorns, his hellfire flickering across the vines as it settles across his brow.

I don't need to think twice as I drop to my knees before him, bowing my head for my king. My husband. My mate. My love.

The crowd erupts again, wild and deafening. Screams, cheers, stomping feet, shaking the floor beneath us. Korithax holds out a hand, helping me rise, and together we turn to face them. My heart pounds, a steady drumbeat against my ribs. These are our people. This is our kingdom. This is our home.

Elyistria steps forward once more, voice ringing like a bell through the air. "All kneel for the Queen and King of Hell."

And they do. Every single person drops to one knee as we sit upon our thrones, side by side, our fingers intertwined. The moment we settle, fire erupts from the spires of our thrones; his roaring in hellfire, mine in divine white flame.

"We did it," I whisper as our guests rise to their feet, cheering for their new rulers.

"We did it, little flower," Korithax murmurs, brushing his thumb along my knuckles.

I glance at him, and he's already watching me. That rare, soft smile playing on his lips. Everything we had faced, everything I had faced... it all felt worth it to be sitting here beside him as his queen. The worries of how well I'll do as a ruler, how well I'll do as the reborn queen, still sit heavily on my shoulders. But for now, I was going to bask in this moment and enjoy this with Korithax.

I lean towards him, placing a soft kiss on his lips, savouring his taste and his touch. I moan softly at the connection, the butterflies in my stomach chaotically dancing as I claim him in front of our kingdom. But just as he pulls me in to deepen the kiss, a violent quake splits the air. We jerk apart quickly, both of our eyes wide.

"What the hell was that?" I ask, scanning the hall as the noise dies.

The doors to the throne room explode open on a blast of wind, every torch sputtering.

"No." I whisper, a wave of ice-cold dread slamming into me as figures step forward through a misty haze.

At the front, clad in silver armour that gleams like moonlight, is Seraphiel.

"What?" She sneers, voice dripping with venom. "No invite for us?"

CHAPTER 57
KORITHAX

The room is still ringing with the echoes of the applause that has only just begun to die down.

I keep Daisy's hand in mine, her touch steadying the storm behind my ribs. We've done it. Crowned in the sight of the realms, bound in blood, in magic, and in soul. She's utterly radiant beside me; my queen, my mate. She pulls me into a soft kiss, her plush lips melting away the remaining sounds of the room as I pull her in closer, deepening the embrace with desperate need for her. Gods, I'll never tire of tasting her mouth on mine.

A sickening quake splits through the floor just before the large doors burst wide. A cold silence swallows the room before the crowd erupts into screams. I stand instantly, pulling Daisy behind me on instinct, my wings bursting free and flexing wide as the stench of divine energy slams into me like a wall. Six figures emerge from the white fog curling through the open doorway.

Seraphiel steps in first. Her silver armour blinding, and her white eyes gleam like polished bone. "What?" She drawls, like bile on her tongue. "No invite for us?"

Behind her, the rest of the Divine Six form in their usual fucking crescent—Calrix with his burning sword drawn already, Mal'Thariel, unmoving, glass-flesh gleaming under the firelight, Amarithe's beauty is venom, her golden aura humming like a curse, Elaron smiling faintly, his lips barely curled in that infuriating way of his, like he knows something we don't. And Velentha—hood up, silent—her face entirely unreadable.

Daisy doesn't move. She stands frozen, small behind me with her fingers locked firmly in mine as she begins to tremble. I squeeze her hand in reassurance, but don't remove my eyes from the assholes in front of me.

"Your timing is fucking shit, Seraphiel," I growl.

"Watch your mouth, Child of Ruin," Calrix snarls.

Seraphiel's gaze flicks to something behind me. "Oh. You brought some little toys," she smirks.

I glance behind me quickly, noticing Ezra and Talia have moved behind us, just a step back. Ezra shields Talia instinctively, but they both shake in terror. Talia's usual tanned complexion looks almost pale as the horror sweeps through her.

"Leave them out of this," I snarl. "This is between us—"

"We warned you not to return, little mortal," Seraphiel interrupts, her eyes locking on Daisy.

I feel her go rigid beside me. Seraphiel takes a lazy step forward, her armour shimmering. "Yet here you are. You defied us. So... let's choose your punishment, shall we?"

Her smile is almost vicious as she raises her hand to point a sharp tipped finger. Then she begins and all the warmth drains from my body. "Eenie..."

"No," I say, voice in low growl. "Don't you fucking dare—"

"Meenie..."

Ezra steps forward. "No. Take me. Don't touch her—"

"Minie..."

Talia clutches Daisy's hand and whispers something I don't catch as I train my focus on Seraphiel.

"Mo." Seraphiel's grin widens, her finger landing on Talia. "Catch a mortal by the toe... if it screams..."

"Stop." I step forward.

"We won't let it go."

"Don't," Daisy chokes out.

"Eenie. Meenie. Minie—"

"No," I snarl.

"—Mo."

She points back at Talia, a vile, high-pitched laugh breaking from her. Talia blinks, going stiff with fear. Seraphiel nods once, and Calrix's dagger flies before I can blink. It plunges straight into Talia's chest, landing with a crunch of bone and a wet, sucking sound. She stumbles, gasping as she looks down at the dagger protruding from her flesh, then collapses into Daisy's arms. Blood pours fast, a river of red soaking the throne room floor as Calrix's laughter booms through the room.

"No. NO!" Daisy's scream tears through the air as she clutches Talia's body. "Talia, no. Please, no... please stay with me..."

But there's nothing left to save. Her eyes are already dimmed, her body sagging and lifeless. I see red, everything in me screaming for vengeance. But I have my Queen breaking beside me, and I have Ezra—

"Aran," I bark.

Aran doesn't hesitate for even a moment. He moves forward quickly and grabs Ezra, who's stands frozen in horror, staring at his lifeless friend. Aran pulls him backwards as a portal rips open behind them, just as Talia's body hits the floor. Ezra shouts Daisy's name, but it's too late. Aran shoves him through the portal with an apologetic look, sealing it shut before Ezra has chance to dive back through.

I offer a small nod to Aran in thanks. We could've run, we could've gone with them. But the Divine Six would chase us down, and bringing their power down on the mortal realm would be utter devastation. At least one of Daisy's friends is safe.

Daisy lowers to the floor, cradling Talia's corpse like a child, her entire body trembling as her gown pools around her, soaked in blood.

Seraphiel tilts her head mockingly. "Such fragile little things," she tuts.

My voice breaks as I stand over Daisy. "Your first mistake was coming here," I say, death in my tone. "Your second was murdering my wife's best friend. I won't let you make a third mistake, you fucking cunt."

Seraphiel raises a brow in a way a mother would scorn her child. "Language."

I bare my teeth, moving slightly to block Daisy. I can't move to her, I can't risk turning my back to them. I quickly glance around the room, the sight of the small children sobbing in their mother's arms making my wings twitch, itching for violence.

"Let my people leave," I say, voice like steel. "This is between us. Not them."

Seraphiel, to my surprise, nods once. With eerie calm, the Divine Six turn to the crowd, and Amarithe lifts a hand, murmuring a spell. The realms' leaders stay put, refusing to move. Even Aran stands his ground. Everyone else vanishes or is ushered out by divine pressure, the door sealing shut behind them.

I use those few precious seconds to move to Daisy's side. She's still kneeling, hands trembling on Talia's blood-drenched chest. I kneel beside her, gently reaching down to lift the girl's broken body, to take her away from this place with some shred of respect.

"No need," Elaron says calmly.

A pulse of light and Talia's corpse evaporates, gone in a flash. Daisy's scream is soul-rending.

"I didn't even get to say goodbye," she whispers, her voice shaking. "You tore everything away from me once... and now you're doing it again."

She stands slowly, her legs unsteady as she takes a single step in front of me. Her crown ignites, white flame bursting from her head like a star exploding in the cosmos. The Divine Six simultaneously freeze, taking in the sight of her. Velentha's the first to move, falling to one knee with her head bowed.

"The Queen born of ash has risen. Reborn as the sun," she whispers. "And she has come to burn us all."

Seraphiel's mouth opens and closes several times like a fucking fish out of water. "No," she mutters. "That does not belong to you."

"Why are you wearing that crown?" Amarithe snarls, her lip curling in disgust.

"That does not belong to you, mortal," Mal'Thariel growls, his otherworldly voice sending a shiver skittering down my spine.

"I believe," Elyistria says calmly, stepping to Daisy's side, "you'll find it does." The two stand together, hand in hand. Sisters, light and rebirth, magic and fire.

"You let her wear Dasmyrin's crown?" Seraphiel spits. "You stand by this mortal and call her your equal? You truly are a fucking idiot, Elyistria."

Elyistria's expression doesn't waver, even when Seraphiel speaks Dasmyrin's name with such hatred it makes my skin prickle. She looks at Daisy, giving her a nod of reassurance. Daisy raises her chin, her spine straightening, and I can't help but smile at my fierce little flower.

"I am not mortal anymore," she says, her voice strong and steady despite the chaos surrounding her. "And I remember what you did to me. Especially you." She raises her hand, pointing a finger at Elaron, venom lacing her tone.

"You cast the soul-erasing spell. But you forgot something, didn't you?" She moves from between Elyistria and me, stepping closer, her fury radiating from her. "I created you."

THE ROOM GOES SO silent I can hear every heartbeat within it; each beat like a war drum, warning of the storm about to break loose.

"You could never truly defeat me," Daisy says, voice like fire. "It was only a matter of time before I returned."

She raises her chin, staring each of the Six down as she squares her shoulders. Her crown blazes on her head like an ancient warning.

Seraphiel's shriek pierces the air. "NO! She's just a weak, pathetic mortal. She is not her!"

Daisy doesn't blink, doesn't falter. And she sure as shit doesn't stutter as she stares down the biggest bitch in the celestial fuckery known as the Divine Six.

"You led the charge to destroy me, Seraphiel. I will not let you succeed a second time. This is my kingdom. This is my universe. And you need to remember, I created you—not the other way around."

Seraphiel staggers back like she's been struck, clutching where her heart could be—if the cold bitch had one. Calrix roars and hurls another blade straight at Daisy's chest.

This time, I don't allow myself to think; I just react. Hellfire surges from my hand, catching the blade mid-air and turning it to ash.

"And that," I say in a calm, deadly voice, "was your third fucking mistake."

I reach my arm up over my shoulder, drawing my sword from the sheath at my back. I move to Daisy's side with Aran, holding the sword in my right hand, the obsidian blade hissing to life as pure black flame licks down its edge.

Sariya moves to Daisy's other side. "This does not have to end in violence. I know what happens if war breaks out, and nobody fares well from that choice."

The Divine Six don't speak. Velentha stays kneeling as the rest of them stand snarling. They had no intention of letting this go; they want war, they want blood, and every single one of us knew it. Sariya lets out an exasperated sigh, knowing they've made their choice.

I feel a presence move behind me and glance sideways—Vor'Khar steps up beside Elyistria, hands crackling with lightning as thunder booms outside of the castle. Another motion draws my eye as Maelkar joins Sariya's side, grinning like a feral beast.

"Well," he drawls, "you fuckers gave up trying to control me long ago. You knew you didn't stand a chance against the Shadow Tongue and his creations. But in case it isn't clear, I stand with Queen Daisy. You fuck with her, you fuck with the shadow realm."

My lip quirks up as I watch him flip off Calrix. Maelkar may have mentally tortured my girl, and I still owed him at least one fucking punch for it. But he stands by her now, so I may just let it slide.

Virena slowly steps forward, taking place beside Vor'Khar. Rain suddenly batters the windows as she speaks.

"I, for one, am real tired of you pretentious assholes. I stand with Queen Daisy."

I snort. The stuck-up leader of Fjellheim Heights just jumped up in my rankings.

I turn to Kaelith. He meets my gaze, and I honestly don't know which way he's going to fall, especially after I set him on fire. I glare, baring my teeth in warning: choose wrong, and I won't hesitate.

He holds his hands up with an eye roll. "I may not forgive you for setting me on fire, Child of Ruin—" I growl at the nickname, "—but, I'd rather set myself on fire and let you piss on me than side with the fucking Divine Six." He stands in line with the rest of us. "I stand with the Queen."

Seraphiel laughs, loud and mocking, shoulders shaking like this is the funniest thing she's ever seen. "We are stronger than all of you fucking fools." She steps forward, a shit eating grin on her stupid fucking face. "One last chance to bow before I eradicate every last one of you."

No one moves. Not a single fucking inch.

Shadows curl around Maelkar, shadow figures dancing around the walls. The whole of Zeriavoss darkens under Kaelith's power.

Thunder and lightning roar from Vor'Khar, and the rain lashes down, thanks to Virena, mist pooling at her feet like a summoning.

Sariya, Daisy, and Elyistria all join hands. The energy pulsing off them vibrates through the air, a god-tier warning none of the Divine Six should ignore.

"Well, you've made your choice." Seraphiel shrugs.

Velentha and Aran gasp in unison. "NO!" Velentha screams, tears welling in her eyes.

Aran surges forward, but he's too late.

Amarithe's magic explodes, and the entire room freezes. I can't move. None of us can. Every person standing against the Six are paralysed under her enchantment. I strain, my muscles screaming as I try to lift my sword.

Sweat pours from Amarithe's brow. "I can't hold them!" She gasps, shaking with effort. "NOW, CALRIX!"

Calrix's laughter echoes around the room. "I've waited a very long time for this, Child of Ruin."

He charges forward, his face split into a grin. I don't think I've ever seen the miserable bastard smile before, and it's a sight that sends shivers down my spine.

I see his sword before I feel it. It slides straight through my armour, sinking into my gut. My eyes widened as he twisted it with another laugh, then rips it free with a sickening, wet shluck.

A roar rips from my throat just as the enchantment breaks. I fall, my knees hitting the stone hard, blood pouring from the wound. My sword clatters beside me, the flames sputtering out. Somethings wrong... the pain is wrong. I'd been stabbed hundreds, if not thousands of times. Something was on that blade, something cursed, something deadly. I could feel it already, spreading like molten acid through my veins. My pulse stutters, and darkness beings to claw at the edge of my vision.

"No!" Daisy screams, the force of her grief shattering the last remaining shreds of the enchantment in the room.

She drops beside me, hands pressing against the gaping wound in my abdomen, desperate to stop the river of blood. It soaks her fingers, joining Talia's blood on her gown and the floor.

"Korithax, look at me. Stay with me." She whispers, her voice frantic.

I try. I turn my head, blinking heavily through the blur. Her face is wrecked, and flame trembles on her crown, pulsing in time with her erratic heartbeat.

"I'm sorry," I whisper, choking on the blood that's bubbling in my throat. "I'm so... sorry."

I can feel the sticky crimson fluid trickling from the corner of my mouth, her thumb brushing it away in desperation, like it would somehow stop my life from fading away.

"No. Don't you dare. Don't you dare say goodbye." Daisy cries.

My hearing warps, her voice distorting like I'm underwater. Was this truly it? Was this how I was to die?

"I need you," she sobs against me. "I need you with me, do you hear me? You're my husband. You're my king, my mate, the other half of my soul. I love you."

I reach out a shaking hand, streaking her ivory skin red as I cup her cheek. "Don't let this be the end of you, sunshine," I rasp. "You were born to reign... not to break."

"No. No, no, no—don't say that. Don't leave me, Korithax. Please."

Her hands press harder into the wound with pure desperation, and I suddenly feel her magic ignite. It explodes from her palms—wild, white-hot fire laced with streaks of darkness, of ash, of something so ancient I can't recognise it.

It surges into me, searching, burning, trying to fix what can't be. But the poison resists, devouring the magic as quickly as she pours it in. Her flame seems to scream with her grief. It surges outwards, not from her hands, but from her body. Flames roar up the walls, melting the stone and scorching the sigils of the Divine Six right from every surface.

Yet still she tries to save me.

"Don't you dare die, Korithax," she weeps. "I can't... I can't lose you. Not now, not when I finally have you as my own."

Her flame responds to her pain, becoming sentient. It curls around her like a living creature—protective, violent, mourning. It lashes out against the room, lacing everything in divine white flame as her anger, her grief, pours out of her.

I was doing this to her. I could see my impending death breaking her to the point of no return. My little flower was burning away, and I was afraid for what was going to be left behind.

"Get rid of him!" Elaron snaps, "so nobody can save him."

"I will end you," Daisy snarls through her sobs. Her voice is layered, sounding so different from the girl I love. Dasmyrin and Daisy seemed to fuse as one, grief-maddened and divine. "You took everything from me once. You won't do it again."

I watch her through bleary eyes, my queen, my love, as the flames dance up her arms and crawl across her body like living armour. She was no longer Daisy, yet she was not Dasmyrin either. She was both, and more. Something entirely unstoppable.

She glows like a dying star on the edge of collapse, but more powerful than anything I'd ever witnessed. I was truly blessed that my last sight before death was seeing my queen transform into the fierce fucking goddess I always knew she could be. What a blessing it is to die in the arms of the one woman that became my peace. She is everything to me. My heart, my soul, my home. I'd spent my life being a cold bastard, a child forged for destruction. And I always foresaw my death on the battlefield, surrounded by my soldiers, nobody truly caring I was dead. Never did I imagine a fate where I died in the arms of an angel who would mourn me so fiercely she set the world alight. My angel. My beautiful, destructive angel.

"I can fix this," she whispers, pressing her forehead to mine. "Just hold on. Just a little longer—"

"I'm fading, sunshine," I murmur. "Let me go."

"No. No, please, don't."

"I love you," I murmur, tasting blood.

And I do love her. So fucking much it hurts.

Her sob tears through the room, louder than the thunder booming outside. She presses her mouth to mine in a desperate kiss. One final, blood-slicked kiss. I exhale into her, giving her my last breath.

Then darkness takes me.

CHAPTER 58
EPILOGUE ONE
ARAN

The throne room reeked of blood and the bitter tang of divine magic.

The air was thick with silence, as if the realm itself had forgotten how to breathe. Daisy knelt over Korithax's body. Her gown, once regal and black with living flame, now hung from her in ruin, drenched in Talia's blood, in Korithax's. Her pale hands trembled as she cradled him, her fingers smeared in crimson, her face carved with a look that held something much worse than grief. Her flame still clung to her like a second skin, breathing and pulsing as if they were alive themselves.

Korithax went still in her arms, and for a breath, the world did too. Then Daisy screamed. It was not a cry; it was not the sound of a woman mourning her love. It was a detonation. Her scream ripped through the throne room like a tidal wave of power—raw and guttural. The sound hit the air with such force that every stained-glass window shattered, raining shards down like multicoloured tears. The mirrors that dotted the walls across the cavernous space cracked from edge to edge, and each column in the room groaned. Every candle in the room extinguished at once, plunging the chamber into darkness broken only by the searing white glow erupting from Daisy's body.

Her hair lifted from her shoulders, fanned by a phantom wind that seemed to spin around her like a storm born from her grief. Her eyes blazed white and her flame—no longer soft or celestial—coiled from her skin in lashing tendrils.

The Divine Six flinched as the blast of her power sent a gust of magic crashing through the air like a living shockwave. The very foundations of Zeriavoss trembled. Kaelith fell to his knees. Vor'Khar staggered back. Even Maelkar's shadows hissed and curled tighter around him in warning.

Seraphiel snarled. "This power—what is this?"

"This isn't normal magic," Calrix muttered, his hand tightening around his sword hilt.

"No," Elyistria said, stepping forward with a trembling voice. "This is hers."

She wasn't referring to Dasmyrin or Daisy. She was referring to the newly formed goddess in front of us. She was something old and something new. Entirely remade, and entirely dangerous.

Daisy's body arched forward as the magic released again in a pulsing ring, the force so violent that every person in the room staggered. Velentha watched without moving, her expression unreadable.

"The Queen born of the ashes has risen," Velentha whispered, her voice barely audible over the storm of power surging through the room. "And her grief will drown the stars."

As the power pulsing throughout the room began to settle, Daisy slowly lifted her gaze. She was not weeping anymore, her face carved from fire and fury. And the Divine Six finally understood. They had not killed anything within this girl. No. They had awakened the goddess within.

I stood frozen a few feet away, my sword still gripped within my hand, though I could barely feel it. All I could hear was the echo of her scream. The way she'd held him, the way she'd kissed him as if her love alone could force life back into his body. Nothing could. Not even her magic, not even her.

A low hum began to grow behind the Divine Six. Mal'Thariel lifted a hand, smooth and crystalline, carved of glass and marble. An unnatural circle of runes spiralled open in the floor beneath Korithax's body, glowing with eerie precision.

"No," I growled, stepping forward. "Don't touch him."

But the Architect had already begun. "The Child of Ruin must not be revived," Mal'Thariel grinds out. "This is a necessity. This is law."

Daisy's lips parted. "What are you doing?" Her voice cracked with raw panic. "No. No, stop. Don't take him from me!"

I lurched forward to help her, but the runes burned with such ferocity I fell backward, my sword clattering to the ground. Velentha's head snapped toward Mal'Thariel, her eyes flaring with something calculating. A whisper, too low for anyone to hear, slipped past her lips. The runes under Korithax's body pulsed... just once, then flickered subtly. No one noticed but me, and I narrowed my eyes on her. What the hell was she up to?

The spell completed, and Korithax's body vanished, his crown falling from him and clattering to the floor with a metallic cry, the last echo of his presence.

"NO!" Daisy screamed, lunging forward.

But it was too late, and her hands reached nothing but the bloodstained floor where his body had been just moments before. She roared, the sound no longer human. The temperature of the room plummeted before spiking into a scorching heat as a final surge of magic exploded outward from her. She threw her hands toward the Divine Six, flame erupting in a blazing spear of pure will—pure, blazing white bright. It collided with their forming forcefield of protection. The energy crackled violently, screaming against the magic holding it back. Cracks spiderwebbed across the shield, but it held as Daisy's power began to drain. She wasn't trained. I had no idea how she was even wielding such magic when she hadn't been taught how to use it. She truly was magnificent.

Seraphiel's eyes widened in alarm. "She's breaking through—"

"We must leave!" Elaron shouted.

Velentha didn't move as her gaze remained fixed on the ground where Korithax had lain, her fingers subtly moving behind her back. Suddenly, a blinding light engulfed the Divine Six.

"No!" Daisy shrieked. Her magic surged again, but it was too late.

They vanished in a burst of divine radiance, the shield disappearing with them. Their exit sent a ripple of silence through the chamber. My gaze whipped to Daisy just as she collapsed, her flames extinguished in an instant. Her body hit the blood-slick floor with a dull thud, her hair fanned around her like a halo of scorched gold. Her hands were still stained with blood, and her crown's fire sputtered and died. I ran to her, barely hearing the others around me. I fell to my knees at her side, reaching for her wrist—a pulse, faint but there. Her breathing was shallow, her body limp, but she was alive.

"Get help!" I shouted, not caring who listened. "Now!"

But even as I held her, I knew that something inside her was so utterly broken. And the girl who rose from this would never be the same again.

~

THE HEALERS HAD CARRIED Daisy's unconscious form from the ruined throne room to her new chambers—the ones that had been prepared for her and Korithax. She hadn't stirred. The girl who had once smiled with sunshine in her eyes was now coated in her best friend's and lover's blood.

The other leaders of their realms dispersed; their own urgencies to attend to. We agreed to reconvene in an hour in the war room to prepare for the inevitable. War was no longer a threat on the horizon. It had well and truly arrived. But there was something I needed to do before then.

~

I WALK ALONG through the deathly quiet halls of Zeriavoss, heading toward the door that had once led directly to the Divine Six's pretentious, sacred realm. It now stood magically sealed, its celestial sigils faintly glowing with power that nobody beside them could breach. I pace before it, my pulse thrumming with anticipation, my thoughts a storm.

A shadow peels through the door, as though it had split like skin. I move fast, closing the distance between us, and pull her into my arms. "Are you okay?" I whisper.

"I'm fine," she replies, but her voice shakes. "I don't have long. If I'm noticed missing, questions will follow."

I nod, but my grip on her doesn't ease.

"That went worse than expected," she murmurs, stepping back enough to look me in the eye. "Much, much worse. There were so many pathways tonight… his death wasn't one I thought likely."

"I had not seen it clearly either," I rasp. "So much so, I ruled it out."

The pain rose again, gnawing at me. I'd spent my entire life watching the threads of fate tangle and snap, but seeing my brother fall… seeing Daisy break. It tore something out of me.

"She has fully awakened now," she breathes shakily. "Dasmyrin reborn. But this version of her? She's something more. The war ahead will be carnage. Too many futures, all of them ending in tragedy."

"I know," I say sombrely. "I can't see the outcome anymore. But with their help, we might chart a path. Do you have it?"

She reaches into her robes and pulls out a thick, rune-covered book. The Divine Six's grimoire. Bound in scales, pulsing with faint light like a living heart. My breath catches as I reach for it.

"They'll kill you if they realise—"

"They'll know it's missing in fourteen hours," she says, cutting me off. "That's how long you have to use it and gather everything you need."

I nod, tucking the book deep into the folds of my cloak. "Are you going to be okay?"

"You know I can't see my own fate any more than you can," she says with a sad smile. "And I suffer the same torture, my love. I can't see you. It terrifies me."

I cup her face, pressing my forehead to hers. "You'll be careful?"

"As careful as a traitor can be." She replies, huffing a laugh.

I kiss her softly, and she sighs into it, like we both know it might be the last. "What did you do in there?" I ask quietly.

She pulls back, her expression unreadable as she softly shakes her head. "I did what had to be done."

I frowned. "But—"

"I must go." She turns back toward the door.

"Velentha. Wait."

She pauses, looking back at me over her shoulder. Her beautiful eyes capture my heart and my soul.

My voice cracks, but I say it anyway. "If they ever find out... You run. You hear me? You run!"

She stares at me, pain flickering in her gaze. Then I whisper the only phrase that means 'I love you' in the way we meant it.

"As the stars remember the dark," I whisper.

She smiles, tears shimmering in her silver eyes. "So do I remember you."

And then she vanishes back through the door, leaving only the silence behind.

CHAPTER 59
EPILOGUE TWO

The door seals behind her, and with it, the sound of a broken kingdom.

She does not look back. She can't, not yet. The grimoire would buy them time, but not mercy.

She walks in silence through the forgotten path, where light does not reach, and the stars do not dare to whisper.

At the realm's edge, the air shimmers, ancient magic pulsing beneath her skin as the gate unlocks with a single breath of her power. This was a place no god of her universe had touched.

The cavern's dark. Silent.

Velentha places the final crystal on the altar, her hands trembling slightly at the fate she was about to seal.

"To unlock the flame, one must burn.
To wake the wolf, the moon must turn.
To free the soul from death's own thread,
A god must fall, and bleed, and beg."

SHE TURNS and does not look back as the door seals closed.

AFTERWORD

So...

Are you okay? Are *we* okay? How are we feeling?

If you've just finished *He Who Holds My Soul* and need a minute to stare into the middle distance, please know this is a safe space. That was... a lot. Phew. What a ride.

I should probably say sorry. And I am. A little bit.

I cried while writing this book. More than once. Sometimes while typing. Sometimes while aggressively staring at the wall afterwards, questioning my own life choices. So if you cried too, just know you weren't alone. I was right there with you, emotionally unwell and fully aware of what I was doing.

That said... I regret nothing. This story was always meant to hurt in order to become something else. Loss matters. Grief changes people. And love—real love—never leaves things untouched.

If you're feeling betrayed, devastated, or slightly feral right now... good. You're exactly where you're meant to be.

As for what comes next... Book Two is waiting. It's darker. It's louder. And yes... I will probably make you cry again. I'm sorry. Truly.

(But also not really.)

Thank you for trusting me with your heart. Thank you for staying to the end. And thank you for walking into the fire with Daisy, even when you knew it would burn.

I'll see you again soon.

—Shannon 🖤

ACKNOWLEDGMENTS

To my street team — **the Chaos Demons** — thank you for the hype, the chaos, and the unwavering support. This book would not exist in the same way without you.

To my Chaos Demons & my Freaky Fucks — my readers. Thank you for choosing dark stories, dangerous love, and emotional devastation. You are exactly my kind of people.

To my husband, thank you for always encouraging me, for believing in me even on the days I didn't, and for cheering on every win, no matter how small. I couldn't do this without you.

To my two children, for being my reason, my grounding, and my reminder of what love looks like in its purest form.

And to my mum, who has always been proud of me, no matter what I'm doing, no matter where life takes me. Your belief in me has meant more than you'll ever know.

About the Author

Shannon V. Velzen is a UK-based author who writes dark romantic books. Stories filled with morally grey characters, dangerous devotion, and love that refuses to be gentle.

She holds a degree in psychology, an influence that shapes her fascination with grief, trauma, power, and the way love can both heal and destroy. Living with a disability, Shannon writes with an intimate understanding of pain, endurance, and the quiet strength it takes to survive becoming something new.

When she isn't writing about demons, gods, and catastrophic emotional choices, she can usually be found juggling motherhood, drinking far too much caffeine, and being supervised by her dog, who firmly believes all writing breaks should involve snacks. She lives in the UK with her husband, her two children, and an ever-growing collection of dark ideas that refuse to stay quiet.

He Who Holds My Soul is the first book in **The Fire and Silence Series**, and her second book to be released.

For more updates
https://svvelzen.com/

instagram.com/shannonv.velzenauthor
facebook.com/Shannonv.velzenauthor
tiktok.com/@shannonv.velzenauthor